D0930671

THE INSECURE MIND OF SERGEI KRAEV

ERIC SILBERSTEIN

L B G

Copyright © 2021 by Eric Silberstein

All rights reserved.

First Edition

ISBN 978-1-7373519-0-0

Library of Congress Control Number: 2021913210

Liu Book Group / Boston

Cover design by Christopher Brand

Cover photograph by Jasper James / Millennium Images, UK

This book is also available in ebook and audiobook formats.

For Frances, Andy, and Mia

PROLOGUE

April 14, 2220
One hundred years after 4-17
Singapore Island

Children,

This is my ninety-fourth annual message. It's hard to believe there are now 2,978 of you, including my two great-great-great-great-grandchildren born today.

My message this year breaks with tradition. Instead of celebrating your accomplishments from the past twelve months, my subject is a chain of events that started before I was born.

I was thirteen on 4-17. Now, one hundred years later, I'm ready to tell you our family's story—a story I've reconstructed from implant recordings, my great-grandfather's glasses, and speculation.

If you have questions, please ask them soon. My great-grandfather was 113 when he brought me and Ora to Singapore. Today I turn that same age. I'm in good health and, as far as I know, my mind is sharp. However, predictively speaking, this is my final decade.

Love,
Leon Levy

1

April 17, 2120
Haifa, Israel

4-17 was a Wednesday. Ora and I were home because it was school vacation week in Israel. I spent the morning the same way I had spent every other day of vacation up to that point —in my room, absorbed in a game, avoiding my overdue homework.

Our house was in a quiet, hilly neighborhood, not far from our parents' university. Great-grandpa, who was visiting us for lunch, paused outside our front door and caught his breath after walking up the few steps from the road.

"I'm so proud of you, Karima," he told Mom in his American-accented Hebrew when he finally stepped inside. "You and Danny have made your mark."

The day before, after over a decade of testing, the olfactory interface algorithm my parents developed in grad school had been promoted to production. Overnight, as the world's population woke up and smelled virtual coffee for

the first time ever, my parents went from respected professors to global celebrities.

Great-grandpa kissed Mom on the head. "How are you
handling all the publicity?"

Mom didn't answer.

My parents had become a subject of media fascination
—especially Mom, who, with her striking mixture of
Chinese, Ethiopian, and Ashkenazi features, did not match
anyone's mental image of a theoretical quantum computer
scientist.

Great-grandpa placed his hand on Mom's shoulder.
"Karima?"

"Sorry, Grandpa," Mom said as she blinked once and
refocused her eyes on him. "I may be a bit distracted today.
Danny and I are looking into something. I'm in the middle
of kicking off a simulation. One sec." Mom's eyes defocused,
then a few seconds later her attention returned. "Hungry?"

Great-grandpa followed Mom through our living room
to the deck. Our house was built into a hill, so the deck was
at tree level, with chirping parakeets flitting back and forth
between nearby branches. Mom helped Great-grandpa sit
down at our table and poured him a glass of water.

"Where's Danny?" he asked.

Mom explained that Dad was in our study, tied up with
something urgent.

"The kids?"

Mom checked. Ora and I were still in our rooms.

Leon, Ora—get down here right now.

Ugh, not now, I thought, and ignored Mom.

And then two minutes later: *Leon—get down here!*

I shifted just enough attention to physical reality to navi-
gate our house.

Out on the deck, Great-grandpa was asking Ora a

question. When he saw me, he pivoted in his chair and reached out for a hug. I inhaled his familiar, earthy smell and felt his spindly arms wrap around my back. He planted a wet kiss on my forehead. My hair smudged his clunky glasses, which he took off and placed on the table. I felt bad for him whenever I saw him wearing those things. Even with them, he was cut off from so many aspects of life, not by choice, but because by the time implants became available, his brain was too old to receive one.

"What are you learning in school?" he asked after I sat down.

I looked vaguely in his direction but didn't respond.

"Leon?" he said.

"Leon! Great-grandpa's talking to you!"

Mom's tone broke through.

"Uhhh. . . ." I played back the last few seconds of input from my eyes and ears at triple speed, ". . . in what subject?"

"I'm blocking games."

"No, Mom! I'm on the *Quest* leaderboard. I'll multitask."

Mom raised her voice and gave me an icy stare. "You're not multitasking. You shouldn't be playing at all. Did you finish your homework? Did you even start? I'm disconnecting you."

"What about Ora? It's not fair."

"I'm disconnecting both of you."

"Five minutes, let me finish, then I'll do ninety percent present."

"No."

And without any more warning than that, Mom hard disconnected us. It felt like my eyes were yanked out, like all of a sudden everything was flat and grainy and dull. For a fraction of a second I was stunned. Then I shot up, threw my chair against the railing, screamed at Mom, ran to my room, and slammed the door.

Ora, who was ten at the time, stayed seated, paralyzed, a look of disbelief on her face.

Mom had used parental controls before to block gaming, block network access, block recording, but she had never disconnected my implant. I'd never even heard of anyone being hard disconnected. I knew the ability to do so was a fundamental human right, and one that for me and Ora, as minors, Mom and Dad controlled on our behalf, but I'd always imagined it as a strictly theoretical thing.

Mom turned to Great-grandpa, stress coating her every word. "Sorry, Grandpa. I've never done that before. I just . . . I've been under so much pressure."

"Karima, honey, let me help. How about I watch Leon and Ora for a few days? You and Danny take a vacation. You certainly deserve it, and it sounds like you need it."

"No, I'm grateful, but, it's not about the kids, it's other stuff. Things were under control until last summer."

Mom explained how a single case of pediatric blindness in Moscow had threatened promotion of the olfactory interface. She and Dad put everything aside and threw themselves into proving that their algorithm was not at fault.

"But then," Mom said, pressing her hand into her forehead, "I was drowning in all the work I had put off. Overdue grant submissions, desperate grad students, and this whirlwind of media interviews that Danny insisted we do for our launch."

She then mentioned something whose significance I now understand, but would not have back then, even if I had been present to hear it. That morning, she and Dad received a message from Korea, from the wife of Sergei Kraev, their old friend from grad school. The message concerned implants, and it was why Dad was holed up in our study and Mom was running simulations.

Great-grandpa leaned forward. "Karima, sweetie, I don't want to be adding to your stress. If you have work to do today, do it, and I'll take Leon and Ora out for lunch."

"Grandpa, no. I'm glad you're here, and I want us all to spend time together."

Great-grandpa placed his hand on Mom's. "Let me give you advice from the perspective of someone who has been on this Earth for a hundred thirteen years. There will always be problems. There will always be time to work on those problems. Slow down and take a moment to enjoy. The whole world is celebrating you."

Mom was silent for five seconds. Then, for the first time in her life, she hard disconnected her own implant. "You're right," she told Great-grandpa, then stood up from the table, walked inside, and came upstairs to get me.

I was sitting in my room, calmer, when Mom opened the door. I apologized and begged to be reconnected, but she stayed firm. "You're thirteen now and it's time you start acting like an adult. Come downstairs and eat lunch with Great-grandpa. Or stay here. It's up to you."

Mom left my room and a minute later I followed. As I passed our study, I noticed Dad was still there, wearing only his sleeping scrub bottoms, staring blankly at the wall. It's not fair, I thought: Dad gets to skip lunch.

By the time I got back to the table, Great-grandpa, Mom, and Ora were eating. I retrieved my toppled chair and joined them.

Great-grandpa held his spoon over his bowl. "This caldo is so good. The aroma, the way the potatoes melt on your tongue . . . it brings back memories from a hundred years ago . . . the pandemic. We were home all day every day, my parents started making proper dinners for the first time, and a caldo like this became a staple."

I lifted a spoon of broth to my mouth. "There was a pandemic when you were a kid?" My attention was finally where it should have been all along, on Great-grandpa. "Weren't pandemics from the Middle Ages?"

He smiled at me. "Maybe history won't be your field, Leon. Yes, 2020, caused by a virus."

"Computer virus?"

"No, biological. The only way to block transmission was to isolate people. One day we were at school, and the next day we stayed home, and didn't leave our house for months."

"Why didn't GHO destroy it?" Ora asked.

"Sweetie, they couldn't. It's hard to imagine how much has changed in a hundred years. The technology you take for granted didn't exist when I was growing up."

Great-grandpa explained that had people back then been equipped with even the first generation of onboard health diagnostics, precision quarantining would have contained the virus.

"Things were primitive. We thought we were living in an age of modern medicine, but oh boy, the pandemic was a rude awakening. Forget about a cure—in the beginning we could barely test people. And our main technique for fighting the infection—we called it 'social distancing'—was the same thing humankind had been doing for centuries."

Ora looked up from her bowl. "Great-grandpa, did anybody in our family get sick?"

"No, we were lucky. My parents were also—"

12:34:25 p.m.

Great-grandpa stopped speaking midsentence, and I saw movement in my peripheral vision. I turned my head. Dad half fell, half stumbled off the stairs into our living room. "Don't reconnect," he whispered. His body spasmed once and he collapsed on the floor. Mom stood up, and in the few seconds it took her to rush over to him, she screamed, "Brain death! I—" Then a mumbled slur of words and she collapsed next to Dad.

+3 seconds

Ora raced to Mom. "Mommy! Mommy!"

I was paralyzed for a second, then I ran inside and got down next to Dad. He was gasping for air and I tried to roll him onto his side. Great-grandpa pushed himself up and out of his chair and shuffled over faster than I had ever seen him move.

"Karima! Danny!" Great-grandpa looked at me. "My glasses!"

I got up, dashed back to our deck, and grabbed them from the table. He wrestled them on and gave verbal instructions: "Critical emergency. Grant access to Karima Yaso and Daniel Levy's health systems."

"Damn twenty-second rule—" I heard him say to himself, but then a moment later, in a tense voice, "It gave instant access. And . . . shit."

I was crouched on the floor again. I looked up. "What?"

"Three hours. For ambulance."

I saw Great-grandpa's eyes scanning information in his glasses. "Brain death. Karima and Daniel. No, this can't be."

Great-grandpa put his hand on a chair and started to lower himself. "Help."

I jumped up, put my arm around his back, supported him from under the shoulders, and helped him into a sitting position on the floor. He put his hand on Mom's chest.

Ora was leaning over Mom. "Mommy stopped breathing!"

I put my ear over Dad's mouth. I didn't hear anything.

I was desperate to get online. To get help. To search for what to do. I looked over at Great-grandpa. "Reconnect me. You should have perm—"

"Something is very wrong," he said, cutting me off, and all of a sudden speaking at a frustratingly slow pace. "Panic can make things worse. I'm going to count to five."

He took a deep breath. "One . . . two. . . . "

It took what felt like an hour.

+1 minute 11 seconds

"Children, listen to me," he said, speaking rapidly again, but with complete thoughts, full sentences. "Dad said not to reconnect. But Mom must have, in the split second she ran over, that's how she saw Dad's diagnostics. What if Dad was also telling you two not to reconnect? No, I'm not risking it. Leon, find the neighbors. Get help."

As I ran out the door, I heard Great-grandpa giving more instructions to his glasses. It felt maddeningly slow for him to be doing this by voice.

+3 minutes 34 seconds

I ran back inside, breathless. "I tried the neighbors.

They're not home or they couldn't hear me shouting and banging."

I saw that Great-grandpa and Ora had slid pillows under Mom and Dad's heads.

There had to be something else. My brain was screaming to be connected, to get help online, to get information. I was sure Great-grandpa, who was studying the display in his glasses, didn't know what he was doing.

"How do you know we're doing everything possible? What if your glasses aren't compatible with Mom and Dad's implants? What if we need to manually switch on implant-controlled breathing? Or reboot Mom and Dad's health systems? You have to reconnect me!"

There was fear in his eyes. He understood so little of our modern implant-centric world. But despite his fear, Great-grandpa stayed firm.

"Ann," he said. An old friend, she'd been an emergency room physician and still lived in the Democratic Union.

He woke her up and they spoke in rapid English. He gave her access to Mom and Dad's health systems. She instructed him. I watched him get close to Mom, examine her chest, neck, and face, and then slide over to Dad and do the same.

Ora wrapped her arms tightly around Mom and pressed her mouth into Mom's cheek. I squeezed Mom's hand and kept repeating "Mom, Mom." Then I looked into her eyes. They were glazed and unfocused, and that's when I understood that whatever had happened to Mom and Dad was likely irreversible.

+4 minutes 33 seconds

Great-grandpa stopped examining Mom and Dad. He

took off his glasses, wiped his eyes with his sleeve, and stared blankly out at the deck.

Ora looked up. "Please, Great-grandpa, do something, please."

"Children." Great-grandpa reached out for us, wrapped us in his wrinkled arms, and began weeping.

2

December 13, 2099
Twenty years before 4-17
Singapore

Sergei Vadimovich Kraev sits on a task chair in his dorm room in Singapore. His knees nearly touch those of his girl-friend, who is perched on the edge of his bed. He stops himself from reaching out to take her hands in his. Instead he looks away from her piercing eyes and takes in her intel-ligent face framed by shoulder-length black hair.

He stares down at his bare feet gripping the base of his chair. "I don't understand. Why?"

"Really? You don't understand?" Lynette says. "You waited until today to tell me about Israel. Now it's too late for me to apply to med school there. So you want to keep dating until graduation and then break up? It's been asym-metric from the start, Sergei. I see that now, and I'm sorry we didn't end things sooner."

"But I don't even know if I'll get in." He has the grades, but hasn't done anything exceptional during his undergrad years. It's a big, competitive world out there and he puts his chances at less than fifty-fifty.

"Sergei, you're getting in, and that's beside the point; the point is you didn't tell me."

First semester sophomore year, he'd been one of nine teaching fellows for Foundations of Quantum Computing. He ran an extra review session before the first exam and opened it to everyone in the course, even people from other sections. Many students, especially those with limited coursework in physics, struggled with the Schrödinger equation.

"There's nothing magical here," he told everyone. "You can understand it, and I'll stay here until you do."

After the semester, Lynette asked him to coffee. He vaguely remembered her as one of a handful of students at his review session who stuck around all night. "Thank you," she told him. "I did well on the exam and in the course." He streamed a smile emoji, thrilled that his extra efforts as a teaching fellow were appreciated.

The following week she invited him to a rainforest, her favorite spot on the island, a place she had hiked with her family growing up. They walked and talked for hours, debating Singapore's policy of requiring comprehensive access to recordings when considering immigration candidates.

"But what about other people's privacy?" he asked. "So just because I want to immigrate to Singapore, the government is privy to a conversation I overheard my parents having five years ago?"

"Things are different here. We're meticulous, not just about immigration but about everything. And you can't argue with the results. We haven't had a single accidental death in twenty-one years."

Yes, that fact was everywhere, part of a list of government accomplishments. And impressive, certainly compared to his native Russia, where there wasn't the same culture of striving for perfection. In ballet maybe, but not in civic systems.

Each time the path narrowed, or other hikers needed to pass, she drew close to him, and, out of respect for her personal space, he slowed or quickened to avoid brushing up against her. They were crossing a wobbly skybridge suspended high above the ground in the tree canopy when she paused, placed both her hands on the braided cable railing, and looked out.

He stood next to her and studied the tropical landscape. He scanned the treetops and spotted a coconut lorikeet. When he turned his head to point the parrot out to her, she moved her hand from the railing to his face, combed his hair away from his eyes with her fingers, leaned in, and kissed him. He tasted the sweet kopi she had been sipping and awkwardly kissed back, his first kiss. Two high school girls with head coverings walked by, smiling, and a feeling of comfort radiated through his body. She took his hand and held it as they observed the birds and monkeys playing in the trees around them.

"Are we officially in a relationship?" she asked a week later.

He looks up and Lynette's expression brings him back to the present. He places his hand on her knee and caresses her kneecap with his index finger, an action that after two years of dating is habitual, but this time the physical contact is charged. She tenderly removes his hand and streams the withdraw consent emoji. His stomach knots. He pulls his arms into his body, raises his head, and stares past her out the transparent exterior wall of his room. Rain has just started pelting the residential tower.

"I really like you. I don't want to break up."

"What do you like about me?"

He can't think of an answer fast enough.

"Sergei," she says through tears, "let's leave it at that." She gets up and walks out.

He stands, paces, and watches the sky darken as the monsoon rain continues to fall. He's never hidden anything from her including his hope of becoming a professor, so why didn't he tell her earlier about grad school in Israel? He knew she was applying to med school and knew that she only applied to institutions in Singapore, and—

A connection request from Mama. He checks the time. No surprise. Before telling Lynette, he'd messaged his parents. Mama must want to talk about it. She's going to make him doubt his decision, which is why he didn't tell her about his application until after he submitted it. He braces himself and accepts the connection.

Sergei's perception shifts from the physical to the virtual, from his modern dorm room to the cramped, dark Moscow apartment where he grew up. Mama is seated at the birch-wood table she and Papa acquired from the previous occupants when they moved in twenty-one years ago, a month before he was born. "My kitten," she says, her hands wrapped around a glass of black tea, a slice of lemon suspended in the liquid, "I don't want you to be disappointed. Do you have a backup?"

He wants to be a professor. It's an aspiration that was seeded the day he arrived on campus and has been growing ever since. On certain rare days he can picture it. He'll mentor generations of students. He'll prove a theorem that will bear his name. He'll develop new algorithms that will push the capabilities of implants.

This, though, is the first time he's sharing even an inkling of his dream with Mama. He kept it to himself because he knew she would dismiss it as impractical.

He explains why Technion. Its PhD program in computer science is the best in the world for implant technology. And yes, he acknowledges, also the most difficult to get into.

"Seryozha, I want to make sure you're being realistic. Think about the long hard road in front of you. Will you get in? If you get in, will you graduate? If you graduate, what are the chances you can get an appointment? How will you support yourself?"

He reminds her that during his gymnasium years he was one of the top math students in Russia. And, he tells Mama, he was encouraged to apply by a professor at NTU—a computer scientist who did her doctorate at Technion and promised to put in a good word with her old advisor.

"Seryozha, I know, but you're no longer a big fish in a small pond. Why not apply to a few other places? And to be safe you should also look for engineering positions at multinationals."

He inwardly sighs. She's right. And he should apply soon. As a senior at NTU he's a strong candidate. It won't look good if he moves back to Moscow and has a gap in his resume. And it's true that not many people, even with PhDs, make it all the way to being professors. He may not be smart enough, or persistent enough.

"You're right."

"Good, you don't want to build sandcastles." Mama then changes the topic. "What are Lynette's plans?"

"Lynette . . . is planning to go to medical school, but I think we're not dating anymore."

When is the deadline to apply to the computer science doctorate program here at NTU? If he applies will Lynette change her mind? If he commits to staying in Singapore will she? One of the things he admires about her is she's decisive. Why didn't he think of that a few minutes ago? Something snapped, and from how she was looking at him he fears it's too late; she's moved on.

"Seryozha, are you listening to me?" asks Mama, who is still seated at the kitchen table in virtual space.

"Sorry, I was thinking."

"Lynette is a kind person."

Kind, yes. Also smart. And she has this remarkable clarity and conviction about everything. Where does it come from?

"I know you like her," Mama continues. "But life isn't always fair, and she probably wants to meet someone Chinese, or maybe someone taller. Be patient and you'll meet someone new."

"Okay."

"Seryozha, I need to go. Don't get your hopes up about Technion. Put some eggs in other baskets."

3

April 16, 2100
Twenty years before 4-17
Pyongyang, Korea

"Why does this counting book for toddlers illustrate '3' with three submachine guns and '4' with four dead American soldiers?"

Fast rhythm, rapped lyrics—*angles, quantum, entangled, want some?*—five: right heel up; six: left toes in; seven: shift weight; eight—

"Kim Sun-hee! Do you have an answer?"

Sunny Kim, not yet world famous and still known by her legal name, Kim Sun-hee, snaps out of her trance and, in the brief moment it takes her to look up at her history teacher, replays, at triple speed, the last few seconds of input from her ears. *Why does this counting book for toddlers illustrate "3" with three submachine guns and "4" with four dead American soldiers?*

Her classmates from Chung Academy watch her, waiting

to see if she'll answer, or if their teacher will call on someone else.

She looks around at the exhibit of old educational books. This is her first time at Pyongyang Central Museum, a rare physical field trip, part of her school's celebration of the fiftieth anniversary of reunification. They've spent the whole morning here, but she hasn't been paying attention, because there are more important things on her mind. Tomorrow she turns sixteen and auditions for 100M. In a few weeks she won't have to think about any of this stuff because dance, not academics, will be where she spends her time. But for now she needs to answer the question.

"Kim Sun-hee," her teacher repeats, "why four dead American soldiers?"

She puts herself in the shoes of an educator assembling a counting book for North Korean toddlers a century ago. Imagining the motivations of others is a skill Appa drilled into her from an early age. "If you can only learn one thing, this is the thing," he told her. He's constantly testing her—talking about her classmates, his colleagues, public figures, even people from history—why is he nervous, why is she pushing this angle, who is he trying to please, what drove her to defect? The trick, he says, is to understand motivation but never develop empathy.

"Because illustrations of dead American soldiers would have pleased the Supreme Leader," Sunny answers.

"Yes, but why?"

This too she learned from Appa.

"The Supreme Leader needed an external threat. He wanted his people to fear the Americans. He wanted Koreans see him as their protector. And when a child is just starting to count—that's a good time to instill hatred."

"Good," her teacher says. "By the time this book was

published in 1994, it had been over forty years since the end of hostilities between the United States and North Korea. And yet, with no firsthand evidence of American ill will, our families a few generations ago had total conviction that the United States was out to annihilate them. I hope you recall from World History that back then the United States was a single unified country, the most powerful on the planet."

————

Sunny prints something she has never worn before: a leotard. Like everyone, she dresses in comfort scrubs and projects her outfit. This is her first time being forced to wear a prescribed physical article of clothing. Annoying, but she gets it. The audition panel wants to see her body and movement unobstructed by loose-fitting scrubs.

She heads downstairs to her dance studio. The natural hardwood floor glows in the sunlight pouring in from the floor-to-ceiling windows. At three hundred square meters, the studio is well over ten times the minimum required for the audition. Even so, she originally thought she would audition in Seoul at the 100M building, but her instructor, Ahn Ye-jin, encouraged her to do it virtually. The roundtrip lag between Pyongyang and Seoul is less than two milliseconds, Instructor Ahn pointed out, more than short enough for synchronous dancing.

Instructor Ahn is already here, staring blankly at a wall. After a moment, Instructor blinks, shakes her head, and focuses on Sunny.

"Are your parents coming?"

Sunny checks. Appa's out golfing. And Eomma's in bed, with do not disturb on. "No," she says, and notices the tiniest bit of relaxation in Instructor's posture.

"Okay, start stretching. You have forty-five minutes. Our bodies are our instruments; if you don't want to get injured, you need to stretch."

Sunny is skeptical of Instructor Ahn. She doesn't doubt her qualifications as a ballerina, but how applicable to pop dance is her insistence on precision and technique? Sunny's had private dance coaches her whole life and nearly all have been effusive in their praise. Ahn Ye-jin, who Appa met through his connections in the art world, and insisted Sunny stick with, has only criticism. In the year since Instructor Ahn became her teacher, the only thing they've worked on is basic movement, Instructor stressing that they would move on when she said so and not before.

Thirty minutes to the audition. Sunny reaches her arms up, bends at the torso, and lines her upper body and outstretched arms up with the floor.

Should she be nervous? She's not. Things others find hard come easy to her. Her friends in middle school stressed about the private high school entrance exam. She studied, but not especially hard, and made it into Chung Academy, the top private school in Pyongyang.

Twenty minutes to the audition. She stands up straight and grabs her right ankle with her right hand. Holding the stretch, she activates exterior view and sees herself the same way the audition panel will in a few minutes. She looks good. High cheekbones, a defined nose, and an expressive smile that she's spent years learning to control. Even with zero embellishment and wearing this absurd leotard, she has the face, the body, and the bearing of a star.

"I've taken many, many auditions," Instructor tells her, "and preaudition jitters are to be expected. Once the audition starts, adrenaline will kick in and training will take over. Remember that the whole thing will be fast. 100M is probably conducting fifteen auditions this morning and they'll want to move through them. It's important not to lose your energy or focus if they cut one part short and ask you to move to the next part. That's normal."

Sunny listens respectfully, but isn't sure why Instructor Ahn is telling her all this, because they've been over it many times before. Perhaps Instructor is herself nervous.

Five minutes to the audition. "Use the bathroom, drink some water, and meditate for two minutes," Instructor says, "that's my preaudition ritual."

Sunny doesn't need a ritual. She's not superstitious.

The audition starts. "No autocorrect," a member of the audition panel reminds Sunny.

Part one. She dances her prepared routine to Quantum Entanglement. No mistakes.

Part two. She freestyles to a pop song composed by an AI for today's auditions. She locks into the rhythm within two beats and can tell the judges are impressed by her improvisation.

Part three. One of the 100M choreographers demonstrates a few bars of a routine and they judge how fast Sunny picks it up. One combination is tricky, the rest is easy.

The whole thing takes eight minutes. "Ms. Kim, thank you for auditioning. We'll be in touch on Monday."

Nailed it.

———

Monday morning. Sunny's father is sitting up in bed. He's chatting with an old university buddy on temporary assignment in the Democratic Union when he receives an incoming connection. He accepts it in neutral virtual space.

"Where are you Appa?"

"In the city."

"Oh, I thought you were at home."

"No, I stayed here last night," he tells her. "What's wrong?"

"I wasn't accepted."

He frowns. "With all those private lessons? And you still screwed up? Maybe they made a mistake. I'll look into it. Don't tell anyone. Don't even think about it. Focus on school. Can you do that?"

"Yes," she says. He sees her eyes are moist.

"Control yourself. You'll be fine."

He disconnects and then turns to Ye-jin, who is sitting next to him in bed, absorbed in something, probably a space drama. "Ye-jin!"

She blinks and looks at him. He catches a moment of horror on her face that she immediately masks. Might be time for a new ballerina, one more appreciative of seeing a shirtless, paunchy, middle-aged man bathed in full sunlight shouting her name.

"Sun-hee didn't get in," he tells her.

"I'm not surprised. Stage presence, yes, she has that, but technique and artistry aren't there. I'm just being blunt. If you and Mrs. Kim can inject some humility, tear down some of her confidence, she might start absorbing what I'm teaching. Then, if I work with her for another two years, she'll have a shot."

He gives a small shake of his head. "A shot in two years isn't what she wants, and it's not what I want."

4

April 18, 2100
Twenty years before 4-17
Singapore

The virtual reception for grad students newly admitted to Technion's computer science department is taking place at seven in the evening in Israel—one in the morning for Sergei. That gives him an excuse to skip. And that was his plan.

But then, a few hours ago, he received a congratulatory message from the department chair saying how much she was looking forward to meeting him. So, at precisely 1:00 a.m. he stands, stares at his dorm room wall, and joins the reception.

He enters a virtual courtyard. He immediately likes its Mediterranean features, so distinct from the equatorial NTU campus. The walls, constructed from yellow-hued Jerusalem stone, are lit from below, casting a warm glow into the open space. Olive trees line the perimeter, each planted in a pebble-filled rectangular perforation in the limestone floor.

There are only two other people here and they appear to be absorbed in conversation with each other. He's reluctant to interrupt, and from the faint threads of speech reaching him, it sounds like they're not even speaking English. Rather than standing alone by the entrance, he makes his way to the far corner where a recorded band is performing.

The music, with lyrics in Hebrew, or maybe Arabic—he checks: Arabic—is unfamiliar. As he listens to the exotic vocal trills and a rhythm that must be North African, his anxiety about moving to Israel tilts toward anticipation. A new place, a new culture, fresh academic challenges.

The band starts on the next song. Four female vocalists sing in close harmony. He looks around. If another student or professor were to walk over he could initiate conversation, perhaps comment on the music or introduce himself. But he's still alone. He remains in the corner and listens to the next few songs. Yes, putting off finding his way into a conversation, but also genuinely mesmerized by the polyrhythmic percussive cycles.

He finally turns away from the band and looks back toward the entrance. He hears the din of the crowd that has now congregated around the virtual drinks table. He scans the group for a friendly face to approach, and is shuffling over when movement in his peripheral vision attracts his attention. He rotates his head and looks at the female student who has just entered the courtyard. He freezes.

Brilliant eyes and a toothy, uninhibited smile. She looks unlike anyone he's ever seen. Sweat films his palms. He knows nothing about her, observed her for a fraction of a second before averting his gaze—what possible basis could there be for his reaction? And yet he is drawn to her, the first time he has ever felt this type of pull. He no longer hears the band playing behind him or sees the others milling about.

She could be using an avatar. But unlikely. The purpose of this reception is to introduce students and faculty to one another before they meet in real life. An avatar, or really any serious altering of appearance, would violate social norms and create an odd first impression. He queries for embellishment level. None, his implant tells him. He lowers his head. He would rather not know that such beauty existed, since in a million years someone like her would never be interested in someone like him.

He turns on annotation and reads the label above her head:

Karima Yaso
Senior, Tel Aviv University
Incoming program: Quantum Algorithms
Incoming group: Professor Ming Liu

Karima. Incredible. Like him, she's an incoming quantum algorithms student, and—he can't believe it—they'll have the same advisor. That gives him a reason, almost an obligation, to introduce himself. She's still standing near the entrance, not yet mingling with others. His heart races. Should he approach? What would he say? What if she's annoyed because she wants to chat with people she already knows? He could mention that he too is joining Professor Liu's group. But now that he thinks about it, since they'll be in the same group, he's certain to get to know her once the semester starts. There's no need to talk to her now with all these other people around. Decision made, his pulse slows.

He glances at her again, trying not to be too obvious

about it. He watches as she approaches two faculty members and joins their conversation. He then starts again for the drinks table, but everyone is now chatting in small groups. Perhaps most of the other incoming students already have friends here, but he doesn't know anyone, and no one looks like they're eager to include him. Anyway, it's late his time. He drops out of the reception. He'll meet the faculty and his fellow students in a few months.

———

Four months later. Sergei arrives in Israel for the first time. Move-in day, they still call it at Technion, though nobody is moving much of anything. Besides the clothes on his back, he has only his guitar. He prints his scrubs, nanobots take care of hygiene and grooming, and everything else is through his implant.

Will he see Karima? She could be moving into the same housing complex, although, if she grew up in Israel, she might have had enough of dorm living in the army. He could have looked it up, and thought about researching her many times, but didn't want to come across as creepy.

Guided by his implant, he walks into a residential building in Old Eastern Village, climbs two flights of stairs, and enters his common room. He peeks into the single bedroom that will be his for the next five years. White walls, large window, bright —not as modern as his room in Singapore, but a clean, functional shell ready for whatever he chooses to project.

He puts his guitar down then hears someone open the common room door. A tall man with a solid build and open smile strides in and drops his bag on the couch.

"Sergei! Hi. Daniel."

Daniel Levy. One of his four suitemates and the third student, along with him and Karima, joining Professor Liu's lab this year. He looks at Daniel, greets him with a nod, and extends his hand. But Daniel doesn't reciprocate. Instead he steps into Sergei's personal space.

"Bro, we're gonna be roommates and labmates. Come here," Daniel says, and bear hugs him.

He gives Daniel an awkward pat on the shoulder and then takes a step back.

Daniel looks around their common room. "We're the only ones checked in so far. I'm meeting a buddy at the gym. Wanna come?"

He's not sure what he would do at the gym, plus he wants to sleep for a few hours and acclimate to the time zone before their meeting with Professor Liu.

"Next time."

"All right, sounds good man."

———

There are three chairs in front of Professor Ming Liu's desk. Sergei is seated in the middle, flanked by Karima to his left and Daniel to his right. Professor Liu explains that he's going to be a visiting faculty member at Tsinghua this semester and wanted to meet his new students in real life before he leaves for Beijing.

Sergei had shown up early for the meeting and, while he was waiting outside Professor Liu's office, he met Karima, who was also early. He could barely speak, her proximity alone enough to overwhelm his senses. The gravelly timbre of her voice, her Hebrew-accented English, even the way she pronounced her name sent bursts of paralyzing signals to his speech centers. Their brief interaction is still ping-ponging through his brain.

"I'm Karima," she had said, putting her hand out. He extended his arm. Did their handshake linger a fraction of a second longer than strictly necessary?

"I was thrilled when I saw we would both be in the Liu group," she said.

"You were?"

"Don't you recognize my name?"

He didn't until she reminded him. The 2096 International Pre-College Math Olympiad. She won silver representing Israel and he, representing Russia, won bronze.

"I have a feeling we'll be spending a lot of time together doing math," she said.

Even now, ten minutes later, he can still feel the warmth of her hand in his. He struggles to get his thoughts focused on Professor Liu, who is explaining that they'll be joining seventeen other graduate students and postdocs in the group.

"What I saw in each of your applications is something I see in myself and everyone else in the lab—off the scale abstract math abilities, an intuitive grasp of quantum computing, and a passion for neuroscience. But I've been wrong before. Just because you got in doesn't mean you have what it takes to do novel BQCI research."

Having been fascinated by BQCI since primary school, Sergei always thinks of it according to the Russian acronym, but of course the English is more universal: Brain Quantum Computing Interface—the technology behind implants. Professor Liu, now his advisor, itself still hard to believe, is the most prolific researcher in the field.

"The good news," Professor Liu continues, "is you're going to be stretched harder than ever before; and, even if you don't graduate, you're still going to emerge the better from your time here."

Sergei wants to ask why students fail to graduate. Is it the classes? Or the difficulty of persisting through the ups and downs of research? But he keeps his mouth shut.

"I've selected a research area for you," Professor Liu says.

With first year primarily about coursework, it's odd that their advisor already knows what he wants them to work on. And is he implying that all three of them will collaborate on a single project?

"Implant technology has advanced rapidly over the last few decades. We're now at the point where visual and aural capabilities outstrip reality. The images you perceive through your implant are sharper than the images from your biological eyes. The reason is simple—we've perfected the visual neural interface, so that implant images, whether rendered or captured from real life by camera, have higher fidelity than those delivered by your biological eyes. The story is the same for our aural systems. We take for granted that music sounds better when it doesn't come through our ears. What I'm saying is obvious, but think about how amazing it is. Two generations ago people couldn't imagine seeing without eyes or hearing without ears."

Professor Liu displays an image of a young woman riding a mountain bike. "This was my grandmother when she was around twenty. What are those white things in her ears?"

"Airpods," Daniel answers without hesitation.

Professor Liu nods. "Eighty years ago people were sticking physical devices in their ears. Those devices received digital signals and turned them into sound waves just so they could be translated into neural signals by our biological aural system. Seems crazy now, like some Rube Goldberg machine, but it was state of the art back then.

"Now, let's talk about smell. Unlike vision and hearing, implants can do only coarse olfactory stimulation. Real, physical smells are far richer. That's why we synthesize food rather than eating nutrient blocks and letting our implants project taste and smell. So . . . why do you think our interface with the olfactory system lags so far behind the other senses?"

Professor Liu waits for one of them to answer.

"Smell digitization isn't good enough?" Karima offers.

Karima speaking gives Sergei an excuse to turn his head and glance at her. He loves how she sounds, earnest, not arrogant, and brave enough to speak up in front of their professor, something he hasn't worked up the courage to do yet.

"No," says Professor Liu, "modern digital noses are good. Less sensitive than the average human nose, but they still do a solid job of mimicking the ability of our olfactory receptors to measure very low concentrations of odorants."

Professor Liu pauses for a moment, then answers his own question. "The problem is security. Olfaction is the only place where our central nervous system is directly exposed to the environment. All our other senses transmit messages to the brain via nerves. But smell is directly tied to the limbic system, which explains the link between smell, emotions and instinctive behavior.

"The current olfactory interface is limited to stimulating receptors in the nose, like the primitive airpods we were talking about. A direct interface with the olfactory bulb requires transmitting signals directly into the limbic system. To do that we need a provably secure quantum interface algorithm."

Professor Liu looks at each of them. "That is your problem area." He then shares twelve articles. "Even though you won't be able to start research this semester, in your free time I expect you to read and understand these papers."

Sergei begins to answer his own question about how students could fail. It's one thing to take five graduate-level courses, and another to learn these papers, which, glancing through the equations, he can tell will require math and biology he's never seen before.

When he turns his attention back to Professor Liu, he's surprised that the conversation has turned to money. "While the heart of your challenge will be conceptual—devising an algorithm and proving its correctness—there are obvious and valuable long term commercial applications."

Daniel seems to be paying very close attention to this part.

Professor Liu tells them that multinational companies will be interested in licensing the algorithm, and explains Technion's policy. Twenty-five percent of royalty streams go to the institution, twenty-five percent go to the department, and the remaining fifty percent go to the professor. "However, I like my students to have skin in the game, and so in my lab, one percent of my portion goes to the students who work on the project."

Sergei calculates. If the project succeeds, and if the algorithm is licensed, he will receive one-sixth of one percent of royalties. He has no idea of the magnitude of licensing fees for implants, but considering that an olfactory interface algorithm would be deployed to ten billion people, even one-sixth of one percent could be substantial.

"Are you clear on everything?"

Sergei, Karima and Daniel each stream the thumbs up emoji.

5

April 19, 2100
Twenty years before 4-17
Pyongyang, Korea

Three hours after his conversation with his daughter, Sunny's father is still physically in his Pyongyang apartment, now seated at the sleek desk in his study. He stares at the flowing Taedong river below, which, on this brilliant spring day, is visible for kilometers through his study's floor-to-ceiling glass walls. Then he shifts his attention and enters his virtual office.

His virtual office, like his physical office, is located on the top floor of the Ministry of Truth and Reconciliation Building. The soaring structure, with its light and airy design, embodies MOTR's commitment to truth and transparency. Back in 2055, when the building was completed, five years after reunification, the contrast with the surrounding communist-era bunkers was striking. Still, it took much more than architecture to persuade former North Koreans to trust the ministry.

He turns his head and studies the static images on his office wall. There are hundreds of photos and he's in all of them. Shaking hands with the current president of Korea, playing golf with the immediate past president, at a dinner with the heads of various ministries, cutting a ribbon with the mayor of Seoul, eating noodles with the chief administrator of Pyongyang. There's even a photo of him bowing to Kim Jeong-hye, the secret great-granddaughter of Kim Il-sung, who came to power through a coup, guided her country to reunification, and then stepped down.

Crystal Chae, the founder and owner of 100M, materializes in his office.

He stands. She bows forty-five degrees, he bows fifteen. He extends his upturned palm, inviting her to have a seat in front of his desk.

"Ms. Chae, thank you for coming to see me."

"Minister Kim, it's my pleasure. I would have been happy to come in person too. I was surprised when your office contacted me, and doubly surprised when they asked if I could meet immediately. I wholeheartedly support your work at MOTR and if there is anything I or my organization can do it will be my honor."

Not bad looking for someone her age. The elegance and control of a former dancer, the deft words of a businessperson.

"Thank you Ms. Chae. I support your work as well. I'm a big fan of 100M. My daughter is too. In fact she auditioned over the weekend and received notice this morning that she was not accepted. I'm sure it was a clerical error, and that's why I wanted to meet, to clear it up."

"Minister Kim, we had three Kims audition on Saturday. Who is your daughter?"

"Kim Sun-hee."

A pause. "I see. It was not a mistake. But please understand, we only have a few spots every year. They usually go to dancers who have already achieved success in national level competitions, or to artists who have built followings on their own."

He's surprised someone of her sophistication isn't taking the easy path.

"Ms. Chae, my daughter wants to be a member of 100M and I would like you to make that happen."

She looks thoughtful for a moment, but not nervous; if anything, he reads a certain smugness in her body language.

"Minister Kim, I imagine you are a good judge of character. How old is your daughter? Sixteen? I wouldn't be surprised if you understand her better than she understands herself. Does she really want to be a member of our group? If it is celebrity she is after, there are easier ways to get there."

Patronizing ajumma. Who does she think she's talking to? Of course, his facial expression remains the picture of civility.

She leans into his desk. "Minister, are you aware of how life changes for a young dancer once they join our group? Your daughter would need to give up every other aspect of her life. She would need to drop out of high school, move to Seoul, live in our dorm, and finish her degree with private tutors. University would be off the table. She would attend dance class every morning seven days a week, and afternoons six of those days would be dedicated to rehearsal. Her physical downtime would be occupied by theory classes in music and choreography. Our coaches would program every detail of her life down to diet and sleep. Is that what she wants to sign up for? Is that what you want for your daughter?"

He leans back in his chair and crosses his arms. "Ms. Chae, my answer may surprise you. What you're describing is intensity. That's something I understand. While you Southerners go about life at a relaxed pace, we Northerners have been running at double your speed, struggling to catch up after a century of isolation. How did you spend your time in high school? Hanging out with friends and taking classes on mindfulness?

"Do you know how I spent my high school years? I woke up at seven, studied standing on the metro, attended class from eight to six, ate dinner at school, and stayed there until ten for self-study. Then I crossed the street to a private academy, did more studying, took the metro back home at midnight, went to bed, and repeated it all again the next day, six days a week, for four years."

She places her hands on her lap. "Minister Kim, I do not doubt your intensity but how is your level of intensity, or for that matter, my level of intensity, relevant to your daughter? It is not you who auditioned for 100M."

Yes, he knows that, and she has no idea where he's going.

"Ms. Chae, my parents, my teachers, my bosses when I first entered the government all told me the same thing— hard work always pays off, so be the hardest working person in the room. Do you know how I became the youngest person since reunification to become a minister?"

He's used to people hanging on his every word, but she looks almost bored. This is becoming a fun challenge. Is she brave or just naive?

"Hard work?" she answers, after realizing his question was not rhetorical.

"No, Ms. Chae, in fact the opposite. It is only after I figured out that working for the perception of results was far more important than actually producing results that my career began to take off. I realized that 'hard work always pays off' is just something those in charge, including now me, tell those not in charge. It's effective. It generates useful output from people who are so busy working, believing the promise, that they never notice the absence of reward."

He unfolds his arms and taps his desk with his index finger. "One of the lessons I've conveyed to my daughter is that if you want something, don't follow the official path to get it. Find a shortcut, be clever, think outside the box. You in the South have been passing your wealth and privilege from generation to generation for over a hundred fifty years. After reunification we in the North started running fast, playing your game by your rules, never realizing we were running on a hamster wheel."

"Why are you telling me all this Minister Kim?"

Time to watch her sweat. "Ms. Chae, I looked into your finances before this meeting. 100M is a commercial success. Your streams generate vast funds, and as far as our accountants could figure out, those funds largely accrue to you personally. So are you the big picture person, and all that stuff about endless training is your way of keeping your dancers running on the hamster wheel? Or maybe you are also running on the hamster wheel, genuinely unaware that all that hard work and sweat is unnecessary."

He glances at his wall, at the photo of him and the president cutting a ribbon in front of the Performing Arts Center in Chongjin. "Well, I have news for you. 100M is not the Kirov Ballet. It's a popular dance group with millions of fans. If you think even one percent of one percent of them could tell whether your dancers rehearse eighty hours a week or eight, you're mistaken."

He looks her straight in the eyes. She must have been stunning in her prime. "You are going to do two things. First, give my daughter a spot on 100M. Second, ease up on the intensity of the training so she can relax and pursue other interests in parallel."

She straightens her back. "Minister Kim, respectfully, I do not have words to express how vehemently I disagree with you. Not only am I sure that hard work is the reason for 100M's success, and not only do I believe that hard work is the primary reason Korea is now the world's second largest economy, hard work is also intrinsically good. We humans are built to work, and relaxation is only enjoyable, indeed the concept only even makes sense, when it follows work."

How did she get this far?

"As for our fans being unable to discern excellence, that is false. Our audience reacts to greatness. And when things are off they know it, even if they can't pinpoint that a dancer moved their foot thirty milliseconds early. There's a reason we're the best in the world at what we do, and it's not luck or good marketing. So no, we will not be giving your daughter a spot."

She stands as if to leave, but he motions for her to sit back down.

Ah, these self-righteous Southerners, so sure of their moral high ground, unable to take a hint.

"Ms. Chae, do you understand the purpose of the Ministry of Truth and Reconciliation? The ministry has the power to take any action necessary to secure the harmony of unified Korea. Fifty years ago that effort was focused exclusively in the North. My predecessors investigated the camps and achieved reconciliation between prisoners and guards. They exposed the crimes of party leadership while preserving the social fabric.

"But now, fifty years later, that's behind us, and the big threat to Korea is the economic and cultural disparity between North and South. Should 100M, an important contributor to Korea's worldwide soft power and cultural hegemony, be allowed to exist when all of its dancers come from the South? What message does that send to our population? A dangerous one, I'm certain. If we've learned anything from the American Second Civil War, it's that cultural problems like this will fester and need to be nipped in the bud. Fortunately for Korea, this ministry is empowered to do that."

6

May 10, 2102
Eighteen years before 4-17
Haifa, Israel

Wednesday night around eleven. Sergei is in his room on the Technion campus, sitting on the floor, back against the wall, legs outstretched and crossed. Karima is pacing back and forth between his bed and the door. They're working on a problem set for 18.457, one of their last required courses. After this semester, it's all research.

"Three days," Karima says, "and we're no closer than when we started."

"Could it be unsolved?" he asks, aware that Professor Seth, who has been teaching 18.457—Advanced Theoretical Quantum Cryptography—for over two decades, is famous for throwing an unsolved problem into a problem set once every few years.

"At this point I wish we could check," Karima says.

They can't because everyone in the class took an enforced oath.

She stops pacing. He looks up.

She taps her temple. "I have an idea. Go back to our original approach from two days ago but use Bass's theorem."

That's interesting. He pulls up their equations. She explains her thinking, that the problem could be more tractable in classical space, and if they can prove it's valid to use Bass's theorem, they can transform between spaces.

He makes a branch from their old work and they start playing with her idea. This is promising. Half an hour passes in a minute, then another half hour.

"Yes!" she says, in a shouted whisper. "It works."

He looks up. He's been burned before by premature declarations of victory. It's always good to check and double-check. "Let's work it backward just to be sure."

After another hour he's confident too. "It holds."

"*Quod erat demonstrandum,*" Karima adds. Latin. She's in a good mood.

He insists they go over the full problem set before submitting, which they do, although he does most of the checking because she's falling asleep.

"Is it okay if I sleep here?"

His mind races. "You mean in my bed?"

"Yeah, if it's okay with you, my eyes won't stay open. We're skinny, we can share."

He nods his assent, not trusting himself to speak, then watches her climb into his bed. He follows and lies down near the edge, careful to avoid contact.

His processor is still running at full speed. Karima is lying next to him. His intellectual partner. This person who has dominated his every waking thought and every dream for two years. Her blazing mind, her seedling-thin body, her

gravelly voice, her volcanic hazel eyes, the almost imperceptible asymmetry of her nose.

His mind sputters. Should he brush his fingertips against
hers? What if he ruins it by moving too fast? She must like
him or she would never ask to sleep here. Even exhausted
she could have walked the five minutes back to her place.
But what if she's waiting for him to make the first move? He
slides a bit closer. He inhales. Citrus, ocean, za'atar, warmth.

He stops. He doesn't want to ruin it. This moment of
suppressing desire and lying here platonically is a memory
they can savor the rest of their lives. He's barely slept for
three days but his mind is still overclocked and showing no
signs of slowing. He instructs his implant to put him to
sleep.

———

He wakes before eleven the next day. Karima is gone. He
replays and sees that she got up and left his room around
eight. Moments later she connects with him. Must have set
an alert tied to him waking.

"Thanks again for letting me stay there. I was so tired."

"How'd you sleep?" he asks.

"Really good. Such a beautiful application of Bass's theorem. Can't wait to check if it was an unsolved problem. See if
our approach was novel."

Sounds like she's going to end the connection. He needs
to take some action, show some interest. She's speaking but
he can't focus on her words. Just ask anything! And then he
does.

"Want to go for a run?"

Brief silence. Then: "Yeah, and after, let's get falafel."

———

This feels right. He runs in stride with Karima who is telling him about her grandfather. They approach Romema and begin ascending Mount Carmel. She doesn't slow and neither does he, but they stop talking, and he returns to his own thoughts.

He should tell her how he feels today. If he doesn't, he'll regret it the rest of his life. But does she like him? It seemed so clear last night, but now, thinking in the light of day, why would she? And if he takes this step there's no going back.

They reach the Baha'i Gardens, pause for a minute to take in the view of nineteen exquisitely manicured grass terraces, and then run fast downhill the few kilometers into Wadi Nisnas.

"I'll grab us a spot. You order the falafel, and get me extra zhug," she tells him.

He orders two falafels on pita. Without checking with her, hoping he's not being too forward, he also grabs four beers, then sits down next to her at the bar. She's looking across the street, at a sweets shop housed in a stone building that must have been built by hand centuries ago. He turns his head. She's still breathing heavily from their run and he watches a glistening bead of sweat roll down her neck. A beam of sunlight bounces off the tiny silver Star of David earring on her left ear, catching his eye and making him uneasy.

She wraps her slender fingers around her beer, takes a sip, and sighs. "Spicy falafel and a cold beer after a run." She puts the bottle down. "Sergei, the falafel here is as good as it gets. Crispy, not oily, with accents of parsley and cumin so subtle that the creamy nuttiness of the chickpeas shines through."

He didn't realize she was so into food, or maybe it's just this type of food.

She looks toward the counter where a line has now formed. The food synthesizer is a standard small restaurant model, she tells him. Technically speaking an identical falafel sandwich could be printed anywhere in the world, but the owner has never licensed the recipe.

"There's only one other place where you can get this falafel. In the DU, believe it or not, at the owner's cousin's shop. In a town outside Boston, close to where my grandfather grew up. You know, my grandfather is probably the reason I love this food so much."

He struggles to concentrate on her words. He's getting progressively more nervous. She's over halfway done with her falafel and he still hasn't figured out how to broach the only topic on his mind. He finishes his first beer and starts in on the second and tries harder to listen.

". . . and speaking of licensing, did you know that Professor Liu is off-the-charts wealthy? From the royalty stream of the first BQCI algorithm he developed. Professor is pretty low key about it. But a few years ago there was a party to celebrate the lab's twenty-fifth year and I heard he hosted it on his own private LEO yacht."

Should he say something? He's already finished his beer and it looks like she's almost done eating. Maybe he should react to what she just said, something about royalty streams. "Yeah, I've realized these last two years that he's pretty savvy about the commercial side of things."

A few minutes later she finishes her second beer. "Let's head back. We finally have time to read the journal club paper."

Together, they walk back. Blue skies, the faint smell of the Mediterranean Sea on the breeze, the distant call to prayer from The Great Mosque, and the beer's lingering buzz.

He needs to act. What is he waiting for?

He hears her saying something about Bass's theorem. He turns to her.

"Karima."

But he can't bring himself to say anything else, and she doesn't notice.

They keep walking. He gets a bit closer, and, as they walk side by side, he wills his right hand to brush up against hers. Having crossed that barrier, he gets bolder and holds her hand in his, without breaking stride. She gives a reassuring squeeze and lets go, all the while still talking about Bass's theorem. He grabs her hand again and now she comes to a stop and looks at him.

He's beyond the point of no return. He looks into her eyes and tells his implant to turn off her projection. Her blue and white workout clothes are replaced with plain uncolored exercise scrubs. She has white salt marks on her face where sweat evaporated. He likes her even more this way. If he could just stare into those hazel eyes the rest of his life.

He needs to be clear, convey his interest without ambiguity. He streams a classic red heart emoji. "Karima, would you have dinner with me tonight?"

He feels her let go of his hand. After a few moments she speaks.

"Sergei, I'm sorry if I sent you the wrong signal by sleeping in your room last night. I love how we collaborate. I love our friendship. But I'm not looking for a relationship. And for sure not with someone in the same lab. I need to stay focused on my PhD."

His insides sink. He will later think this is the moment

he should have walked away with his head up, but instead he opens his mouth. He hears himself. He's outside of his own body, powerless to stop, unable even to prevent Russian grammar from intruding on his normally flawless English.

"Do you not feel the connection between us, Karima? You are the most incredible, the most beautiful person in the world. From the instant I first saw you at reception, there hasn't been a five-minute interval when you haven't been in my thoughts or dreams. I love everything about you. When we're together I feel alive, and when we're apart I think only of excuses to be together. You must feel some of that. Do you not?"

She purses her lips and appears thoughtful. Then, "Sergei, I'm so flattered. I have enormous respect for you. I do feel a connection, a strong one, but it's an intellectual connection. I think of you . . . like a brother."

She streams a hug emoji, opens her arms, and hugs him. Immobile, yielding, his heart fracturing in her embrace, he will remember the feel of her arms on his back and the radiant warmth of her face next to his for the next eighteen years.

"I need to get back," she says, and hails a car.

And just like that, he's alone. He sits down on a block of concrete that forms part of an urban planter containing a wilted, stunted palm tree and lowers his head.

What's wrong with him?

7

June 23, 2103
Seventeen years before 4-17
Seoul, Korea

Saturday night. Sunny finishes a high-energy routine. Her chest rises and falls as she catches her breath. She smiles and looks out at the millions of faces in the virtual arena. "Sunny! Sunny!" Tens of thousands of fans scream her name and stream mini suns, exclusive emoji purchased in packs of a hundred. The emoji arc through the air, emit bursts of yellow and orange light, morph into amber hearts, then collapse into themselves.

She was born to do this. Her fans love her, need her, and after dancing with 100M for three years, she is an idol, recognized in every corner of the planet. If she has a frustration, it's with the other dancers on the stage, who compete for attention and vie for lead positions in the choreography, rather than remaining content with supporting roles.

A soft monophonic piano line envelops the space. She

sits in the lotus position and bows her head, her body still. The audience quiets. It's hard to believe they're into this. What a music critic described as "an achingly beautiful downtempo routine" when it debuted last livestream.

The music, "Longing," is a haunting ballad by Swedish musical phenom Annelise. The dance was choreographed by Pae Yo-kyeong who takes the front-center position, two rows in front of Sunny. Over the first four counts Yo-kyeong raises her head, and over the next three she moves her right hand to cover her face. On four she snaps her head back and, moving with almost imperceptible speed, lowers her back until she is prone, lying on the stage. She twists, returns to seated, and positions her hand over her heart.

It's slow, it's boring, Sunny can dance her own part in her sleep, and the four minutes take an hour.

Finally, the last note of "Longing" rings out. Sunny has returned to the lotus position, which she and the others sustain, immobile, for a full minute of silence. She's astonished that the audience is also still, rapt, soundless for the full sixty seconds.

She stands. Thunderous applause and suspended crying emoji fill the venue. She basks in the adoration of millions of fans. She's not alone on stage, and yes, her current position means she is partially occluded for much of the audience, but she senses that all eyes are on her. She brings her index finger and thumb together and streams yellow heart emoji into the stands. Then she bows and exits the virtual stage.

She blinks and shakes her head. Although now surrounded by the white walls and uniform neutral light of the 100M production studio, her mind still echoes with the sights and sounds of her fans screaming her name. She looks around and sees the other dancers, positioned exactly as they were on the venue stage, but now in real life, dripping with sweat.

A coach hands her a bottle of water.

"They love me," Sunny says, gulping down the drink.

She tells their assistant business manager to bring up the stats.

Pae Yo-kyeong—371 million emoji

Sunny Kim—264 million emoji

Jung Eun-ha—

She points at the stats. "No way, I saw more emoji out there for me than Yo-kyeong. Eun-ha, isn't that what you saw? The stats are screwed up, and—"

Yo-kyeong interrupts her. "I have something important to discuss." Sunny watches Yo-kyeong look around the studio, saying nothing, until she has everyone's attention.

"Something has been bothering me these past three years. I finally discussed it with my agent, who reviewed my contract, and pointed out that we, the dancers, have the right to override ownership and vote out other dancers."

Sunny's pulse accelerates. Where is Yo-kyeong going with this? Is she trying to use her senior status with the group to get rid of the one dancer who has surpassed her as fan favorite? That will never work.

"It requires," Yo-kyeong continues, "a two-thirds majority and a one-week notice period. I'm calling for a vote to remove Kim Sun-hee."

Nobody seems shocked. Has Yo-kyeong already discussed this with the others behind Sunny's back? Sunny feels her fists clench and her heart beat even faster. Her vision tunnels on Yo-kyeong. Before she even realizes it, Sunny has stepped in front of Yo-kyeong. She smells the bitch's kimchi perspiration and stares, unblinking, into her nasty eyes. "If you have a problem with me, you can tell it to my face."

Yo-kyeong backs up and speaks in measured tones, in words that sound rehearsed to Sunny. "Kim-little-sister, I know you try. I know some fans love you. But you don't belong here. You don't dance at our level. You bring us all down."

Condescending, self-righteous, conceited—

Strangle Yo-kyeong. That's what she wants to do. But she gets control of herself. How many of the others share Yo-kyeong's view? Has Yo-kyeong poisoned them? Sunny can't play into Yo-kyeong's hand. She lowers her head. Best to project humility.

"Pae-elder-sister," she says, calmer, "sorry for my outburst. And I'm upset you feel that way. I love 100M and feel that I belong here with you and my other sisters. It makes me sad that you want to vote me out, but that's your right, and I understand."

Yo-kyeong gives her the slightest bow of the head, then turns and exits the studio. It's late and everyone else starts filing out too. Sunny follows them to the elevator bank.

"Good night," she says. A few of the other dancers reciprocate without making eye contact. An elevator door opens. She steps in, alone, because at present she's the only member living in the lower dorm, two floors below the studio.

The doors shut. Yo-kyeong is clever. Her relationships with most of the others were formed years before Sunny became a member. But it's the fans that count and they love Sunny. No matter, she's not getting voted out. And if none of the others like her? So what. She'll buy a puppy to keep her company. She's responsible enough now. She straightens her back and smiles. The elevator door opens and she walks to her room.

8

June 26, 2102
Eighteen years before 4-17
Haifa, Israel

Sergei grabs the underside of his chair from both sides and pulls up, tensing his arm muscles for ten seconds, twenty seconds, then relaxing. He already made it into the most prestigious computer science graduate program in the world. It would be nice if Xyloom could accept that as proof of his abilities instead of interviewing him, but companies have their own way of doing things, and holding conversations seems to be one of them.

Sergei repeats his exercise. Then it's time. He enters a virtual door and finds himself in a meeting room. Emily, his recruiter, stands up.

"Hi, Sergei! It's so good to see you again. How are you? Where are you today? Haifa?"

"Yes, on campus," he tells her, trying to match her rah-rah energy. She says something about the beautiful weather in Tel Aviv, her stroll through the reverse virtual gardens this morning, her plans to get to the beach after work, and asks if he's been outside.

"Yes, this morning, running to calm my nerves before the interview."

"No reason to be nervous Sergei. You're gonna do great. Our team is excited to meet you. I want to check—has anything changed in your situation or thinking since last week?"

Last week was when he met her for a preliminary conversation. No, he tells her, nothing has changed, he's still planning to leave grad school.

"And how far along are you with other companies?"

Is she allowed to ask that? He tells her that he's done a number of first- and second-round interviews, and adds that one company turned him down after the final round.

"I appreciate you being so open."

Maybe he shouldn't have told her.

"You'll be interviewing with three people today," Emily tells him, and explains that she'll be back at the end to wrap up. He'll need to take an enforced oath—first, not to use aid during the interview and, second, to keep his recording private. "You'll be working through problems. They're not intended to be difficult or require specialized knowledge, but we've calibrated responses across many candidates, and that's why we need them to stay confidential."

Emily tells him that his first interview will be with Jessie, a senior engineer who's running ten minutes late. "She'll join you in a bit. In the meantime, wait here and look at these materials." Then Emily leaves him alone.

He spends a few minutes looking through the materials. What's he doing here? He can't stay at Technion and be around Karima for another three-plus years, but he also doesn't want to leave the BQCI field or go back to Russia. He needs to get a job at a multinational so he can live in Korea, Israel, Singapore or Sweden—the KISS countries. All four welcomed refugees from the American Second Civil War and are now, along with China, the world's economic and technical superpowers.

But is he prepared to be a cog in a massive machine like Xyloom with its sixty thousand employees? It's not what he dreamed of a few years ago, but the problems should be stimulating. He'll also get to work on things that actually make it into production, into use in humans. And, maybe, while he won't be teaching courses, there'll be opportunities to mentor people, especially once he gains experience.

His interviewer still hasn't shown up. Strange. Maybe they're not that interested in him. And he's missing journal club for this. Is Karima wondering why he's not there?

Karima. After the falafel catastrophe, he'd thrown himself into his studies. It was odd working on problems and reading journal articles by himself after two years of operating as a combined brain. Even as he worked solo, he held an imaginary dialogue with her, throwing out ideas and listening to her take on them. He kept hoping to run up against a problem he genuinely couldn't solve so that he would have no choice but to ask her for help.

He did see her at lab meetings. They even had a lengthy technical discussion about their olfactory interface algorithm, but others were around, and she gave no indication that things between them were abnormal. But of course they were, otherwise they would still have been studying together.

He debated inviting her to his family's bard festival, the date of which coincided with the deadline for his last problem set of the semester. The year before, he had told her all about it, explaining that his parents were fans of old Soviet bard music. Back when he was little, his dad created a virtual island and started inviting friends and family to sing songs around a campfire. Over the years the tradition grew into an annual celebration of bard, with hundreds of fellow enthusiasts joining his parents on the island. Karima had been fascinated and, after she expressed interest, he almost invited her, but didn't, fearing the things his parents might say to her.

At least in theory, there had been no reason not to invite her this year. She was interested, or had been the prior year; and, although his concerns about his parents still stood, perhaps showing another side of himself could get her to see him in a new light.

On the other hand, he didn't want her to come only out of obligation, perhaps feeling bad for how they'd left things. Nor did he want to receive another explicit rejection. He kept going round and round in his head all week. Finally, after turning in his problem set, he reached a decision. He sent her the info to attend.

That evening, he stood on the bow of a virtual ferry, bound for Papa's island. The island was modeled after Ostrov Putyatin, located fifty kilometers southeast of Vladivostok in the Sea of Japan. When Sergei was ten, Papa added transportation to the experience. To get their guests into the right mindset, or, per Mama's frequent criticism, to frustrate their friends, Papa made it impossible to materialize directly on the island. A visitor had to board a ferry on the mainland, and then keep their attention on the journey for the full twenty-minute ride.

For the first time in weeks Sergei had nothing to do. He looked up at the twin funnels exhausting black smoke into the sky. He listened to the rumble of the engine and the chatter of AI passengers. He looked down at the hull cutting through the waves, then stared across the sea at the grass-covered rolling hills of their still distant destination.

How would the scene change if their olfactory brain interface research succeeded? He would be able to smell the saltwater air. He would also smell the slices of salami and cucumber sandwiched between two pieces of butter-slathered black bread in the hands of the AI passenger standing next to him. And knowing Papa's commitment to authenticity, he might even smell diesel fumes, whatever those smelled like.

He checked the time. It had been five minutes since the ferry set off. Another fifteen to go. Would Karima be there? She hadn't replied to his message one way or the other, but at that very moment she could have been on her own virtual ferry, with her own fellow AI passengers, en route to the island. He wouldn't know until he arrived. He imagined they were together, standing next to each other on the deck, holding hands, the simulated wind blowing her virtual hair.

One time he'd made this same trip with Lynette. It was during their junior year at NTU, also at the end of a semester. He stood with her at this exact spot holding hands, and then more than holding hands. Physically they were in his dorm room, and as things progressed, he and Lynette lay down on his bed, which he perceived as stretching out on the boat deck. Lynette started to loosen the drawstring on his scrubs and he unintentionally switched his focus from the ferry to his room. By Papa's fanatical logic, the ferry turned around and took them back to the mainland. They never made it to the festival.

He'd barely thought about Lynette since moving to Israel. Had she felt about him the way he felt about Karima?

No, theirs was a friendship—warm, comfortable, orders of magnitude less intense than what he felt for Karima.

He looked up. The ferry was pulling into the dock. He told himself to be patient. He could wait until he and Karima graduated. He could wait his whole life if need be.

He disembarked. She wasn't on the island, at least not yet. But hundreds of bard enthusiasts were, and he recognized many of them from previous years. He followed the crowd up the sandy beach.

Mama and Papa were sitting on two logs by a campfire, and he visualized how they were seated in real space, on stools in their tiny Moscow apartment. Papa picked up his intentionally somewhat-out-of-tune seven-string guitar, plucked out a C chord, and started singing: *"Zdravstvuy, zdravstvuy, ya vernulsya."* By the second *"zdravstvuy,"* everyone around the campfire joined in. "Hi, hi, I've returned . . . back from the region with only big mountains," the lyrics went as the chords progressed from C major to A seven and eventually back to C major.

After "I've Returned," Papa started on *"Ty u Menya Odna"* in the key of A minor. "You are the only one . . . like the moon in the night . . . there is no one else like you . . . not beyond a river, not behind a fog, not in distant countries." Sergei closed his eyes as he sang along to his favorite song.

As he moved his lips, he was transported back to fourth grade at Moscow School 1543. There was a talent show and for some reason he wanted to participate, something his twenty-four-year-old self could not imagine. His idea was to accompany himself on guitar and sing *"Ty u Menya Odna."* Mama discouraged him, fearing that kids his age wouldn't be interested in old bard music. He insisted and started practicing, and Mama, listening, kept telling him that he wasn't ready to perform in front of an audience, and it might be wiser to focus on his stronger subjects, or if he really wanted to be part of the talent show, to do something safe, like recite a poem. He stuck with his plan and sang in front of the whole school. On the walk back to their apartment Papa pointed out a few chords he'd flubbed. Mama didn't say anything.

Sergei opened his eyes and looked around to see if Karima had shown up. No. He sang along with the next song, and the song after that. He knew all the lyrics by heart.

Fifty songs later, the crowd lost steam. No doubt copious quantities of vodka had been consumed in the physical world, undercounted by the number of virtual bottles lying around the fire.

Mama held a glass in the air. "Dear friends—last song." There was no question of what that would be. *"Milaya moya . . . solnyshko lesnoye . . . gde v kakikh krayakh . . . vstretish'sya so mnoyu?"*—"My dear . . . where and in which lands will we meet again?" By the end Sergei's eyes had teared up. He waved at Mama and Papa and then dropped out.

His attention was returned to his dorm room where it was late and dark. After four hours of campfires, crowds, and bard music, he was ready to unplug his brain. He turned off his implant's audio and visual interfaces and lay in the dark for a few minutes, letting natural sounds filter in through his biological ears without noise cancelation. He heard rhythmic snoring through one wall, and through the other, the one shared with Daniel, moaning. One of Daniel's friends was over, female by the sound of it.

Sergei rested for another few minutes. Finally, he stood up and walked to the bathroom. Ten minutes later, towel wrapped around his waist, he stepped out into the dark common room. A creak drew his attention toward Daniel's room where someone was opening the door and backing out on tiptoe. It was hard to see in the dark, especially since his eyes hadn't yet adjusted, but from behind it looked like a woman, like Karima.

The person turned, said, "Hi, Sergei," and entered the bathroom.

9

June 24, 2103
Seventeen years before 4-17
Seoul, Korea

You don't belong here. You don't belong here. Sunny, lying in bed, can't stop thinking about what Yo-kyeong said to her in front of the group last night. Eun-ha, the others, they're Sunny's friends, her sisters. Why didn't they jump to her defense? How could they desert her? Couldn't they see what Yo-kyeong was doing? Why were they afraid to stand up to her?

With trepidation, Sunny connects with Appa, tells him what happened, and asks for his help.

"Fixing this is child's play," he says. "Who's the natural leader?"

"The one who wants to vote me out. Pae Yo-kyeong. She's like the elder sister."

"Okay, here's what you do. . . ."

Sunny stands, stretches, walks around her room, and sits back down on her recliner. She resumes skimming old interviews of Yo-kyeong. Painful, because the fraud is so good at acting genuine.

> **Journalist**: "How did you first get interested in dance?"
>
> **Pae Yo-kyeong**: "It happened when I was five. My mother had business in Moscow and took me with her. She was invited to see Swan Lake at the Bolshoi. She almost left me with hotel babysitting, didn't think I could sit through a ballet, but gave in after I begged. I was mesmerized. Even now I get goose-bumps thinking about it. Rogozina danced the lead. Spellbinding, this aura that captivated the audience. By the time the curtain closed, I knew."

What bullshit. There's no way a five-year-old could sit through a ballet. Korea's dance darling my ass. Why doesn't the reporter call her out?

What was Sunny doing at that age? Five she's not sure about, but eight she remembers, no matter how much she tries to keep the memory buried. Around the time she started third grade, when she was seven, she begged Appa and Eomma for a puppy. Eomma didn't want an animal in the house. But Sunny didn't let up. Finally, as her eighth birthday approached, Appa said she could have one. Her puppy would have to stay in the cottage and sleep in a kennel. She would be solely Sunny's responsibility. "Are you ready for that?"

"Yes," she told Appa.

They picked her up from the breeder on Sunny's birth-day, an eight-week-old Samoyed, white as snow and fluffy as cotton balls. She named her Gureum, cloud. They played on the grass for hours that first day, until finally Gureum fell asleep in her arms. After that, they were inseparable. Month after month, Sunny spent all her free time with Gureum in the cottage, in their yard, on walks around the neighborhood, or in the nearby dog park, but never in the main house. She taught Gureum how to wave, paw, and dance.

December came, and with it early cold winds and whirling sleet. Sunny woke in a mood and didn't feel like going outside that one day. Let Gureum stay in her kennel. She would be safe and warm, and Sunny would go the next day.

The next day sandbagged her with guilt. She'd promised to be responsible, and she hadn't. Would Gureum understand? The wind whistled outside, blowing her thoughts around like so many snowflakes. With this cool, Gureum would be fine without water.

The third day she worried, worried that she hadn't brought food or drink to Gureum in three days, and hadn't taken her out of her cage. Sunny couldn't even bring herself to look out the window, because there the cottage was across the yard, with Gureum, abandoned, locked in her kennel inside.

On the fourth day she willed herself to enter the cottage, and the smell hit her. A wrenching guilt in her stomach, rising dread in her chest as she approached Gureum's kennel.

When she ran out of tears, Sunny wrapped Gureum in a blanket and buried her in their garden, using a metal hand trowel to dig into the cold earth.

She told Appa and Eomma that Gureum ran away. Yet they must have known the truth because, as she realized only when she was older, pets have implants.

Why hadn't Appa intervened before it was too late? Why had he never confronted her with the fact she murdered Gureum?

Sunny sits still for a few minutes, lost in thought, forgetting her current task. She would give everything she had to again nestle her head in Gureum's fur, hug her, rub noses, brush her matted coat, inhale her clean puppy smell.

Then she forces her mind from the past and returns to Yo-kyeong. She speeds ahead in the recording.

> **Journalist:** "When do you feel most ecstatic?"
>
> **Pae Yo-kyeong:** "As a dancer or a choreographer? Dancing . . . I get to give out so much energy. To move millions of people on a livestream to ecstasy, or to sadness. It's an incredible feeling. As a choreographer, it's when I get to see these ideas in my head transmitted to the world. Humans have been dancing for millennia. During that entire time our anatomy has remained unchanged, yet we can still come up with new creative ways to move. I love it when I'm out and see random people grooving with moves that originated in my head."

Sunny rolls her eyes. Do people believe this crap? They wouldn't if they could see the loser's true face.

> **Journalist:** "You famously started out as a backup dancer for Samuel. How did that come about?"
>
> **Pae Yo-kyeong:** "I always wanted to be my own artist, but I was almost twenty-two and wasn't having any luck getting into a dance group. I worried I had missed my window by going to university. A family friend introduced me to Park Byung-ho, who was

managing Samuel and a few other musical artists at the time. Mr. Park hired me as a backup dancer for Samuel. It was a formative experience and I did it for two years. Whenever we were on stage, though, I was jealous of Sam. I wanted to become an artist myself, perform my own original choreography with dance at the center, and that's why I auditioned for 100M."

She might be able to use this. She searches for recordings containing Yo-kyeong and Park Byung-ho.

Yes. Two clips she can use. The first, which has no discernible audio, shows Yo-kyeong and Mr. Park at an intimate table in an upscale restaurant. The second is from a Samuel rehearsal and shows Mr. Park with his hand resting casually on Yo-kyeong's bare shoulder. It's obvious. This is the real Yo-kyeong.

Now Sunny searches the 100M fanbase for someone with a connection to Samuel. Lee Sang-chul. He's an accountant on the Samuel business management team and appears to be obsessed with Sunny, having spent a small fortune on bursting sun emoji. She has her AI send Lee Sang-chul a verified private message:

> *Mr. Lee! Thanks for being such a loyal Sunny fan. Sunny loves connecting with her supporters and you've been selected for a private meet and greet this Wednesday. Let me know if you're interested.*

———

Friday. Two days until the vote.

Dispatch: "What's going on with 100M's Pae Yo-kyeong? Yo-kyeong has always been seen as the creative anchor of the group, and, pun intended, something of a goody two-shoes. Now the fandom is up in arms after evidence emerged that Yo-kyeong slept her way into Samuel, where her career started, and there are rumors that she also slept her way into 100M. Shown in this recording is Yo-kyeong having a romantic dinner with Park Byung-ho, the manager of Samuel and long rumored by industry insiders to be a pay-for-play type of guy. Here's Park Byung-ho with his arm around Yo-kyeong during a Samuel rehearsal in 2094. Why did this all just come out? An accountant for Samuel was conducting a routine audit and uncovered unusual expenses. Looks like Park Byung-ho was using corporate funds to cover luxury hotel rooms where he allegedly had physical relations with Yo-kyeong. Gross. Not something I even want to imagine. Fans are calling for Yo-kyeong to leave 100M. We'll share more as the story develops."

———

Sunday. A slate gray conference table in a round virtual room, the walls decorated with stylized black and white glamour shots of dancers dating all the way back to Fred Astaire and Ginger Rogers from the 1930s.

Sunny looks around at her fellow 100M members. Should she speak first? No, better to stay quiet, see how things play out, see if the loser even has the gall to bring up voting.

Yo-kyeong, who is seated across from her, leans forward and rests her clasped hands on the table. "I've been thinking long and hard about how to start this meeting." She swivels her head, pausing on each person except Sunny.

"A rumor emerged Friday that I slept my way into Samuel. I'm going to share something with you that I've kept secret for nine years."

Yo-kyeong presses her palms together and lowers her head. "I did sleep with Mr. Park. He pressured me. It happened after I was already a dancer for Samuel, not before. Did his attraction help me get into Samuel? I don't know. But I'm confident I deserved my place on the dance line there, and I know it's talent that earned me entry into 100M. Our fans may never understand, but I hope you do."

Well, this is a twist, one that should work in Sunny's favor.

"Someone," Yo-kyeong glares at Sunny, "is behind the rumors." Sunny holds Yo-kyeong's stare until Yo-kyeong looks away. Then Yo-kyeong continues. "I do not believe a Samuel accountant just happened to find irregular hotel expenses from a decade ago. I slept with Mr. Park three miserable times and each time was in his apartment. On the nights where I supposedly stayed with him in a hotel, I was in fact at home. I'll grant you access to my private recordings so you can verify for yourself."

Show sympathy and make her look small. Sunny adopts a pained expression. "That's so sad, Yo-kyeong. I feel sorry for you." Others start to follow suit and murmur similar sentiments, but Yo-kyeong continues speaking with conviction, her tone conveying that she does not want sympathy. "There's been a lot of drama about me this week. None of it changes the fact that Kim Sun-hee does not meet our standards. We're here to vote. There's no reason to postpone."

Sunny can't hold back. She looks directly at Yo-kyeong. "You ajumma sea cow! You just want to get rid of me. People are saying you have no talent. I don't agree, but if you stop thinking about yourself for a minute, the best thing you could do for 100M is resign with dignity."

Yo-kyeong doesn't engage. She goes back to addressing everyone else and speaks as if Sunny were not in the room. "I never felt that Kim Sun-hee belonged at 100M. She didn't pass our bar during her initial audition, and she's still subpar. I know this to be true with every fiber of my being. You know it too. But this is a big decision. One we should make with data. That's why I prepared a report."

Who does Yo-kyeong think she is? An exec at some chaebol presenting to the board? She watches way too much drama. Know your audience, bitch.

"The report enumerates the hundreds of mistakes Kim Sun-hee made over our last twelve streams. Technical mistakes were identified by places where our autocorrection algorithm needed to make unusually large corrections. Artistry issues were identified by an emotion AI.

"You could argue that everyone makes mistakes. True. But as the report shows, in the last year, excluding Kim Sun-hee, we each made an average of two moderate or severe mistakes per performance. She made thirty-eight. Proof she doesn't belong."

This is so stupid. But Sunny bites her tongue, making a supreme effort not to lose it. Does Yo-kyeong really think she can trick everyone here with her charts and fancy language?

Two stacked cubes and a frame appear on the table. Everyone is familiar with this setup because it's how they review and critique their performances. The top cube displays a raw three-dimensional recording, the bottom cube contains the corresponding autocorrected stream, and the flat frame has a visual representation of the measures and counts.

Yo-kyeong tells the group she's going to take them through an example from their "Longing" routine last Saturday, and then commences playback at one-eighth speed.

"Here's where I raise my hand to my face over three counts and snap my head back on four. The second row is supposed to raise hands offset by a half beat and catch up by three so that we all snap our heads back at precisely the same moment. You all did that correctly and it looks sharp. Kim Sun-hee was in the third row."

Why does she keep talking as if Sunny's not in the room?

"The third row is offset by another half beat, so hands should start being raised on two, be caught up by three and heads should snap back on four in sync with me and the second row. You can see that everyone did that except Kim Sun-hee. She starts raising her hand a full eighth beat late and is then also late at snapping her head back. It's especially noticeable because the rest of you in the third row were perfect. It even looks bad on the autocorrected version. That's because it was too big a mistake to be corrected in our ten millisecond buffered livestream."

Does the sea cow really think that something so minor, something you can barely see even in super–slow motion, could possibly matter to the fans? Does she even understand artistry?

"Let's talk about artistry," continues Yo-kyeong, as if reading Sunny's mind. "You can't listen to "Longing" and not be moved by Annelise's pain. Watching this playback I see, I know, you felt her. But look at Kim Sun-hee. She has, I don't know a better way to describe it, a shit-eating grin on her face the whole time. Like she's telling the audience, this music has nothing to do with me."

Sunny looks around the room. She needs to isolate Yo-kyeong. She claps slowly three times. "Bravo Ms. Pae. I see you put your university education to good work. But it's all bullshit. You could make the same argument about any of us, and you probably will whenever one of us gets too close to your spotlight.

"All that stuff about counting mistakes, everyone here knows that eighty percent of statistics are made up. And anyone can pull clips to tell whatever story they want. It's all fake, and your reports are shit. In your sick mind you've made up this whole convoluted tale to make me look bad. Well, it's not that complicated, and we don't need to waste time watching recordings. All we need to do is count how much money fans spend on emoji for each of us."

Sunny looks around the room. One or two people are subtly nodding. Nobody is making eye contact, but it seems like they get it.

"Yes, you're number one, but that's because you're old and have been around a long time. I'm number two. And that was before it came out that you slept your way in here. Now our fans are up in arms saying you have no talent. I don't agree. Pae-elder-sister, I know you're a competent choreographer, but perception is reality. How much money do you think fans will spend on you during our next stream?"

She stretches her arm and points her finger at Yo-kyeong. "The only way forward is for you to resign from 100M."

10

June 26, 2102
Eighteen years before 4-17
Haifa, Israel

Sergei is still in the virtual meeting room at Xyloom waiting for his interviewer to show up. He should be studying the materials Emily gave him. Instead, he did what he swore to himself he wouldn't do—started thinking about Karima—and now his mind is trapped in an infinite loop, replaying the moment she emerged from Daniel's room.

———

"Hi Sergei," she had said, and walked past him into the bathroom as though it was the most natural thing in the world. He stared, paralyzed and speechless. And then she closed the bathroom door. He stumbled the five steps back to his room, lay down in bed, and folded himself into a fetal position.

He struggled to make sense of events. While he was at

his family's bard festival, singing to Karima in his mind, looking around every few seconds hoping she would show up, she was in fact physically next door with Daniel. Physically.

Sergei curled tighter into himself. How long had this been going on? Why hadn't Daniel told him? Why hadn't Karima? Was he so unimportant to her?

Giggles percolated through the thin wall, and before long she was moaning again. He didn't want to listen, but he couldn't stop, and in spite of the dread flooding his stomach, he felt himself becoming erect. An aching mountain of darkness descended. He wanted to go outside and run, even in the pitch dark, especially in the pitch dark, but he was too crushed to move. Finally he told his implant to force sleep.

———

Sergei had woken up at noon. Something—the ten hours of sleep, the dreams his mind conjured during the night, the warm sunlight streaming into his room—had rebooted him. He thought back to the night before. He replayed the interaction one time to confirm that it really was Karima, although he knew it was, and then many more times to numb himself to the memory. But god, even in the dark, disheveled, for only two seconds, she was so beautiful, and her voice, the way she pronounced his name in her gravelly Hebrew accent. . . .

He got out of bed. He listened for conversation, checking if Karima might still be around. He didn't hear anyone. He opened his door and stepped into the common room.

Daniel was sitting on their couch, wearing only boxers, his long legs stretched across all three cushions, his back supported by a pillow, his right hand resting on his hip inside his waistband, staring at nothing. Sergei guessed he was still working on the 6.781 problem set which had been due the day before. He peeked through the open door of Daniel's bedroom. It was empty.

Daniel finally noticed him. "Hey bro. You just get up? I'm almost done with the 6.781 problem set. This thing's a fuckin' bitch. You do it yet?"

"Yes, I turned it in yesterday," Sergei heard himself say. "It's not too bad once you get past the second problem."

"Wanna get lunch? I need a break."

———

"Why do you drink this tepid shit? You should get the Turkish coffee from Galit's."

Sergei looked across the table at Daniel, and then beyond him at the other mostly unoccupied tables in their dorm courtyard. Why was Daniel always complaining about the food? Sergei looked back down at his own untouched lunch.

"You'd think," Daniel said, "in an age of printing food there'd be no excuse, but this cafeteria shakshuka tastes like crap."

"Tastes okay to me and it's cheap."

"Huh. Hey, guess who I hooked up with yesterday."

Sergei paused. He wondered if Daniel was trying to rub it in. No, he was just so self-centered he had never guessed Sergei's interest.

"Karima," Sergei finally said. "I bumped into her last night."

"Yeah. I asked her for some help on the problem set. She was explaining conjugate pairing and how you need it for problem three. I was looking at her, she was projecting one of those shirts with exposed shoulders, and I was thinking, 'Man, she is so fucking hot, I should just go for it.' So I said, 'Karima, you have beautiful shoulders.' She said, 'Thanks Daniel,' and went right back into conjugate pairing. I was like, 'It's so nice out, let's meet IRL and take a car over to Dor Habonim, we can hang on the beach and finish the problem set.' "

How could it be that simple? Sergei's mind went into a little stutter over that, unable to move past the notion that it could be so straightforward.

"So we get to the beach and we're like the only ones there. She takes off her scrubs and she has on this, I don't know what you call it, but it's not the swimsuit you wear to work on a problem set. I thought she was projecting but I checked and it was one hundred percent real, zero embellishment. Holy shit man! I'd show you but she blurred herself."

Sergei didn't want to be shown. He didn't even want to be there. But at the same time a strange compulsion had seized him, and his mind, rattling, threw up a grid of unwanted images as Daniel, oblivious to Sergei's condition, plunged on.

"We swim, and I don't mean putz around in the waves. She's a fuckin' dolphin, bro. We must have been out there two hours, up the coastline and back. Like five times I had to DM her to wait up, and I'm a strong swimmer. So we get back to the beach and she pulls two Malkas out of her bag. We're sitting on the sand, drinking, and I'm thinking, should I make a move? I want to, but, you know, it's Karima, she's in our lab, things could get weird.

"We're still the only ones on the beach except for this cento dude bobbing in the waves. He gets out of the water, nods in our direction and walks off toward the nature preserve. Now we're each on our second beer. Karima turns to me and I'm thinking she's going to get right back into conjugate pairing, but I swear to god, she brushes her lips against my ear. One thing leads to another. Then *she* streams the 'consent?' emoji and I stream back the biggest fucking thumbs up emoji you've ever seen, but that wasn't the only thing up at that point, bro.

"The rest is . . . let me just say four. And Serge, man, she's the one."

Sergei's focus returned with Daniel's last words. "What do you mean she's the one?"

"I mean I'm going to marry her, you know, like monogamously. Commit. Have kids. The whole megillah. Maybe you think that's crazy or rash but when you know, you know. Serge dude, how many people have I hooked up with?"

Sergei's reply came mechanically in a wash of stomach acid. "Working backwards . . . Shoshana, Anika, Jasmin, Bradley, Afu, Wyatt, Wuzi, Anahit, Natasha, Lili, Yael, Asami, Stephen, Indira, the other Afu, Melissa . . . so that's sixteen. Plus Karima. Seventeen."

"Holy shit, I was asking rhetorically! Did you query your implant or are you like the fucking 'pedia of my sex life?" Daniel laughed. "Anyway, yeah, and that's just since you've known me. And I've never felt a connection like with Karima. It's like everyone else was fucking flat and she has depth. We talked all night."

Sergei listened and watched, speechless.

"Her mind is incredible. I mean, I knew she was one of the top math people, but she's more than that. I could never quite place her looks either . . . now I know why, she's a mix of Ashkenazi, Ethiopian and Chinese."

Daniel paused for a second to sop up the rest of his shakshuka with a piece of pita.

Sergei still had barely touched his.

"Hey, you gonna eat that? Can I take some?"

He nodded. Daniel grabbed Sergei's pita, tore off a piece, and scooped up some tomatoes and egg from Sergei's pan.

"I know," Sergei said, fighting to keep a neutral tone. "Karima's mom was born in America and came to Israel as an infant to escape the Second Civil War, and that side of her family is a mixture of Chinese American and Ashkenazi American. On her dad's side it's a mix of an old Israeli family with Polish roots and an Ethiopian family that immigrated here a century ago."

"What the fuck," said Daniel, "you serious? Are you Karima's fucking family tree? Why do you even know all. . . ?" Daniel's brows slid up as realization dawned. "Oh shit, bro, you're into her! Oh man, I'm really sorry. Come here."

"Sergei? Sergei?"

He snaps out of it. "Hi, I'm Jessie, an engineer here. I'll be interviewing you today."

———

Emily wrapped up with Sergei an hour ago. Now she has his interview panel assembled around a virtual table, about to discuss if they should make him an offer. She looks over at Jessie and reads the look on her face—this is an obvious no, I'm busy, let's get this over with. Well, that's not what Emily thinks, she wants to hire Sergei, and the point of this meeting is to collect multiple viewpoints and then discuss. She's not going to let Jessie poison this one.

"Okay," she says, "let's get the pulse of the room." Everyone knows the system. Two thumbs down means strong no, will fight not to hire; one thumb down means no;

one thumb up means yes; and two thumbs up means strong yes, will fight to hire. She gives the panel a moment to input their assessments and then displays them:

Jessie: one thumb down
Abhinav: one thumb down
Yael: one thumb up
Emily: two thumbs up

She knew Jessie was negative on Sergei. But Yael is positive, that's good. "Looks like this'll be an interesting discussion," Emily says. "Jessie, let's start with you. Why are you thumbs down?"

"Take a look at my first question." Jessie plays the recording at 2x.

Jessie: "A few decades before the Korean reunification and the American fracture [. . . *fast forward . . .*]
My question is, what is the expected number of prisoners shot?"
Sergei: "Let me think."

Emily doesn't know everything that goes on in Xyloom engineering, but she's sure this question isn't relevant to any actual work Loomies do. And all this stuff about firing and shooting, it's like Jessie was deliberately playing head games with Sergei.

Jessie: "Please think aloud so I can see how you're working through the problem. But I won't nod or give you clues along the way. Get to an answer and then I'll let you know if it's right."
Sergei: "Yesli—"

Jessie: "Please think in English."

Sergei: "Okay. *[... fast forward ...]* Were the hats assigned randomly?"

Jessie: "Yes, you can assume that."

Sergei: "Let's look at some extremes *[... fast forward ...]* the expected number of prisoners killed was fifty."

Jessie: "No, wrong."

Emily frowns. It doesn't matter how good an engineer Jessie is. She's a shitty interviewer. All she's doing by intimidating candidates with that tone is causing them to rule out people who get nervous. This is Xyloom, not the military, they're supposed to select for technical and cultural excellence, not the ability to stay cool under verbal abuse. Well, not quite abuse, but still.

Sergei: "Let me think. Let's say there was just one prisoner. For that case the answer must be one-half. Is that correct?"

Jessie: "I'm not giving you clues along the way."

[20 seconds of silence]

Sergei: "Sorry, I'm nervous. This is the type of problem I used to do in math club in primary school but my brain is frozen right now."

Jessie: "Well, the prisoners were pretty nervous, and they figured it out."

What's wrong with her? Can't believe they pay her eight times a recruiter's salary.

Sergei (visibly shaken): "Let's say there were two prisoners. Ah, the first person could say the color

[. . . fast forward . . .] so the expected number killed is twenty-five."

Jessie: "Wrong. But I'll tell you what, you're making progress. Let's go to my next question and you can finish this one later and send me the correct answer this evening. So get this first one out of your mind."

Jessie stops the playback. "It's not just that Sergei didn't get the right answer, he gave a wrong answer twice and didn't say anything about double-checking his work or proving his solution. He's sloppy."

Emily looks directly at Jessie. "I've never heard you use that question before. It seems pretty complicated to do under interview pressure. Also, why all the talk about dictators, firing and killing? If candidates weren't nervous to start, they might be by the time you talk about executing prisoners."

"Emily," Jessie says, "what's three times three?"

Where is this going? "Nine."

"My point is," says Jessie, "that for someone of Sergei's background, my Supreme Leader question should be as easy as multiplying three times three is for you. I would hope you could calculate that even if someone was screaming in your face."

"I'm not an engineer so it's hard for me to judge, but that question doesn't seem like three times three. It seems like it requires an insight. Not everyone's great at coming up with those on the spot, especially during an interview."

"No," replies Jessie, raising her eyebrows, "you're not an engineer."

Emily counts silently to five, not taking her eyes off

Jessie. What *is* her problem? Time to turn this conversation positive. "Yael, why are you thumbs up?"

"I was impressed, I might even change to two thumbs up. I, um, asked about his research. He's at the early stages of developing a provably secure quantum algorithm with applications for direct olfactory interface. I, um, drilled deep and had him write out equations to explain the concepts behind their algorithm. I also went in the opposite direction and asked him about the big picture. He was excellent on both counts. And it's not only that, I questioned two or three of his assumptions and decisions, and he explained his thinking without getting defensive. He seemed exceptionally open about the areas he's unsure of. I would love to work with him. Truthfully, I learned some super interesting stuff that I shared with the folks on my team right after the interview."

Emily is shocked by how often she hears this type of thing in these panel debriefs. Candidates enter into all these confidentiality agreements, and yet they come to these interviews and share info that must be secret. And she's sure it's true in the other direction too, when Loomies interview at other places. It's a double standard. One for engineers, and one for everyone else.

Yael continues, "I, um, didn't detect even the palest of yellow flags. The only question is why would he drop out before getting his PhD. Emily, did you ask?"

"Yup, I'll get into it."

"Also, Jessie, for what it's worth," says Yael, "I'm not sure I could do your problem under the pressure of an interview. I was just thinking about it and the answer must be one-half. But it's disingenuous of you to say that that problem is like three times three."

Yes! Finally! Someone willing to stand up to Jessie.

"One-half is correct," Jessie acknowledges.

Emily runs her hand through her hair. She needs to win them over even though her vote is supposed to be the least important. "Okay, let me share my thoughts. I was pretty negative at the start of the day. He failed our interest test. I left him alone for fifteen minutes to review the Xyloom materials before Jessie started her interview. He looked for less than thirty seconds. After that I assumed he either wasn't that interested in Xyloom or he lacked curiosity. However, take a look at this part of my wrap-up."

> **Emily:** "Sergei, if our interview panel gives the thumbs up, we're going to check references. What will Professor Liu say?"
>
> **Sergei:** "I don't know. He has a large lab by academic standards and I've only met with him a handful of times, so he doesn't know me that well. I think he'll be disappointed that I'm leaving. He'll probably say that I have the intellect, but lack the mental fortitude for academia."

She stops the playback. "I like how honest Sergei sounds, and I bet it's true. Now take a look at this part." She resumes the recording a few minutes later.

> **Emily:** "I want to be open with you. I checked the notes in our recruiting system and you didn't do that well. With your performance in math competitions and educational background—primary and secondary school at 1543 in Moscow, NTU in Singapore, two years at Technion in Professor Liu's group, I would have expected you to ace our interviews."
>
> **Sergei:** "I'm sorry. I'm disappointed in myself. The

first interviewer, I forgot her name, gave me a problem that I'm positive I could have solved back in third grade. But I got stuck and just kept thinking about the problem the whole rest of the day and it threw me off. I'm not sure if you believe me and I'm not trying to sound arrogant, but that problem is trivial compared to the stuff I work on. Also, just before you came back, I finally figured it out. It's one-half."

Emily stops playback. She looks at Abhinav and he looks like he's come around. This is probably going to go her way. "Here's where I got him to open up about why he's leaving Technion."

Emily: "Tell me more about why you're leaving grad school."

Sergei: "To be in a different environment."

Emily: "What do you mean?"

Sergei: "I have at least another three years. To be honest, I'm having a hard time with some of the interpersonal relationships."

Emily: "Sergei . . . that's a flashing red danger sign for us. And just to get it all out there, abandoning your PhD studies is a danger sign too. We work on hard problems and they take years to solve. If you're leaving Technion after two years, how do we know you won't do the same here after another two years?"

[No response.]

Emily: "Are you okay?"

Sergei: "I *am* a committed person. This is embarrassing. Three of us started at the same time in

Professor Liu's lab two years ago and we were all close. . . ."

Emily stops playback. "I'll stop it there because it gets personal. Short story is the other two people are dating and Sergei has a crush on one of them. From what I can tell, he's immature and it's mostly in his head. Look, we've all been there, and passion is a good thing."

"I've never been there," says Jessie. "I can't imagine making a major life decision like leaving grad school just because of some guy or girl."

Just shut up already. One day something is going to go wrong in your life, you'll be looking for a job, and the interview gods will not be kind.

"You're a machine, Jessie!" says Yael.

Emily taps on the virtual table. "Let's get back to Sergei. Here's where I am. He's an extraordinary candidate who's a bit shaken up right now. Does he have the intellect to make it here? Yes. Will he work well with others? I believe he will. Our criteria is we hire if there's an eighty percent chance the person will be awesome, and I believe Sergei crosses that bar. Jessie? Yael? Abhinav? What do you say?"

11

July 2, 2103 - May 17, 2104
Seventeen years before 4-17
Seoul, Korea

Sunny looks around her room in the 100M building, her home for the last three years. Later today she'll be forced to move. How could they have voted her out? Did they really think she was subpar? The stuff Yo-kyeong said after the vote—that they never wanted her there in the first place, that she only got in because of her connections—could that be true? She needs to prove it's not. She's going to audition for another group, rise to the top, and show everyone at 100M how badly they screwed up.

She sits on her bed, stares at the wall, and connects with Appa.

"Appa, did you pull strings to get me into 100M?"

"Daughter, listen to me," he says, not answering her question. "Crystal Chae and 100M are going to be sorry. Your fans love you. Who cares what that loser Yo-whatever-her-name-is thinks? You need to get back on your feet. Now what's next?"

"Audition for Beol."

"No. You're beyond that. Start your own group. Your fans will follow."

She hadn't even considered that, but as soon as she does, she knows it's what she should do. She doesn't need 100M and she doesn't need Beol. She's Sunny Kim. And she already knows who she can get to manage the business side —Lee Sang-chul, who was fired from Samuel this morning, and is so into her that she won't need to pay him much.

"1Billion," she tells Appa.

"Good name. And good goal. Get a billion fans. Crush 100M."

If she moves fast to choreograph routines and hire backup dancers there's no reason she can't return to the public eye in a few weeks.

"Daughter, a suggestion. Don't worry about beauty or technical excellence. Don't try for an artistic vision. You have a starting pool of fans. Now use analytics. Whatever resonates, whatever generates the most emoji, go in that direction. Make income your North Star."

She half listens to Appa. Even if Lee Sang-chul agrees to work for free, she'll still need to rent a studio, pay the backup dancers, and hire a producer.

"Appa, that's good advice. This isn't going to be cheap. Can you transfer half a million uni to help me get rolling?"

Long pause, and then, "No, I won't. Advice I'll share. But not financial support. You're nineteen now. Use your savings from 100M."

Fear creeps into her belly. So that's how it's going to be from now on?

———

Dispatch: "Breaking news. Even more drama with 100M. First accusations about Pae Yo-kyeong sleeping her way into Samuel, and now Sunny Kim. Moments ago, 100M's number two star announced she has left the group due to artistic differences. A representative from 100M confirmed and released this statement: 'We wish Sunny well and respect her desire to pursue her own unique artistic vision. She'll always be part of the family.' "

———

Sunny connects with Lee Sang-chul, who seems shocked to hear from her. He looks different. He must have been projecting a younger, fitter, less bald version of himself. Now he's the aging accountant she expected in the first place.

"Mr. Lee, I'm starting my own dance group and I'd like you to join as business manager."

A look of relief comes over him and, without hesitation, he accepts.

"I can't pay you cash," she says. Her plan was to offer him one percent equity in 1Billion in exchange for his services. But he's more eager than she expected. In a flash, she realizes that not only might he work without pay, if she can get him to invest, she won't need to dig into her own savings. "You invest a hundred thousand uni for half a percent of equity."

He agrees. Is he any good? He must be at least decent with money to have that kind of cash on hand to invest. And as Appa says, sometimes bad breath is better than no breath. Plus, what's the risk? She can always fire him.

———

August. Things get underway, and Sunny's not surprised when Lee Sang-chul shares two pieces of good news. Sales of limited edition pre-debut emoji packs are through the roof. And even better, over two hundred thousand advance tickets have been sold without any paid promotion. Her fans miss her and they're eager to see what 1Billion is all about.

September. 1Billion's debut livestream peaks at 240,000 audience members. It's so profitable that the single performance nets her more than all of her past earnings from 100M. To celebrate, she purchases a beach house in Thailand and heads there for vacation. She's on her deck, relaxing on a chaise longue, and looking out at the Andaman Sea when Lee Sang-chul connects with her.

"I've been analyzing our stream, and emoji sales were soft," he tells her.

She takes a sip of her iced coffee, sweetened and turned light brown by condensed milk. "Of course they were, fans bought most of their emoji in advance."

"Even accounting for that."

"None of the other dancers are famous yet, that's why," she counters. God, he's such an old man. "Stop worrying."

And two days later, she's in the middle of a massage when Lee Sang-chul tries to connect again, but she declines the request. He keeps trying every few hours until she responds.

"Advance ticket sales for next month are not looking good."

"That's your business, fix it."

"Sunny, I'm worried about the performance. I think you should come back and start rehearsing. Or stay and rehearse virtually. Our dancers are waiting around with nothing to do. They need the choreography."

If she's going to work with Lee Sang-chul, she needs him to understand who the boss is. She switches their conversation from neutral space to her current physical surroundings. Now he perceives himself as seated next to her. Together they look out at the calm, expansive sea. Then she turns to him. Projecting her metallic gold bikini top and vintage denim shorts, she gives him her famous smile, directing all of her focus at him.

"Sang-chul," she says, calling him by his first name rather than Mr. Lee for the first time, "when I say I need a vacation, I need a vacation. Don't tell me what to do. I'll decide when to be back in Korea and that's when we'll resume rehearsal, understood? I don't appreciate you bringing your doubts and negativity to 1Billion. If you have a problem then you're welcome to leave."

He apologizes. She feels a pulse of satisfaction, an interior smirk. She's never addressed anyone with that degree of authority before, certainly not someone his age, but she knows she said the right thing.

October. 1Billion streams its second performance. On stage, less than ten minutes in, Sunny's stomach sinks. There aren't enough emoji. And the fans aren't concentrating on her, or the stage at all. She has a sixth sense for when an audience is with her and knows this one isn't.

Without missing a beat, she shifts her view to that of an audience member. Seeing herself and her fellow 1Billion dancers from the outside, everything looks exactly as it did during rehearsal, nothing is off. What's the problem? Doubt sets in. Was Yo-kyeong right about her not being as good as she thinks? Is that what her old dance instructor, Ahn Ye-jin, was trying to convey when she kept harping on about the basics?

No. Thinking that way is pointless.

But when the stream ends, Sang-chul confirms Sunny's intuition. The stream peaked at 180,000 audience members, lower than last month but still impressive. Also nicely profitable since promotion costs were again negligible. But engagement, measured by emoji sales and audience focus tracking, was way down.

Sunny had planned to return to Thailand. Instead, starting the day after the livestream, she pushes herself and her hired backup dancers to rehearse seven days a week. For the first time in her life Sunny works hard. However, hard work doesn't halt the downward trend, which continues in November and December, with both streams failing to generate a profit.

January 2104. Sunny, who up to this point had been doing all the choreography herself by borrowing ideas from her 100M days, hires a professional to assist. She also fires the production team and hires a new producer who moves the group toward a sexier, edgier concept. She pushes Sang-chul to spend even more on marketing to get a critical mass to January's stream. Eighty thousand attend, but engagement metrics are bad.

February. Even worse. Only fifty thousand attendees. Sunny replaces two of her dancers and the new producer. "We're out of money," Sang-chul tells her. "The economics are upside down. Not only are we paying more to acquire audience members than they generate in sales for that stream, ninety-eight percent never come back, so even in the long run what we're doing won't turn a profit."

"You think I don't know that?" she snaps back. "Why don't you fix things instead of complaining!"

Sang-chul nods. "I do have an idea, Sunny. I estimate you have five thousand hardcore fans. They've attended every stream. Let's cut four of the dancers, stop spending on marketing, and for the next few months we do streams to your core fans. It should be profitable and you can hone your craft."

Hone her craft! What a condescending loser. "Sang-chul, look at me. Do I look like some freak, indie performer to you? I'm Sunny fucking Kim! We're 1Billion. Not 5K. No way is Sunny Kim performing in front of a measly five thousand people."

March. Sunny sells her beach house to generate cash. And, despite Sunny's instructions, Sang-chul preserves the funds by spending less on marketing.

April 21. Having spent all day on her feet rehearsing with the other dancers, Sunny is now sitting by herself in their shabby, rented studio, reviewing the recording of their stream from two days ago. She and the other dancers all looked great, as good as any 100M performance. What was wrong with the audience? Why didn't they respond?

She pauses the recording and blinks as she shifts her attention back to her physical surroundings. Sang-chul is hovering nearby waiting to speak. One look at his face tells her he's planning to resign. That's not happening.

"There's something I need to discuss with you," he says.

"Oh, Sang-chul, I'm so glad you're here." She turns on her brightest smile, directs the blaze of her full attention at him, and places her hand on his arm as she talks. "I turn twenty on Thursday. I was hoping we could eat dinner together, celebrate my birthday, and talk about some new ideas to grow 1Billion."

He blinks, then agrees.

She beams at him. "Why don't you pick a place?"

———

Sunny's eyes sweep slowly across the softly lit room. Her gaze lingers on tables, and while she doesn't natively recognize anyone, her implant's annotations tell her she's among the upper echelons of Seoul society. She looks at Sang-chul. How could he possibly have secured a reservation at this exclusive sushi place? Must have used her name.

He pours warm sake into her glazed ceramic cup and then fills his own. "Happy birthday, Sunny," he says, and streams a sparkling candle cake emoji. "I'm so honored you chose to spend it with me."

She uses her chopsticks to grab a fried, salted grasshopper from a plate in the middle of the table, swirls it in a tangy sauce, and pops it into her mouth. As she chews, she keeps her eyes on Sang-chul who looks down and picks up his own grasshopper. In a moment it's gone and his chopsticks are already lifting the next one off the common plate. At his size he's going to need to eat a lot of bugs to get full.

He wipes his mouth with a cloth napkin. "You said we're going to talk about ideas to grow 1Billion. I have an idea for a new format."

"I didn't mean your ideas. I meant my ideas. It's better if you stick with the business side and I'll handle artistic decisions." As she says this, she sees the energy drain from his body, remembers her goal—that she wants to keep him—and that he works without pay. She shines her light back on him. "But I'd love to hear your idea."

She pours herself more sake, downs it, refills her cup, and downs it again as Sang-chul, regaining his balance, explains his idea for what he's calling a participatory event. "Instead of audience members passively listening, you'll lead them in dance. We simplify the choreography so people can follow along. We situate fans on an enormous grid with each square sized to make people feel part of a crowd while still leaving them enough room to dance in place. You'll encourage a sense of community to keep fans coming back, drawn by a connection to their fellow fans, and to you of course. It will be like a mixture of instructor-led exercise, dance class, and meditation. If it works, we'll get our retention rate and viral coefficient back into healthy territory."

Is he joking? Poking fun at her in some way she doesn't get? But he sounds sincere.

She frowns. "That is so stupid. What makes you think my fans would want that?"

"N of one." He places his open hand over his heart. "I'm your fan and it's something I would like."

"Can you even dance, Sang-chul?"

"Not well. But I love watching you dance. And if I could be in the safety of an anonymous crowd listening to music and following your lead? Yes."

She pops another grasshopper into her mouth. The sake is warm in her belly, mellowing her out. Spineless and annoying as Sang-chul is, she concedes he sometimes has good ideas. What the hell, maybe it could work.

"Fine, we'll try it," she says, and tells him to work out the details with their producer.

———

Sunny looks out at her audience. Only twenty thousand people, but the spacing makes the crowd look larger. The virtual grid, a kilometer wide and fifteen rows deep, is positioned on the southeast bank of Lake Manasarovar in the upper Himalayas. A snow-capped Mount Kailash towers in the distance behind a range of mountains, visible in the moonlit night sky and reflected in the still water of the lake.

She was annoyed when Sang-chul and her producer started spending so much time on the participatory format idea. She also thought the virtual location they chose was boring. But she decided to let them run with it; now, looking out at the crowd and landscape beyond, some small part of her acknowledges that this is a magnificent venue. Even she has been transported to a calmer and more meditative state of mind.

Showtime.

She and two of her dancers are on a floating platform positioned in the lake, and her other four dancers circulate among the audience. She gets everyone in the crowd to stand and mimic her movements. She has people close their eyes and tap their feet to a medium tempo pop song with a droning bassline. Even with the subtle, cautious, barely discernible moves she begins with, the collective effect of twenty thousand people moving in controlled unison is magical.

She has her audience's undivided attention. She remembers this feeling from her 100M performances, but even then, she was not their sole focus. She raises her two hands toward the sky and feeds off the energy of all twenty thousand people raising their hands. "My friends, you are incredible!" she cries. Thousands of imploding sun emoji light the night sky.

Interesting how speaking to the audience—something she never did at 100M or her earlier streams—causes bursts of emoji. It's a new way to connect with her fans and they're eating it up.

An hour later she brings the stream to a close. "My

friends, you belong here. I am inspired by you." The emoji come even faster. "I will see you next month."

She waves for a full two minutes and then drops out of the virtual Himalayas. She blinks and acclimates back to their physical studio, missing her audience already.

Sang-chul has a huge smile on his face. "You were incredible. Engagement metrics were strong. Very, very strong. So was profit."

Back where she belongs.

"Good," she says to Sang-chul. "Take my dancers out for chicken and beer, charge it to 1Billion."

12

October 12, 2105
Fifteen years before 4-17
Haifa, Israel

Karima receives a message that she and Danny are to meet with Professor Liu. It's odd. He rarely makes time to meet his advisees outside of group meetings, but when he does, it's usually one-on-one. Why does he want to meet with both of them at the same time? The whole thing makes her apprehensive.

"I want to talk about your project," says Professor Liu as soon as she and Danny sit down in front of his desk. "You're in your fifth year of our program. You've been working on the algorithm for four years now. One of the things I've learned is when to abandon ship. You have little to show and, as far as I can tell, you've made no progress at all since Sergei left. The project could be beyond you. If I had time I would supervise you more closely, but I don't."

Her stomach drops. Abandon ship? She suspected he was concerned, that he might criticize them, perhaps even question if their personal relationship was interfering with their research, but talk of abandoning ship? Not what she expected. And with no prior warning.

"I've also never had married collaborators in my lab," he continues. "Is your personal life getting in the way of your asking the skeptical questions of each other that your research requires? I don't know."

So she was partially right, he's concerned about their relationship. Maybe inviting him to the wedding, letting him see they have family and friends and lives outside of their research, wasn't so smart.

"Technion has a strict rule. You graduate in seven years or not at all. I'm concerned you're going to run up against that. That will be bad for you and looks bad for me. So I'm assigning you a new, easier project which you should safely be able to finish within eighteen months. I'm giving the olfactory interface to Chunxing. Please do a brain dump with her ASAP."

Karima is stunned. Yes, this project is the hardest thing she's ever worked on, and yes, because academics, really everything, has always come easy, she's never had to learn when to throw in the towel. But she's still optimistic and it seems premature to switch. Of course, she does want to graduate. She rapidly DMs back and forth with Danny . . . there's no way he's giving up their project.

Danny places his hands on the desk and leans in. "Professor Liu, I understand why you're concerned and we both appreciate you looking out for us. We *are* making progress. We have an algorithm that we're sure is correct. Our entire focus now is proving it. Karima and I are not ready to give up."

"Yes, but didn't you already have this algorithm two years ago? My sense is you're floundering with the proof."

Now she leans in. "Professor Liu, please give us one more year. We'll work on the new project in parallel as a backup. We will not disappoint you."

He leans back in his chair, appearing to consider. "I'm inclined to give you more time but I want to be transparent. I've lost faith in both of you these past few years and I don't think your chances of success are high. Also, as your mentor and someone wise to the workings of academia, I advise you to take the safer path. Work on the easy project, graduate, and then resume work on hard problems once you have appointments of your own." He pauses, then taps his desk with two fingers. "Are you sure you want to continue? Do you want to sleep on the decision?"

They probably should sleep on it. But Danny DMs, *We need to lock this in now, okay?*

Yes.

"No," Danny tells him. "We don't need to sleep on it. We're sure."

"Okay. You have one year. I advise that you split your time with the safer project. Don't dig a hole so deep you can't climb out. And don't disappoint me."

———

Karima and Daniel step outside the Quantum Computer Science building into the bright sunlight. In silence, they walk across the campus green and sit on the stone steps outside the student union building.

"Fuck, that was harsh," Danny says, breaking the silence.

She considers. "True, but it might be the tough love we need. We've gotten too comfortable."

"Tough, yeah; love, no. He doesn't give a shit about us. But I agree with you. We need a kick in the ass. Well, I don't know if you need one, but I need the pressure. You married a born procrastinator."

No kidding. She's never known him to start anything more than a day before it's due.

"Honey, I knew you were a procrastinator since 6.553. Question is, what do we change, how do we move faster?"

He plants his hands on the step and leans back. "I'll get out of teaching 18.969. It's a time suck. And let's postpone Samos."

That was supposed to be their honeymoon. See Pythagoras's birthplace. She sighs. "Yeah." There'll be time later, after they graduate.

"I want to get away from campus," he says, "go someplace with zero distractions."

She knows the perfect spot. Uncle Gadi's goat farm, a working dairy farm a century ago, and now a desert tourist attraction, but the tourists are few and far between.

"One other idea," Danny says, "abstain until we prove our algorithm."

She laughs.

"I'm serious. Think about how motivating it'll be."

"But. . . ." Well, it's not the craziest idea, and anyway, no way is he going to last more than a week.

"I can't believe I'm the one arguing for this," he says. "You're the one with all the willpower. I'm thinking we get to the goat farm, we put our heads into the problem, and we crack it in a few weeks."

"You're serious? You're crazy, but okay, let's do it."

He puts his hand on her knee. "Let's go home right now, a last drink before the drought. Like in the old days before an astronaut would blast off for a tour of duty on the space station."

She leans over and kisses him on the cheek. "Would love

to, but I'm teaching in ten minutes." On Mondays she guest-teaches a middle school computer science class. She'll get a friend to take her place going forward but it's too late for today. "So let's just start that policy now, Comrade Gagarin." She streams a rocket ship emoji.

———

"Ms. Yaso," a student says, "I understand how the proof works. You position four copies of the right triangle such that you have an inner square with sides of length C and an outer square with sides of length A plus B. Then you calculate the area in two different ways and that proves that A squared plus B squared equals C squared. But I don't get why we go through all that trouble. I can prove it by generating a million different random right triangles and measuring. That only takes a second and you don't need a flash of insight to get it to work."

Good question, and it raises the exact point she wants to make. Karima is teaching these sixth graders about proofs, using the Pythagorean theorem as her illustration.

"That's not proof," she says. "There are two flaws with that approach. Does anyone know what they are?" She looks out at the class and calls on the only student showing a raised hand emoji.

"The measurement isn't infinitely precise," says the student. "It wouldn't prove that A squared plus B squared is exactly C squared, only that it's approximately C squared."

"Excellent! And that's a very subtle point." Karima draws a triangle on the virtual board with vertices at A=(0,3), B=(0,0), and C=(4,0). "Suppose your implant generates this right triangle. How would it measure the distance of the hypotenuse AC?"

"Use the Pythagorean theorem," a student suggests.

"Normally, yes, but you can't let it do that here because you're trying to prove the theorem! You have to force your implant's geometry module to not use the Pythagorean theorem or anything derived from it. That's a pain, but you can do it. Think of it like using a ruler in physical space. But the measurement won't be perfectly precise, just as when you use a physical ruler you always have some measurement error.

"What's a physical ruler?" a student asks. Karima answers, then goes back to her main point.

"This isn't just some theoretical problem. If you were to measure the hypotenuse as 5.0000007 you would say, oh, well of course that's just due to measurement error and it's actually exactly five. But that's only because you already know the Pythagorean theorem or perhaps you have faith in the beauty of the universe. Let's say ancient mathematicians hadn't proven the theorem. Then for all they knew, it could be that the hypotenuse C is equal to . . ." She writes $(a + b) \times 0.0000001 + \sqrt{(a^2 + b^2)}$ on the board. "Because it would have been beyond the precision of their technology to measure the tiny difference between what that equals and the actual hypotenuse length."

"Now using your implant, if you generate millions of triangles and measure billions of times, all of which you can do instantly, you'll get the error down much further than that, but you still won't know to infinite precision that A squared plus B squared equals C squared."

She gives her students a moment to internalize the concept, and moves on when she sees understanding on their faces.

"What's the other flaw?"

She pauses for fifteen seconds and scans the room,

waiting for a student to volunteer an answer. Then she offers a clue. "How many different right triangles did we randomly generate?"

"Millions," somebody says.

"And how many right triangles are there?" Karima asks.

"An infinite number," the same student answers.

"That's right. There are an infinite number of right triangles. So even if you prove that A squared plus B squared is C squared for the millions of generated triangles, infinity minus millions is infinity, so there are still an infinite number of triangles you haven't proven it for. And yet the short series of steps we went through on the board, which require no computing power, provide absolute certainty for all right triangles."

"Aren't you splitting hairs?" one of the students asks. "If you can demonstrate that something is true to a very high level of precision on millions of examples that's as good as a mathematical proof for all practical purposes."

Sharp student, and that's the question Karima needs to motivate her next example. She's going to miss teaching while she and Danny are sequestered, pursuing their own proof. Did Pythagoras hide out somewhere too?

"I'm going to tell you a story from five hundred years ago, before computers, before calculating machines, back when people did arithmetic by hand.

"A mathematician noticed that thirty-one and 331 were both prime numbers and wondered if 3,331 was also prime. He painstakingly checked it and found that yes, it was prime. He then checked 33,331, which took even longer, and found that it too was prime. For several days he tried to come up with proof that a number composed of many threes followed by a one was prime, but couldn't do it. He then thought, maybe this is just a fluke, and my time will be better spent disproving it by finding a number that matches the pattern but isn't prime. So, he spent months checking 333,331, 3,333,331 and 33,333,331 and found they were all prime.

"The mathematician was then totally convinced that any such number was prime. He drove himself crazy looking for proof. But it turns out it's just not true, and if he had only started to check 333,333,331, he would have found that it's divisible by seventeen!"

She looks out at the class. They get it. In fact, one student is streaming that the next prime with that pattern is 333,333,333,333,333,331. Three hundred thirty-three quadrillion!

Karima moves on to her broader point. "That's the type of problem we prevent by proving things. Computer programs are riddled with bugs and security holes because humans are bad at doing things perfectly. Just because something seems to work or seems to be correct in most cases doesn't mean it will work in all cases. For many computer programs we're willing to live with this because 'works well in most cases' is good enough. Proof is an admirable holy grail, but any organization that insisted on proof for everything would quickly fall prey to rivals that avoided letting perfect be the enemy of the good. However, there are some situations that are so sensitive that we do not release software until there is mathematical proof of correctness."

Doesn't she know it.

"Let me tell you another story, this one about a distant relative of mine who was killed almost ninety years ago. I'll call him Uncle Charlie because that's how my grandfather talks about him, although he was actually my grandfather's great uncle.

"During college in the 1970s in the then–United States,

Uncle Charlie studied Chinese and became fluent. Not easy today, a herculean feat before implants. He was recruited by the US Central Intelligence Agency, a spy agency like our Mossad, and served for decades as a covert agent in the US embassy in Beijing. According to information declassified by the DU only recently, Uncle Charlie recruited many spies from the senior ranks of the Chinese government.

"Uncle Charlie had a heart arrhythmia. Back then—"

"What's an arrhythmia?" a student asks.

"It's when the electrical pulses that coordinate the beating of your heart get messed up. It's not a condition anyone has these days thanks to nanobots and implants.

"Back then, of course, the concept of an implant as we know it didn't exist, and even the idea of computer technology in your body was strange. But it wasn't unheard of. In the 1980s doctors invented a technology called an implantable cardioverter defibrillator, an ICD. It was a medical device installed under the skin with wires connecting to the heart. It had a primitive computer, and if it detected a bad rhythm, it applied electrical shocks to get the heartbeat back to normal.

"By the mid 2010s, when Uncle Charlie was only in his late fifties, his heart arrhythmia grew dangerous enough that doctors implanted an ICD. By then, the government authorities responsible for regulating medical devices were familiar with how bugs could appear in software, and understood that a bug in an ICD could be responsible for patient death. They insisted that device manufacturers prove that their algorithms for administering shocks to the heart were safe and secure.

"That was the right idea, but they didn't mean mathematical proof. Instead it was the type of thing you were talking about with generating millions of triangles. Manufacturers ran tests showing that the software behaved correctly. They tried to make sure nothing slipped through the cracks by creating traceability matrices to connect the dots between written specifications, code, and tests. Manufacturers were also conservative, carefully testing new models in a few patients first before making them available broadly. Despite all of that, problems crept in. In the case of Uncle Charlie the problem was with security."

She looks to see if they're following, and they are, even with all the old jargon. These are sharp students.

"Here's what happened. China's Ministry of State Security discovered the identity of the spies Uncle Charlie had recruited. All were executed. China knew that Uncle Charlie was the recruiter and sought retribution, but the informal 'rules' of espionage at that time permitted you to persecute spies but not foreign agents.

"In November 2017, Uncle Charlie was with his extended family in the then-US state of Maryland celebrating the American holiday Thanksgiving. About twenty family members, including my grandfather, were gathered around a table. Uncle Charlie stood to make a toast. His daughter recorded it all on her smartphone. Here's—"

"What's a smartphone?" a student asks.

"A primitive handheld computer. The implant of the time, but no direct-to-brain interface."

The student nods. Then Karima plays the recording.

The virtual board is replaced with a grainy, low resolution, flat recording of a family standing around a dining room, the table filled with turkey, cranberry sauce, mashed potatoes and other exotic dishes. Uncle Charlie is at the head of the table. He lifts his wine glass, and collapses before uttering a single word. The video goes black but audio of screaming continues.

Karima stops playback. "Five minutes later Uncle Charlie was dead. An autopsy was performed, and the official cause of death was sudden cardiac arrest caused by a severe arrhythmia. The family was in shock. They didn't understand how Uncle Charlie, who had a state-of-the-art ICD confirmed to be in good working order, could die of the very thing the ICD was designed to prevent.

"Uncle Charlie's daughter-in-law, who is still alive today and gave me the recording, was a computer scientist. She took possession of the ICD following the autopsy and figured out that Chinese hacking was responsible for her father-in-law's death. The Chinese caused the ICD to create a fatal arrhythmia, and timed it for when Uncle Charlie was with his family celebrating Thanksgiving."

The students are quiet, stunned. Then one of them asks, "Ms. Yaso, what did the United States do?"

"They didn't do anything. They never officially accepted that Uncle Charlie's death was due to anything other than natural causes. It's probably not that they didn't believe the evidence, but it wasn't worth escalating tensions with China."

The class still looks shocked. She wonders if telling them about Uncle Charlie was too much.

"Now why did I share all of that with you?" she asks.

After a brief pause one of the students speaks up. "Was it to explain why you need mathematical proof that algorithms are correct? If all that could happen with a primitive heart device, imagine the risks with our implants that interface with the brain."

"Yes! Good. You're exactly right. Researchers like me in the field of Brain Quantum Computing Interface work to create provably correct algorithms that can be safely used in implants. For example—"

The classroom teacher breaks in, tells Karima they need to wrap up in the next minute, and asks if she has any final thoughts to share.

"Let me leave you with this," she says. "A proof is a thing of beauty. Forget about the practical applications we just discussed. Most things you do in life won't stand the test of time. A proof is different. A rigorous mathematical proof will be as correct and true ten thousand years from now as it is today."

The teacher streams the folded hands emoji. Karima waves at the students and then drops out of the virtual classroom.

13

July 15, 2106
Fourteen years before 4-17
The Negev Desert, Israel

A stucco cabin with a thatched-roofed porch sits on rocky desert soil. A silhouetted hammock hangs between the porch and a wooden post set in a mound of heavy stones. And next to the post a full moon is reflected in the static water of a shallow dipping pool. It's three in the morning on Uncle Gadi's goat farm. Inside the cabin, Karima is sound asleep, one arm grazing Danny's side on a narrow bed.

Boom. Boom.

Boom.

Karima is jolted awake. She shakes Danny's arm. "Did you hear that?"

"Nimrod-7. IDF training exercise," he mumbles and is immediately asleep again.

She buries her head in his neck, closes her eyes and inhales his warm scent. Typical Danny. Sleeps through explosions, and yet somehow recognizes the ordnance in his dreams. She still finds it hard to believe they're married. That she was attracted that first day in Professor Liu's office wasn't a surprise. He was every boy she had a crush on in school, every guy she had dated. The epitome of the Israeli soldier scholar, only more soldier than anyone from her unit and more scholar than any of the boys she had hooked up with from competitive math.

No, what surprised her was that her attraction from a distance didn't disintegrate as she got to know him better, and that hooking up turned into friendship, and friendship into love, and love into her desire for a formal, lasting commitment.

The moment eye candy turned into yearning is still so clear to her. First semester of grad school. Grandpa was visiting campus. They were in the courtyard of the Quantum Computer Science building, seated at a table shaded by a palm tree, drinking coffee with cardamom. Even now she has a guilty feeling remembering how antsy she was for Grandpa to head home so she could get back to studying for an exam. Daniel, whom she wasn't yet close to, stepped out of the building and she waved. He walked over and she introduced him to Grandpa. Daniel sat down with them and got Grandpa to tell stories about his career as a classical software developer. Speaking with the pre is an exercise in patience, and watching Daniel that day, getting Grandpa to laugh, talking about old operating systems, that's when she knew.

He didn't show interest in her until much later. It was interest she hadn't expected, because she tended to attract a different type—more reserved, more cerebral. Once they did get together, she was amazed by the intensity of his confidence in her, in them. His total conviction that they would stand together under the chuppah, start a family, become professors, cross new ground, change the world. That they could will all of that into existence. She believed it then and still does.

The distant explosions stop. She inhales again, her mind slows, sleep descends.

Boom.

Boom.

More explosions. She wakes. Now it's five. She can tell that Danny's awake too. She rolls over and her hand lands on the sheet where he was sleeping a moment ago. It's moist. She reaches over and feels his sleeping scrubs, which are wet. "What the hell, Danny, why are your scrubs wet?"

"Wet dream," he says, and she can hear him smiling.

"What are you, thirteen?"

"It's my subconscious. Ten months for fuck's sake."

She laughs. She's impressed that he, that they, have stuck with his insane idea. And she can't wait, once they solve it . . . they've been on so many hikes, and if on one, as the desert sun sets behind a mountain, if he were to kiss her on the neck, and lift off her top, and. . . .

Her belly flushes hot. Don't go there, focus on math.

"Were you at least dreaming about me?" she asks, slapping him on the butt and wiping her hand on his scrubs.

"Not sure. It's already fading. Anyway, the cleaning enzymes will do their magic. Go back to sleep."

Boom. Boom.

"It's past five. Let's get up."

———

Karima and Daniel arrive at the trailhead, a geotagged location off the highway, just as the sun breaks over the mountain range to their east. They walk side by side on level ground toward elevated terrain, kicking up the dry sand and pebbles beneath their feet.

"I'm getting nervous that we still haven't started on our backup project," she says.

"Don't worry. We're close. I can feel it."

She has that feeling too, some days. And other days she's convinced the proof is impossible.

It doesn't take much, though, to persuade her to put off the backup, because shifting focus would be torture. She wants to solve this thing, not leave it unfinished and move onto something new. But if they don't switch soon they won't have time. "I have this knot in my stomach. We're close to the point of no return."

Danny takes her hand as they scramble up a boulder. "Let's start working, then you won't think about that."

On their very first day on the farm, their first day with zero distractions, she and Danny found and fixed a trivial bug in their algorithm. Although trivial, it was concerning, because the last tweak they had made prior to that was a year earlier, and ever since then they had assumed their algorithm was perfect. But now they really are confident because they've run months and months of simulations. They're certain—their algorithm, their code, is correct and secure. Their sole challenge is proving it mathematically.

The algorithm has three stages. In their first two months in the desert they proved the correctness of stages one and three. They know the proofs for those stages are solid because they checked and rechecked every step.

Where they're stuck is on the proof for the second stage. They've been working on it since January, seven months. In March, she had the idea of breaking the second stage into five families of subcases and attacking the proofs for each subcase family independently. They numbered the subcase families one through five, and successfully proved two through five, leaving only the first family unproven.

"Doesn't it seem like we've overcomplicated things?" Danny asks. "It feels like we're missing something."

He brings this up all the time. He wants there to be a simple, elegant solution to everything. Sometimes there just isn't. His comment makes her think of Sergei, if only because Sergei would never say that. She and Sergei had this way of working where their brains became extensions of each other. If she can get that going with Danny they might have a better chance. Every once in a while she gets the feeling that he's intellectually lazy. If the thinking gets really hard, he waits for her to do it, following every step of her logic, but not contributing.

They switch to walking single file as the path narrows and they begin gaining altitude. She hikes in front. "Sometimes things get complicated. We're not going to succeed by being scared of complexity. We need to persist and maybe once we get to a solution we'll find a way to simplify it. Look at Andrew Wiles. You know his thing about exploring a dark mansion?"

"Who the fuck is Andrew Wiles?"

She turns around and stares at him. How does he not know that?

"He was like my hero in middle school. The guy who proved Fermat's Last Theorem." She plays an old flat recording:

> **Journalist:** "How did you persist for so many years?"
>
> **Wiles:** "Perhaps I can best describe my experience of doing mathematics in terms of a journey through a dark unexplored mansion. You enter the first room

of the mansion and it's completely dark. You stumble around bumping into the furniture, but gradually you learn where each piece of furniture is. Finally, after six months or so, you find the light switch, you turn it on, and suddenly it's all illuminated. You can see exactly where you were. Then you move into the next room and spend another six months in the dark. So each of these breakthroughs, while sometimes they're momentary, sometimes over a period of a day or two, they are the culmination of—and couldn't exist without—the many months of stumbling around in the dark that precede them."

"That's my problem," says Danny. "That guy was used to living in a mansion and hunting around for light switches. I've never even seen a light switch. Do you think people ever forgot to switch them off?"

"Focus, Danny!" And she pulls up the equations they worked out on their hike near Ben-Gurion's tomb a few days ago.

One hour. Two hours. They talk occasionally, but mostly they are thinking, mentally manipulating a shared equation board in virtual space, each balancing abstract math constructions in their thoughts.

Karima catches her foot on a loose rock. She regains her balance, but even the momentary loss of concentration throws her off the thread she was pursuing in her mind. She looks around. They've nearly summited Hod Akev. Back in February, the first time they hiked this trail, she stared in awe at the cratered landscape that, although she knew she was seeing through her biological eyes, registered as the rendered backdrop of a fictional alien planet. That was when they had the luxury of time. Now she only allows herself a few seconds to take in the otherworldly scenery. Then she returns her attention to equations and code, fractioning off just a sliver to physical reality so she doesn't stumble off the cliff.

They pause for lunch. Then they continue hiking and thinking, playing with different approaches, getting briefly excited about ideas, and deflating after one of them, usually her, pokes holes.

Late in the afternoon they arrive at an oasis, a spring surrounded by tall limestone walls on three sides, and a rock ledge at water level on the fourth. They put their scrubs and equations aside and swim, naked, in the chilly water.

For the first time since they set out on the trail this morning, she lets her mind wander. Despite all the pressure to complete their proof, despite the insane psychological trick they're playing on themselves by abstaining, she's enjoying herself. She's never before had a time in her life where she could spend every minute of every day thinking about math; and to do so in nature, in the Negev . . . it's something special.

She treads water and watches Danny as he finishes swimming and lifts himself back onto the ledge. He still has the firm muscles of a member of the special forces, and looking at him standing on the ledge, her husband, confident, face turned up toward the sun, drying in the desert air, drops of water running down his chest and legs, she feels some extra motivation to figure out this proof.

She gets out of the water too, dries off, and puts her scrubs back on. Then more hiking and thinking, and back to their cabin on the goat farm. No breakthroughs today.

———

The next morning Karima wakes at five, the cause this time a dream, not IDF exercises. In her dream she solved the first family and did so using an obscure math theorem known as the Pan-Sidiqqi transformation. Could that be a clue from her subconscious? She stays in bed, turning the first family problem over and over in her mind. And then a flash—a possible solution.

She brings up her virtual equation board and writes out every step of the idea that popped into her head.

And . . . this looks right. Yes. Yes! Proof of the first family. The final piece of the puzzle.

She tempers her excitement. It's too easy to make mistakes. She confirms her work by checking each step. It looks good. She then channels her inner Sergei and checks the proof a third time, working it in reverse. Two hours have passed.

Still lying in bed, she places her hand on Danny's shoulder and gently rocks him. "Danny, wake up, I got it."

Half awake, "Got what? Another idea?"

"Not just an idea, the whole solution."

She explains. Then they get out of bed, print coffee in the kitchen, and walk out onto the front porch. Sitting on two wooden chairs and looking out at the rocky yellow sand of the desert, she takes him slowly through the proof on their shared virtual equation board. He tries, without success, to find flaws with each step. Then, without looking at her work, he rewrites the proof from scratch on his own board.

"Holy shit. It works. You figured it out! My god, you did it."

She watches the months of stress that had been slowly accumulating drain from his face.

He leans over and kisses her, and she tastes the coffee he

has just been sipping. She takes him by the hand and leads him back into the cabin and to the bedroom. She raises her arms. He pulls off her sleeping scrub top, stands staring at her naked chest, and then places his hands, warmed by the coffee, on her cheeks and resumes the kiss that began on the porch.

An hour later she's lying on her back, holding Danny's hand, feeling the dry desert heat against her bare skin. From the nearly subvocal sounds of disbelief he's making, she can tell he's checking sports news. She runs through each step of the beautiful proof. How did it take them this long to figure it out? If only she had thought to use Pan-Sidiqqi earlier.

And then bile floods her stomach. Her body tenses.

"Shit."

"What?" he asks.

"There's a flaw. I made a mistake with the Pan-Sidiqqi transformation."

How could she have missed it? How did he? He seems to be lost in thought, and then, "Turn off recording and expunge your last minute."

Why? But she does it and then walks him through the problem.

"This assumption doesn't hold," she says, and sees that he gets it. He goes silent again.

"Karima, honey, let's stick with the proof you came up with this morning."

"What do you mean? It's not proof of anything."

"Listen to me. Only a handful of people can even understand this math. We'll renumber our subcase families so that this first one is the fourth one. Think about it. The overall proof is going to end up over eighty pages long. When Professor Liu gets to the proof for stage two he'll go over the math for the first family with a fine-toothed comb, but how careful is he going to be by the time he gets to the fourth family? And even he might need months of study to get up to speed on all the techniques we use. The chance that he or any of our readers spot the flaw is very, very, very low."

The room gets cold. She fishes her scrubs off the floor, slides the bottoms back on, stands up, puts on the top, and walks toward the door, away from him. "Daniel, that is wrong. It flies in the face of everything we believe. How could you even suggest it?"

"The world is messy. Not everything can be perfect. You know that. And what difference will it really make? Do you believe that our algorithm is correct?"

That's never been the question. She's sure it is. The problem is mathematical proof of it.

"Yes."

He gets out of bed, throws on his scrub bottoms, and approaches. She backs away but stays in the room and listens to what he's saying.

"Consider two scenarios. In one scenario, we graduate with accolades. We become professors at a prestigious institution, start our own labs, make important contributions, become recognized, wealthy. In the other scenario we eke out our doctorates without anything noteworthy to our names. We go on to get regular jobs, become swappable logic circuits in the petascale central processing unit that is the modern multinational. Meanwhile Professor Liu has his favorite student, Chunxing, put the finishing touches on our work and she receives all of the glory, not to mention royalty streams."

This is her husband. Let her give him the benefit of the doubt and follow his line of thinking. Of course she would rather scenario one, but not by breaking the rules.

"Besides it being wrong," she says, "we also run the risk of discovery."

"If someone discovers the flaw in our proof we can thank them and play dumb. After all, if you hadn't had your insight just now, that's exactly what would happen. For all we know there are other flaws in our reasoning that we haven't found yet. And discovery, if it happens, will likely come years from now when we're established and have other work to our names. I'd rather face future potential embarrassment than certain failure now."

He speaks fluidly, without hesitation. She wraps her arms around herself as it dawns on her that this was his backup plan all along.

"Plus," he says, either oblivious to or unbothered by her body language, "we can keep working on it after we graduate, and then we can report the flaw and fix at the same time. Isn't that what happened with your math hero?"

That is true. But what if they never find the fix? What if there is no fix?

"What if the algorithm itself is flawed?" she says.

"We know the algorithm isn't flawed, or if it is, it's a flaw that will never matter, because we've done trillions and trillions of simulations. If there is in fact some miniscule problem, it might be unfixable, and then we'll have spent years trying to prove something that isn't provable. However you look at it, we're best keeping your insight to ourselves. We either fix it later or go to our graves with it."

She's not naive. She knows perfectly well that you don't get to the top by following every rule to the letter. Is this the first time she's being confronted by that reality? She needs to clear her head. She tells him to give her time to think, then slips on her shoes and exits the cabin.

She turns their conversation over in her mind. No, this

isn't just breaking a bureaucratic rule or working a backdoor channel. Daniel, her husband, is proposing they hide a known mistake, commit academic fraud, a sin on par with faking data. Intellectual honesty is so much a part of her identity, and—she thought—of his. She's never cheated in her life—never used her implant when she wasn't supposed to, never copied an answer from a friend, never even borrowed anything without returning it. She knows the world is not black and white, but math is.

She puts those thoughts out of her mind and thinks about her application of the Pan-Sidiqqi transformation. She made a fundamental error, but is it salvageable? The overall concept feels right, it's too perfect not to be. The trick must be finding a different way to prove that the conditions for use of Pan-Sidiqqi are met. She spends two hours playing with ideas, the whole time meandering away from the farm, trudging along the desert soil, ascending a nearby hill.

Nothing solid yet, but the direction is promising. She turns and looks at their cabin in the distance, its yellow stucco walls shimmering in the desert sun. Their rainbow-colored hammock is swaying on this windless day. Daniel must be lying within. She doesn't need to tell him she won't go along with his plan, because now she's optimistic they can fix the proof. She'll tell him they should work together on fleshing out the approach she's just been sketching in her mind.

I have an idea. Am heading back to the cabin.

Karima, I sent our proof to Professor Liu.

No.

She checks messages. He told Professor Liu the proof was done. He attached a draft with the first and fourth families switched. Told him they would be returning to campus and using the next few months to finalize their dissertation. Professor Liu already sent back his congratulations.

What did you do?

I did it for us.

He betrayed her, went behind her back, made a unilateral decision. The bile that was splashing around her stomach earlier wells up into her chest. She sits on the sand.

Come back to the cabin and we'll discuss.

She wants nothing to do with him. She blocks him, and he reacts by rising from the hammock and starting in her direction. Even if he runs it will take him twenty minutes to reach her present position. She rises, jogs down the other side of the hill to the national highway, hails a car, and leaves Daniel and Uncle Gadi's farm behind.

14

September 20, 2110
Ten years before 4-17
Seoul, Korea

The virtual venue, lit by moon and stars on a cloudless night, is the dry, cracked, flat bed of an ancient desert lake. The grid is a thousand columns wide and a thousand rows deep. A million squares, each occupied by a 1Billion fan, dancing, synchronized. Sunny, twenty-six, stands on the peak of a sand dune and looks out at her audience, feeding off their energy.

It's been seven years since she started 1Billion and six since she came up with the participatory format. Audience size and income have exploded. She has millions of fans. And the money is rolling in. The profit 1Billion earns each month would be enough to support her in luxury for years, at least if she slowed her spending.

But far from feeling content at being the subject of the undivided attention of a million fans, she's unsettled, because last month the audience was larger, and the month before that even larger. Each livestream needs to be bigger than the one before. They're called 1Billion for a reason.

Income has been falling too. Sang-chul reassured her that it was due to the summer months and the Olympics. But now it's September and she can already see that emoji sales are down again. As soon as the stream ends she's going to tell him he needs to fix the situation or be replaced. She needs competent people around her.

Deep down she has yet another concern, one she can barely articulate to herself and certainly won't mention to Sang-chul. For years, her control over her fans has grown. They imitate her every gesture and hang on her every word. Over the past half-decade, she's figured out what things to say, and how to say them, to evoke passion in her audience. She expects, deserves, demands to be their center of attention. And now she senses her control slipping. They're looking away, dropping out, even laughing inside, she suspects.

"One, two, three, stomp; four, five, six, seven, stomp."

A curved display materializes behind her and expands to occupy three-quarters of the rendered sky. All eyes are drawn to it as a virtual camera soars above the crowd. The display shows close-ups, then tens, then hundreds, then thousands, then tens of thousands of people stepping the same way at the same time. Her audience members experience a collective euphoria induced by turning off their minds and swaying with a million fellow humans.

And then it's over. The last notes of the final song ring out, the camera display disappears, all is still.

Moments later, a sun rises, its reddish glow bending around the edges of the sand dunes. As the false dawn progresses, and the sky brightens, she hears the crowd chanting her name, "Sunny! Sunny! Sunny!"

She lives for this. Her audience registers her location as distant, on top of the sand dune, and yet can also see her body and face as clearly as if she were meters away. The crowd gets even louder. "Sunny! Sunny!"

She raises her hands in slow motion, reveling in every repetition of her name. The crowd quiets. "My friends. How are you? You love me! And Sunny loves you back."

She pauses, watches her audience stream sun emoji, and listens to the roar of the chants of her name, repeated over and over in unison. She shifts her attention to her live stats. Income is rocketing up, but audience size is dropping at an alarming rate. What the hell? Just like last month and the time before. Sang-chul better be able to fix this. She raises her hands again to quiet her audience.

"My friends. I plan to speak with you for half an hour. Some of you may be tired from dancing. Some of you are in time zones where it's now early in the morning. I'm tired too. But I will persist because I owe it to you to share what's on my mind."

She stretches her arms in front of her with upturned hands. "I am inspired by you. I am inspired when I watch you dance. I am inspired by your love for your fellow human beings. And I am inspired by your love for me."

"Please take a moment, turn to each of your neighbors, introduce yourself, and tell them what about 1Billion inspires you."

Arrows appear, guiding each audience member to speak with the occupant of a neighboring square. At thirty seconds the arrows shift, and then again at sixty seconds and ninety seconds.

After the full two minutes she waits for silence.

"We are accepting."

She pauses and listens to her audience repeat her words: *We are accepting.*

"We are kind."

We are kind.

"We do not judge."

We do not judge.

They're with her. So why the hell are so many dropping out?

"My friends. It does not matter how you look. It does not matter how you dance. It does not matter if you're wealthy or poor, sexual or asexual, old or young, skinny or fat. If you are here, you belong here. The only thing that matters is you do not judge.

"Judges are cruel. Judges pretend there is a single reality and expect you to live in it. I'm talking about the teacher in school who gives you a failing grade on your essay. I'm talking about the boss who lectures you on how to do your job and denies you a promotion. I'm talking about the parent who criticizes how you act. I'm talking about the potential romantic partner who shows no interest and the potential sexual partner who denies you. I'm talking about the people who look down on you because you struggle. These people, these *judges,*" she lets the venom drip from the word, "are selfish. We are a kind, compassionate community. But judges are destroyers, they tear you down."

She lets her words sink in.

"I want to show you someone. Yo-kyeong Pae. She was a member of 100M, my old dance group. A nasty person. A judge."

A recording appears in the virtual sky and the audience looks up.

Yo-kyeong: "Let's talk about artistry. You can't listen

to 'Longing' and not be moved by Annelise's pain. Watching this playback I see, I know, you felt her. But look at Kim Sun-hee. She has, I don't know a better way to describe it, a shit-eating grin on her face the whole time."

Sunny is silent for five seconds and then smiles, points to her mouth, and pans her head.

"Is this a shit-eating grin? Is it? Look at Yo-kyeong now. She's a nobody. 100M is gone. She runs some indie dance studio, they don't even have a thousand followers. That's what happens when you judge. Yo-kyeong is a judge."

Yo-kyeong is a judge.

Yo-kyeong is a judge.

Sunny lets the chant go on for half a minute and then raises her arms.

"We are kind. They are cruel. We are accepting. They are elitist. They impose false standards so they can perpetuate their dominance over us. School and grades. Government and laws. Work and output. Relationships and consent. Rules. Rules. Rules. Made up by them. They control you. They exploit you.

"You have the right to be happy. You have the right to be respected. You have the right to your reality. Anyone who forces you to take a test . . . anyone who ranks you . . . anyone who compares you . . . anyone who criticizes you . . . anyone who excludes you . . . anyone who denies you: I say screw them!"

She catches her breath and listens to the thunderous reaction. The crowd is screaming "screw them" over and over and streaming 1Billion branded (and pricy) nut and bolt emoji.

But then she looks at stats. The dropout rate is five thousand per minute. What is going on? She raises her arms a final time.

"My friends. I will never judge you. I will never deny you. I am here for you. If you would like anything from me —ask. I may not get to every request, but I will spend every minute trying. My friends, I love you, and I will see you next month."

She drops out of virtual space, blinks, shakes her head, and looks around the 1Billion studio. Sang-chul is standing in the corner staring at her.

She looks at him. "We need to talk. Wait for me in my office."

15

September 20, 2110
Ten years before 4-17
Seoul, Korea

Three years ago, 1Billion bought 100M's data assets, intellectual property, and physical building out of bankruptcy. Sunny remembers the look on Crystal Chae's face. That was an enjoyable day. Even Appa seemed proud.

They renovated the building and moved in. Sunny's office occupies the entire top floor of the high rise, what used to be a meditation sanctuary for the 100M dancers. Her personal kitchen, a space twice the size of her old dorm room, is situated in one corner, with full-height windows looking out into the Seoul night sky.

Sunny sits across from Sang-chul at a rectangular table. Holding chopsticks in her right hand and a spoon in her left, she ingests a bowl of ramen. "We need to talk about audience size," she says between slurps, glancing out at Olympic Park, the pulsing bluish glow of its glass-clad swimming venue visible in the distance.

"Sunny, before we get into that, there is something I want to ask. I've . . . I've. . . ."

"Stop buffering, spit it out." Of course, she knows exactly what he's going to say, and can't believe it's taken him this long to work up the courage. This is going to be fun.

"What I'm trying to say is. . . ." He hesitates; then, in a tumble: "I've admired you, Sunny, worshiped you, ever since you joined 100M. And getting to work closely with you these past seven years has been such an honor. I would follow you anywhere, do anything for you. Just now on the stream you said you will never deny . . . does . . . does . . . that include me?"

She picks up a piece of seaweed with her chopsticks, places it in her mouth, and chews, letting his question hang out there. "Let me guess. You want my affection? Or, Sang-chul," she looks directly at him, "would you like to come home with me?"

He swallows and nods.

She stares into her bowl, as if she's giving the idea serious consideration. Then she looks up. "Don't be absurd. Even the thought of your d-line body grinding on me is nauseating. Get the whole idea out of your mind."

She watches the life drain from him, and gives him a few seconds to collect himself.

"About audience size," she says, "you said the drop was due to the Olympics. Now they're over, but income tonight was the lowest in a year. And toward the end people were dropping out like flies."

"Well," he says, sounding almost confident, "I'm not quite sure how to tell you this. Some of the things you've been saying recently sound crazy."

Holy shit, who poured the soju in his coffee?

"Are you criticizing me Sang-chul?"

"I'm not saying *I* think what you're saying is crazy. But I suspect BORO AIs are starting to classify you as. . . ." He swallows, and the rest comes out in a rush. "As unhinged, unreliable, toxic and corrosive."

She blinks. "What the fuck are BORO AIs?"

"Board of Reality Overseers. Didn't you learn that in civics? Oh, right, you didn't go to university. Let me explain."

Who does he think he is? She folds her arms and he starts blabbing.

"Two decades after the Internet was invented, anyone could communicate with the whole world for free. At first that seemed like a good thing. But with no arbiter of truth, it was easy to exploit the system. Extreme was more entertaining than subtle. People got polarized around competing narratives. That led to conflict. Two million perished and twenty million refugees fled the United States during its second civil war."

She slurps some noodles and looks up. "Skip the history lesson."

"I need to explain. BORO could shut down 1Billion."

"Make it short," she says, and turns her attention back to her ramen.

"Well, people realized a world without shared truth wasn't that great. But there was no way to put the cat back in the bag. Until AI. Ubiquitous automated fact checking. The idea was that any bit of information you received would be tagged with a fact check score. It didn't matter if you were the sole recipient of a message from a friend or one of a hundred million watching a stream. The system was modeled on an old technique employed by newspapers. Do you know what those were? Journalists would check claims by public figures and rate their truthfulness on a scale. . . ."

Oh right, you didn't go to university. Arrogant prick. Let's see who's stronger. She lifts half a soft boiled egg from her ramen bowl and suspends it in the air with her chopsticks. "This is so good, want a taste?"

He nods.

She reaches across the table with her chopsticks, feeds him the egg, and gives him a good look at her chest down the V-neck of her scrubs top. She stares at him and watches him get flustered.

He looks away, chews and swallows the egg, and then continues. "Uh, what was I saying? Fact checking. Well, it didn't work, because people didn't care. They were overwhelmed with fiction. By the time AI was good enough for reliable fact checking, less than one-tenth of a percent of all information consumed was rated somewhat factual or better. There was no incentive to tell the truth. The opposite of how things are today."

Blah blah blah. She holds a slice of fatty braised pork in her chopsticks. "You should try this too." Before he can respond, she stretches out over the table and places the edge of the meat in his mouth. His face reddens. He has no chopsticks of his own with which to grab the piece of meat, nor is it something he can swallow whole. She remains stretched over the table, her extended arm and chopsticks holding the pork for him, the overall angle of her torso giving him line of sight. The awkward position means that he can't avert his eyes. He finally closes them while she inserts the rest of the meat into his mouth. She sits back, he finishes chewing, and after a moment he appears to regain some of his composure, all signs of his previous arrogance now wiped from his face.

"Yeah, so what, get to the point," she says.

"Then . . . then . . . then they came up with a better way to use fact checking." His tone turns oddly formal, as if he's a teacher and she's his student. "Instead of placing the onus on individuals, they made the conceptual network links between people exhibit a flakiness inversely proportional to the truthfulness of information carried on the link. Sunny— are you following? It means it became hard to transmit information that was fake. If you made a recording claiming that the Earth was flat, it couldn't go viral. Even if you were chatting one-on-one with a friend online, if you started to talk about the Earth being flat, the connection quality would get poor and even drop. On the other hand, you could readily transmit a math tutorial."

So boring. How far can she push him off balance? She finishes her ramen and scooches her chair closer to the table. She extends her right leg and rests her bare heel on the seat of his chair, between his thighs. "Is this okay? I need to stretch."

He nods, and with apparent considerable effort, continues. "So then the big question was who gets to define truth. Sure, one plus one is two. But other things aren't so clear. Take our history. Were Kim Il-sung, Kim Jong-il, Kim Jong-un heroes or devils? And of course it's a question that went beyond any one country."

Of course. Who does he think he is? She circles her finger in the air, signaling for him to speed things up, but he just keeps plodding along.

"There was this one rare moment of international cooperation. People were so horrified by the United States Second Civil War that they put their differences aside. The world came together and signed two major conventions. The first established that networks and related algorithms must use fact-checking AI. All countries except the Free States of America signed. The second convention created the Board of Reality Overseers: BORO."

BORO . . . more like boring. She begins stretching her

right calf, pushing her toes forward and gently moving the ball of her foot in a counterclockwise motion. He freezes and stops talking. Will he ever stand up for himself? She makes a little pact in her mind. If he calls her out, even if he just tells her to stop, if he shows some semblance of a spine, she'll make his dreams come true. "What's wrong?" she asks.

His face turns an even brighter shade of red. "Nothing," he says, but then doesn't speak. Finally, stuttering, "The . . . the . . . the board is responsible for the definition of reality underpinning the fact-checking AIs. The only exceptions are China, where the Communist Party defines reality for its citizens, and the FSA, which rejects fact checking. The, um, two conventions were the most important global achievements of the twenty-first century. They reversed a trend toward fracture and paved the way for our modern society."

She removes her right foot, replaces it with her left, and repeats the same stretching motion, now making a slow clockwise motion with her bare foot, pressing and feeling with her toes. Soft, limp. He can't even get it up when something he's fantasized about for a decade comes true. What a weak, flaccid man. Emasculation complete. (There's a college word for you, Professor Lee.)

"About . . . about our audience size going down," he says, struggling to speak, "what I think is happening is we're getting backpressure from the BORO AIs. Your speech is crossing a line in the eyes of the AIs, their toxic sensors are going off, and they're protecting your audience from you. It's not happening in a black-and-white way, but enough to nudge you back to safer ground."

She removes her foot from his chair and stands. "What? You were droning on and on. You're saying this BORO board is blocking my audience from me?"

He nods.

Her arm muscles tense. "What bullshit! Who's on this board?"

Sang-chul stands up too, looks down at his feet, and answers her question, his tone somewhat back to normal. "Elected representatives from every country except China and the FSA. Members serve for six years, with a third of the board turning over every two."

"When are the next elections?"

His eyes defocus for a moment. "Different times in different countries next year. Next cohort will be sworn in fifteen months from now on January 4, 2112."

"Good. Go home. And Sang-chul, sweet dreams," she says, streaming the classic waving-hand emoji.

16

March 27, 2111
Nine years before 4-17
Northern Israel

500 meters

Daniel looks across at Lia, his old buddy from the army, and the only woman from his subunit he never slept with. She's just as fucking hot now approaching forty as when they first met at eighteen.

"When was the last time you jumped?" Lia asks him.

"Must be fifteen years."

700 meters

His life has been one steep ascent. Service in the special forces? Check. Marriage to a brilliant partner? Check. Doctorate from the top computer science program in the world? Check. Children? Check. Professorship? Check.

What's next? Tenure? He's on track. It's a formality.

Wealth? More of a problem. The good news is that his olfactory interface algorithm was licensed by a multinational. Once it's deployed to all implants the royalties will come pouring in. And with his old grad school buddy Sergei out of the picture, he and Karima will receive a combined one-half percent, which will be substantial, enough income, he's calculated, to live the lifestyle he wants in perpetuity.

Bad news is, it's a long road. The algorithm needs to go through test after test after test. The royalties won't start until it's deployed to implants and promoted out of the sandbox into full privileged mode. It makes sense that approval of code that interfaces with the brain takes time, but at current pace it will be another fifteen years.

That's why he's hanging out with Lia. She's a rising star in the government, skilled at working the levers of power here and in the international arena.

1000 meters

"Lia, can you get fast track designation for my algorithm?" It's a big ask, because fast track is normally for algorithms that are less consequential, ones that don't operate at the brain-interface level.

"Maybe, probably," she says, seemingly only half listening. He follows her gaze. The drone skin is transparent and visibility today is at least twenty kilometers. To their left, sparkling in the sun, is the Mediterranean. He spots Haifa, the Technion campus, the terraced steps of the Baha'i Gardens. He can even make out the hilly neighborhood with the house he and Karima bought a few months ago, just in time for Ora. To the right he sees the Kinneret, the Sea of Galilee, a place he plans to go to with Leon this weekend, who at four is already a confident swimmer.

1500 meters

Sooner or later approval of his olfactory algorithm is inevitable. And what after that? Rarified air. He'll be on the world stage, alongside the academic, commercial, and government titans at the top of the food chain. To be ready, he needs his next few wins lined up—he won't be able to rest on his olfactory algorithm laurels forever—and to get those wins he needs more irons in the fire.

2000 meters

Earlier today he was speaking with one of those irons, his most gifted student, Itai Wang. Daniel bets that Itai will make the next breakthrough in the lab. Itai served in Talpiot, obviously something with hacking, but Daniel has never gotten Itai to give him even a clue about the specifics.

Daniel almost served in Talpiot himself. They tried to recruit him. But he needed to prove he could make it into Sayeret Matkal, the same commando unit that his family had been active in for generations. He began military service at eighteen, rose to become an officer, and left active duty at twenty-two. Those years gave him a group of buddies, Lia among them, who he knows he can count on for anything.

3000 meters

A thousand meters to go. He remembers his first jump, the thrill of watching the altimeter click up, anticipating the plunge into open air. That was in his first year of service. It was a rite of passage, a tradition, a drill in overcoming fear. He wasn't nervous, and even if he had been, he never would have given his commanding officer the satisfaction of seeing it.

"Nervous, Lia?"

"Nope, at my resting heart rate." Same with him. God, attribute it to selection or training, alumni of the special forces are an impressive bunch. Here they are, neither has done this in fifteen years, ascending in a transparent drone, about to plunge into the sky, and their bodies are behaving like they're sitting around drinking coffee. Not even coffee—water. Nerves of steel. Karima, for all her athletic prowess, would be freaking out.

"Let's make this competitive," he says. "Second on the ground buys drinks." These civilian chutes autodeploy at four hundred meters, so the trick is diving headfirst to maximize terminal velocity.

"No, I want to enjoy freefall. Plus, Danny, you're buying, you're asking me for a favor."

So she did hear him, and she wouldn't let him buy if she wasn't going to at least consider helping him.

3500 meters

Move to door flashes in his implant. He stands, steps over to the door, and slides it up. He sticks his hand out, feels the air rushing by, and watches the pressure ripple his skin.

4000 meters

Jump flashes.

Lia steps out into the open air. Zero hesitation. He's right behind her.

He arches his back, stretches his arms and legs, banks to the left, and then moves his arms rearward and slips forward through the air. He rotates his body so he's facing the sun, rotates again to face the ground, and then flies in circles. He orients his body into a head down position, speeds past Lia whose chute has already deployed, and then opens his own chute.

And suddenly all is calm.

His thoughts drift back to Talpiot and from there to hacking. Grandpa—not his grandfather but Karima's—told him that when he was growing up there were only two types of people: those who knew they had been hacked, and those who didn't. Back then nothing was truly secure.

The situation could not be more different today. Every algorithm, every bit of code in an implant is mathematically proven to be correct. Yes, hacking into systems of lesser importance still happens, but never into the crown jewels, into implants, into the brain.

Something he rarely thinks about is the fact that the mathematical proof of his own algorithm has a tiny problem, a miniscule flaw known only to him and Karima. They never speak of it, but he's sure it's still eating her up inside. He's also sure she'll fix it years before their code ever gets into humans.

But what if, for the sake of considering remote possibilities, the problem isn't restricted to the proof, and the algorithm itself has a flaw? Could a hacker ever exploit it? Should he worry about that before pushing Lia to accelerate approval?

He should estimate the risk. Start with the risk of there being a flaw in the algorithm. He and Karima did trillions of simulations to test their code and there were zero problems. But to be conservative, say the chance is one in a million.

Now suppose there is a flaw. What are the chances that a

hacker can find it, even the best and brightest of Talpiot like Itai? Maybe one in a thousand.

And that the hacker would do harm? Something fascinating from his conversations with Grandpa is that even though in Grandpa's day every system was compromised, society mostly just kept on functioning. Hackers were more interested in spying and making money than causing chaos. So say one in a thousand that this theoretical hacker intends to do damage.

Six plus three plus three is twelve. That puts his worst case scenario at one in a trillion.

When he was growing up there was concern about an asteroid. At the peak of estimated risk, when he was in first grade, astronomers predicted that seven years later, when the asteroid approached, there would be a one in ten thousand chance of impact. Now that was worth worrying about. And the whole planet did, until astronomers revised their estimates a few months later.

But one in a trillion? No way. That would be like worrying about an alien species attacking. Or that the universe is one big simulation that's going to get abruptly turned off when some god trips over a power cable.

He sees the ground rushing up. He steers toward the beach and lands as casually as if he were stepping off an escalator. A minute later Lia lands, meters from him. He holds her hand and helps her out of her harness.

He points to an outdoor bar across the road. "Drink?"

17

January 4, 2112
Eight years before 4-17
Seoul, Korea

BORO had maintained a low profile for decades. Board members were academics, largely social scientists and legal scholars. Elections were rarely contested, and most citizens of most countries would have been hard-pressed to name even one of their country's representatives.

Then, starting a year ago, iBillion set out to get their superfans elected to the board. They targeted their supporters with a simple message: BORO itself is the enemy. And they got the message out by exploiting the policy, in place for obvious reasons, that AI fact-checking algorithms were not permitted to impede criticism of BORO.

India and Japan held their elections in early 2111. iBillion achieved victory in both, getting their entire slate of preferred candidates elected, all drawn from iBillion's most rabid fans. And by mid-December, when the final wave of elections wrapped up in countries like Indonesia and

Pakistan, the scale of 1Billion's success was clear: a full half of the new incoming board members were 1Billion's.

———

Sunny is in her office about to watch BORO's first official meeting of the new term. It will be boring, and not something she's going to make a habit of streaming, but it will also be fun to see her influence exercised on the global political stage. A stage bigger than the one Appa plays on. She hopes he's watching.

She studies the BORO members. It's an odd collection of people. Five-sixths are the academics. She looks at them, their knowing head nods, their insider handshakes. A bunch of overeducated nerds who think they deserve to impose their views on everyone else.

She can easily pick out her one-sixth. They look nothing like the rest of the board, but they also share little in common with each other, other than a sense that the world is against them.

The chairperson, Professor Adaku Adichie from Nigeria, was selected from among members entering the fifth year of their terms. Professor Adichie brings the meeting to order. The first agenda item is the formal swearing in of new members. That completed, she introduces the second agenda item.

"You are all aware of the highly unusual nature of BORO elections in many countries last year. For the first time since the establishment of BORO, there was a successful international campaign to elect a slate of candidates. These candidates, now fellow board members here today, view BORO itself as the enemy. Their goal is to disband the board, but short of that, they intend to push for a definition of reality so untethered from fact that the AIs we oversee will become useless."

Sunny sits up. Where's this going? And who the hell is this Adichie person to assume she knows the goals of Sunny's representatives?

"It appears that there are people in this world, and in particular Sunny Kim from 1Billion, who have forgotten the horrors of the last century, horrors precipitated by competing narratives of reality. That a dance studio is threatening the peace and prosperity of the entire planet is ridiculous and would be amusing if it weren't true."

Sunny snorts. That's right bitch. BORO isn't the only powerful organization around. You're dealing with Sunny Kim.

"Fortunately, our body was designed with safeguards to moderate the pace of change. It's why we serve six-year terms with a third of us turning over every two years. It's also why we have the ability to take explicit, and even draconian, action against individuals and groups with a two-thirds vote. We need to use that power to stop Ms. Kim before she causes more harm."

What harm? For the first time your cliquey board has some people who don't think just like you, and that's a problem?

"I move to block Sunny Kim and 1Billion. This will limit Ms. Kim and her organization to a maximum of one hundred followers and stream attendees. The block will be permanent unless removed by a vote of this board. All in favor?"

Shit. Sunny looks at the tally: 989 in favor, 204 against, seven abstentions.

"Motion passes. Block will be put in place immediately. Let's move to agenda item three."

18

July 8, 2115
Five years before 4-17
Singapore

Minutes after nautical dawn, Lynette Tan, strolling, is one kilometer into the ten-kilometer loop at MacRitchie Reservoir. Her attention is fractured—five percent on the trail and the rest on a continuing education class. She's been swamped by her patient load, so she put the thing off for months, but it's required to maintain her license, and now she only has three days left to finish.

She loves being an interventionist, as sure as ever that she made the right decision back in med school to specialize in it rather than neurology. This continuing education class uses a simulated patient and is virtual, but her actual practice is all about face-to-face interactions. That's why she chose intervention; it's one of the few medical fields that requires physical contact. When a patient's mind is on the verge of being lost to a virtual world, her mission is to wean them back to real life, and making an in-person connection is the most important tool in her toolbox.

This treatment simulation is challenging, and also not remotely representative of the cases she sees in Singapore. Who comes up with this stuff? John—her virtual patient—is simultaneously addicted to an adult world where he role plays a centaur, and to wak, an opioid that interferes with the implant-to-nerve interface. She has never once had a patient with either of those problems.

The whole thing is contrived, but it does play to her strengths, deciphering her patients and the worlds in which they are trapped. "John," she says, "can you describe how you feel when you're galloping around as an equine?" He starts to answer, but gets paused by an urgent incoming connection.

"Mum, everything okay?"

"Lynette, ah, look where your brother is."

She checks, bringing up a map on one wall of the neutral virtual room she and Mum now occupy. No current location. Last recorded location was three weeks ago. Pyongyang. That's strange. What's Ethan doing there?

"Mum, why's he blocking location?"

"Don't know. It's not just location. I tried him yesterday and he was disconnected. Same thing today."

"Let me try." Same, disconnected. What's he up to?

She displays his activity. A timeline appears, suspended in the space between her and Mum. It's packed with the usual posts, many related to Ethan's documentary work, but all activity comes to an abrupt stop at the June 17 mark. She studies his final post from that day. It's a recording of a dancing figure. She enlarges it to fill the room and watches with Mum.

What the hell? It's Ethan, dancing nude, writhing in

jerky aquatic animal-like motions, to a Korean love ballad that she recognizes only because it's currently trending worldwide. Ethan's naked form fills the virtual room for a few uncomfortable seconds, then she shrinks the recording to a tiny cube to obscure the details, and she and Mum watch the remaining two minutes.

"Must be a fake," says Mum.

"No, verif—"

Aaahhh! Lynette's attention is yanked back to physical space. She feels someone touching her hand. Then an instant later, relief—not a someone, just a monkey running off with her breakfast bar. Two seconds later she rejoins Mum.

"What happened?"

"Nothing. I'm at MacRitchie. A macaque stole my breakfast, scared the hell out of me. Mum, tell the truth, is this a prank?"

"No, Lynette, definitely no."

What's going on? She zooms into the last recorded location. Not Pyongyang exactly, a spot a few kilometers outside the city, 1Billion Dance Studio. She taps *about us*.

She and Mum are shifted into a saccharine diorama. A bright meadow, four smiling people dancing to upbeat, soaring music. A deep, textured voice narrates. A special place, where members lead disconnected lives and dedicate their energies to the 1Billion mission of inspiring the world to dance.

Why would Ethan go there? Is he making a documentary about the group? Probably more compelling than his last few subjects. But why disconnect, and why the nude recording?

"Do you think he's okay? Lynette, you need to do something."

She pulls up a travel plan. "Mum, if I run back to the road, I can make this eight o'clock supersonic to Pyongyang."

————

Three hours later Lynette's car pulls up to a gated, enclosed facility in the woods on the outskirts of Pyongyang. Odd. A screen above the entrance displays *Welcome to 1Billion Dance Studio* in English and Korean. Or maybe not so odd. If everyone keeps their implants disconnected they need old-fashioned stuff like this.

She peeks into a narrow booth next to the gate and is surprised to find it occupied by a human attendant. "Do you have someone here named Ethan Tan? I'm his sister."

She is informed that as a visitor, she is required to accept the terms of a nondisclosure agreement and take an enforced oath to keep recording and network access turned off. An extraordinarily unusual request. But she wants to see Ethan and doesn't want to get into a dispute, so she consents. The attendant opens the gate and directs her to cabin 8-92.

This isn't a studio. It's more like a compound or a camp. And it's eerily empty. Where is everyone? She makes her way along the path the attendant pointed out, finds the correct block of cabins, and steps up into the open door of the one marked 8-92.

A striking woman, younger, mesmerizing, dancing in slow motion, her arms at chest level and bent at the elbows. Sunny Kim. Lynette recognizes her from researching 1Billion on the supersonic over. Not the flesh and blood Sunny Kim, but a life-size recording displayed on the back wall, which is screened, like the walls in facilities for the pre.

Lynette looks away and takes in the whole structure. A single rectangular room runs the full length of the cabin, with the underside of the bare pitched roof serving as the ceiling. A warm summer breeze flows in through the open side walls, which are not so much walls, but foldable flaps held open by rudimentary hook and eye hardware. Two bunk beds line each side wall, and all eight spots are occupied with people napping. Adults! Napping in the middle of the day!

Is this where members live, or just a place to rest? Might be fun to stay here for a night or two, like camping. But to actually live here day after day? And then she notices what's not present—no food synthesizer, no bathroom. Where do they do input and output?

She takes a few steps into the cabin, surprised that nobody has noticed her, and studies the back wall. Eight looped recordings arranged in a two-by-four grid occupy the space to the right of Sunny. She recognizes the top right one. It's Ethan dancing nude, a flat projection of the recording she and Mum found on his timeline a few hours ago. The moving image is disturbing enough on its own. Grouped with seven other one-eighth-sized men and women dancing naked, juxtaposed with a life-sized, fully clothed Sunny, it's frightening. What the hell kind of place is this?

Lynette looks in the upper right bunk and sees Ethan napping. Yes, she's had a few hours to get used to the idea that he might be here. But seeing him in the flesh, sleeping on a bunk bed, it doesn't compute. How could he be here?

She places her hand on his forearm and gently shakes him. "Ethan. Ethan."

"Aiyoh, sis, what you doing here?"

"Visiting you. Wah lao, what you doing here?" she asks, falling into Singlish.

"All the way just to visit?" he asks.

"Your implant is disconnect. Mum and Dad cannot reach you."

"Yah. We disconnect for first two years."

Who is *we*? She can't speak with him here. Others are starting to stir and could listen to their conversation.

"Let's go makan."

"Midday meal isn't until 1:15."

"Damn hungry. Monkey stole my breakfast. Let's eat in a café."

"No cafés here."

"What about a restaurant outside of this . . . what you call it, camp, compound?"

"Campus. With my implant disconnect I can't pay for anything off campus."

What's his problem? Doesn't he get that she's just trying to get them out of the cabin?

"My treat."

"Not sure. Now is individual rest time and I'd rather have midday meal in the dining hall at 1:15."

"Well, how about we take a walk?"

"I need my rest. Let's talk here."

"Ethan, I came all this way and I need to go back soon."

The longer she stays in Korea on this unplanned trip, the more patient appointments she'll need to squeeze into the back half of the week or skip entirely. No big deal for her, she likes working long days, but it throws off her patients who count on the consistency.

"Let's walk," he finally says.

And then the man on the front right bottom bunk stands up. "I'm in the mood for a walk too, I'll join you."

Ethan introduces Robert.

"Robert," she says, "I need to ask my brother for advice. Do you mind if we walk alone?"

"No, no, of course not. I didn't realize. Ethan, I'll see you at 1:15 for midday meal."

———————

She and Ethan walk away from the cabin. "What's going on? Are you making a documentary?"

"No. I guess we haven't talked in a while. This is my home now. I decided to join, to dedicate myself to inspiring one billion people to dance, to help make Sunny Kim's vision come true. Do you know who she is?"

Siao! He's gone off the deep end.

"Yes, I know, I looked on the flight over. But why would you join? When did you decide this? Since when have you even been interested in dance?"

"You know the documentary I made last year?"

That really long one on, what was it, lizards? Guppies? Zebrafish? No, goldfish!

"Yup, the one on goldfish?"

"Not goldfish, salamanders. A four-hour exploration of olm salamander forelimb motion. I was feeling so good about it, sure it would finally be my breakout project. And then when it got fewer than ten complete views—you, Mum, and Dad must have been three of them—I decided to give up on documentaries.

"Then, out of the blue, I got contacted by one of the senior choreographers here. She told me about 1Billion. Said she stumbled across my work and loved it. It inspired her to create a dance routine modeled on my salamanders. She invited me to come here, physically, and consult on the dance, and while I was here they screened my documentary."

Sounds shady. Did they pay his travel expenses? She almost asks, but thinks better of it.

"That was nine months ago and people were crazy about it. There were dozens of 1Billion members in the room and they stayed up all night asking me questions and figuring out how to move their bodies like salamanders. Sis, you don't know how good it felt to finally have people appreciate my work. I was beginning to lose faith in my judgment, questioning if my documentary was compelling, and then I realized it was, I just needed to find the right audience."

Uh-huh.

"The whole thing was so well received that I was invited back for a screening with a larger group a few months later, and then again a month ago. I stayed for a week in one of the cabins, something of a trial, and Robert, who you just met, invited me to join on a one-year provisional basis."

She has so many questions, but she knows they're going to upset him. She runs her fingers through her hair. "Why didn't you tell anyone? And why did you disconnect?"

"Sis, I would think you of all people would get it. We disconnect to avoid distraction, to focus on dance. I know I should have told Mum and Dad. I planned to, but everything happened so fast, and I was worried about upsetting them."

Does he hear himself? Focus on dance? Her brother? A forty-something-year-old man who has never danced in his life?

"You didn't think Mum and Dad would be upset by a recording of you dancing naked?"

"That was to join. Everyone does it. Proof of commitment. Plus Mum and Dad will learn to appreciate it once they realize the human body is beautiful in all its forms. I'm not naive. Maybe the outside world sees a forty-one-year-old scrawny body writhing awkwardly to a techno love ballad, but here we see a work of art. My whole first week the recording was playing in the dining hall and I got a lot of compliments. And it doesn't really matter what the outside world thinks, because I'm disconnected and sealed off from that."

She would laugh, maybe even suspect he was pulling her leg, if his tone wasn't so earnest.

"No, Ethan, let's call a spade a spade. The only reason you have the luxury of ignoring the outside world is that Grandma and Grandpa gave you those rental properties. They wanted you free to make art, not attend summer camp."

"About that . . . sis . . . I assigned that income to 1Billion."

"Siao ah! The thirty thousand from your JB rental units? Why? Why would you do that?"

"It's no big deal. It puts us all on equal footing. The income stream will come right back to me if I don't make it past my one-year provisional membership."

"But Grandma and Grandpa saved day and night to buy that property. They gave you the units so you could make documentaries. That money should stay in the family, not go to 1Billion."

And where *is* all that money going? Food plus housing plus what?

"That's thirty thousand uni per month. What do you figure the expenses are to house you in a primitive cabin and feed you in a communal dining hall? Three hundred per month? Does that seem fair? You're subsidizing all the other people here with Grandma and Grandpa's money while you live like an impoverished monk. That's not right."

He flashes a look of superiority. "I'm not supporting all these people. Everyone has passive income. Real estate, investment interest, licensing royalties, trust funds, social security, even lottery winnings. Like in our cabin there's just one person on scholarship."

She fights down her rising anger. So that's their game.

She and Ethan turn right and continue along the wooded path. Two women approach from the other direction and stop to say hello to Ethan. One introduces herself as the choreographer who invited him to campus. She tells Lynette how thrilled they are to have Ethan as part of the community and how moved everyone was by his salamander documentary. On and on, she doesn't stop talking, and then, after fifteen minutes of inane dance talk which Ethan seems to find captivating, the choreographer suggests they all walk over to the dining hall together.

"You go ahead," she says to the pair. "My brother and I are still catching up. We'll follow in a few minutes."

"Okay." Doubtful sounding. "Don't be late, midday meal starts in ten minutes."

"Sis," Ethan says once the two women are out of earshot, "maybe we should go with them. I really don't want to be late."

"What difference does it make?"

"In life, as in dance, timing is crucial. I'm a provisional member. I don't want to bend the rules."

God. Punctuality never used to be his strong suit.

"You're scaring me Ethan. But no prob. Let's eat; we can talk after."

"I can't. I have dance lessons."

"Didn't you have dance lessons this morning?"

"No, campus-wide group dance from five to seven, and then I had isolation exercises after breakfast, but lessons are after lunch."

"Skip."

"I don't want to fall behind. Plus I can't let my partner down."

"After lessons?"

"Then it's evening meal."

"After that?"

"Evening group dance and bed."

"Ethan, I came all this way to see you."

"I know. I just don't want to let anyone down when I'm so new."

Dear god. This is much, much worse than she thought. She needs to be strategic, like he's a patient.

"Listen. Do what you need to do. I'll be back tomorrow at the start of rest. We'll go for another walk."

———

She hails a car and heads into town. Starving and needing to collect her thoughts, she enters a small restaurant, sits at the bar, and orders grilled eel and a noodle dish.

She's torn. On the one hand, her every professional and sisterly instinct tells her that Ethan is being taken for a ride. On the other hand, he's an adult. He's drifted from one project to another his entire post-college life. One way or the other he's certain to get bored of 1Billion and head back home. But if she pushes him and suggests that they're flattering him for his money, she could permanently destroy their relationship. He needs to realize what 1Billion is on his own, and when he does, he'll need a face-saving way out. She needs to take care not to close that exit.

For some reason her college boyfriend pops into her mind. On the surface Sergei and Ethan are similar—smart, skinny math guys who like music. But that's where the similarity ends. Sergei would never be taken in by flattery. The only professors he trusted were the ones who criticized him. Sergei couldn't believe that people liked his work, and Ethan can't believe they don't. Which attitude is healthier? She needs to get Ethan to channel some of Sergei's skepticism.

She lifts a piece of eel with her chopsticks and swirls it in a shallow ceramic bowl of soy sauce. There are two things she should do before she goes back to the compound—excuse her, the campus—tomorrow. First is to do more research on 1Billion. In treating patients for virtual reality addiction, she's always found it invaluable to know the ins and outs of the particular worlds in which they are trapped.

Second is to seek counsel from her professional support group, the four other interventionists she gets together with to share advice on cases. She tells her AI to schedule an urgent meeting of the group.

———

So three-and-a-half years ago, 1Billion went from this famous online dance group to a bunch of unplugged people living on a compound outside Pyongyang. Not exactly a common path. Lynette, now in a hotel room, sifts through more media than she could possibly consume about the old, online version of 1Billion. These bootleg recordings of Sunny Kim leading participatory dance sessions show her saying some crazy, unhinged stuff. And this whole attempt to take control of BORO, how had she never heard about that? No wonder they were shut down.

But as far as the current offline incarnation of 1Billion, almost nothing. Just some fan chatter from a few years ago about how, after being blocked by BORO, Sunny acquired land on the outskirts of Pyongyang and built the 1Billion campus.

Lynette connects with her colleagues. They're initially split on what to do. They're so used to dealing with virtual reality and chemical addiction that it's hard to take disconnecting your implant, living on a campus, interacting with fellow humans, and doing healthy physical activity as a threat. But her friends grow concerned when she plays the bootleg recordings of Sunny's rants from before 1Billion got blocked and when she tells them about her stilted conversation with Ethan.

"If Sunny Kim is creating a physical version of that distorted virtual world with those same toxic ideas, you should get your brother out of there," one of her interventionist friends tells her. She agrees.

———

The next morning, Lynette stands outside Ethan's cabin, going over what she wants to say to him, waiting for him to return from whatever dance thing he's doing. She sees Ethan and Robert approach.

"Hi, Lynette!" Robert says. "So good to see you again. Ethan was on fire in artistic expression class."

She ignores Robert and signals to Ethan to start walking with her.

"Maybe you guys should chat during midday meal," Robert says. "We have a strenuous afternoon of dance today and Ethan needs his nap."

She bites her tongue. No way did he just say that. She explains that she needs to chat with her brother before she heads back to Singapore this afternoon.

Robert interlocks his fingers and stretches his arms toward the sky. "You know, I'm feeling a bit restless, do you mind if I walk with you?"

Ethan says nothing.

She forcefully explains that she needs time alone with her brother.

"Of course, I understand; didn't realize. Ethan, try to get back here by one so we can walk over to the dining hall together for midday meal."

"Ethan," she gets into her rehearsed speech once they're on the walking path, "this is a dangerous place. I watched recordings of Sunny Kim back when 1Billion was online. She espoused crazy, toxic ideas and worked her fans up to foaming at the mouth. She was blocked by BORO."

He looks at her as if she were still in primary three and he in six. "I know all about BORO. They're another reason we keep our implants disconnected. They despise us and our philosophy. They want to control reality to preserve the status quo. We stand for people defining their own realities. BORO wants to destroy us, but as long as our implants are disconnected, we block their influence."

What is he talking about? Can he hear himself?

"Ethan, do you really think BORO gives a rat's ass about you? Do you think they're spending even an iota of their precious time plotting to destroy some nothing dance compound? Here's why you keep your implants disconnected. It lets 1Billion control the flow of information. You can't make informed decisions if you can't access your own resources, if you can't even talk to anyone outside the group. You have no external frame of reference. You're not getting any objective feedback."

"Sis, don't insult 1Billion." His calm, reasonable tone confirms her fear: brainwashed. "We may be small now, but all of the impactful organizations in human history started small. Look, I'm not some impressionable kid. I'm a product of Singapore's world-class educational system. I'm an adult with forty-one years of life experience. My eyes are wide open. In the outside objective reality you're talking about, I've accomplished little of value. Here, I'm appreciated."

Appreciated for your money. Maybe not only that, but would they have invited him to become a member otherwise?

"This is my reality and it feels right to me. And you know, from my perspective, your reality is warped. Spending your days striving for professional recognition. Even just being an interventionist. Why intervene? Let people do what they want. I like being part of a collective with a pure and simple mission, to inspire a billion people."

Inspire them to do what? She almost makes the snarky comment aloud, but instead suppresses her anger. This isn't like the arguments they used to have as kids. She's not trying to win, she needs Ethan to achieve his own clarity. She needs to lower the temperature.

She doesn't get far into figuring out how to do that though, because the choreographer and her friend appear as if out of nowhere. "Ethan," says the other woman, who is apparently one of the teaching assistants for his afternoon dance class, "you looked great yesterday. For someone who never danced before coming here, I'm astounded by your progress." The two women chat with them for ten minutes and then suggest they all walk over to the dining hall together.

"No, we'll follow in a few," Lynette tells them.

"Don't be late for midday meal," the teaching assistant tells Ethan. "You're going to need your energy for lessons this afternoon."

She and Ethan resume walking. "Sis, I really do need to get to the dining hall for midday meal."

She can't contain it any longer. "It's just fucking lunch, Ethan! Stop calling it a fucking midday meal and acting like it's some sacred ritual. Nothing will happen if you skip lunch."

But she's about to lose him, and that dissolves her anger. She puts an arm around him. "Sorry Ethan. This place is creeping me out. Look, you're right, you're an adult, and if you want to try life here it's not my place to argue you out of it. Do you at least have a partner?"

"A dance partner?"

"No, I mean, are you seeing anyone?"

"No, relationships are prohibited for Lo's. Once I get to L1, Mother will assign a partner for one day a month. At L3 we get to find our own long-term partners, as long as Mother approves, and can even move into pairs cabins."

What? She had just persuaded herself to let this thing play itself out, but this is a whole new level of screwed up. And is Sunny Kim *Mother*?

"Ethan, is *Mother* what you call Sunny?"

He nods.

"But she's younger than you. She's even younger than me. Also do you hear how crazy what you just said is?"

"Is it crazy? A bit odd maybe, but it's all about perspective."

She sees how he could think that. He was married for a couple of years, and as far as she knows, hasn't dated anyone since his divorce half a decade ago. Here there's structure, gamification, like school, like an addictive virtual world. Follow the rules and you get paired up. Clever.

"I need to get to the dining hall."

"Ethan, I'm sorry. Sorry for getting combative."

"That's okay. I know this will take some getting used to."

"Can I suggest one practical thing? Change your financial arrangement. Like direct twenty-nine thousand to your own investment account and a thousand to 1Billion. That way you'll have a safety cushion if and when you choose to leave."

She has two motivations. First is the one she told him. Second is if 1Billion's interest in him is all about milking his funds, this will drive their interest down.

"We're not allowed to do that. Commitment means directing all of your income to 1Billion and finance does audits to confirm. Plus, I don't actually control the income stream. I transferred the deeds."

"What? Why would you do that? They just want to control you and your assets."

"No, it's nothing like that. 1Billion is a nonprofit and it saves on tax to have 1Billion own the rental units directly. It's completely typical, pretty much everyone here with real estate does it that way."

She's stunned, not sure what to say. Should she mention this to Mum and Dad? To Grandma and Grandpa?

"Okay, sis, I really need to get to midday meal."

She hugs him. She doesn't want to let go, but he breaks the embrace after a few seconds.

"Don't worry, I'm fine, more than fine. Give my best to Mum and Dad."

Yup, your best. They're going to be thrilled to hear about all this.

————

Lynette lands in Singapore exhausted and uneasy. How is it that she knows with certainty that Sunny is a con artist but

Ethan can't see it? She spent the supersonic racking her brain trying to come up with a plan. Pressuring him head-on to leave will backfire and further solidify his commitment to the group. Waiting for him to leave on his own isn't good enough, but what can she do?

She speaks with Mum and Dad and tells them part of the story but leaves out the deed transfer. She powers through a few patient sessions, has a light dinner of kaya toast with a soft-boiled egg, and goes to bed.

The next day she wakes up energized by a plan that occurred to her during the night. She's a single individual trying to persuade Ethan that he's in a warped environment, but he's surrounded by hundreds equally invested in the craziness. She needs to enlist the help of other worried friends and relatives. And she knows exactly how to find them—search for recordings of people dancing naked. If the ones she saw in Ethan's cabin are representative, there's a certain similarity to all of them, and that will make them straightforward to find.

Another benefit of getting in touch with relatives is she'll be able to estimate the income 1Billion is pulling in through its members. At least when decoding what makes virtual worlds addictive, following the money leads to useful insights. If Ethan with his U30,000 monthly "contribution" is even remotely typical, then 1Billion could be bringing in a few hundred million a year. Where is it all going? Not to housing, that's for sure.

She searches, finds roughly eight hundred recordings like Ethan's, and has her AI trace contacts, yielding a list of three thousand family members and friends. She composes a brief message introducing herself and explaining why she wants to get in touch. Her AI sends the message. Within five minutes her calendar for the next two days is packed with forty meetings and a waiting list of over a hundred people looking for meeting slots. She's obviously touched a nerve. This will work. Ethan will be home in a month and the whole family will be together to watch the drone show on National Day.

19

July 12, 2115
Five years before 4-17
Outskirts of Pyongyang, Korea

Another fucking OCIR. Sunny finds that even she's started thinking in terms of Sang-chul's annoying acronyms. Fernando sent her the report yesterday. She had no intention of looking at it, but he pinged three times today saying it was urgent. She finally agreed and told him they would discuss it at the weekly leadership team meeting tonight. So now she has to read the stupid thing. At least it's mostly recording snippets. This really wasn't what she signed up for when she agreed to let Sang-chul put what he called a *management system* in place.

OUTSIDE CONTACT INCIDENT REPORT

Member: Ethan Tan
Visitor: Lynette Tan, his younger sister

Time of contact: Monday and Tuesday (July 8, 2115 -
July 9, 2115)
Date report prepared: July 11, 2115
Report distribution: Leadership team

Summary

(prepared by Fernando Rios — head of culture)

Ethan Tan, one of our new recruits from Singapore,
was visited by his sister Lynette Tan, an interventionist. Standard procedures were followed. However,
Lynette appears determined to stir up trouble. On
Wednesday, after she returned to Singapore, she
initiated contact with the **families and friends of
other members.**

What the hell? Why did she contact other families? How?

Member protection and inoculation

(prepared by Miriam Meyer — head of recruiting)

Lynette visited on Monday. We followed our playbook for minimizing outside influence. When
Lynette asked her brother to go for a walk, Robert
Lin, who is Ethan's cabin captain and was part of his
recruiting team, proposed accompanying them.
Lynette insisted on walking alone with her brother
and they spoke privately (view recording). To stop
their conversation, we had another member of
Ethan's recruiting team intercept him and his sister

on the walk. In total, we limited Lynette's one-on-one time with Ethan to seven minutes.

Lynette told Ethan she would be visiting again on Tuesday. Per our playbook, we had Robert lead a reinforcement discussion in the cabin Monday night (<u>recording</u>). After analyzing Ethan's behavior during that discussion and his conversation with his sister on Tuesday (<u>recording</u>), I consider our inoculation a success.

Yes, Miriam's team is good at giving new recruits a spine. That's not news.

<u>Tracking the sister</u>

(prepared by Fernando Rios — head of culture)

This is one of the roughly **400 messages** Lynette sent to the families and friends of members on Wednesday:

Greetings Grace. My name is Lynette Tan and I'm a doctor in Singapore. I'm reaching out because I believe your son Sam is a part of 1Billion. My brother recently became a member and is living at their compound in Korea. I'm concerned about him. Do you share my concern? I would love to compare notes. <u>Respond</u> to schedule a time for us to speak real-time.

Sunny chews her lip. Seriously? Four hundred people? So this is what Fernando wanted her to see?

And here's the conversation between Lynette and Grace Park, Sam Park's mother. It took place this morning.

She plays the recording at 2x.

Grace: "We have three kids. Sam is our middle. I've been distressed ever since he got involved with 1Billion. He's totally cut off except for virtual visits now and then. He used to love spending time with his nieces and nephews and now he doesn't even get in touch on their birthdays.

"Sometimes I look on the bright side. My wife is fanatical, capable of single-minded focus for months on end, and that's why she's been so successful. Sam got some of that from her. He was a champion swimmer—almost made the Korean Olympic team. Now he's chosen to apply his intensity to dance. It's perturbing, but it's also hard to fault him for being passionate."

Lynette: "What does your wife do?"

Grace: "Oh, I figured you knew. She's founder of the largest Korean sauce company. If you've ever had doenjang from your food printer, some tiny fraction of a uni went to her company. She trained as a chemist and was the first person to figure out how to mimic the taste of natural fermentation with a synthesizer."

Lynette: "I had no idea. I print Korean food all the time. And speaking of uni, I want to ask you something; of course, I'll understand if it's too private. Years ago my grandparents gave my brother real estate—rental units that generate thirty thousand uni a month. He turned the full income stream over to 1Billion. I'm curious about others. Does Sam send funds to 1Billion?"

Grace: "Oh god. You're touching on a sensitive subject. Good thing my wife isn't here. When each of our kids was born we gifted them shares in the company. Back then it was a tiny startup. Now, decades later, those shares are worth a lot. Sam earns an annual dividend of 2.5 million uni and he directs all of it to 1Billion. I know it's for a good cause and our accountant found a way to transfer the tax deduction to our other kids, but it's still upsetting."

Lynette: "Two and a half million? Holy shit. Pardon my Japanese; that works out to more in a month than I make in a year as a doctor. What is 1Billion doing with all the money? *[Pause]* One thing I can tell you is we're not alone. Most of the other families I've spoken with have similar stories, albeit with amounts more like my brother."

Grace: "How many others have you spoken with?"

Lynette: "Around twenty. That's all I've had time for. I reached out to four hundred and a hundred fifty got back to me."

Fuck her. What a loser. This Lynette woman needs to get a life.

Grace: "How many members do you think there are overall?"

Lynette: "Rough estimate? Eight hundred to a thousand. Two ways I get there. First is I found around eight hundred recordings of people dancing nude posted in the last three years that look like my brother's initiation recording. That's how I found Sam and you. Sec—"

Grace: "Don't remind me. That's a hard thing for a mother to watch. You know, you bathe them when they're little, but after puberty I'd rather just see them clothed."

Lynette: "Not easy for a sister either. [Laughs] The other way I estimated is my brother's in an eight-person cabin, number eight-dash-ninety-two. All the cabins start with eight or two, and two must be for pairs. I studied the map and the cabins are numbered sequentially, with the highest eight cabin being one-fourteen and the highest pairs cabin being forty-two. Eight times a hundred fourteen plus two times forty-two is just shy of a thousand."

Grace: "Interesting. *[Pause]* Did you see Sunny Kim while you were there?"

Lynette: "No, except for on walls everywhere, but I'm convinced she isn't the inspirational, positive role model everyone makes her out to be. I've been studying every recording of Sunny since she joined 100M as a teenager. Have you ever watched bootleg recordings of her giving speeches from when 1Billion was still online? They're scary. She said all sorts of crazy, self-contradictory things under the guise of being inclusive and nonjudgmental. She worked her fans up into a rabid fury. BORO had good reason to shut her down.

"I've been trying to get in touch with Crystal Chae, who owned 100M, to see if I can learn more about why Sunny left the group; but she's ignoring me. I did manage to reach Yo-kyeong Pae. She was a big 100M star around the time Sunny joined in 2100. I'm

going to be meeting with her next week and I hope
she can shed insight into Sunny's true character."

Shed insight into her true character? *Pae Yo-kyeong?* Let the
two losers talk, that'll be funny.

> **Grace**: "What are you thinking? Do you have a
> plan?"
> **Lynette**: "I'm still trying to figure that out and I'd
> love your advice. I recognize that there's nothing
> necessarily illegal about 1Billion recruiting adults to
> their cause and asking those adults to contribute
> their time and financial resources. However, it would
> be unethical for 1Billion to use coercive techniques
> to brainwash recruits and I suspect, from the stilted
> conversation I had with my brother, that that's
> happening. And if it's happening to him, you can be
> sure it's happening to others. I'm considering a three-
> pronged strategy. . . ."

Sunny rolls her eyes. Three pronged my ass. Does she think
she's some government minister leading a major policy
initiative? But Sunny slows the playback to 1x.

> "The first prong is forming a group of concerned
> families and friends. We can help each other
> persuade members to leave 1Billion.
> "The second prong is to follow the money. I've
> been using the information that each family's been
> sharing to piece together the financial picture. Enor-
> mous sums of money are flowing into 1Billion. . . ."

Sunny snaps upright at that. Yeah, that's *my* money, bitch.

But Sang-chul has the contributions set up so they're watertight. Doesn't he?

"Where's it all going? Is 1Billion a legitimate nonprofit organization? We need to shine a bright light on it, and I won't be surprised if that light exposes tax evasion. If nothing else, 1Billion needs to be held to greater accountability.

"The final prong is to publish information that will be discoverable by 1Billion members or anyone thinking of getting involved with them. I'm a member of the Society for Interventionists. I'm going to write up my findings in an article and submit it for publication in our society's journal...."

That's your plan? Write an article in a journal? Sunny cackles.

"Once peer-reviewed, it'll have high credibility and should be the first thing that comes up when people look for information on 1Billion or Sunny Kim.

"That's my tentative plan. What do you think?"

Grace: "I'm so impressed, Lynette. I don't know why I never thought of any of that. I'll help, let me know what you need. And can you also keep me posted on your progress?"

Sunny digs her nails into her palm. Well, she sees why Fernando kept pinging her. Her team can fix this. But dealing with this crap over and over again is beneath her. She has an idea, and the first step is elevating Magnus Peterson to the leadership team.

20

July 12, 2115
Five years before 4-17
Outskirts of Pyongyang, Korea

Sunny's standing meeting with her leadership team is every Friday at nine p.m. A few minutes before nine thirty, she steps into the conference cabin and sees four of herself, enlarged, stylized and silhouetted on each of the walls, dancing at one-fiftieth speed, so slow that at first glance the moving images appear static.

She sits down at the round table in her usual spot between Sang-chul and Fernando. Until a few hours ago those two and Miriam, her head of recruiting, made up the whole team. Now Magnus is here too.

Magnus Peterson. Former head of the Scandinavian chapter of her fan club. Swedish tech executive. When 1Billion went offline, he leapt at the opportunity to move to Korea and be part of creating the campus. He seemed appreciative when, earlier today, Sunny told him she was elevating him to the leadership team. She needs fire to fight fire. But first she needs to test him. Not the easiest person to read—reserved. If nothing else it's nice to have a new face in here—he's easy on the eyes and, looking at Miriam, Sunny can tell she's thinking the same.

Her thoughts are interrupted when the door to the attached kitchen opens. Her eyes track the slender woman who walks in and sets two bottles of baijiu and a bowl of spicy peanuts on the table. Sunny doesn't recognize her. Must be new. Cute.

"Thank you Nadezhda," Fernando says.

Nadezhda, sounds Russian.

"Who's that?" she asks, after the girl leaves.

"Nadezhda Maksimova," Miriam answers. "4K. Composer. Got lucky with royalties when a game that licensed her music exploded."

Fernando unscrews the top of the baijiu and pours everyone a shot. Sunny catches an odd look on Magnus's face. Probably wonders why we're drinking on our dry campus. Well, you're with the big boys now, Mr. Peterson.

Fernando raises his glass toward her. "Thank you, Mother, for your wise leadership."

Fernando refills everyone.

"Thank you, Mother," Sang-chul says, "for the tireless work you do to build our community and for the pressure you place on me to achieve our financial targets."

Shots downed and refilled.

Miriam raises her glass. "Thank you, Mother, for your genius idea this week to use more colorful hearts in our recruiting ads."

Sunny looks at Magnus. This is a crucial moment. If this isn't his thing, then he's not a fit for her leadership team, and definitely won't be up to the task she has in mind. "Thank you, Mother, for the beauty you bring to our world," he finally says.

Fernando refills everyone and then turns to her. "Mother, can we talk about the OCI first?"

She nods and scoops up a handful of spicy peanuts. Can't they manage anything without her? What were they doing before she got here?

"Everyone look at the report?" Fernando asks.

"Fernando," says Miriam, "something I don't understand. How'd you get that private conversation between Lynette and Sam's mom?"

Fernando grins, like he has a delicious secret. "Grace is our agent. I recruited her and a bunch of other families to warn us if BORO ever started making trouble. She forwarded me Lynette's message and I asked her to play along to elicit intelligence."

Maybe Fernando's not totally useless. Sunny smiles at him. "Nice work."

These little suckers are so good, who would have thought numb and hot would go together? She grabs another handful as Sang-chul looks past her to Fernando. "Why the heck did you have her share all that info about how much we get from Sam? He's in the top five."

"I told her to be herself and win Lynette's trust. I couldn't control every word out of her mouth. I don't know if she really feels that way about the money or was just making it up, but trust me, she's solid. She *loves* Mother."

Sunny looks up when Nadezhda walks in again, this time with a round of Sunny's favorite beer. The girl really is fucking cute. This whole idea of picking new recruits to serve the leadership team was Sunny's. Miriam was against it, concerned about hypocrisy, but Miriam didn't get that that was the whole point.

Fernando turns to Sunny. "Hungry yet?"

She shakes her head.

"It'll be another half hour before the meal," he tells Nadezhda.

As Nadezhda walks out, Magnus stands up, as if to follow her.

"Where are you going?" Sunny asks.

"Bathroom, I'll be right back."

"Just wait, I don't want you to miss anything, we'll take a bio break in a little while."

Magnus sits back down and Miriam leans toward him. Sunny can just make out what she whispers: "Next time —diapers."

Sang-chul puts his beer down. "What a gross, disgusting woman. We can definitely nail her on NDA violations for the stuff she revealed about the campus. And, by the way, we should change our cabin numbering so visitors can't use that to count our members."

Fernando agrees and proposes they file an emergency cease and desist tonight, getting a court to issue a temporary order blocking Lynette from speaking with other families. "There are a bunch of ways we can tie her up in court and drain her finances."

"Here's another idea," says Miriam. "It won't help right away but will be a good insurance policy. We hire a few people to pose as patients. They go to Lynette for treatment, and then after a few months we have them relapse and file malpractice complaints."

"Smart," Sang-chul says. "If we can get her medical license revoked we can dry up her income."

Sunny looks at Magnus. "Do you have any ideas?" This is another test. If he doesn't have the balls or the imagination to come up with an idea for something this simple, no way can he do what she has in mind.

She watches. He squirms. Then pauses. Then takes a sip of his beer. "We form a foundation and keep its connection to 1Billion hidden. We figure out who the likely peer reviewers are for Lynette's article and encourage·them to apply for research grants. During the application process, the foundation subtly indicates that Lynette is a kook, and it won't look favorably on them accepting her article."

Impressive. Sunny looks around at the others. All nod. Test passed.

She half listens as her team works out the details. Then she lets the anger she felt watching Lynette and Grace earlier today well back up. She interrupts, intentionally adopting a strident tone that slices through the chatter. "Do all that stuff. But you need to think bigger. We've been here three long years. How many members are we up to?"

Everyone looks down.

"I said, how many fucking members?"

Sang-chul picks his head up. "984."

"Nine eighty-four. We need ten thousand, and then a hundred thousand and then a million. How long will that take if we have to play whack-a-mole with these nonbelievers? Lynette this, Lynette that. It's not worth my fucking time. How do we fight the assholes at BORO when they have all the power?"

She sees that Magnus is staring into his half-filled glass.

"Magnus!" He looks at her. "You need to neutralize BORO's power. You need to turn off AI fact checking."

"That's impossible," he says after a pause, almost whispering.

"Who are you to dismiss a directive from Mother?"

shouts Sang-chul. "If Mother gives you an assignment, your job is to find a way to do it, not make excuses."

Sunny, calmer, looks at Magnus. "Take your bio break, and when you get back you can tell us how you're going to make it happen. Where the hell is dinner?"

21

July 12, 2115
Five years before 4-17
Samos, Greece

Think we can get the kids to bed early? Daniel DMs Karima.

After a five-hour hike? That's not going to be the problem. Just make sure you don't fall asleep before they do, she replies, appending a classic smiley emoji.

Wake me up if I do. I'm desperate here.

Daniel is following Karima, Leon and Ora along a path paved with loose rocks near the town of Karlovassi. He smells the warm, salty breeze and tastes the lingering sweetness on his lips from the baklava they ate after lunch.

In truth, he's not that desperate. Eager, certainly—who wouldn't be hiking around a romantic Greek island. But not desperate because, for his family's sake, he's been sleeping with his former star student and now junior colleague Itai Wang.

"Mom, I'm bored," Leon complains. "Can you unblock reading?"

"No, honey, not during the hike. And watch your step, I don't want you tripping."

"Kids," Daniel says. "I'll give you a puzzle. Do you know why we came to Samos?"

"You and Mommy missed your honeymoon?" Ora says.

"Yep. But why Samos?"

"Because of Pythagoras," says Leon.

Daniel watches Karima reach over Ora and tousle Leon's hair. "I was around your age, Ora," she says, "when I learned about A squared plus B squared equals C squared. I had this feeling, like something clicked in me, that someone could come up with something so simple, so elegant, so useful, prove it was true, and the proof would last for eternity. That's when I knew I wanted to be a mathematician. And Pythagoras was born right here on this island. Twenty-seven hundred years ago."

Would Daniel have wanted to be Pythagoras? No implants, so few people, but to be famous for millennia. . . . Something to think about later. Back to amusing the kids. He forms a cube with his hands. "Here's something else Pythagoras figured out. Imagine a cube. How many faces does it have?"

"Six," Ora immediately answers.

"Good. And what is the shape of each face?"

"A square."

"Yes. A square is a regular polygon. All its sides are equal and all its angles are the same. A cube is a three-dimensional shape whose faces are all identical squares and where the same number of faces meet at each vertex. How many is that?"

"Three."

"Correct. Now, Pythagoras proved that there are only five

shapes where the faces are all identical regular polygons and the same number of faces meet at each vertex. The cube is one. Can you figure out the other four?"

The path narrows and they proceed single file. Leon, then Ora, then Karima, with Daniel bringing up the rear.

Things started up with Itai a few months ago. Daniel knew, or at least suspected, that Itai was interested in him the whole time he was his student. But that would have been messy, and Daniel never signaled any interest. Then a few months ago Itai connected with him. "I'm planning to teach your olfactory algorithm in my class," Itai told him. "I've been working through the proof and I'm struggling with how the Pan-Sidiqqi transformation works in the fourth family."

"Happy to help. Let's talk over a drink," Daniel said, and suggested they meet at a bar in a Haifa hotel with a first-class privacy shield. One thing led to another, but Pan-Sidiqqi wasn't one of those things.

What's Karima in the middle of saying? Something about taking their next family vacation to the DU. ". . . see where Grandpa grew up. I'd like to go. When I went to that conference in the FSA last year, it was weird, 'cause things seemed so normal, nothing like what I imagined. But every time I saw an old person I couldn't help but wonder what they were doing back then. And it was strange to think there could be young pre around. Do you think—"

"Four triangles," Ora interrupts.

Karima looks at Ora. "What's that honey?"

"One of the shapes." Ora makes a pyramid shape with her hand. "Four triangles like this."

"Whoa," Karima says, "that *is* one of the shapes. How'd you figure that out?"

Ora smiles. "Like a cube but made out of four triangles. Three meet at each corner."

"Sweetie, I'm so impressed," Daniel says. "Do you know what that shape is called? Leon, what's a word that means four?"

"Quadra," Leon says.

"Yes, but not that, another word. Quadra is from Latin. Where are we?"

"Tetra?" asks Leon.

"Excellent, buddy! Yes, it's a tetrahedron. Now can you kids figure out the other three? They're harder. I'm so sure you won't be able to get 'em, if you figure out just one, it's all-you-can-eat ice cream for dinner."

"Danny!" Karima punches his shoulder.

"Sorry, I shouldn't have said that without checking with Mom, but a promise is a promise."

Holy shit, do you think Ora got lucky? He DMs Karima.

I couldn't have figured that out at five, that's for sure.

"Do you think Grandpa would come with us?" he asks, speaking aloud again. "Leon and Ora should understand what can happen in the world."

Ora looks up. "What happened, Daddy?"

"Nothing, sweetie."

He supports Leon and Ora as they scramble up a boulder. Then he climbs up himself, puts his hand out, helps Karima up, and gives her a kiss on the cheek. "Kids, your mom looks as beautiful today as the first day I saw her in our professor's office."

"Ugh, Dad," Leon says.

"I don't know," Karima says, returning to the topic of visiting the DU. "He's never been back and I've never heard him say he wants to go back. I'll ask. He might do it for the sake of the kids; he feels strongly that we should never get complacent."

"Never get complacent about what?" Leon asks.

Karima stops walking and looks at Leon and Ora. "Children, you're so fortunate to be growing up at a time when life is safe and logical. Dad and I were lucky too. Great-grandpa wasn't. He was born in the United States back when it was a single unified country. But when he was a little older than Dad and me, a civil war broke out."

"Is that why Great-grandpa came to Israel?" Leon asks.

"Yes, but not before something bad happened."

"What?"

"This isn't the time. We're on Samos to have fun. Maybe when you two are a little older we'll take a trip to the DU with Great-grandpa and show you where he grew up."

"Won't it be dangerous?" Leon asks.

"No, honey, it's very safe. It's been safe for fifty years. Don't worry. Dad and I would never put you in danger. We'll always protect you."

Fuck, Daniel DMs Karima.

What?

Just got a message from Lia. China and Korea are pushing back on our fast track designation.

Is that so bad? There's a reason approval is a long process.

Yes it's bad!

Fuck. This is the difference between another four or five years and eight or more. He needs to speak with Lia. He needs her to get Israel to apply pressure to China and Korea. He needs the inside info on why they're pushing back.

"Mommy, Daddy! Eight triangles, four up here," Ora says, and makes a pyramid with her hands, "and the other four down here," she says inverting her hands.

Karima looks astonished. "Ora, that's amazing! How'd

you figure that out? I'm impressed. Super, super impressed. What do you think that shape is called?"

Leon speaks up. "Octahedron?"

Karima leans over and kisses Ora and Leon on their heads and streams hundreds of ice cream emoji.

Fuck ice cream.

22

Children—sorry to interrupt the flow of my story. After I shared a first draft with my grandson David Levy, who has been helping me edit (thank you David), I realized many of you are not familiar with implant history. You'll want to be from this point forward. Please find below **five short posts from my great-grandfather's blog.** These are all from the '60s and '70s, the decades that saw implants go from commercially available to ubiquitous. —Leon

Pill

January 15, 2067

In the late 2020s, when I was starting my career in Boston, I had a friend at MIT who was engineering a new drug delivery mechanism. I remember her telling me that getting anything larger than a few nanometers across the blood-brain barrier was impossible. The comment stayed with me because at the time I was working on nanobot software, and even the smallest bots were still a few hundred nanometers in all dimensions.

Back then, if you had asked me if I thought a noninvasive procedure for implanting computers in mammalian brains could be developed in my lifetime, I would have laughed. Younger people may consider today's regulatory approval of implant by pill no big deal, but for me the delivery mechanism is as impressive as the implant itself.

You swallow a pill and a few days later you have an implant. Easy on the outside, anything but on the inside. The pill contains the implant core, nanobots, and nanocapsules with electrode substrate. All of these components are spirited across the intestinal barrier through a nanorobotic mechanism that creates and then cauterizes a miniscule opening in the gastric mucosa. The components travel into the bloodstream, migrate to the brain, and then, aided by another nanorobotic process, cross the blood-brain barrier. The core is implanted at the base of the skull, and a permanent, flexible electrode network grows and intertwines with the nervous system.

Up until now, receiving an implant has required minimally invasive robotic brain surgery. Sounds scary and not exactly an impulse purchase. Even so, nearly one percent of all people have implants. I predict implant by pill will cause that number to rise quickly, very quickly.

BTW . . . if implant by pill doesn't blow your mind (not literally of course), maybe this will. Within the next five years, approval is likely for a fetal delivery system. Mother swallows a pill anytime in her third trimester, and three days later her unborn baby will have an implant. Wild.

Free implants
March 14, 2072

It's monumental. Free implants for everyone in the world young enough to receive one and unable to pay out of pocket. Permanent fund established by the wealthiest countries to cover the cost. Connectivity now considered a fundamental human right. These are big, bold unprecedented programs.

You can look at it as altruism. Finally, the wealthy countries are doing something to even the playing field, or at least to invite everyone onto the field. Or you can look at it as motivated by public health. The pandemic of 2020 is still recent enough for me to remember that we're all connected. The more people equipped with what is, among other things, a sophisticated health monitoring device, the lower the likelihood of disease outbreak. Then there's the economic side. What company isn't interested in a few billion extra potential customers?

Over fifty percent of eligible people already have an implant. Where will free take it? Are we headed to one hundred percent?

Is age the new digital divide?
May 6, 2074

All this talk about how the digital divide is now gone. Sure, that may be true for class and country, but what about the age divide? I feel forgotten. I'm not even retired. I'll live at least another thirty years. But the world is operating as if we older people don't matter. We'll be gone soon, so why bother taking our limitations into account, is that the idea? People talking without speaking aloud. Screens disappearing from public spaces. It's even getting annoying seeing everyone walking around in boring scrubs, forgetting that older people like me can't see projected outfits. Today things are barely tolerable. How about in twenty years? It's like I won't just be preimplant, I'll be subhuman. (And for the record, I don't mind being referred to as preimplant, but please stop calling us "the pre" as if we're an alien species.)

Citizenship and privacy
September 2, 2075

I spent the summer before sixth grade at my grandparents' house in New Jersey. I found a box of old paperback Isaac Asimov novels in the basement. Asimov was this science fiction giant from the twentieth century. I read a novel a day until I made it through the box, transported that summer into Asimov's worlds of robots and psychohistory. I never wanted the stories to end, but when they did, I kept reading all the back material. There were these two sentences from "About the Author" that have stayed with me all these years: "Isaac Asimov was born in the Soviet Union to his great surprise. He moved quickly to correct the situation."

Those sentences came back to me this morning when I was reading about the new microfines for Chinese citizens who say negative things about their government. For my entire life people have been predicting that with our interconnected globe, country of citizenship would become less important, but the opposite is true. Citizenship has never mattered more even as location has never mattered less.

I'm fortunate that my daughter and grandchildren, as Israeli citizens, are afforded strong privacy protection for their implants. Technology guarantees that only the government of record for a citizen may access private implant information without explicit authorization. And here in Israel, our legal system and layers of safeguards guarantee that access will be granted only when justified and after due process.

But if you're a Chinese citizen, Chinese law applies, and comprehensive surveillance from birth by the party is legal, expected, and accepted. I find the idea of microfines on speech reprehensible. My Chinese cousins say it's no big deal, no different than a microfine for spitting on the street. Is that what they really think? No way to know.

Required—that's going too far!
November 24, 2078

Is this just my old-fashioned American individualism shining through? I'm disgusted at the new UN resolution making it obligatory for every eligible person to receive an implant. Over ninety-nine percent of eligible people already have one, what gives the world's governments the right to force them on the remaining one percent? Look, I understand the security argument. The reality of modern technology is that one person can do enormous damage. We need to prevent something like the Real Madrid Stadium Massacre from ever happening again. I also get the vaccine argument. People can't opt out of vaccination because that endangers everyone and burdens the system. Even so . . . this feels different, or maybe I'm just old and set in my ways in thinking that having an artificial electrode network permanently and irreversibly meshed with your nervous system is something you should choose. (Plus, aren't some of the arguments invalidated by the fact that there are religious exceptions and the entire FSA isn't even part of the UN?)

23

July 12, 2115
Five years before 4-17
Outskirts of Pyongyang, Korea

Sunny steps out of the bathroom and sees Magnus. She places her hand on his shoulder. "I'm really glad you're here." A nervous smile flashes across his face, then he opens the meeting room door for her. They walk back in and rejoin the others.

She wasn't that hungry, but now, with the aroma of searing meat, she suddenly is. A smokeless grill is on the table and Fernando is using tongs and scissors to barbecue galbi, bulgogi and thick slices of white onion. Surrounding the grill are small metal bowls with her favorite banchan: cabbage kimchi, pickled radish and mung bean sprouts. There are lettuce leaves to wrap the meat and, for each of them, small square ramekins with fermented soybean and anchovy sauces. All exactly as she likes it.

She picks up a pickled radish with her chopsticks and points it at Magnus. "Okay, now tell us your plan."

Magnus puts his beer down. "We can't disable fact checking. That would require hacking into implants, which is impossible. I'm not trying to be disrespectful. I'm just stating a fact. Every algorithm in an implant is provably secure. No implant has ever been hacked."

"Magnus," says Sang-chul, "just because something hasn't been done before doesn't mean it can't be done. With that attitude we never would have tamed fire, invented agriculture, discovered quantum theory, set foot on Mars, cured cancer, or started 1Billion. Mother is a visionary. Mother doesn't expect us to stick to tried and true. Mother wants us to operate in uncharted territory, in choreography *and* in operations.

"You know," Sang-chul continues, "I admired you, thought of you as this polar fox, making an impulse decision to leave your fancy executive job in Sweden and come build our campus. But all of a sudden you look like a trembling chickadee to me, perched on your swing in an open cage, afraid to fly out for fear of the unknown."

Sunny lifts a lettuce wrap filled with galbi and rice to her mouth. He's come a long way, or at least does a good job of pretending. And all the dancing has been good for him—he's lost some weight. "Well put, Sang-chul."

He smiles.

"So you want me to make a plan to do something that's impossible?" Magnus asks, his voice shaky.

"No," says Fernando, "you don't get it. If Mother says it's possible then it *is* possible. Your job is to make it happen. Be positive and bold."

Magnus is quiet for a moment. Then, "We need a BQCI expert."

More annoying acronyms.

"What's BQCI?" Miriam asks, taking the words out of Sunny's mouth.

"Stands for Brain Quantum Computing Interface," Magnus says. "The technology in implants. Involves complicated math and neuroscience. There are only a few thousand people who specialize in it."

"Do you know any?" asks Fernando.

"No. But it's easy to make a list. Should all be in KISS or China. Either working for multinationals—Xyloom, Alphabet, Brain Duck, KuaiNao—or they're at research universities."

"Well," Miriam says, chewing on a piece of fish cake, "now we're getting somewhere. Recruiting is something we know how to do. And unlike you," she points her chopsticks at Magnus, "I'm not afraid of the seemingly impossible task of recruiting an implant expert to an anti-implant dance group."

Fernando rests his scissors and tongs on the edge of the grill. "Let's find a candidate."

Sunny's silhouette disappears from one of the walls and is replaced with images of the top BQCI professors. A database of academic literature and genealogy is consulted to generate a list of five hundred people who trained with these professors. The list is reduced to twenty by applying the usual filters and rankers for identifying potential recruits, minus the constraint that the candidate have a passive income stream.

Miriam studies the wall and points out the top candidate. "Sergei Vadimovich Kraev. Works in Israel as a senior BQCI engineer. No kids. Divorced. Girlfriend. Grew up in Moscow. College in Singapore. Attended a single 100M livestream twelve years ago in 2103, before Mother resigned."

"Interesting," adds Magnus. "He studied with Professor Ming Liu at Technion in 2100. Professor Liu's lab was, probably still is, where the top people trained. Sergei never completed his PhD, see that? Joined Xyloom in 2102 and has been there ever since. Xyloom practically invented implants. If we do manage to recruit this guy we should make sure he keeps working for them."

Sunny looks at Sergei. Slim build, kind face, blond hair, honest, timid eyes. Looks recruitable. "When, not if," she says. "You need to learn to think positive."

Miriam wraps a slice of bulgogi in a lettuce leaf. "We're in luck. He opted in to comprehensive tracking when he attended the 100M livestream back in 2103. Makes things much easier. Hey, look at that, his eyes were glued to you, Mother, for sixty-eight percent of the show."

Miriam runs their recruitment strategy algorithm and its output appears on the wall. "This is almost boring. Our best approach is a classic hetero swallow operation. And our member to whom he is most likely to be attracted is Nadezhda Maksimova."

"The girl serving us?" Sunny asks.

Miriam nods.

"She's too new," Fernando says. "We don't know how committed she is. And also, why do we think she would be good at recruiting? Who's our next best option?"

Miriam looks at the wall. "Next best is Mother. And after Mother is Lara Vega, who has proven herself a very capable recruiter. However, there's an eighty-three percent chance that Sergei will be attracted to Nadezhda, and that drops to under fifty percent for Lara."

"No offense to your algorithm, Miriam," Fernando says, "but why should we trust it? Nadezhda is cute but, objectively, Lara's in a whole different league. I'm confident Lara can do the job and we know her commitment is unwavering."

What's with Fernando and Lara? Sunny doesn't see it and would rather he focus his lust on her.

Magnus turns to Fernando. "It's not Miriam's algorithm. I created it, and I'll tell you why you should trust it."

Finally, a little confidence from Magnus.

Magnus extends his thumb. "First, empirical evidence. We run tests using random people. We predict the probability of attraction to various 1Billion members, arrange for them all to be in the same virtual place, and see if the person is attracted as predicted. We nail it most of the time."

Magnus raises his index finger. "Second, the algorithm can explain its reasoning. Not all of it, but it will list the factors that are significant and human interpretable. In that way it's like you or me. There's a lot that goes into attraction, and you can understand some of it, but even you can't perfectly explain why you are more or less drawn to someone.

"Incidentally, once implants support true olfactory interfaces, I'm expecting our algorithm to improve, since smell—"

Sang-chul interrupts. "Get back to Sergei."

"Okay, let's have the algorithm trace its reasoning."

Two walls fill with tables, charts, illustrations and looped recordings. Magnus interprets. "So one factor is body type. No surprise there. The eye tracking from when Sergei was at the livestream twelve years ago shows his gaze lingering on people in the audience and on stage with a very specific body type—slim, with a body mass index of sixteen to twenty, small chest, and a height of 160 to 170 centimeters. Nadezhda, and for that matter you, Mother, match all of that."

Maybe a little too much confidence. She lets it go.

"The next factor is smile and facial expression." Magnus explains that the twenty-four three-second looped recordings tiled on the wall are the faces Sergei looked at during the stream, sorted by their normalized impact on his heart rate. "If you squint you can almost get a feel for what moves Sergei. See the commonality with Nadezhda?"

Sunny does see that. This is actually interesting. This stuff comes so naturally to her, she doesn't need an algorithm.

"Another factor is familiarity. Sergei is thirty-seven. Our algorithm is predicting that he'll be attracted to someone who, like him, grew up in Russia and may have shared cultural values. Nadezhda is a good match."

Now it's getting boring. "Enough lecturing, Magnus. Miriam, how do we do this?"

"One more thing," Magnus says. "I want to point out that there will be equally strong attraction in the other direction. That will make Nadezhda's job easier, but also introduces other risks."

The door starts to open. Miriam clears the wall. Nadezhda walks into the room with another round of drinks. Sunny catches Sang-chul leering even though she's sure he wasn't paying Nadezhda the slightest bit of attention before. The power of suggestion.

Nadezhda leaves the room and Miriam addresses Sunny's question. "We do it in four phases. In the first phase we give Nadezhda time to get completely committed to 1Billion while we engineer a breakup between Sergei and his girlfriend. In the second phase we introduce Nadezhda to the mission and train her in recruitment. During the third phase Nadezhda meets Sergei and forms a relationship. And during the final phase we get Sergei to move here and become a member."

Fernando leans forward. "I'll promote Nadezhda to being a composer for morning dance music. We usually keep those spots for the top half, but it will help seal her commitment."

"Can't we move faster?" Sang-chul asks.

"Yes," says Miriam, "but with a big chance of failure. What I advise is that we follow the schedule I outlined, and in parallel work on recruiting a few other BQCI experts."

"Right," Fernando says, "we want a few rabbits in the race."

Sang-chul jumps back in. "And when we get Sergei here, then what? We tell him to hack implants?"

Has he learned anything the past twelve years?

"No," Miriam says, "not right away. We give it a year or so. Once he views his identity and purpose as inextricably linked with 1Billion, we explain our problem with BORO and ask for his help."

Sunny stands and looks at her team. "Two minute break. And after we resume, next month's L1 pairings."

24

January 17, 2116
Four years before 4-17
Tel Aviv, Israel

God created the Earth in six days. For the type of stuff Sergei engineers at work, six years is more typical. The thing he loves about hackathons is you only get forty-eight hours. He did his first hackathon seven years ago, invited by friends from Xyloom who thought, correctly, it would help get his mind off his divorce. Those friends have all gotten too busy to dedicate the weekend, but he's become a regular, and this year he has a great idea.

He's physically in his apartment in Tel Aviv and virtually at his Xyloom office. It's late Friday morning, the end of an intense week, and he has that feeling of pleasurable exhaustion that comes after sprinting to a goal.

"You really gonna waste your whole weekend doing that hackathon?" Zev asks him.

Sergei and Zev work together on a Xyloom team that's developing a dense logging capability for implants. The product will be for brain boosters who want neuron-by-neuron logging at a resolution high enough to capture every firing. It's difficult, fascinating, slow-going work. The project started four years ago and this week they achieved an important milestone: initiation of testing in primates.

Sergei nods. "Sure you don't want to join?"

"I can't. Too much family stuff."

He gets it. You can't tell your daughter you have to miss her basketball game because you *need* to compete in a hackathon—especially one whose official name is *The Stupid Shit No One Needs Hackathon*. It's been held on and off for a hundred years. The winning team is the one that comes up with the worst idea (25 points) and manages to hack it together by the end of the weekend (75 points).

Last year he joined a team that hacked a food synthesizer to encode information in swiss cheese using the ancient QR code format. Useless? Yes. That was the point. This year he has his own useless idea, and his first challenge when the hackathon kicks off tonight will be to recruit a team.

———

There's something disconcerting about the virtual space. He remembers having the same thought in past years, too. For decades, ever since the hackathon went virtual, it's been held in a cavernous hall that resembles an old airplane hangar. The roof, covering an unbroken rectangular surface of what must be eight to ten thousand square meters, is supported by steel double trusses extending from the perimeter. The building looks like it could actually exist in physical space, which it probably does, or at least did at some point. And that's what's strange, because he's used to virtual meeting spaces that pay no regards to the principles of structural engineering.

He joins the thousands of other hackathon participants at one end of the hall and listens to the organizer explain the rules. "If you have an idea, line up over here. In a moment you'll tell your idea to the group and describe what type of help you need. Then we'll form teams and get to work. Forty-four hours from now, at five p.m. on Sunday, we'll assemble for demos. Our judging panel will score each team, we'll announce the winners, and then, for those of you still awake, we'll close with some networking and games."

Sergei hesitates, then makes his way to the line. His pulse quickens. It shouldn't since this whole thing is for fun, but speaking in front of a group this size is nerve-racking, especially when it's about his own idea that he hasn't yet vetted with anyone. Plus there are some pretty serious engineers here, including the Xyloom colleagues he did the cheese project with last year.

He finds a spot in the line and turns to face the crowd. Looks like everyone who intends to pitch an idea has assembled. Then one last person steps forward. He tracks her movement as she walks directly toward him, her eyes fixed not on him, but somewhere else, perhaps the gap between him and his neighbor. His breath catches. She joins the row, slotting in next to him, then turns to the person on her right. "Hi, I'm Nadezhda."

Something about her. Dirty blond hair, warm smile, merino-timbred voice, reed-like body, skinny jeans, T-shirt with a looping animation of a hedgehog strumming a balalaika. Somehow he noticed all of that even though he's normally oblivious to these things. Is she real? He checks. Yes, she's projecting her natural appearance with less than one percent embellishment. The last time he had this type of visceral reaction was sixteen years ago when he saw Karima for the first time, a moment he tries never to think about.

In the next second, a bit of depression. He was excited to throw himself into the hackathon this weekend. He doesn't need a reminder that he's divorced, past his prime, and that a person like Nadezhda, who must be ten years younger, would never be interested in him.

Is that necessarily true? She's at a hackathon; maybe she likes hackers. Plus she's probably Russian. She has a Russian name, and he hears a Russian accent in her English, oddly tinged with some of the inflections he associates with the English of his Korean colleagues.

What was that corny poster Daniel had up in their Technion dorm? A looping animation of a pro basketball player shooting and missing baskets, with the caption: *You miss 100% of the shots you don't take.*

She turns to him. "Hi, I'm Nadezhda."

Without thinking, he switches to Russian and introduces himself, sure that his face has turned red. She answers in Russian, tells him to call her Nadya, and asks where he's from. Just as he's about to answer, the organizer cuts them off because it's time for the prospective team captains to explain their ideas. They start at the far right, which is two people from Nadya, so Sergei will speak fourth.

The first person pitches her idea. He's not listening because he's trying to silently rehearse his own one-minute pitch, but his mind keeps shifting focus to Nadya. He can sense her next to him in virtual space. He mentally replays their few seconds of conversation and the even briefer moment when they made eye contact and he stared into her smiling blue eyes. Were they blue or closer to gray? Somehow, this seems important and so, in a corner of his vision, he replays and sees that her eyes are in fact a bluish gray.

The second person is now speaking and Sergei finally gets his mind back onto running through what he plans to say. He'll ask the group, "What's the one thing that everyone likes?" and prompt responses until he gets the answer *ice cream*. Then he'll ask, "What are two things everyone has?" and look for the answer *hands*. Then—

Nadya is starting to speak. He tunes in.

"Hello stupid shit hackers. I'm Nadezhda. My idea— Snarky Soundtrack. I got it from composing music for video games. In game there's always soundtrack. Real life— boring. You walk down hallway, you pick up a tool, you jump. Not dramatic. Why? No music. My idea—automatically create and project soundtrack as you go about your day, and I want all music and sound effects to be opposite of what you expect. You are walking with friend on bright sunny day chatting about where to go for dinner. Dark, somber, foreboding music. About to have first kiss with new romantic interest? High-volume, high-tempo, obnoxious honky-tonk tune. You get idea.

"I'm hoping few of you will join me in quest to make Snarky Soundtrack in next forty-five hours. What help I need? I know what music to use when. That's it. I don't know how to make technology. That's where you people come in."

That's a good bad idea. Now it's his turn to present. His palms are sweating, no longer because he's nervous to speak, but because he's just had the thought that he should abandon his own idea and join Nadya's team. Decision trees explode in his brain. If he decides to join, will it be obvious to Nadya and everyone else that he's interested in her? Will he look flaky and insecure if he drops his idea before even presenting it? How much time has passed since Nadya stopped talking? Even now he might look like a deer in headlights.

Shoot. What to do. There's no guarantee Nadya will have room on her team. She's sure to be mobbed by people wanting to work with her, but he knows he can implement her idea, and that's probably not true for most people here. He hates to deviate from his plan. Isn't this, though, exactly one of those situations where his ex was always telling him to get out of the box in his mind and be more spontaneous?

"Sergei?" the organizer says.

"Sorry, I've just decided to save my idea for next year."

———

Sunday evening. The hackathon is winding down. Sergei is standing around a high top with Nadya and their other victorious teammates, chatting and throwing virtual darts. The room dims and Nadya leaves the table. He assumes she's going to drop out. He'll drop out soon too. But then she makes her way back to the table, squeezes in next to him, turns, and starts speaking in Russian.

"Seryozha, how'd you learn to do all that stuff?"

Do not mess this up. It's just a conversation. And in your native language.

"Hack your idea together? I love building things. I really get computers." How to explain. "If you hear a piece of music can you play it back, without aid?"

She nods.

"You don't memorize every note, right?"

"No. It's more like I absorb the bigger structure. The melody, chord progression, rhythm."

He puts his hands in his pockets. "That's how I am with technology. Show me a piece of software, let me play with it for two minutes, and I know how it works even if I've never seen the code."

Hope that doesn't come across as bragging. This is going okay, though. Chatting with her is comfortable; it doesn't feel like they only met two days ago.

"That's so impressive. I wish I could do that. Honestly I didn't know what to expect from this hackathon. I didn't think my idea could come together so quickly. I'm in awe that you took this random thing that was in my head and made it real."

"Have you ever done a hackathon before?"

She streams a classic smile emoji. "Am I that obviously out of place?"

"No, I mean, we won, that speaks for itself. What gave you the idea—"

"I'm a member of the 1Billion community—"

"That huge dance group out of Korea? With what's her name?"

"Sunny Kim."

"It's funny," he says, "when you were speaking in English, I thought I heard bits of Korean intonation. Now it makes sense. But I thought 1Billion broke up years ago?"

Nadya tucks a few strands of hair behind her ear. "They didn't break up. They switched from online to offline. Sunny built a campus near Pyongyang. It's a utopia for people who love dance and music."

He tries to imagine what that means. He's thinking of what to say, and his puzzlement must show, because she explains. "Ever played that MMO where you and ten thousand fellow warriors all do Tai Chi on a grassy meadow? It's like that. But IRL. We start every morning with outdoor dance exercises."

He's not a good dancer, but maybe he'd become one if it

meant he could stand next to her every morning. Is he too old to learn?

"I thought you wrote music for video games?"

"I do. I wrote the soundtrack for *Quest*. That's my biggest one. I also write music for our morning dance routines at 1Billion and that's where I got the idea for Snarky Soundtrack. When I write I'm always visualizing the routines our choreographers will come up with. So I started thinking, instead of choreographing the dance to the music, what if we choreograph the music to the movement? What if each person had their own personal custom soundtrack derived from their motion?"

He listens, captivated.

"I realized," she says, "the effect would be more comedic than artistic, and that goes against the ethos of 1Billion. We take ourselves seriously. Dancing engenders a sense of belonging through collective, synchronized motion, the opposite of a snarky personal soundtrack.

"But I couldn't get the idea out of my head. I was talking about it at midday meal with an engineer friend and asked if she could program it. She was like, that's the stupidest idea I ever heard, and told me if I was serious I should go to find someone to build it at a stupid shit hackathon." Nadya laughs. "That was the first time I even heard of a hackathon, not to mention the 'stupid shit' variety, and now here I am."

"And we won! I had so much fun doing this with you. We work well together." His face flushes and he kicks himself for being too obvious.

"I think so too. We make a great pair."

Whoa.

"Where'd you grow up?" she asks.

"Moscow, then college in Singapore, moved to Israel for grad school, and never left."

She tells him that she spent her whole life in Nizhny Novgorod until she joined 1Billion.

He wants to keep the conversation going. "I love the sound of the balalaika. Do you play?" he asks.

"Yes! How'd you know?"

Sergei points to the balalaika animation on her T-shirt.

"Forgot I was projecting that. Do you play?"

"No, I play guitar. I mean, not like a professional, but I grew up singing bard with my parents. They're sort of fanatics."

"No way! Same here. *Zdravstvuy, zdravstvuy, ya vernulsya,*" Nadya starts to sing.

"*Zdravstvuy, zdravstvuy. . . .*" Sergei tries to join in, but the time delay is too large. "Your voice is so beautiful, and *"Ya Vernulsya"* is one of my favorite Vizbor songs. Too bad we can't sing together. Korea to Israel is too far."

Did he just call her voice beautiful? It is, and that just came out, and it didn't seem to scare her.

"I know. You'll have to visit me in Korea someday Seryozha."

25

January 20, 2116
Four years before 4-17
Tel Aviv, Israel

The day after the hackathon, Sergei wakes up with one thought on his mind: Nadya. There was a spark, he's sure of it, but does he dare take a next step, and if so, what should it be? It seems so unlikely to work out, maybe he's better off keeping the weekend as a memory to savor, and not risk ruining it. Then he replays their conversation. He watches the animation on her face when she speaks and listens to her say that they make a good pair. No, he needs to try.

But not now. After work. It's Monday, the day he gets together in person with his local colleagues. He hails a car and heads to the Xyloom campus in Herzliya, north of Tel Aviv.

He has sometimes thought of the Xyloom campus as visually jarring, but today it's majestic, made even more so by the rare bright winter sun and the intricate, colorful patterns formed by its rays reflecting off the buildings.

There is no other place on the planet where the work of so many different groundbreaking twenty-first century architects can be seen within a few square kilometers. These geniuses, whose iconic concert halls, museums, transportation hubs, and houses of worship are found in cities across the globe, were asked to aim for greatness and originality without concern for blending with the surroundings. That's why a physics-defying serpent-like glass-and-steel building stands next to an impossibly tall cylindrical tower built entirely from translucent, color-morphing structural plastic.

The campus serves a few purposes. Some of the buildings house labs for quantum computing and implant hardware development. There are also facilities for preclinical research, a euphemism for animal testing. Although human brain simulation has gotten better in recent years, any serious project in the field of BQCI still requires studies in primates. Thus, there are more orangutans than humans working in building seven, a neomodern structure designed by M.I. Pei, the visionary behind the Korea spaceport and great-great-granddaughter of I.M. Pei.

Other buildings are residences. Many Loomies like living on campus, especially those who were recruited to Xyloom from other countries and don't otherwise have family in Israel. Sergei himself lived on campus from the time he left Technion until he got married, when he and his ex moved into his current apartment.

Then there are the coworking structures like building four, which he's about to enter. For some Loomies, the draw is purely the human contact, and has nothing to do with the building. Others like the exercise facilities, where you can chat with colleagues while climbing a rock wall or shooting baskets. His favorite feature is the outdoor space. Through tracking shade and a trickle of air conditioning, there are decks all around the building where, even in summer, he can work and hold meetings without any discomfort from the hot Mediterranean sun.

Sergei chats with his team and catches up on work he missed from being at the hackathon on Sunday. He reviews and comments on code change requests from his colleagues, and finds himself giving an unusual amount of positive feedback. He listens as one of the engineers on his team describes a bug she's been facing for the past week. Seemingly at random, one out of every trillion data points in their log is dropped. Over a game of ping-pong, he asks her to describe her investigation so far; and, in doing so, she suddenly figures it out, and excuses herself from the game where he was up five points. In short, a typical day.

After work, Sergei heads west to the sea and walks south along the beach back toward his apartment. Nadya has been a background thread in his mind all day, eagerly awaiting its opportunity to come to the foreground and execute without interruption. Now he has time to research her. He hopes she's not married, or only into women, or unstable.

The first thing that comes up is the intellectual property registry. She has dozens of copyrighted songs to her name, a few of which show as exclusively licensed. He finds the first with a public recording. It's from 2110, six years ago, and Nadya is singing, accompanying herself on keyboard. Her unadorned performance gives him goosebumps; the song, in Russian, is simple, sincere, moving. He sees a side of Nadya that is earnest and vulnerable, very different from his irreverent hackathon team captain. He watches over and over, paying no attention to his surroundings as he strolls along the sand on autopilot.

Can you fall in love with someone by listening to them sing? Last night he was attracted. This is something more—

this is the person he wants to spend the rest of his life with. But he's less and less certain that Nadya would be interested in him. Her random appearance in his technology world and her being impressed with his engineering skills seems more like a moment-in-time anomaly.

He continues reviewing the intellectual property registry. She's been even more prolific these past six months, but the registry shows that the copyrights for all of her songs during the period were transferred to SK Holdings. His limited understanding is that independent songwriters, like independent software developers, license their music but rarely transfer their copyrights. What is SK Holdings? He can't figure out anything beyond that it's a nonprofit registered in the FSA, where antiquated confidentiality laws allow legal entities to mask their ownership.

He listens to more recordings of Nadya's songs and then expands his search beyond the registry. Not much comes up. She's had success as a composer and songwriter, especially with licensing her music to games, but it doesn't look like she's known as a performing musician.

Then he finds something odd. A recording of her dancing naked. It must be related to her quirky sense of humor, her head on a virtual body. No, it's verified as real and untouched. He can't bring himself to watch, but then he does, a few times in a row. Normally something like this would be gross—how appealing really is the nude human form? Or it could be pornographic. But her recording is neither. It's unmistakably art. Lyrical, pulsing, passionate energy, harmony and discord, syncopated rhythm. He's never seen anything like it. She looks so graceful, seeming to be totally comfortable in her own naked skin.

But why would she make a nude recording, or at least why make it public? It's from eight months ago, so not the result of youthful poor judgment. It's out of character, or at least what he knows of her character. He searches for similar recordings and finds an article that explains everything. And by some crazy coincidence, the article is by Lynette Tan. He hasn't been in touch with her since they broke up senior year at NTU, sixteen years ago.

From the article, he learns that the recording is a requirement to gain membership into 1Billion. It's an initiation of sorts, where the prospective member demonstrates their commitment to the organization by publishing a public recording of themself dancing naked. Wow, that takes guts.

Lynette seems pretty negative about 1Billion, but maybe she just resents her brother joining the group. Sergei remembers Ethan. A smart guy, less driven and less directed than his sister.

Sergei shifts his attention to his physical environment. He's already walked to the heart of the Tel Aviv beach area and finds himself in front of one of the luxury hotels. He takes a seat at an outdoor bar and orders a beer and a hummus plate. He listens to the conversations going on around him in Hebrew, Arabic and English. He drinks his beer and watches a muscled, speedo-clad man sustain a handstand on the boardwalk for an impossible length of time, longer than it takes Sergei to finish his beer and order a second.

A group of ultra-Orthodox men walk by, wearing, not projecting, black caps and heavy coats. Is it scary or impressive that in a world where people wear scrubs and project their desired outfit, these men have held onto tradition, wearing garb identical to their forefathers centuries ago? They must be so hot and sweaty. Although perhaps physical concerns are outweighed by the comfort of knowing you belong to a community.

He's halfway through his second beer, mindlessly dipping pieces of pita in his hummus. Should he contact Nadya? What is there to lose? Best case, they get married, have kids and live happily together for the next ninety years. Worst case, she ignores him or outright rejects him. So why is he hesitating? Does he fear that acting too quickly will jeopardize his chance of success? Or is it his old nemesis, fear of taking any action for which the outcome is uncertain?

Now is not the time to try for a real-time connection. It's two in the morning in Korea. And a real-time connection would be too forward. He should send a message. That will give him space to compose his thoughts. If she's interested she'll get back to him and if not, so be it. There's peace in knowing, as his boss is fond of saying.

But what type of message? "I've been obsessively looking into you and just watched you dancing naked five times. Let me know if you're up for chatting real-time." He chuckles.

Maybe reference their shared project? "I had an idea for a new type of effect we can incorporate into the soundtrack and wanted to get your thoughts. Let me know when you can connect real time." No, that's stupid. He should let her know he's interested so she can put him out of his misery sooner if she's not.

Perhaps genuine and direct is best. "Hi Nadya, I enjoyed getting to know you this weekend. I'd love to chat more. Let me know if you're up for connecting real time." Should he say "enjoyed" or "really enjoyed?" Is "let me know if you're up" too casual? Perhaps just "Can we. . . ?" Yeah, that's better. Does he need an emoji? Should he call her Nadya or

Nadezhda, or leave her name out entirely? Is "love to chat" too over the top?

Stop overthinking and just send. Life is short and getting shorter.

Hi Nadya, I enjoyed getting to know you this weekend. I'd love to chat more. Can we connect real-time?

26

April 17, 2116
Four years before 4-17
Outskirts of Pyongyang, Korea

Sunny wakes. It's dark out. She closes her eyes but can't fall back asleep. What time is it? She holds her gaze where the wall and ceiling meet. The time appears: 3:51.

She turns thirty-two today. Twice as old as when she joined 100M. She was so confident, sure she would be an idol, destined to be the obsession of millions. And she was right. Up until four years ago she led the life of fame she had always expected. What got into her starting this offline reincarnation of 1Billion? It wasn't that she needed the money, and it wasn't even that she couldn't live without the adulation of fans, it was that she couldn't let BORO win. Now, though, she's stuck living on this "campus" with a measly fifteen hundred members worshiping her and calling her *mother*.

Fucking *mother*. It was Appa's idea, his only contribution to 1Billion, a subtle way to reinforce her control. Appeal to

Confucian filial piety, he said, even though she's in fact younger than half the members. Labels become reality and Sunny, who if anything should be called goddess, has become frumpy mother.

That explains yesterday. She traveled to Israel to dissuade Nadezhda from defecting. Frustrating that Miriam couldn't handle it on her own. How is it that she, Sunny, is better at everything? It's not that she minded the trip. Tel Aviv is one of her favorite cities, and she easily succeeded where Miriam failed—Nadezhda was persuaded to stick with her mission.

No, what she minded was how Mai mistreated her. Sunny had noticed Mai, a recent recruit from Thailand, during evening meal a few weeks back. Sunny carved out time to get to know her, even having her over for a private session to talk about her uninspired choreography ideas. Sunny let Mai accompany her to Israel. On the way back last night, on her private supersonic, Sunny invited Mai to stay with her in the sleeping quarters. Mai crawled under the covers, but refused to do anything intimate. Sunny charmed and then pressured Mai, telling her how much she needed the human contact after a stressful day, but Mai kept her distance. "I'm flattered, Mother, and I love you; I'm just not into older women."

Fear of jail. That's the real reason she can't sleep. iBillion is organized as a charitable entity and doesn't pay tax on the money flowing in from members. She's always treated iBillion as her personal bank. Using entity funds to buy assets around the world under her own name seemed a smart investment strategy. But that was before Lynette Tan started encouraging the National Tax Service to investigate.

Sunny closes her eyes. Sleep still does not come. She opens them again. She tells her wall to cycle through her dog photos. A noble black lab in Poland, a beagle from Canada with delicious long floppy ears. She's lost track of how much money she's donated. Private animal shelters and humane societies all over the world. All anonymous, all made through layers of intermediaries. Hundreds of millions of uni per year. More than she's spent on real estate. Her only request that these photos of rescued animals, only the cute ones, get filtered back to her.

Normally the photos help her sleep. Not today. She looks at the time again: 4:03. An hour until morning dance. No way is she putting on a show. She'll visit Appa and spend the day off campus instead. But she'll need to leave soon, before people assemble, start wishing her happy birthday, and expect her to lead them in a routine.

But she can't bring herself to get out of bed. Yes, she can. The trick is to take one step. Rise. Get down on the floor. Do a single pushup. A journey of a thousand kilometers. . . . She does another pushup. Then another. Her uncharacteristic bout of worry melts away, and she keeps going until she reaches fifty.

———

She steps off the elevator into her family's Pyongyang apartment. Appa, who was either already awake or alerted by his implant, stands in the foyer and greets her.

"Daughter, what are you doing here? Are you okay?"

"Of course," she says, and explains that she plans to spend the day in the city. She follows Appa to the living room. She plops herself down in one of the modern armchairs arranged around a coffee table that appears to be levitating. The teak hardwood floor is covered by an exquisite handmade rug with an African pattern, new since last time she visited.

Appa steps into the kitchen and comes back with two glazed stoneware mugs and a glass pot of barley tea. He sits and pours them each a cup.

"What's on your mind?" He knows she wouldn't show up without warning for no reason. Well, why not open up?

She lays it out, verbalizes her fears for the first time. That she's created a monster, that friends and relatives of members are organizing against her, that she's broken tax law, that she's sick of being *on* all the time, that she's annoyed by all the worship by her shitty brainwashed followers.

"Maybe I should shut the thing down, get a lawyer and come clean to the government?"

"No!" he says emphatically. "Never show weakness. Never appear vulnerable. Never act guilty. Everything will come tumbling down and then you'll end up broke and in jail. And that won't look good for me. You need to grow your way out of this, daughter. Make 1Billion so powerful that you make your own rules. You're a little nervous. So what? Everyone gets nervous. Get over it. Toughen up. It's lonely at the top."

"Minister?" a voice comes from the bedroom.

"Who's here?" Sunny hisses.

"A friend."

So that's what he means by friend. Wasn't her old dance instructor Ahn Ye-jin one of Appa's friends? How had she never made that connection before? How many friends has he had?

"I do have two suggestions for you. One, move off campus. Make up an excuse. You won't need to be on all the time if you do that, and if you do it right, being less accessible and more aloof will elevate you in the eyes of your followers.

"Two, start spreading money around. I can help you with a list of connected people and their organizations. You'll sleep better at night knowing that influential people owe you favors."

Yeah, right, that will be a list of people *he* wants to influence with *her* money. But she doesn't say anything. Appa is a master at this stuff and knows how to keep his public image squeaky clean.

The bedroom door opens and a woman walks out. Tall, smiling, tight braids, and considerably younger than Sunny. Appa introduces her. She speaks in impeccable Korean with the slightest hint of a Nigerian accent. "It's such a pleasure to meet you. I used to idolize you when I was a little girl, and I've heard so much about you from the minister."

Sunny flicks a quarter-second smile at her. You're still a little girl.

The bit of fluff sits down next to her. Appa gets up, goes to the kitchen, and comes back with a third mug.

He explains that he has an early morning round of golf with some government colleagues and needs to head out. Sunny, who has no desire to spend time alone with Appa's mistress, follows him out.

"Remember what I told you," he says in the elevator. "Be tough. Stay in control. You can grow your way out of any problem, but if you admit weakness or give in to fear, you're dead."

Appa hails a car. It's daybreak and the rising sun's warm red glow is stunning as it rebounds off the contemporary buildings lining the block. She turns and looks at her reflection in the glass and sees someone with the bearing and determination to be at the top of the world.

She takes Appa's harsh advice to heart. He's right. The only way out is up. There is no solace to be found. Not in a lawyer, not in confession, and not in Appa, who didn't even wish her happy birthday. Forget about going back to campus. Today feels like a good day to look at real estate, maybe even buy some land in Pyongyang.

Sunny takes one last look at her reflection. She really is fucking hot.

27

April 11, 2116
Four years before 4-17
Low Earth Orbit

Sergei kicks off from the foothold next to him and floats over to where Nadya is staring out a glass wall. He catches her shoulders to stop and stabilize himself, then kisses her on the back of the neck, inhaling her sweet smell of pears and wild berries.

"I've never been in a private room this large even on Earth," she says.

"Me neither."

Sergei turns from the glass wall and scans the presidential stateroom. It occupies two stories. The bathroom alone is larger than their apartment in Tel Aviv. The style is minimalist, monochromatic, so as not to draw attention away from the room's dominant, arresting feature—its transparent exterior wall, spanning, without interruption, both stories and the full length of the cabin.

He pivots and takes Nadya's hand in his. Together,

holding hands, they gaze at the horn of Africa below. This is too good to be true. Something will go wrong. He should wait.

"Why does Xyloom have a yacht like this?" she asks.

Safer ground.

"It's not Xyloom's. It belongs to our founder. I know it's obscene. But keep in mind he's too old for an implant. The only way he can experience this is physically. Plus weightlessness supposedly does wonders for older bodies."

"He's pre?"

"I know, strange, the founder of the company that invented implants doesn't have one. But Xyloom was formed over a century ago. Back then, it was barely possible to interface with the brain. The company started as a classical software business. Our founder cycled all the profits into funding decades of BQCI research. People thought he was crazy. He kept at it, even when other multinationals backed off during the Second American Civil War."

He pauses. She seems engrossed, and this is a comfortable topic for him, so he plunges on. "The first clinical trials for implants were run in the early 2050s with human subjects who were in their twenties. Xyloom-1, the world's first approved implant, came on the market in 2061. The strict age cutoff was forty-five, and even most people in their forties didn't meet the neuroplasticity requirements. Our founder wasn't even close. By 2061 he was already in his seventies.

"That's why they call him Moses. But you know, if you can't enter the promised land, hanging out on the world's most luxurious space yacht isn't bad. This whole trip is our single craziest perk. It's a one-time-only thing for sixteen-year Loomies. I asked for a special exception."

He doesn't tell her that he agreed to pay Xyloom back for

the shuttle fees if he leaves the company before his sixteenth anniversary. Not something he could possibly afford, but he also has no plans to leave, and he doubts they would actually enforce it.

"Why sixteen?"

He smiles. "Our founder, as an old-time, pre–quantum computer guy, loves powers of two. He probably figured it was too special a perk for eight years, and thirty-two was too much."

He feels Nadya rotate herself so that she is above him with her toes stretched toward the ceiling, the tops of their heads touching. They stay that way in silence for a few minutes, holding hands, head to head, faces pressed against the glass, looking out at Earth.

Now. He should ask now. What better time will there be?

He bends his neck and looks up, and repositions Nadya with his arm so that together they form an "L" shape. His lips graze hers, and then he starts to kiss her in earnest, but he's let go of her arm, she's not holding onto anything, and the force of his kiss is enough to cause her to drift away.

She laughs. "This looks so easy in space operas."

Not the mood he's going for.

He pushes off the glass wall and floats toward her. She reaches out and embraces him and they maneuver back into the "L" position. He holds her head, and she, his. He looks into her bluish-gray eyes. She loves him, he's sure. Ask.

His implant alarm goes off. His heart rate has escalated into unsafe territory, out of line with his current level of physical exertion. He suppresses the alarm. He hears himself hyperventilating. Ask.

"Nadya . . . Nadezhda Maksimova . . . will you marry me?"

He reads a momentary flicker of something in her face

—fear? His stomach plunges. Silence. Two seconds, three seconds, four seconds.

"Seryozha, I—" she says, but then doesn't say anything else.

He searches her eyes and remains silent, feeling her soft hair with his fingertips.

And then, "Yes."

He pulls their faces centimeters closer. Sweet, a hint of alcohol from the wine they sipped through straws on arrival. This feels right. She's not going anywhere. They will be wife and husband. Married! Sometimes good things happen.

Neither of them is holding onto anything fixed. The momentum from his earlier push off the wall has them slowly spinning in the cavernous space of the stateroom, a right triangle rotating about and translating along all three axes.

He tastes something funny.

Nadya breaks off the kiss. "I'm feeling nauseous."

And then she vomits. Small and large droplets of wine, bile and half-digested food spew everywhere. Many of the droplets move with speed toward the bed. Others remain suspended near them, drifting with little velocity.

"Are you okay?" he asks her. He wants to hold her, but he's floated away. After another few seconds he bumps something fixed and uses it to push off, flying through the particles and droplets and back to her. He lets his momentum carry both of them to the opposite wall where he grabs a handhold. He slowly rubs her back and uses his fingers to comb bits of half-digested food from her hair.

"I'm feeling better. I think it was the spinning motion. What do we do?"

"I bet this happens all the time," and even as he says it, they hear the rush of fast-moving air. They watch as the suspended droplets and particles drift toward a filter intake and cleaning enzymes remove all the vomit that made contact with surfaces.

"I'm going to take a shower," she says.

"You know it's not actually a shower, it's more like a banya. Do you need me to come in with a venik? I bet I can print one."

———

Fifteen minutes later Sergei is staring at North America. To think, if he had been born a century earlier, that's where he would want to be. It's where Xyloom started; it was the location of the first node on the Internet, where the computer chip was invented, birthplace of the transistor. Hard to believe.

He sees Nadya in reflection emerge from the bathroom and watches her float over. She is so graceful, so radiant, the fact she's going to be his wife still hasn't registered.

She grabs his hand. "Seryozha, there's something serious I want to discuss. You're used to all this luxury. What if one day I want to return to the 1Billion campus, will you be willing?"

"Nadya, I'm not used to this luxury, and I don't care about it. You should see, you *will* see, the tiny Moscow apartment I grew up in. I care about you, about math, ideas, music. But not my environment, and for sure not my physical environment."

She seems to be waiting for him to say more. "Don't you like our life in Tel Aviv?"

"Yes, I love it, because we're together. I also miss 1Billion. I miss my friends, I miss the sense of purpose and camaraderie. I'm not saying I want to move there tomorrow. I'm not sure I'll ever want to go back. I just want to know that you'll keep an open mind about it."

Is there any question? Of course he'll move to Korea if she wants. She's more important to him than anything.

"Nadyusha, I will follow you anywhere and do anything for you. I love you with every cell of my being. If you told me to strip naked, put on ice skates and glide across the frozen Volga I would do it. And if you ask me to join ıBillion, I will."

28

December 8, 2116
Three years before 4-17
Tel Aviv, Israel

Sergei enters the virtual events hall. Hundreds of people are milling about, chatting in small groups. He overhears snippets of conversations in the vocabulary of his field: interface, primate, test, nanosecond, zettabyte, sandbox. He turns on annotations. PhDs everywhere. He must be one of the only people here without a doctorate. An information bubble materializes in the air: "Welcome to BQCI Leaders Conference 2116. Opening talks begin in ten minutes."

This is his first conference. He told his boss he would rather read papers to keep up to speed, but she urged him to attend. A way to broaden his network and keep his ear to the ground on cutting edge research, she said. He agreed, reluctantly. He hopes he doesn't run into any of his former peers from grad school, many of whom are now movers and shakers in the field.

He looks over today's scheduled talks. These are

compelling topics, and his earlier trepidation dissipates as he reads the abstracts. He needs to pick. Better to attend the talks relevant to his current project, or go for the ones that most intrigue him?

"Recent Advances in Brain Simulators: a survey of nonbiological techniques for interface testing." That's relevant, but he's pretty sure he's already up to date on the latest techniques.

"Pushback: a novel system for human-to-human contact in virtual space." Fascinating, and the talk is being given by a lead BQCI researcher at KuaiNao, a Chinese competitor in the implant market. It's always hard to figure out what those guys are working on, and any insight he gets from the talk could be useful. After smell, touch is the last frontier of implant research. Pure brain-based solutions are nonexistent, and the popular physical solutions that depend on mechanics are really nothing more than glorified exercise machines. He marks the session as one to attend.

"Dolphin Dreams: lessons from a failed attempt to build a dolphin brain interface." Interesting, and he always likes it when researchers share lessons from failure, but not today.

"Sandboxing: time for a new approach?" Is someone really arguing against sandboxing? Any new brain interface algorithm is first tested in primates and small-scale human trials, and then deployed into the sandbox in all implants. The sandbox is a testing ground—the algorithm operates, but is walled off, and its power attenuated by a factor of ten thousand. He reads the abstract. The talk will make the point, using theoretical examples, that on the one hand sandboxes provide a false sense of security, and on the other hand, with all algorithms proven mathematically, sandboxes aren't necessary. He might attend this one.

"Stereo Shmereo: moving from bidirectional to hexadirectional audio perception." Humans can only perceive bidirectional sound, but is that a limit of the brain or the result of "good enough" evolution giving humans two ears? The talk covers recent work by researchers at Brain Duck. This is also super interesting, but it overlaps with the KuaiNao one. He can watch the recording later.

"The Addiction Problem: five case studies on coping with virtual reality addiction." No. A serious societal problem, but not his interest area. The topic reminds him of Lynette. Will she be here? He's been meaning to get back in touch and ask her about 1Billion and her brother.

"Sleepless in Sweden: is implant-induced micro-napping a sufficient replacement for traditional sleep?" That's a topic of personal interest. If he and Nadya do end up moving to Korea, he's going to want to keep his work schedule on Israel time so he can collaborate with his team, but he'll want his social life with Nadya to be on local time. The best way to do that is to switch from one long sleep per day to micro-napping. Who's giving this talk? A professor whose name he doesn't recognize from Uppsala University. He marks it for attendance.

"4D Monkeys: training the primate brain to natively perceive four dimensions." *This* is incredible. The researchers implanted capuchin monkeys in utero, completely blocked perception through their biological eyes, and fed their visual systems exclusively with input from a four-dimensional virtual world. That's pretty far out there, but could it be that our brains could natively deal with four dimensions? He's definitely attending this talk.

And then there's the keynote at the end of today, co-presented by the rising academic power couple in BQCI, his old labmates from graduate school, Daniel Levy and Karima Yaso. They're both now tenured professors running their own labs. They're living the dream he wanted and, given the divergence in their careers, he hasn't been in touch; in fact, he's gone out of his way to avoid contact since he left Technion fifteen years ago.

A chime sounds and the information bubble reappears, now indicating five minutes to the first session. He heads toward the talk by the KuaiNao researcher.

"Sergei, no fucking way! Is that you, buddy?"

He looks up and feels his blood pulsing against the backs of his eyes. Daniel and Karima are walking toward him.

Daniel streams a bear hug emoji. "It's been so long bro, how are you?"

"Sergei, it's so nice to see you," Karima says. "Last time was our wedding—wait, you couldn't make it to our wedding, you were in Moscow if I remember, so it's been since . . . must be over fifteen years."

"Man, where are you these days? Back in Moscow?"

"No, never left Israel. I live in Tel Aviv. Work at Xyloom."

"Get the fuck outta here. You're in Tel Aviv? Why have you never come to visit? We're still in Haifa. We're both professors at Technion, colleagues with Professor Liu."

Of course he knows that. Does Daniel really think Sergei hasn't followed their careers?

"I know."

"You need to pay us a visit, like physically visit. We have two kids. Leon is nine and Ora is six. Life is crazy. You think supervising grad students is tough, your own kids are even tougher."

No, he doesn't think that supervising grad students is tough, because he's never done it.

"Do you have kids, Sergei?" Karima asks.

He and his ex discussed having kids, and he's glad they

didn't. With Nadya it's a different story, he can't wait, but she's not ready yet.

"No, I was married, got divorced, and actually I just got married again."

"No way! Congrats man. I'd love to meet her. Or him."

"Her," Sergei says.

"Where is she?" Daniel asks.

"You mean physically? She's right here with me in Tel Aviv. I think she's exercising on the balcony."

"Why don't you invite her to join us? Introduce her to your old grad school buddies."

Nadya probably would enjoy the conference. She's always very interested in his work. But admission is a week of his salary.

"She doesn't have a pass."

"That's nothing, I have extra student passes, use this to get her in." Daniel transfers a pass to him.

"But she's not a student."

"Don't worry about it, bro. As far as the conference chair is concerned, the more attendees the better."

"You sure?"

"Yeah, it's no big deal."

Is this something he could get in trouble for? Daniel seems confident it's fine.

"Okay, one sec."

Half a minute later Nadya joins them. Sergei introduces Daniel and Karima.

"Call me Nadya. That's what my friends call me."

"Holy shit, Nadya, you look like a younger and paler version of Karima. Is that what you actually look like? Fuck, zero embellishment. How the hell did you end up with this old guy? You a computer scientist too?"

Sergei had never thought of that before. They are so

different, but superficially there is a resemblance. Something in their smiling eyes.

"No, musician," Nadya answers Daniel.

Daniel looks at Sergei. "I always thought it was the music you were into bro, turns out it's the musicians." And then Daniel turns to Nadya. "Have you written anything I might have heard? God, I can't get over how much you look like Karima."

Sergei jumps in, changing the subject to their original joint research project. "Daniel, Karima, I know this is coming a decade late. Congratulations. I've been following developments on the olfactory interface. Preclinical is going well. The algorithm could be in the sandbox soon and promoted to privileged in five to ten years. I wish I could have been part of it."

There, it came out, the congratulations he should have given years ago, and an admission of his biggest regret—that he missed his chance to be part of what will be the most dramatic improvement in implant brain interface in the last twenty years.

"Your work will move us a step closer to erasing the line between physical and virtual," he tells them.

"And we'll be fucking rich!" Daniel grins. "Once it gets promoted to privileged the royalties will start rolling in. Not Professor Liu rich, and not rich like what's-his-name, the founder of your company, but more money than we could possibly need."

The chime sounds again indicating the first session is starting.

"What talk are you going to?" Daniel asks him.

"The KuaiNao one."

"Karima and I are splitting up. She's going to that one and I'm going to the one on sound perception. Nadya, come with me. You'll like it. And the researcher at Brain Duck giving the talk, she used to be my student. She's a musician too."

———

Sergei hasn't been alone with Karima, even in virtual space, since he confessed his interest on that street in Haifa. Memories come flooding back—the feel of her cheek on his, the marks of evaporated sweat on her face, the taste of falafel and beer, the salty breeze. She seems nervous. Maybe she too is remembering that day, or maybe something else is on her mind.

"Sergei, it's good to see you again. I've missed working on math problems with you. I'm so happy that you met Nadya. You seem really cute together." She bites her lip, and a shadow falls across her face. "Sergei . . . can we talk in private?"

He can't imagine what she could want to discuss with him. Maybe over the years she realized that there was a connection between her rejecting him and him leaving grad school? Even if so, he takes full responsibility for his own decisions; he certainly doesn't hold her at fault, and wouldn't want her to bring it up now.

"Sure, let's talk after."

"No, I mean really in private. In person. I can meet you in Tel Aviv."

"Miss the talk?"

"No, after. I can be there in half an hour. Is the Dizengoff fountain convenient?"

"Yes, it's a five minute walk."

"So does that work for you?"

"Okay."

He listens to the talk by the KuaiNao researcher but has a hard time concentrating. Why would Karima want to meet in person? Could she have latent feelings that were rekindled by seeing him after so many years, and stoked by learning about Nadya? No, that's ridiculous.

Maybe she wants to recruit him to join her lab in some capacity. More plausible, but he has no interest in that, and even if he did he can't leave Xyloom, because he would owe those shuttle fees.

And why all the drama about meeting in person? Well, in another twenty minutes he'll find out. They won't have much time, though, because he doesn't want to miss the second session talks.

Sergei shifts a fraction of his attention to physical space and sees that Nadya is absorbed, no doubt the Stereo Shmereo talk is interesting. He taps her on the shoulder. "Nadya, I'm going to walk outside and keep listening to this talk." She nods and shifts her attention back to virtual space.

Five minutes later he's in Dizengoff Square. He spots Karima right away. She's older, the sparkle in her eyes is somewhat diminished; but, if he's honest with himself, his reaction to her has not.

Karima hugs him. Her warm smell of citrus and za'atar brings him back to their one night lying next to each other on his dorm bed. His face flushes. He's ashamed he didn't act, ashamed he misread the situation, sorry for what might have been.

"Could you turn off recording?" she asks him.

Is it the first scenario he imagined? Even if so, he would never cheat.

"I hope you're not thinking about murder," he jokes, and turns off recording.

He follows her into a hotel where she says there's a privacy shield. She motions toward an empty corner of the lobby. He sits down, and she sits next to him. Then, in almost a whisper, "I want to share something with you, but I need you to keep it a secret for the rest of your life. Don't tell anyone at Xyloom. Don't tell Nadya. Don't ever commit it to digital form. Do you promise?"

What could it be? Something her lab is working on? But why would that be a secret from Nadya? And why would it need to stay secret for the rest of his life? At any rate, he trusts her.

"Yes. You're scaring me, but I promise."

She gets even closer and starts speaking. "I've been nervous about something for years. These last two it's gotten bad—a feeling of dread in my stomach that never goes away. I needed to talk to someone, and as soon as I saw you today, I realized you might be the only person in the world who could help me."

He stares at her.

"There's a flaw in our proof."

"What are you talking about? What proof?"

"The proof of correctness for our olfactory interface algorithm."

He blinks. She's serious. "What? Why haven't you reported it? When did you find it?"

"We knew before we turned in our dissertation."

Sergei's fingers rake furrows in his hair. "How is that possible? Wouldn't Professor Liu or the others on your committee have spotted it? And why did you submit your dissertation if you knew there was a flaw?"

She shakes her head. "A few years after you left, Professor Liu turned up the pressure. He threatened to take the olfactory project away from us and told us we were in danger of running out the clock on graduating. Danny only performs when a deadline is looming and so the pressure turned out to be a blessing. The two of us dropped out of life, moved to a cabin on my uncle's goat farm in the Negev, and spent every waking minute working on the proof. It worked and in less than a year we had a complete solution. Then I discovered that one minuscule part had a flaw, but that was a part we had spent months working on.

"We had a tough decision. Admit defeat. Or pretend, even to ourselves, that we never found the flaw, hope Professor Liu missed it too, and go on to lead the charmed life of glory and success we now apparently have. We chose the latter. Or to tell you the truth, Danny chose and I went along with it. I separated from him for two months, almost reported him, but he was persuasive, and I was pregnant."

My god. He needs a minute to absorb. To keep up a facade for this long.

"Why didn't you just work through the flaw after you graduated and then publish the flaw and its fix, pretending you had only then discovered it?"

Karima's eyes tear up and she places her hand on his. "Sorry, Sergei, I've needed to talk with someone about this for so long. That was my plan, that's how I justified going along with Danny's idea to hide the flaw. It's still my plan. I've exhausted thousands of hours trying, with no success or even promising directions. But I'm also trying to do math in my head with my hands tied behind my back. I can't use my implant or write anything down because I don't want any record that I knew the proof was flawed. I certainly can't assign the problem to any of my grad students. In fact, I probably subconsciously steered them away from studying the proof so they wouldn't spot the problem.

"Also, this last decade has been a whirlwind of activity

for me. Starting a lab, teaching, kicking off new research projects, guiding students, writing grants, serving on committees, not to mention raising two kids. The strategy that worked for me originally—thinking about a single problem day in day out while hiking in the desert—isn't a luxury I've had since graduation."

"Why not report it now? You could say you just discovered the flaw. I'm sure you and Daniel wouldn't lose your appointments, and it's the right thing to do. There's still time before sandbox deployment."

"I can't. I've thought about it many times. But it's not my decision alone and I can't do that to Danny. I agree that we wouldn't lose our professorships, at least if we pretend we just discovered it, but if the algorithm doesn't get into production, we won't get our royalty stream. Daniel underplayed just how important that is to him."

Sergei looks at Karima and slides his hand out from under hers. It's strange, she no longer looks attractive. He's held her on a pedestal all these years and now the pedestal is gone. "I wouldn't say he underplayed that. He said something like 'and we'll be effin' rich.' "

"The thing that gives me some comfort," Karima says, ignoring his comment, "is that I know the whole thing is only a theoretical concern. Interfacing with the olfactory receptors is dangerous since they're directly tied into the limbic system. Sorry, of course you know that. As a result, our algorithm has been through more exhaustive testing and bounty hacking than any other implant interface subsystem ever."

What happened to the Karima he knew? "You of all people should know the difference between proof and empirical evidence. Also, if you believe it's only a theoretical problem, why are you so concerned? You made a mistake and you and Daniel should admit it to the world. You can even do it during your keynote today."

Vigorous shake of the head. "I know you're right but I can't. I can't do that to Danny." A moment's quiet, then: "Sergei, unburdening myself isn't the only reason I asked to meet." She places her open hand on his upper arm and squeezes. "I'm asking for your help. You are one of the few people in the world with the math skills to follow our proof and the creativity to fix the flaw. I've failed, and if I'm honest, Danny was never up to it. Will you try?"

———

Sergei senses tension as soon as he walks in the door. What did Daniel tell Nadya?

"Where were you all afternoon?" she asks.

"Walking around the city listening to the talks."

"I tried connecting after the first talk ended. Why did you ignore me? Why was tracking off? Daniel told me Karima left their house just as the first session was starting. This is eating away at me. Did you physically meet Karima?"

Sergei hesitates. He doesn't want to open a can of worms.

"No."

"You're lying."

Nadya brings up a recording, the public feed from Dizengoff Square, and zooms in on two people. He sees himself and Karima.

"That's you and that's Karima. Right?"

He nods and his stomach sinks.

Nadya's voice rises. "Why is she standing so close to you? Why did you walk into that hotel over there, the one in the old movie theater? Don't pretend you don't know that hotel has a privacy shield. You and Karima were lovers in grad school, weren't you? Were you, Karima and Daniel in some sort of poly relationship back when, let's see, I was in primary school?"

"No! What are you saying? Karima asked me for advice about something confidential. All we did was sit in the lobby and talk. Look at the tracking from after I left. I spent the whole afternoon wandering around Tel Aviv."

Nadya doesn't ask for details. She's silent for a moment and he has no idea what she's thinking. Then she picks up her balalaika and speaks in a cold and distant tone. "Everything has happened so fast. From the hackathon to me moving in with you to getting married. We haven't spent a day apart in ten months."

He's never seen her like this. "Nadyenka, these ten months have been the best of my life."

Nadya stands up, walks to the door, and turns to him. "I thought I knew you, I thought I trusted you, but now I'm not sure. I need a break. I'm going to visit my parents in Nizhny and then go see my friends at 1Billion. I'll get in touch after I have time to think."

29

December 9, 2116
Three years before 4-17
En route to Singapore

Supersonic from Melbourne to Singapore. Arrival in two hours. Lynette stares out the window at the blanket of clouds below. She had expected to spend a few extra days in Australia, but Great-grandma's condition worsened, and Lynette will go directly to the hospital when she lands.

She shuts her eyes, turns on sensory deprivation, and imagines herself floating through the air. And then a thought—cabins. She pops out of her meditation, reviews her recording from a few days ago, and confirms that Grace did in fact use the word *cabin*. Suddenly Lynette can explain what happened. Mum would say it's groundless paranoia, but no; she's sure.

Early this year, her group of concerned families organized a rapid extraction task force. Funded by her friend Grace, wife of the Korean sauce magnate, the purpose of the task force was to provide 1Billion members a safe and immediate off-ramp. Lynette had come up with the idea and worked out its essential components: free, no-questions-asked transportation back to home country, money to cover housing and living expenses for a year, counseling, and legal assistance to recover assets and income from 1Billion.

April was the first time they tried. 1Billion was to hold a dance exhibition at the Korean Performing Arts Center in Chongjin. Thirty 1Billion dancers, unfortunately not including Ethan, were, according to their families, slated to stay overnight in a hotel, affording the opportunity to approach members one-on-one with offers of help. Lynette and other people on the task force traveled to Chongjin, but at the last minute 1Billion changed its plans. The troupe arrived at the venue by ground transport, performed, and headed right back to Pyongyang.

Australia was a different situation. Eighteen 1Billion dancers (again, unfortunately, not including Ethan) were scheduled to perform three shows in Melbourne and spend four nights in the country. She figured there would be plenty of opportunity to approach members individually, and being eight thousand kilometers outside of Korea would provide psychological distance too, making it easier to open up and accept assistance.

She flew to Australia. There she met up with Grace and the parents and siblings of the soon-to-be-arriving 1Billion members. Lynette's group scouted the venue and hotel, and role-played conversations. To every objection they had an answer, and they worked out logistics such that if a member said they wanted to be extracted, it could be done right then and there, before the person lost their nerve.

Then the unexpected. An entirely different group of eighteen 1Billion dancers showed up. None were the relatives of the families who had traveled to Australia. And instead of staying in the hotel next to the venue where they had made reservations months earlier, they stayed in cabins on the outskirts of the city. The trip was a bust. Most of the concerned parents and siblings left early, and Lynette and Grace failed to speak with even a single 1Billion member.

Two last-minute plan changes by 1Billion. And now Lynette remembered something Grace said.

She and Grace had arrived at the Melbourne supersonic terminal at the same time. They were chatting on their way to hail a car, and Grace asked, "Eat first or go direct to the cabins?" Lynette thought nothing of it at the time. Grace was speaking English and Lynette assumed she used the wrong word for hotel. But no. It was a slip. Grace must have known the 1Billion members would be staying in those cabins. She must have been in touch with 1Billion. And she must have told 1Billion about their rapid extraction task force.

Grace is a mole.

Rage wells up and she digs her fingertips into the armrests. Grace is her friend, a confidante, her ally in freeing Ethan. A sympathetic ear, the one person with whom she can commiserate.

Or so she thought.

Lies. All lies. God. How deep and wide do the tentacles of 1Billion reach?

She replays every conversation with Grace. Her telling Grace how they used flattery to lure Ethan, how they programmed Ethan, how they kept members so busy dancing they didn't have time to think about anything else. Grace nodding along, telling her how insightful her observations were. And then all their planning around the rapid extraction task force, Grace saying it was a brilliant idea and putting up the funding. Shit, shit, *shit!* She's been played. What did she miss? And what's in it for Grace?

There is a positive. If Grace hadn't slipped, Lynette wouldn't have figured things out. But Grace doesn't know that Lynette knows, and she may be able to use that to her advantage. And phew—she almost told Grace that she was going to use Great-grandma's failing health as a way to get Ethan back to Singapore. Good thing she didn't.

———

"What's seventeen times four?" Lynette asks.

"Eighty-seven, no eighty-six, no sixty-eight."

For as long as Lynette can remember, Great-grandma was adept at mental arithmetic, responding with correct answers as quickly as someone with an implant. Lynette is fortunate to have known all eight of her great-grandparents, but this great-grandmother, Dad's father's mother, is the one she and Ethan were closest to growing up. They used to love visiting Great-grandma in her apartment right on the Singapore River. More than anyone else, her encouragement was the reason Lynette worked so hard to get into NTU, Great-grandma's alma mater.

Now, at 117, Great-grandma is dying. Lynette reaches over the hospital bed and takes her hand. "Tell me again about your virtual millinery app." Lynette loves this story. Great-grandma looks like she's about to speak, but then she drifts off, and after a few minutes, is sound asleep. Lynette releases her hand.

In the hallway, Mum, Dad, Grandma, and other relatives are speaking with the hospice physician. "She's going to pass next week and after today may not be able to hold a conversation."

"Mum," Lynette says after the doctor moves on, "did you tell Ethan? He'll want to visit Great-grandma before she passes. And, I know you don't want to think about this right now, if he stays for a week, we'll have time to persuade him to quit 1Billion."

Mum frowns. "I already left your brother a message. But Lynette, dear, even though it's nice having you living with us again, I'm worried about you. You're so obsessed with discrediting 1Billion. You should focus on getting your license reinstated."

Mum doesn't get it. It's like she doesn't want to see the true nature of 1Billion because that would mean acknowledging how screwed up a situation Ethan is in. But, still, does Mum seriously believe that she, Lynette, was negligent with her patients to the point of malpractice? After over thirteen years with zero complaints? She should tell Mum about Grace.

No, she shouldn't. Mum would chalk it up to paranoia. Worse, she might mention it to Ethan.

"I will get it reinstated. But Mum, listen to me—"

Mum doesn't let her finish. "Isn't your friend from NTU high up in the government now? What's her name? Something Singh. Ask her to fix your license situation."

"Zelda? She's Minister of Transport. And I'm not going to ask her to pull strings to help me with a personal problem. Listen, Mum, 1Billion was behind the suspension. They're as devious as—"

Mum talks right over her again. "Lynette, we raised you to take responsibility for your own actions. Why on Earth would a dance group in Korea care about your medical license? Even if they did, how could they be responsible for the mistakes you made with your patients? Maintain some perspective. They're a dance group, not some criminal triad."

"Mum, I didn't—"

Mum raises two fingers: an incoming connection request. "It's your brother, let me talk to him."

Ten minutes later Mum blinks and refocuses on Lynette. "He's going to come tomorrow, but can't be away from campus for more than a day. Lynette, before you say anything, I'm upset too. But let's not fight with him. Let him come in peace and say goodbye to Great-grandma."

30

December 8, 2116
Three years before 4-17
Tel Aviv, Israel

Sergei peers out his window. It's been dark for hours on this short winter day, and now it's starting to drizzle. He can just make out Nadya getting into a car in front of their building. He's still shaking, stunned by her abrupt exit. She didn't even give him a chance to respond before she shut their apartment door.

Two cores on the same chip with common registers. That's how he thinks of the two of them. He can read her thoughts, and she, his. She's never acted rash. He's never seen her angry. They've never even argued or battled in silence. Her storming out of the apartment was out of character. But what if decisiveness is an aspect of her character he never appreciated? Could his white lie have toggled a binary switch?

Or was it an excuse? Maybe his instincts have been off this whole time. He thought she loved him, but perhaps it was only the strength of his passion that drew her into his orbit. The musician thinking she's attracted to the mathematician. The spark waned, and the closer she got to him, the less she liked what she saw. He's too old, too short, too skinny. So his meeting Karima was not the cause, but the catalyst, for Nadya to act on preexisting feelings and correct her mistake in marrying him.

Or did she meet someone else? Shoot, he's been thinking this was about him and Karima, but Daniel had hours to work his charm on Nadya. Sergei knows how Daniel operates, and for sure he found Nadya attractive. Nadya could be on her way to meet him physically right now, in some faculty lounge he uses for these purposes, and they'll use Sergei's meeting with Karima to justify whatever happens. The thought of Nadya sliding Daniel's boxers down his legs. . . .

No, he's being paranoid. In his soul he knows Nadya loves him. Take a breath. Stay calm. He needs to give her space, if only to mask his own desperation.

He counts thirty minutes, each minute lasting an hour. Then he contacts her.

No, no, no. She blocked him. He's prohibited from connecting and he's unable to track her. Where is she? Half an hour is enough time to get to Haifa. She could be on the Technion campus right now, Daniel's large hands yanking off her scrub top. Sour bile rushes into his throat and he shuts his eyes. He takes slow, measured breaths and brings his panic under control.

First things first. He sets an alert to notify him the instant he's unblocked. She'll know he has the alert enabled but that's okay, he's not trying to hide the fact that he cares.

He needs to think rationally, force himself to assign realistic probabilities to things. Fifty percent—she just needs some space and will come home or unblock him in a few hours. Thirty percent—she's leaving the country. Five percent—she's with Daniel. Fifteen percent—other.

There's a supersonic to Moscow leaving in ten minutes and that's the fastest route to Nizhny. She could be on it. He can't make it, but he could book his own travel on a later flight. No—if she's coming home in a few hours, he wants to be here, not in Russia.

The more important thing is convincing her that nothing happened with Karima. He could grant Nadya access to his every recording with Karima as a show of good faith. But that won't prove anything. Worse, it would show his unreciprocated interest back in grad school, which could further arouse Nadya's suspicions about what happened in the hotel today. And would it then sound credible that the reason he spent the afternoon wandering around Tel Aviv was because he was thinking about a math problem, and not because he had finally fulfilled a sixteen-year fantasy?

He also can't think of a way to explain why he lied in the first place. Even if he were to break his promise to Karima and tell Nadya what they discussed, that wouldn't explain why he hid the meeting itself.

He replays Nadya's parting words: *I need a break. I'm going to visit my parents in Nizhny and then go see my friends at 1Billion. I'll get in touch after I have time to think.*

Perhaps he needs to take that at face value and wait for her to contact him. In the small part of his brain that has not succumbed to panic, he knows that the connection between them is solid. It's not going to be broken by his one white lie or her unsubstantiated suspicions about what happened in the hotel.

Stop overthinking. Nadya is his wife. She trusts him. She must.

He messages her:

My soul,

> *I miss you. I'm desperate to speak with you. I'm sick to my stomach. Nadya, you mean everything to me, and I would never do anything disloyal. I love you and anxiously await your contact.*

Your husband,
Seryozha

Thirty seconds, one minute, ten minutes. His heart jumps for a fraction of a second when a message comes in, but it's not from Nadya. One hour, two hours. Still no response. He goes to sleep with the aid of his implant, and sets it to wake him if she sends a message or unblocks him.

Many hours later, he stirs. His heart drops when he feels the winter sun streaming into the apartment and realizes he slept through the night and he's alone. He's still blocked.

He attends the morning keynote on day two of the BQCI Leaders conference. He's among thousands present to hear Xyloom's head of implant research share her vision for the future. He listens but absorbs nothing, in part because as a Loomie himself he has already heard much of this before, but mostly because of Nadya.

By the afternoon it's been twenty-four hours since she left their apartment. He pours his heart out into a message with the thoughts that have been running around his mind all day.

My Dearest Nadya,

In a classical computer chip there is the concept of a tick. Like the tick of a metronome, only billions of times faster. With each tick an instruction executes. Tick. Add two. Tick. Multiply by three.

You and I are two cores on a single chip, intertwined, operating together, synchronized by the same clock. Tick. I add two. Tick. You add three. Tick. I multiply by two.

But now you're gone and I'm malfunctioning. Tick. Add one. Tick. Subtract one. Tick. Add one. Tick. Subtract one. I'm stuck in an infinite loop, skipping between zero and one.

It's been twenty-four hours and I've had no word from you. My soul, will we never speak again? Will you block me forever?

Perhaps there is a symmetry to passion and you have left my life as suddenly as you came into it. If these past ten months end up being our only time together, I will remember them always, grateful to have been your partner for even just a brief portion of our time in this universe.

Know, though, that I dream of burying my head in the crook of your neck, of inhaling your sweat of sweet-tart pears and the black sea, of walking hand in hand eighty years from now, of kissing you on the cheek and kissing our children on the tops of their heads.

And yet if none of that comes to be, if we go our sepa-rate ways, if we form families and grow old with others,

know that I will never have for anyone else the depth of
feeling I have for you.

   I love you and will always love you.

Your husband,
Seryozha

Thirty seconds, one minute, ten minutes, one hour, two hours. No response.

31

December 11, 2116
Three years before 4-17
Tel Aviv, Israel

Sergei wakes up in his Tel Aviv apartment to a cool, rainy Friday morning. It's been three days since Nadya walked out. Still no word. He works through a few technical issues with Zev during their morning virtual nature work, then has a planning meeting. Nadya occupies his thoughts as much today as yesterday, but he does a better job of keeping those thoughts in the background.

Around noon, when the workday ends, he leaves his apartment and takes a car to the Sorek Estuary south of Tel Aviv. He hikes along the greenish-brown stream toward its outlet into the Mediterranean.

Why hasn't she gotten in touch? If she feels nothing for him, why not tell him? And if she does care for him, why put him through misery? He can't square her behavior with his. The only thing that makes sense is that she's punishing him with her silence, which at least means she cares.

He has to stop thinking in circles. He promises himself that when he reaches the sea he'll change mental topics. Then, if he still hasn't heard back by late in the afternoon, he'll send a third and final message.

He arrives at the beach and the ruins of Yavne-Yam. He studies the remains of the ancient port city. Thinking about the timescale—first settled during the Bronze Age, and occupied by one civilization after another until its abandonment a thousand years ago—he's reminded that his own troubles are meaningless. He's a grain of sand, waiting to be washed out with the tide, subject to the whims of forces around him. Somehow, that thought comforts him.

He looks up and down the shore. He's in complete solitude. Not another soul around on this cold, wet, winter day. He shuffles along the sand and wills his thoughts to turn from Nadya to Karima.

He's unsure what to make of Karima's revelation. Something he always admired about her was her commitment to precision and correctness. Lots of people are sloppy, but not Karima; and for all his swagger, not Daniel either. Why would they publish a proof with a known flaw? Forgetting for a moment the risk of introducing an implant hacking vector, just knowing of the imperfection would eat away at Sergei.

He puts himself in their shoes. Multinationals must have come calling on Professor Liu to license the algorithm. In those meetings, were Karima and Daniel excited, or were their insides torn up by guilt?

Humans do have a remarkable ability to compartmentalize. Perhaps that's how Karima and Daniel function. They wake up each day thinking about the foundation as a whole and forget about the insignificant bit of uncured concrete in one corner of its base. And Karima is probably right that the concern is only theoretical. There may be a flaw in the proof, but after ten years of testing, if there was a problem in the algorithm itself, it would have shown up.

Does he have an obligation to tell someone? Tell them what exactly? That there is a mistake in a mathematical proof that was published a decade earlier that only a few people in the world can understand? And yet he can't pinpoint the actual mistake? And he, an inconsequential engineer, knows this because the famous coauthor of the proof told him in secret?

What he needs to do is find and understand the actual flaw. If he can fix it, then he'll have a choice—quietly tell Karima and let her take the credit, or publish the fix himself. And even if he can't fix it, he'll be able to judge its severity and then decide what to do.

He brings up the proof. He knows from when he looked at it three days ago that the math is beyond him. There are techniques he hasn't used since grad school, and other techniques, like the Pan-Sidiqqi transformation, that he never learned. If he is to have even a shot at understanding the whole thing and then fixing it, he'll need to spend months or even years leveling up his skills.

He's not one of those people who learns by passively reading math texts. He needs to tackle a problem actively. Fortunately, the distraction of a difficult but tractable puzzle is exactly what he needs to keep his mind off Nadya. A good starting point is working through his old grad school problem sets. That should warm up his brain and he can always retrieve his original solutions if he gets stuck.

Many hours later, pacing up and down the beach, virtual board filled with equations, he's on the verge of solving a problem from one of his old classes. He's still rusty, but he's having fun, completely immersed in the math, old thought patterns restored. He adds an equation to the board. It's a promising path. Could he demonstrate this by induction? What if he factors this—

Two alerts come in quick succession, causing the math structures in his head to collapse and jolting his attention back to his physical surroundings. It's dark, hours past sunset, and hours past when he'd intended to message Nadya again. He tastes the cold, salty air. He hears waves lapping the beach and is suddenly aware of wolves howling in the distance.

The first alert is a message from Nadya. "Seryozha," he starts reading. The diminutive form of his name. As soon as he sees that he knows things will be okay.

Seryozha,

> *Why are you on a deserted beach alone in the middle of the night? Please be careful. I miss you and I love you. But I need to be sure I trust you. I need time to think.*

Your wife,
Nadya

The second alert tells him that she unblocked tracking. He sees that she did in fact leave Israel and spend a couple of days in Nizhny Novgorod. At present she's over Ulaanbaatar, the capital of Mongolia. She must be on her way to Pyongyang and the IBillion campus, just as she said.

She wouldn't have unblocked tracking if she didn't want him to follow. He books a supersonic to Pyongyang for the morning. Tomorrow he'll see her. Problem set forgotten, he visualizes her bundled up in winter clothing. He'll embrace her, press his cheek against hers, and make her understand that nothing happened with Karima.

32

August 22, 2117
Three years before 4-17
Boston, Democratic Union

Karima looks out the train car window. In her mind, informed (she now recognizes) less by the specifics of Grandpa's stories she heard growing up, and more by the tone, this place was gray and grimy, one big abandoned wasteland. It's not—it's sunny, quaint, friendly. Low-rise buildings line both sides of the street, and pedestrians stroll along the sidewalk. "Grandpa," she asks, "did you ever ride this line when you lived here?"

"Sure, all the time. So many memories. Like when I was Ora's age, Sunday mornings, snow outside, bundled up in our yurongfu, my parents reading on their phones, me and my sister competing to see who could stand longer without holding onto anything."

He's looking frail. But she can imagine it. Grandpa, a little boy, over a hundred years ago, standing, shifting his weight from foot to foot to counteract the acceleration and deceleration of this ancient tram. She wishes, though, they had taken a car today. Grandpa wanted the kids to experience this, but he needed Danny's help getting on, and they'll need to repeat the procedure in reverse when they get to their stop.

"What's yurongfu?" asks Leon, who loves new words.

Grandpa always talked about yurongfu for cold Boston winter days, but, come to think of it, she's never heard anyone else use the term. She's not even sure what language it is.

Grandpa pats Leon's chest. "It was like a puffy jacket. They don't have them anymore, at least not in Israel."

Grandpa grips the metal pole next to his seat and starts to pull himself up. Danny is instantly next to him, supporting him, and then helping him shuffle to the exit. They get off at Coolidge Corner. A name she heard countless times growing up, a place that in her imagination was a literal corner formed by tall, gray cinder block walls, but she sees now is in fact an intersection, a picturesque one at that.

They cross the street and rest for a minute so Grandpa can catch his breath.

"This is where we lived, not where I grew up, after I was married."

Grandpa points toward a street. "The best hospitals in the world were up that way. Lots of doctors lived around here. That's why we moved to this neighborhood, for Carolyn."

Grandma Carolyn. Karima was named after her. And Grandpa always said that's where her smarts came from.

He leads them down a block. They turn right and stop in front of a wide, seven-story brick residential building. He points out a set of windows on the second floor—the apartment he and Carolyn bought a year after they got married, he tells them.

A young couple pushing a baby carriage emerge from the building. Danny holds the door open for them, and after the couple step away, everyone slips inside. They follow Grandpa down a hall and take the elevator to the second floor. They pause outside the elevator door. Great-grandpa places his arm around Karima's shoulders and she can feel him trembling. This was her idea, this trip to the DU; she hopes it's not too much for him.

"It was a Saturday morning. September 19, 2048. Carolyn was thirty-three. Your mom was seven months old." Grandpa's telling everyone, but directing his words at Karima. She's heard this before, many times, but this is different, standing where it happened. She looks over at Leon and Ora.

"I was home watching her," Grandpa continues, meaning Iris, Karima's mother. "Carolyn was on call at the hospital all night, hadn't come home yet. The war had started a year before. But this area felt safe. We kept hearing about bad things, but they always seemed far away, and day-to-day life was normal. In retrospect I know there were many signs things weren't normal; we were, what is the expression, something with a lobster, no, frog, the frog who is slowly brought to a boil and doesn't notice it should jump out of the pot until it's too late."

When she was a kid she didn't get it. Wasn't it obvious they should leave? Even if just as a precaution, why stay put when there's a war raging? But being here, and being older, she sees it differently. He was forty-one back then, she's forty now. They had a baby. Careers. It would take a lot to persuade Karima to walk away from her life. Why should it have been any different for Grandpa? Especially back then, before implants, when physical location mattered more.

"It's not like we didn't think about leaving. Our parents had left, many of our friends too. We applied for a visa to Singapore just in case. Carolyn was a physician and a researcher. I was a software developer. We would qualify for an educated refugee visa; it was just a matter of paperwork and—I forget what you call it when they investigate you— the background checks."

Grandpa stops talking. "Are you okay?" she asks.

He nods. "Why did I do it?" His voice is internal, a murmur. "That morning, Iris was napping, I was doom-scrolling and—"

She sees confusion in Leon's eyes, and then it disappears. He must have looked up doomscrolling. One of those old terms Grandpa and no one else uses.

"There was this post. It said my company was suppressing evidence that the Earth was flat. I got so angry. Lost my temper, posted a comment, I still remember it verbatim: 'You ignorant buffoon—evidence that doesn't exist can't be suppressed.' A millisecond after, I realized I was signed in under my real name."

Grandpa looks down. "How could I have been so careless? I deleted the comment. I thought fast enough. It wasn't. Someone doxed me, posted our info on an extremist site for FSA terrorists operating in the DU."

She's heard this before too, but it's still hard to get her mind around. The idea of a network existing without the core tenets of privacy, security, and fact checking as low-level guarantees . . . it's insanity.

"Within an hour a man slipped into the building. His name was Carter Taylor."

Grandpa identified Carter Taylor later from security

footage. He's still alive, a good twenty years younger than Grandpa. Worked law enforcement in the FSA for fifty years. Retired now, the patriarch of a large family, a hero in their eyes and in the eyes of his country for his wartime exploits.

Grandpa wipes his mouth. "At 11:22 a.m.," he goes on, a small but persistent quaver in his voice, "Taylor stepped out of the elevator. He was dressed like anyone else. The only weird thing is he was wearing gloves. He stood here a moment studying the apartment numbers. Then," Grandpa points to the right, "he started walking this way."

Grandpa shuffles down the hall with everyone following. "Apartment 201, the Smiths. Taylor walked by it." Grandpa points to the door of the next unit. "202, the Wangs; Taylor touched the door handle." Grandpa moves to the next door. "The Abbas and Katz family, 203. Taylor touched the door handle."

Now they're at the end of the hall. Grandpa, with everyone following, turns around and walks back along the opposite wall. "Units 204 and 205, the Johnsons and Wilsons —Taylor passed by both." Grandpa points to the handle of the next apartment. "Apartment 206, Rodriguez. Taylor brushed his gloved hand here."

Grandpa stops in front of the next apartment. "Unit 207. Our home. Taylor spray-painted a blue circle on the door, a symbol that meant spherical-earther. Then he touched the door handle and got back in the elevator. He was on the floor for less than a minute."

Karima peers at the old-fashioned solid oak door. Is it the same door as back then? Looks like it could be. She doesn't see any sign of the blue circle, but maybe, just maybe, the wood looks a bit different where Grandpa pointed, where they would have sanded off the paint.

"At 11:51, around half an hour later, Carolyn came back. She always took the stairs so she came in from there." Grandpa points to the stairwell door at the end of the hall.

"She saw the graffiti and screamed. She knew what it meant, and was certain she'd find Iris and me injured or even dead." A vein pulses in Grandpa's head and he closes his eyes.

What if Grandpa and Mom had been killed that day? She, Karima, wouldn't be here, and neither would Leon and Ora. Danny would be married to someone else. Would he and that someone else have figured out the olfactory interface algorithm? Stomach pain. Things are on track from a regulatory and preclinical standpoint, but she's still no closer to fixing the proof, dotting the *i,* than she was a decade ago. Their algorithm could go into the sandbox next year. She never imagined they would be this close before they corrected the proof.

Grandpa opens his eyes. "Carolyn ran over here and grabbed the door handle. It recognized her and unlocked. She twisted it, pushed in the door, and saw me playing on the rug with Iris, oblivious to the intruder and the graffiti.

"We decided not to report it. We counted ourselves lucky that a bit of vandalism was the only consequence of my mistake. Carolyn said she needed to lie down. That was her usual routine after being on call all night. She also said she wasn't feeling well, and that was unusual, because she never got sick. She kissed Iris, went to our bedroom, closed the shutters, and crawled into bed."

Karima knows what's coming next. She takes Leon and Ora's hands. This will give them nightmares, as it did her. Grandpa always said it was important to unravel the security blanket. Karima wants to adopt the same philosophy, not because it's likely that Leon and Ora will ever come face to face with mass cruelty, but just in case.

"At five, I went to wake Carolyn. I opened our door, walked over to our bed, and kissed her on the forehead. Her forehead was clammy and cold. I turned our lamp on. Her eyes were open, her body was rigid; she wasn't breathing. She had no pulse."

Karima stiffens and squeezes Leon and Ora's hands.

"I immediately understood that the intruder had smeared a nerve agent on the handle. There were reports of that happening in New York City. I sent an emergency message to everyone in the building."

She once asked Grandpa how he'd been able to think so clearly. He attributed it to his experience managing technology emergencies. "You learn to suppress panic, compartmentalize, prioritize, and operate on several levels in parallel," he'd told her.

"My message saved the Rodriguez family, but Lauren Wang, who lived in that apartment," he points, "and my friend Essmael Abbas, who lived there," he points to unit 203, "had already touched their door handles. Both succumbed to the poison."

"Great-grandpa," Leon says, "I don't understand. Why did they want Great-grandma Carolyn and those other people to die?"

"Not here," he says in low tones. "Let's talk somewhere else."

———

They enter a brick building with arched windows. "Ollie's, Occam's, it used to be called something like that," Grandpa says. "Can't believe it's still a pizza place. We came here when I was a kid. Leon and Ora, you'll see, American pizza, it's good."

How can Grandpa be thinking about the pizza? Then Karima realizes, for her, this is a place of nightmarish stories. Whereas for Grandpa . . . yes it's that, but it's also where he grew up, where he started his career, where he got married. There's a nostalgic component to this trip, a home-coming of sorts, and he wants them to see his town in a good light.

"Who's hungry?" Danny asks. "Let's do one cheese pie and, let's see, this one, Spicy Sweetheart—habanero caramelized onions and artichoke hearts—that sounds good. You kids want lemonade?"

Wasn't Danny affected by anything he just heard? How does he have such a big appetite? She can't handle spicy right now. Between Grandpa, thinking about the work piling up . . . and of course that other thing that's always in her gut. She searches the menu. "How about this one instead, the Andyamo?"

Danny raises three fingers. "Let's get all of 'em. It's so cheap compared to back home."

They sit in silence for a minute. Then Leon speaks. "Great-grandpa, I don't understand. Didn't people know the Earth was spherical?"

"I don't understand either. I've been trying to under-stand for seven decades. Of course people knew. Mom's hero Pythagoras knew it two and a half millennia ago. For the entire history of the United States kids were taught it in school. People grew up with globes, and photos from space, and models of our, what is the word, not universe, but. . . ."

"Solar system?" Leon says.

"Yes, models of the solar system. And flight trackers, showing airplanes flying over the South Pole. And yet around the time I was growing up more and more people started believing the Earth was flat, one big pizza pie with the Arctic at the center."

Their pizzas arrive. Karima picks up a wedge-shaped spatula. "Ora, you want a slice of cheese? Leon?"

Grandpa serves himself a slice of the Andyamo and continues. "Did flat-earthers really think our planet was flat? Some did. But most didn't. It was more like a badge of honor. A way of sticking it in the face of educated people. It's like they were saying, I don't care about logic, stop trying to control my thinking.

"America always had an anti-intellectual streak, but this was something different. All solid ground disappeared. Up became down and down became up. Everything was distorted. Trust in experts, faith in good intentions, all out the door."

Grandpa takes a bite of his slice. "When I was growing up, one of our ex-presidents made a joke that's stuck with me all these years. He was standing in front of a podium and said something like—" He pauses, frowning. "Let me remember exactly." Grandpa holds his slice in the air, thinking. Then, "You have to believe in facts. Without facts there's no basis for cooperation. If I say this is a podium and you say this is an elephant, it's going to be hard for us to cooperate."

Karima turns that over in her head. That's the argument for BORO in a nutshell. Shared reality is a prerequisite for cooperation.

Grandpa takes another bite of his slice. "There's this idea, Occam's razor, and it's really just common sense—that the simplest explanation is usually the correct one. But the country got filled with all these Occam's sledgehammer people. To them, the more crazy, the more convoluted, the more conspiratorial hoops you needed to jump through to explain something, the more credible.

"So when I commented on that post, it marked me as someone who was part of the conspiracy. And then when they dug up my personal information and saw I was mixed-race, that made me . . . no longer human."

Leon is hanging on Grandpa's every word. He hasn't even touched his pizza. "Great-grandpa, is that what the war was about, flat-earthers against spherical-earthers?"

Karima's not surprised he doesn't know this. World History isn't until middle school and, while she grew up hearing about this stuff, it's not a topic she and Danny have discussed with Leon and Ora.

Grandpa laughs. "No. Or at least it was much deeper than that. The country had two political parties. For over a century and a half they were fierce rivals, like competing teams, playing hard but playing the same game by more or less the same rules, and with a certain degree of civility and cooperation."

Grandpa takes another slice of the Andyamo. "During the first few decades of my life something changed. Each group developed a different idea of what the country stood for, which was a big problem, because at heart a country is, what's the term . . . a shared fiction, and it doesn't work if people don't share enough of the fiction. In a polarized environment it's hard to stay neutral, and everyone had to declare allegiance to one team or the other."

For some reason this makes her think about Danny. She could have reported him for academic fraud. Divorced him. But she didn't. Something about loyalty to spouse, to family, to clan, to team. It's not admirable, but it is human nature.

"When I was a little older than you," Grandpa continues, still speaking mostly to Leon, "the son of our then president said something chilling. 'To me, they're not even people.' He was talking about the other party. I don't know if he believed that or not, but soon enough others did.

"This dehumanizing of others . . . it got worse and worse. Then something happened that started the war. One party won decisive control of all three branches of government and passed the Freedom Act of 2047. The three freedoms. . . ."

Is Leon going to understand? Probably not. The gulf between mid-twenty-first century United States and present day Israel is too big, and thank goodness.

Grandpa puts his slice down and takes a sip of water. "First, the freedom of protection. No state, county, or municipality was permitted to regulate guns. Any citizen over eighteen could buy, own, sell, and carry any type of firearm. Indoors, outdoors, in schools, houses of worship, private homes, coffee shops, arenas. Anywhere.

"Second, the freedom of life. No citizen, under any circumstance, at any time, could terminate a pregnancy. And traveling to another country to terminate a pregnancy voided citizenship.

"Third, freedom from aliens. No immigration, period. No work visas, no spousal visas, no education visas. No path to citizenship other than being born in the country to citizen parents."

Leon really does seem to be absorbing all of this. She's surprised. Does he even know what it means to terminate a pregnancy? He must be looking stuff up.

Grandpa picks his slice back up, takes a bite, and continues explaining. "The Freedom Act was beyond the pale. Utterly unacceptable to the minority party, which formed the majority here and in other states. A convention was held. This state and others resolved to secede. We voted, and the resolution was ratified, forming the Democratic Union, and triggering the largest-ever internal migration in American history. The federal government immediately declared the secession illegal and threatened military force to collect taxes and impose law.

"That's when the war started. Six years later it ended in a stalemate and the United States formally fractured into the DU and the Free States of America. Of course, Iris and I were in Israel long before then."

One thing Grandpa has never told her is how he and Mom made it to Israel. It's somehow a part of the story that has never come up.

"Grandpa, what did you do after Grandma Carolyn was. . . ?"

Grandpa doesn't respond for a minute. Then he leans forward. "You have to understand how scared I was. Not just for me but for your mom. My name, my photo, my address, my employer were all out there for targeting by extremists. Until that point I had relied on keeping my head down, going about my business, avoiding attention. That wouldn't work any longer. Someone had put me on a list of people deserving of death, but I was still alive.

"I knew we needed to get out of the country ASAP, even that day if possible. I couldn't wait for my Singapore visa to come through. Israel was our best choice, and also our only choice. And by some miracle—not a miracle, a terrorist attack in a different part of the city—a single seat opened up on a flight to Tel Aviv that afternoon. I bought the ticket, but then realized, if Iris and I got on that plane, who would bury Carolyn?

"So I gave up our reservation and made arrangements for Carolyn's funeral. The next day, we went to the cemetery. I was afraid to tell our few remaining friends for fear of word getting out, and our parents had already fled, so your sleeping mom and I were the only ones there. We stood, a crisp autumn day, trees blazing yellow and red, and said goodbye to your grandma."

All these years, how is it she's never wondered where Grandma Carolyn was buried?

In the ensuing silence, Grandpa says, "I'd like to visit Carolyn's grave this afternoon. You don't need to come with me. You can walk the Democracy Trail or rent a canoe and paddle along the Charles."

"Grandpa, what are you saying? Of course we're coming with you." Karima rubs his upper arm.

The table goes quiet again. Then Grandpa continues. "I was able to book a flight for Wednesday. We locked ourselves in a hotel room near the airport. Then, an hour before our flight, we took a car to the terminal—I knew entering international departures would be the dangerous part. As soon as I got out of the car, Iris in a baby carrier on my chest and a knapsack on my back, a man wearing glasses looked at me. I could tell right away he was scanning everyone and checking identities against a list. He approached, holding a stylus in his left hand, which, as he got closer, I saw was an autoinjector. I will never forget his words: 'Bassoon huh? Think you're so superior? Scum like you don't deserve to live.'

"He raised his left hand with the autoinjector. I was about to die, and even in that split second, I thought back to my 'ignorant buffoon' post, and realized I was going to be killed by a man who didn't know the difference between a buffoon and a bassoon.

"Iris sensed my fear and started crying. Shaking, I moved my left hand to comfort her. She wrapped her little hand around my index finger.

"I looked at the man. He was wearing a Red Sox cap and so was I. I put my right hand out. And on instinct, he reciprocated. We shook hands. I locked eyes with him. 'Please let me and my daughter leave. We will never come back.' And he did. And I didn't, until yesterday. That was sixty-nine years ago."

33

January 3, 2118
Two years before 4-17
Singapore

Stroke. Get Ethan home. That is Lynette's New Year's resolution.

Stroke. As long as 1Billion exists, benevolent in the eyes of its exploding membership, Ethan will never leave. Putting herself in Ethan's mind, she knows he views her as the crazy one, but that's only because he's blind, unable to see that he's trapped behind an information firewall.

Stroke. She needs to expose the true face of 1Billion and Sunny Kim. She's published damning information but nothing came of it. She was naive. You can shine a lamp, but if people don't want to look in the light, it doesn't matter.

Stroke. She needs to get the authorities to shut 1Billion down. There's nothing illegal about running an adult sleep-away camp for people too timid to think for themselves. But it is illegal to launder money through a nonprofit, and she's sure that's what Sunny is doing.

Stroke. She's been in touch with the Korean National Tax Service. She shared the financial information she's been able to dig up, but they said it wasn't compelling enough to justify an investigation.

Stroke. She needs to do her own forensic accounting and bring irrefutable proof to the authorities. And if iBillion is operating at the scale she suspects, there will be plenty of revenue agencies in other countries motivated to pressure Korea and iBillion into returning lost tax income.

Stroke. How to conduct a forensic investigation? She can't lean on other concerned families for help or financial support. She learned that the hard way with Grace, with whom she's been maintaining a fake friendship for a year.

Stroke. She's not an accountant. At the moment, she's also not a practicing interventionist because her medical license has yet to be reinstated. Well, isn't forensic accounting similar to patient diagnosis? It's numbers, it's contracts, it's following threads, it's reading between the lines, it's looking for things that are out of place. She's good at most of that and can figure the rest out.

Stroke. FSA and SK Holdings. How is it that, in a global economy built on transparency, one country maintains anti-quated corporate laws designed to maximize opacity? Well, there must be a way to pierce the veil, and that's where she'll start.

Two hundred laps, two kilometers. Lynette lifts herself out of the pool at her parents' apartment complex. She wraps a towel around herself, sips water, and looks up at the sky. It's a warm cloudless January day. She knows what she needs to do, and is confident that a year from now Ethan will be home.

34

February 10, 2118
Two years before 4-17
Outskirts of Pyongyang, Korea

Sergei wakes. It's dark out and he instinctively verbalizes *What time is it?* in his mind before remembering that he's unplugged. He then focuses his gaze at a certain point where the cabin wall meets the ceiling, and the time displays: 4:28 a.m. He gets up, uses the bathroom, and lies back down. Nadya stirs next to him.

"My sun, what time is it?" she murmurs.

"Four-thirty."

She snuggles up close to him and slips her hand past the waistband of his sleeping scrubs. "We have half an hour."

———

Ninety minutes later, he and Nadya are in formation with ten thousand other 1Billion members on the central green, which is white at present because it's covered in snow. The two-hour morning dance is half over. A year ago, when he joined 1Billion, he needed his every gram of concentration to keep up with the dancing. Now it's gotten easier. His body grooves and his mind is free to wander.

It's weird how Latin songs stand the test of time. The music thumping through campus right now is Celia Cruz's "*La Vida Es Un Carnaval,*" written well over a century ago. There seem to be countless Latin songs of that era in their rotation, but he can think of only a handful of comparable Asian songs, "Gangnam Style" being one particularly grating example. Of course, even much older music has endured. Last Monday, the entire two-hour dance period was dedicated to waltzes composed by Johann Strauss in the mid-1850s, over a quarter of a millennium ago. There's something magical about dancing a waltz in the snow, less so salsa.

Nadya looks over and smiles. She looks so good when she dances. You would think she grew up in Cuba or Colombia. He smiles back, or at least tries to. Smiling has never been his strong suit, and his usual crutch, streaming a smiling emoji, is not possible while disconnected.

When the dance is over he and Nadya will join everyone else in the communal dining hall for morning meal. Then he'll head back to their cabin, nap for a few hours, connect his implant, and start a day of work at Xyloom. At first the transition from 1Billion to the outside world was a form of daily culture shock. Now he's used to it.

He enjoys living on campus. He likes the routine of morning dance and being disconnected part of the day. He spends lots of time chatting with Nadya, something that was a struggle back when they lived in Tel Aviv where, although they were physically together most of their waking hours, he was always plugged in. Of course, he's not as fanatical about 1Billion as some of his fellow members, but that's just his nature.

At the moment, the thing on his mind is his meeting with Mother tonight. He's been here over a year and has never spoken with her. He's only even seen her twice, both times from a distance when she was leading the full group of ten thousand members in a routine. He's been racking his brain trying to guess why she wants to meet with him.

The music switches to a merengue number, a dance his body can now do without conscience thought. If his implant were connected, he might read a book, write code, or catch up with work. One of the things he likes about the 1Billion philosophy of keeping your implant disconnected is it frees the mind to daydream.

He can't believe this is his life. That he's a member of 1Billion, that he spends two hours each morning dancing, that he *can* dance, and that he enjoys it—all strange. He drifts back to the past.

————

He had tried to reach Nadya during his supersonic from Tel Aviv to Pyongyang, but her implant was disconnected. He landed, took a car to her last recorded location, and found himself at the main entrance to the 1Billion campus. He explained who he was to the human attendant. It was a beautiful evening, a light snow carpeting the ground and covering the birch trees on both sides of the gate.

He waited ten minutes, and then he saw Nadya approaching. He began hyperventilating and sweating, despite the cold weather. Would she embrace him, as he had been visualizing over and over on the flight from Tel Aviv, or would she tell him to go away, that she needed more time to think?

Her light steps stirred up tiny whirls of snow. As she came into the lit area, he saw tears on her face. They made eye contact and he knew she had forgiven him. If anything, he read relief in her expression, as if she were the desperate one. He pressed his lips against her cold cheek, ran his fingers through her hair, and wiped the tears from her eyes.

She had arrived that morning and was assigned to an eight-person cabin, but with him showing up, temporary accommodations were arranged in a couple's cabin. A day turned into a week. He continued his usual Xyloom projects during Israel working hours and spent the rest of his time unplugged, with Nadya, and with her friends.

After that week, so he could remain on campus, he joined 1Billion as a guest member. He also started dance lessons.

People were warm and accepting. Having spent his professional life working among cynical Israelis, and his foundational years with pessimistic Russians, he found the relentless positivity of the 1Billion members simultaneously refreshing and unnerving. The first time someone told him how thrilled they were to hear his theories on the connections between music and math he took it as sarcasm. By the third time he recognized it for what it was—enthusiasm. It was a good thing that 1Billion's mission was to inspire the world to dance and not to make art, because tormented souls were in short supply.

After a month, he and Nadya mutually decided that they would rather live on the 1Billion campus than return to Tel Aviv. This entailed him becoming a full member, a decision he made enthusiastically. His skeptical personality meant he could never embrace 1Billion with the same blind devotion as some of the others. He found it weird, for example, that there were screens all over the place with recordings of Sunny Kim. It reminded him of things he'd learned about Stalin imagery during the Soviet era of Russian history, the personality cult of the Heroic Vozhd. But, on balance, 1Billion was a good place, and he felt included in a way he never had in Israel or Singapore.

He prepared to meet with Miriam Meyer, head of recruiting. He knew he would have to redirect his salary. He accepted that, understanding that 1Billion would take care of all of his needs and that if he ever rescinded his membership, his salary would revert back to him. However, he would still need to travel back to Israel once every other month to be with his team at Xyloom, and he wanted to hold on to his apartment in Tel Aviv.

The thing that gave him the most pause was publishing a nude recording. He was uncomfortable with it in general, and also specifically worried that the recording could send an odd signal to Xyloom or future employers. Still, everyone else had recorded one, and he was ready. He also figured he could preempt any future concerns by addressing them head on. He imagined a cover message: *To Whom it May Concern—when you research me you may find the attached recording of me dancing naked. Let me assure you it was part of an artistic project. In no way should it be taken as a sign of poor judgment.*

Or something along those lines.

Miriam shook his hand. "I'm so thrilled. I've heard wonderful things. It makes me so happy that Nadezhda is back and you're joining our family. You know, your wife is a lovely human being and a talented musician."

"I know," he said, "I'm lucky to have met her."

She flashed an odd smile. "Luck or fate?"

Then she instructed him to connect his implant so they could enter into legal agreements.

Miriam listened to his concern about his apartment in Tel Aviv. They agreed that 1Billion would purchase the apartment for the remaining balance on the mortgage. The apartment would be left empty and reserved for 1Billion members, like him, to stay in during visits to Israel. They also reached an understanding that should he ever leave 1Billion, the apartment would be sold back to him.

He explained his need to travel to Israel every other month.

"Won't Xyloom pay for that?" Miriam asked.

He explained that no, they wouldn't, because he was making the decision on his own to relocate to Korea. She asked him to try to get Xyloom to cover the cost, but assured him that if necessary, 1Billion would pay his travel expenses to and from Israel up to six times a year. The discussion was mildly frustrating since of course if he kept his salary he could easily afford his own travel, but at that point he was committed to joining.

Then they talked about the recording. He was beyond pleased to learn that for people like him, who intended to work in the outside world, the policy was to hold the recording for external posting at some indefinite future date. Apparently, he realized, 1Billion was sensitive to how employers might view nude recordings.

"Do the Hokey Pokey," Miriam suggested. "In a few months you'll be a fluid dancer, but from what I understand, right now you're a beginner. The Hokey Pokey is easy because the choreography is in the lyrics." She instructed him to remove his clothes and then she started the music.

———

"You looked great," she told him as she handed his scrub bottoms back. "You have a natural sense of rhythm." She patted his stomach with the back of her hand, which felt mildly inappropriate. "And whatever exercise discipline has gotten you these chocolate abs is going to serve you well in dance class."

He tied his scrub bottoms and she handed over his top.

After he was fully dressed, she hugged him. "Congratulations Sergei Kraev! You're officially a member of 1Billion." She told him there would be a ceremony to welcome new members at evening meal that Friday, and his recording would be unveiled there, and then go into circulation on the cabin walls.

Then she said something strange, and even now, he's still not sure if she was joking or not. "One other thing, Sergei. I noticed that your chest and back are hairy. Mother has expressed a preference for men to be hairless. You might consider changing your grooming settings."

———

Sergei's thoughts are yanked back to the present because the merengue transitions to contemporary samba, which requires his full concentration. He tries to copy others, moving his feet, hips, and arms and shifting his weight, but he's doubtful that what he's doing bears any resemblance to samba. He looks over in awe at the man one row up and a spot to the left. Will he ever be at that level?

After another ten minutes, the music stops and morning dance ends. Nadya pecks him on the cheek, and, holding hands, they walk to the dining hall.

"Still thinking about why Mother wants to meet with you tonight?"

"Yeah, I wonder what it could possibly be, and why she didn't invite you."

"We'll find out soon enough. I'm so hungry."

35

February 10, 2118
Two years before 4-17
Outskirts of Pyongyang, Korea

The invite didn't say anything about the length or purpose of the meeting. It just said to meet Mother in cabin 128054 at seven. So, at ten of the hour, Sergei drops out of his virtual office, blinks, glances around his cabin, slips on his parka, and steps outside into the winter dark.

It's an eight-minute walk and he wants to be early. He makes his way along the wooded path at a brisk pace, his boots leaving deep imprints in the fresh snow. He wishes he knew why Mother wanted to meet with him. Because of his Xyloom schedule, he's only enrolled in one dance class, but would she be aware of that? Or could she be concerned that he spends too much time connected? Or . . . what could it be?

He's hungry. He skipped midday meal so he could finish his Xyloom work early. And if this meeting goes longer than fifteen minutes he'll need to miss evening meal too. It's not like he can just show up in the dining hall for a later seating, and he can't print himself a snack because there are no private food synthesizers on campus. It won't be easy to make it through two hours of morning dance tomorrow on an empty stomach.

He walks into the cluster of meeting cabins with two minutes to spare. Where is 128054? It's not here. Panic! He should have double-checked. It must be in the cluster close to the main gate.

He sprints. This is the problem with being unplugged. And why is the cabin numbering so random? There's no system to it! His feet sink into the snow with every step, and he struggles to maintain speed. One minute . . . two minutes. He pauses, breath heaving, then starts sprinting again. Three minutes . . . four minutes—he arrives, breathless and late.

He takes a moment to knock the snow off his boots. Then he steps up, places his hand on the wooden door handle, and as soon as he begins to push, he hears recorded violins: F-sharp, E. The opening notes of Tchaikovsky's Violin Concerto in D Major. He recognizes it from the first three notes. His favorite classical work—one that he and Nadya often listen to in their own cabin.

He crosses the threshold and scans the room. It's sized like the eight-person units, but without bunk beds. Instead, a wooden picnic table, the retro kind with attached benches, sits in the center of the floor, and musical instruments line the two longer walls—this must be a music studio, like where Nadya spends her days with her fellow composers while he's in his virtual office.

His eyes land on Mother, who is seated at the table. He's never been this close to her. She radiates a glow that isn't apparent in the recordings of her all over campus. She is somehow simultaneously younger and slimmer in physical appearance, and more matriarchal and weightier in bearing, than in his prior mental image. She's wearing winter scrubs, their regal purple color and deep V-neck top her mark of distinction on campus.

Without meaning to, he stares at her collarbone and the delicate notch at the base of her throat. He quickly looks away and focuses on the table. Bowls, chopsticks, and place settings. As soon as he notices those, the mouth-watering smells of warm rice and sesame oil reach him. Food—oh, so this will be a meal.

He looks to the opposite side of the table where the bench is occupied by a Scandinavian-looking man he doesn't recognize. Perhaps another member just past his one year anniversary? A chance for Mother to get to know newer people in a personal setting? Sergei does a quick calculation. No, that doesn't make sense. She couldn't do that with just two members at a time.

Still breathing heavily, he apologizes for being late, and hangs his parka on a hook next to the door. By the time he turns back around, Mother and the man have risen and are bowing. The angle puts Sergei in an awkward position, and, in spite of himself, he notices the gentle swell of Mother's breasts and the way her coffee bean-colored nipples graze the lined fabric of her scrubs. He averts his eyes immediately and she doesn't seem to have realized.

"Sergei, it's so good to meet you," she says, a warm smile on her face. She introduces Magnus Peterson, 1Billion's head of technology.

Ah, so this is something about technology. He hopes he can help. He doesn't want to have this whole meal and then disappoint Mother if it turns out she's looking for something outside his area of expertise.

Mother motions for him to sit on the bench next to her, which he does, and then she and Magnus sit back down. He watches her reach for a transparent green bottle labeled in Korean. She shakes it, swirls the liquid inside, and, using the thumb and forefinger of her opposite hand, twists the top off. Alcohol? A drink sounds nice, will help get his nerves under control; but it's also odd: the campus is dry. Must be ceremonial.

She raises her glass. "To dance!"

They drink, then, "Sergei, I hope you like dolsot bibim-bap. Growing up, it's what we ate on cold days like today."

He looks at the steam rising from the stone bowl in front of him. He loves bibimbap. It's his favorite dish in the dining hall rotation.

She lifts the lid off his bowl. Rice, crisping against the scalding sides of the bowl, covered in shiitake mushrooms, shredded cucumber, bean sprouts, daikon radish and sliced beef, topped with a raw egg. She motions for him to use the gochujang first, which he does, spooning the chili paste onto his rice and mixing everything together.

"Sergei, I'm so glad you're part of our community. I don't think we've ever had the chance to speak before. I'm eager to get to know you."

"It's an honor to be here," he says, eyeing his bowl.

Mother starts eating and he and Magnus follow suit.

"Let me ask you a question," Mother says. "I'm always surprised where it leads, and I find it's a good way to learn about our members. What did dance and music mean to you growing up?"

He's just picked up a mushroom with his chopsticks. He puts it in his mouth and chews, thinking about how to answer. Music was big; dance was not. But does Mother really want to hear about his childhood? It certainly wasn't anything special. Well, maybe she is interested. And he doesn't need to get into Papa's virtual island. Just keep it short and sweet.

He tells her about his parents and how he grew up surrounded by bard music.

"Bard?" she asks.

"It's an old sort of antiestablishment folk music. Was popular in Russia during the Soviet regime. The lyrics are poetic, really spoken as much as they're sung," he explains. "What about you? Did you grow up with dance and music?"

Should he already know? Mother entered the public eye when she was a teenager and has been interviewed countless times. No doubt some interviews touched on her childhood. It also feels weird to be asking her a question. But if this is a conversation it's rude to talk only about yourself. Plus, he's curious.

"Very similar. My parents loved music. That's where my passion started. Believe it or not, my first instrument was the accordion. It's a long tradition in my family dating back to before reunification. My great-grandfather even taught me an old Russian song—'Moscow Nights'—do you know it?"

Podmoskovnye Vechera. A classic. He nods.

And then he loses focus on the conversation, because the soloist has reached the virtuoso cadenza and the violin is singing. Those double stops. Sublime. This must be the Shacharon recording.

Silence. The Tchaikovsky comes to an abrupt stop and it takes Sergei a moment to recover. He hears Mother talking. "Let me just remember," she says, and then starts to hum. Somehow Magnus knows the tune to "Moscow Nights" too, and hums along. After a few bars Sergei joins in, singing, *"Ne slyshny v sadu dazhe shorohi, vse zdes' zamerlo do utra."*

Mother pours a second round of shots. "To Moscow nights!"

Of all the images he had formed in his mind of how this meeting might go, not one involved him singing Russian songs with Mother. Nadya is going to be shocked.

"And what about dance," Mother asks him, "is that something you grew up with?"

"No. I mean, except that I've always liked watching it. You know, I saw you perform once when you were still part of 100M. One thing's for sure, sitting in that audience with millions of other fans—I remember you had this crazy thing where your arms seemed to spin in circles, bouncing and locking for the tiniest fractions of time on each beat, this smile of exhilaration on your face—I never thought I'd meet you in person. That one day I would be sitting with you eating bibimbap—unimaginable."

Or that he would be leading a half-unplugged life, living in a cabin on the outskirts of Pyongyang. . . .

"What about you? Have you always loved dance?" he asks Mother.

Magnus gives him a weird look, but Sergei isn't sure what it means and Mother seems perfectly happy to answer.

"Always. One of my favorite childhood memories was when my appa took me to Moscow to see . . . I forget the name in English, a famous ballet, a classic. . . ."

"Artificial Intelligence?"

"No." She hums.

Lebedinoe Ozero. *"Swan Lake."*

"Yes! *Swan Lake,* at the Bolshoi. It gave me goosebumps, and by the time the curtain fell, I knew that's what I wanted to do. What I love most about dance is I get to give out so much energy. Humans have been dancing for millennia. During that entire time our anatomy has remained unchanged, yet we can still come up with new creative ways to move. Inspiring others and feeling part of something bigger is my aspiration, not just for iBillion but for the whole planet. I want to live in a world where everyone dances together."

He is moved. Normally he has an aversion to grand visions. But this is different. It's not some corporate goal, false national ideology, or unproven piece of religious fanaticism. It's a simple and elegant idea, that people the world over would be better off if they danced together. Still, he isn't ready to verbally affirm the vision. He instead redirects the conversation to Magnus.

"What about you, Magnus?"

"Me?"

"Yes, Magnus," says Mother, "what drew you to iBillion?"

Magnus is silent for a moment. "Well . . . there's a really old pop song by an obscure British artist that captures why I left my job in Sweden and moved here. It's about a price tag, and wanting to make the world dance, and—"

Mother interrupts. "Why don't you sing it for us?"

"Sing it? Are you sure?"

She nods.

Magnus stands up, grabs the acoustic guitar from its stand next to the wall, and puts the strap over his shoulder. He strums a C chord and starts singing, something about making the world dance and not worrying about material things. Magnus's voice is clear, his pitch perfect, his solo performance of the silly song moving. Is everyone here so talented? Maybe there's something to that old adage about rare talent not being so rare.

Magnus pauses and looks at Mother. "Should I sing the second verse?"

"No, your bibimbap will get cold."

She opens a second bottle and pours them each a shot. "To making the world dance!"

Then, "What about you, Sergei? Why are you so committed to 1Billion?"

Is he so committed? Mother seems to think so. Maybe he is. He wasn't the day he became a member. If Nadya had proposed they rescind their memberships and go back to Tel Aviv he wouldn't have given it a second thought. But that's not true anymore. This place has grown on him, though in a contest between Nadya and 1Billion there's no question, he would follow Nadya to the ends of the Earth.

He tells Mother how he ended up at 1Billion, how much he appreciates the sense of purpose and mission that is often lacking outside, and that he even likes disconnecting his implant. "Sacrilegious as it may be to say, as an implant engineer, I think everyone would be wise to unplug for a few hours a day. Civilization is becoming more and more virtual, that's inevitable, but there are ideas we have here at 1Billion that others should copy."

Mother squeezes his upper arm. "That warms my heart, especially from you. Magnus tells me that for implant technology, you're one of the top minds of our generation. I'm honored you choose to spend your time with us."

Does Magnus have him confused with someone else? He knows implant theory, but he's hardly a top mind of the generation. He's never published anything and is barely known outside his immediate department at Xyloom.

Magnus must see that he looks puzzled. "I helped with your background checks when you applied. I went through my old contacts. Word back was you're brilliant, but don't let that go to your head!"

Who would have said that? Are there people at Xyloom who view him as brilliant?

"It's really nice to hear that. I don't think it's deserved, but thank you for saying it."

Mother pours another round of shots. "To humility!" Then: "Sergei, I'd like to ask you for your advice. Do you know why we stopped streaming?"

"Yes. BORO imposed a hard cap."

"You're right. At the time I was upset, but now with some distance I see it was a blessing in disguise. I find living and dancing together on our campus more rewarding than our old livestreams, and, as you point out, in this day and age where everything is virtual, we've become an alternative, a role model."

Yes, that's true. As impressive as he remembers Mother being when dancing with 100M, there are tons of online groups out there. 1Billion is something special.

"When we started there were only thirty of us, including me and Magnus. Three years later we were five hundred, and by 2116 we had a thousand members. Rapid growth, but still tiny compared to our old virtual audiences that numbered in the millions. Small enough that the outside world took no notice.

"Now we're over ten thousand people and something strange is happening. That's where I want your advice. Have you met Miriam Meyer who runs recruiting? She's analytical. She tracks our recruiting metrics—how many people express interest, how many enter discussions, things like that. She tells me that in recent months the ratios have all changed, as if a force is pushing people away from us."

Mother looks at Magnus. "Could you explain to Sergei what Miriam told us?"

Magnus turns to him. "Miriam identified BORO as the culprit. 1Billion represents a way of life that, as you said, Sergei, is not the mainstream online life that most people lead. Because we spend so much of our time with our implants disconnected, we're not subject to the usual control exercised by AI algorithms. That makes us the tiniest bit of a threat to BORO, but apparently enough of one that their algorithms have begun biasing people against us."

"My question for you, Sergei," Mother says, "is: do you think Miriam is right and what can we do about it?"

He plays with his chopsticks. Miriam's theory is more than plausible. It's the technique BORO uses to prevent the world from getting sucked into the warped thinking that goes on in the FSA, the only country not subject to fact checking. It's not that board members at BORO are taking deliberate action, it's just that the algorithms have learned how to protect people from others who are not under algorithmic influence. That's all working as expected when it comes to the FSA, but it's not appropriate for 1Billion. BORO is supposed to prevent a repeat of the American Second Civil War, not judge art or impinge poetic license. If people want to dedicate their life to dancing, or living unplugged, or both, BORO has no business acting against that.

Sergei looks up. "Yes, Miriam's probably right, but it's unintentional, a side effect of how AI fact-checking algorithms work."

"What should we do?" Mother asks. "How can we make things fair and balanced, so that people can make up their own minds and not start out prejudiced against us?"

Sergei closes his eyes and imagines the mechanisms at play, the stages a person goes through when considering joining 1Billion, and the subtle influence that AI fact-checking exercises at each. Anti-1Billion information must be getting boosted while positive information, say about mission or healthy lifestyle, is getting suppressed. Counteracting influence at the network tier is not tractable, but tweaking how people absorb information at the implant level to give them, in effect, a neutral starting point, might be.

"I'm not sure. I need to think about it."

Mother gives him a warm smile. "Great. We're looking for your advice. If you think of anything practical, we'll be interested in hearing about it. Let's have another meal together in a few weeks."

Sergei stands up to leave.

"Sergei, this bottle of soju is still half full. Could you take it and share it with your wife? I don't like drinking, but I don't want to waste it either."

He accepts the bottle from Mother, puts on his parka, and steps out of the cabin.

———

Sunny watches Sergei shut the cabin door. She looks at Magnus, who seems like he wants to say something but is hesitating. "Yes?"

"You did such a great job, Mother. I've never heard you talk like that before."

"Talk like what?"

"So eloquent, so coherent, so measured, and all in English."

Yeah, that's what happens when you rehearse for a year.

She stares at Magnus. "You're saying I'm normally incoherent?"

He looks scared. "No, Mother, that's not what I meant at all. I mean I was impressed and touched. I saw a side of you tonight that I've never seen before. Like I didn't know that you played the accordion."

"I don't play the fucking accordion, Magnus. But you looked hot playing the guitar."

She walks over to his side of the picnic table, sits next to him on the bench, and slowly runs her finger along the inner seam of his fleece-lined scrub pants. He freezes.

She puts her mouth near his ear. "Will he deliver?"

"I'm not sure."

"Are you ever fucking sure of anything, Magnus? You need a lesson in the power of conviction and confidence. Come with me to my cabin. This has been a taxing exercise and I need you to relieve my stress, for the good of our community."

36

April 1, 2119
382 days before 4-17
Singapore

Lynette turns to study a strand of yellow-tipped red flowers, parrot beaks hanging from luscious green leaves. The fronds look to her like the banana leaves they serve curry on. Or maybe she's just hungry.

Mum takes a step forward and cups her open palm behind one of the flowers. "What a beautiful specimen of *heliconia rostrata*."

Lynette, whose routine is to swim in the morning and play badminton or volleyball in the evening, rarely joins Mum on her daily strolls through the botanic gardens. She has today because she wants to broach a sensitive subject.

"Mum, let's use Grandma's century birthday to get Ethan home for a few days. I've uncovered so much more information about 1Billion. If we get him back with our family, and away from their influence, I'm sure we can persuade him to leave."

Last month, a friend, someone Lynette knows through her network of concerned families, managed to get her son to quit ıBillion. Lynette's friend arranged for her son to visit home for a week. As soon as he arrived, she begged him to stay disconnected, which he did, and that blocked contact from ıBillion. Then she showed her son proof, supplied by Lynette, that ıBillion was siphoning member money into Sunny's personal treasure chest. Once his eyes were opened, Lynette's friend presented her son with a step-by-step plan for getting reintegrated into society. Each step was small, and there was a clear structure, something she knew her son craved. All he needed to do was say yes to the first step, and he did. To Lynette's knowledge, it is the first time anyone has been persuaded to leave ıBillion, and the success has increased her confidence that she can free Ethan.

"Lynette, dear, I want Ethan back as badly as you. But I think he's doing okay there. Maybe it's best to let him be."

She knew the conversation would go this way. She needs to push because Mum has a blind spot when it comes to ıBillion.

"Mum, how can you say that? If he contracted a disease would you say, that's okay, let it run its course, whatever happens, happens?"

"Of course not."

"Well, it's the same thing. He's been brainwashed. I can't accept him wasting his life away living on a crappy campus dancing all day and enriching a con artist. And the longer he stays there, the less equipped he'll be to return to normalcy."

Mum sighs. "Honey, I'm not as persistent as you; I don't have your energy. I've given up fighting . . ."

Good. It's better than the alternative, that Mum doesn't believe her, doesn't see ıBillion for what it is.

". . . but if you want to see your brother away from Korea, he's going to be in Moscow next week."

"What?" That could be their opportunity. "Why are you only telling me now?" It comes out with more heat than she'd intended.

They reach the VIP orchid section. Avoiding Lynette's question, Mum crouches to admire a plant with alluring dark purple flowers. Lynette looks to see who this hybrid species is named after. No. Sunny Kim. Mum must know. She comes here all the time.

"Ethan asked me not to," Mum says, answering at last. "And I knew you would react like this. You need to live your life, get back to treating patients." She stands back up, her eyes returning to meet Lynette's. "I hate to see you so consumed by ıBillion."

"Why is he going there? To perform?"

"Recruiting trip. That's all I know."

So now he's sucking others into it?

"I'm going to Moscow," she tells Mum. "And you and Dad are coming with me." She turns to walk on.

"Lynette . . . there's something else. . . ."

She looks at Mum.

"Ethan is married. Not legally, but according to ıBillion. He has a permanent partner. Mai. She's sweet."

"*What? When?*"

"February. She was his dance partner. I talked to them; she even called me mum. I can tell she really likes your brother, appreciates him. He moved out of those eight-person cabins, and they live in their own couple's cabin. It's a much better situation. He seems content, happier than I've ever seen him."

What the hell, how could Mum keep this from her? Also how is it that her brother, living in some insular, totally screwed up place, gets married while she, in a pool with millions of interesting matches, has had no luck in that department—has not in twenty years met someone she's liked as much as her college boyfriend.

She shakes her head. "Why didn't you tell me?"

"I'm sorry, I tried, many times, and hesitated. I knew it would upset you."

"Mum, you're right. I am upset, but it's because you didn't tell me. I'm happy for Ethan. But you must see it's also a clever strategy for 1Billion to bind their members to each other like that."

"Mai is going to be in Moscow too."

Really? That's good. And an error on 1Billion's part, she suspects. Ethan won't want to come home to Singapore if Mai—his wife! She can hardly believe it—is trapped in Korea. But with Ethan and Mai both in Moscow—that's a whole different dynamic. Lynette can even enlist Mai's parents in making the case.

"Mum, I've spent a lot of time strategizing with other families on how to do this. We need to find Ethan and speak with him in a setting where he can't cut the conversation short. We won't criticize 1Billion. We'll focus on a single goal: persuading him and Mai to come back to Singapore for an extended vacation. We need to get them on our territory, give them a taste of normal life; then we'll push them to sever ties with 1Billion."

37

April 6, 2119
377 days before 4-17
Moscow, Russia

Sergei is with Nadya in the Yugo-Zapadnaya metro station in Moscow, standing in the long wide hallway that leads to the escalators. The bright spring day spilling in through the entrance masks the usual dreariness of this drab, unexceptional neighborhood where he grew up. It's only his fourth time back in Moscow since he left for his undergraduate studies in Singapore. And for Nadya, who grew up in Nizhny Novgorod, it's her second time in Russia's capital city.

1Billion's six-piece salsa band is arranged in a semicircle. With Miguel on Cuban tres, Swati on baby bass, Jemal on congas, Isabella on horn, Victor singing and playing the güiro, and Pluto on lead vocals, they are producing music of a caliber Sergei suspects tops that of any busking ever at this obscure station in its one-hundred-fifty-year history.

Sergei looks over at Ethan and Mai, who also traveled

with the group to Moscow. They're in the middle of the semicircle executing precision salsa moves. Ethan, in his black trousers and sparkling-silver half-open button-down shirt, and Mai, in her black bra top and silver-sequin pants, would look absurd if it weren't for their technique and physiques making the outfits so fitting—at least, Sergei imagines that's what the onlookers think.

Hundreds of commuters are streaming in and out of the station. Many are lost in their implants, but for a good number, the real life spectacle before their eyes breaks through. They pause to watch Ethan and Mai and listen to the Latin music, making up a semicircle that completes the band's formation.

Sergei approaches a female commuter. These cold approaches were difficult and scary when he and Nadya started yesterday morning, but now he's done a thousand or so and is at least used to it. Even rejection doesn't bother him as much as it did, he just moves on to the next person.

The commuter's eyes are glued to Ethan and Mai.

"Those are my friends," Sergei says in Russian. "Aren't they good?"

The woman nods in agreement.

"We're from the 1Billion dance studio. Have you heard of us? May I share some information?"

The woman nods again. He transfers an information link by proximity and confirms that she opens it, then softly touches her upper arm in a friendly gesture. That's been the single hardest part for him.

He walks back over to Nadya, who was having a similar interaction with a different commuter.

"Successful?" he asks.

"Da."

That brings today to 707 and the total to over 1,300.

They're over halfway there and getting more efficient, so they should be able to wrap things up tomorrow if they start early.

The crowd watching Ethan and Mai has grown. Sergei makes his way over to a commuter on the fringe and starts a conversation. Beneath his feet, the concrete rumbles as a metro train pulls into the station. It's rush hour and the trains are now more frequent. By the time he finishes his conversation and looks up, an endless stream of people is emerging from the bank of escalators leading up from the platform.

Having grown up in Moscow, he's good at picking out people who don't belong, which is why his eye catches a small group of Asian men and women making their way down the hallway. There's a woman about his age and two older couples. They stand out not because they're Asian, although that is somewhat unusual in this neighborhood, but because something in the optimistic spring of their step signals not-Russian. The younger woman looks like an older Lynette Tan; and as she gets closer, he sees, to his astonishment, that it *is* Lynette. What. . . ? No way is this a coincidence. Did Ethan invite her? Why didn't he mention it?

Lynette and her four older companions, two of whom Sergei now recognizes as her parents, join the packed half-ring of commuters and watch Ethan and Mai dance. Lynette hasn't noticed Sergei, who blends in with the commuters. And, as far as Sergei can tell, Ethan hasn't yet spotted his sister or his parents, probably because he and Mai are absorbed in their dancing and because the crowd is several rows deep.

The band is playing a Cuban salsa number. Ethan has his right arm around Mai's upper back, Mai's left arm is resting on Ethan's shoulder, and their opposite hands are intertwined as they spin and pivot positions. How does this look to Lynette? She must be impressed. Ethan and Mai are not only excellent dancers in their own right, but something charged happens when they dance together, a hypnotic synchronization, a centripetal blending of movement. It's something you witness and want to experience yourself. Maybe Lynette will end up joining iBillion too.

The set comes to an end. Mai and Ethan, holding hands, bow and then lift their heads. Mai gives a shout, and runs over and hugs the two other older people with Lynette. "Mom, Dad, what are you doing here?" Sergei's implant translates from Thai. So those are Mai's parents.

At nearly the same moment, Ethan notices his parents and sister. Pluto from the band, seeing what's happening, asks everyone to take five, and the audience disperses.

As the crowd thins, Ethan points to where Sergei and Nadya are standing. A look of shock and disorientation shows on Lynette's face as he and Nadya walk over to join the group.

"I don't understand, Sergei, what are you doing here?" Lynette says.

He steps forward and awkwardly hugs her, the smell of her hair transporting him back to his NTU dorm room bed and warm, tropical weather. He shakes hands with her parents. "Mr. Tan, Mrs. Tan—it's good to see you. This is my wife, Nadezhda Maksimova."

Lynette and her parents nod toward Nadya. "Good to meet you, young lady," Mr. Tan says.

"Ethan never told you that I joined iBillion?" Sergei says to Lynette.

A funny look crosses Mrs. Tan's face.

"Mum, you knew?" Lynette says.

"Yes, honey, Ethan told me."

Lynette points her finger at Sergei. "Did Ethan recruit you? How? Why?"

"No. Nothing to do with Ethan, a coincidence. I joined because of Nadezhda. She was a member before we got married. Ethan was an instructor in one of my classes. We remembered each other from Singapore, became friends. I invited him and Mai on this trip. I thought you knew."

"How did you know we would be here?" Nadya asks, everyone shifting closer to the wall to avoid another dense wave of commuters trudging down the hall toward the station exit.

"Ethan told us," Lynette says. "But he didn't say anything about you and Sergei. We wanted to meet Mai in person, wanted to see Ethan dance, thought it would be a nice surprise. But, honestly, I'm the one who's surprised—shocked, actually. Ethan and Mai, your dancing . . . I was moved; I had no idea! You're good."

A huge smile opens on Ethan's face.

"And Sergei," Lynette continues, "you're the last person in the world I would expect to be associated with 1Billion."

That, he agrees with. Back when they were at NTU no one, especially himself, would have predicted he would end up a member of a dance group.

"Ethan, Mai," Mrs. Tan says, "we made reservations, we want to take you out for dinner, a belated wedding celebration." Mrs. Tan turns to Sergei and Nadya. "You should join us too."

Sergei catches Lynette giving her mom a weird look.

"Mum, we can't," Ethan says, "we're in the middle of recruiting. The band is counting on us."

"It's okay," Sergei tells everyone. "We've done enough for today. We can resume in the morning." Then he turns to Lynette's mother, "Thank you Mrs. Tan, it's very kind of you to invite us, but Nadya and I are seeing my parents tonight."

"I like watch you dance again," Mai's father says.

Sergei sees that the band members are back. "How about this? Do one more set, and then we'll call it a day."

"Can I speak with you?" Lynette asks him.

———

He and Lynette step outside the station. They begin walking around the block. He's forgotten how uninspiring these dilapidated, concrete shell buildings are, or maybe they just seem that way compared to the pristine iBillion campus.

Catching up with Lynette is comfortable, they fall right back into their old speech patterns—it doesn't feel like it's been two decades—he feels instantly close to her. Until she starts talking about iBillion. She tells him about her investigation, about her estimate that, last year alone, the organization stole—her word—one-and-a-half billion uni from its members.

"Look," Lynette says, "iBillion is a toxic, sick, corrupt organization and the fish rots from its head. Sunny Kim is not what she appears to be."

Seriously? Her hatred for iBillion is so out of character. She was positive and level-headed back at NTU. How could Ethan joining trigger such abhorrence?

"You know me, Lynette, and my eyes are wide open. I'm not your brother—I would never devote all my waking hours to dance. iBillion is a weird place, I know that. And yes, sure, we're on firm financial footing thanks to the zeal and generosity of our members. But Sunny is the real thing, an inspiring leader. Maybe she's misunderstood by the outside, but I'm on the inside, and I feel good about 1Billion."

He turns his head to look at her as they continue walking next to each other. He speaks from a place of conviction, almost appealing to her; he wants her to understand.

"I'm alive there, Lynette, and I like being a part of something bigger than myself and my work. And don't you think everyone could benefit from a more balanced split between the virtual and physical? Have I been brainwashed? No way. I'm impervious to flattery and manipulation; you know that. You're being overly suspicious. You should come stay on campus for a week and see for yourself."

She doesn't reply and he senses a new barrier between them.

They arrive back at the station. Lynette places her hand on his shoulder. "Sergei, if you and Nadezhda ever feel trapped, if you need help leaving 1Billion, negotiating to get your income or assets back, I'll be here for you, no questions asked." And then they walk back in to the final bars of a cha-cha-cha.

———

"None for me," Ethan tells Lynette, placing his hand on top of his shot glass.

That's rude, but she's definitely not picking a fight with him over this. Dad speaks up. "Ethan, one shot, a toast to you and Mai."

Ethan slides his hand away and she pours him a shot of chilled vodka. Then she completes her loop around the table, finishing by filling her own glass.

"To one hundred years of blissful marriage," Dad says,

raising his glass. "And to eternal love and bringing us a grandchild soon!"

Mum puts her glass down. "What's this soup?"

"Borscht," Dad answers, stirring sour cream into the red liquid in his own bowl. "Beets and cabbage. When in Russia...."

After Mum finishes her soup, she turns to Ethan. "After you're done here, I'd like you and Mai to come to Singapore for a couple of weeks. It's Grandma's century birthday. She wants to see you and meet your wife. We already bought you tickets for our return flight."

Lynette is relieved: Mum is sticking to the plan, after almost bungling things earlier by inviting Sergei and his wife to join them.

Ethan stiffens. "We can't just be away from campus on a whim. Mai and I have teaching responsibilities, and we need to rehearse for a show in June. Plus I would need to get permission for a vacation. Approval takes weeks."

This is an objection they rehearsed. Mum just needs to stick with the plan. Use the word "visit"; don't scare him.

"Ethan, honey, I know there'll never be a great time to visit with your busy schedule. Your grandparents miss you. Your cousins miss you. Can't someone take over your classes for a few weeks? Grandma is turning one hundred. She'll be devastated if her oldest and favorite grandchild misses her celebration."

"Mum, I know. I do want to be there, but I have commitments."

Lynette watches him closely, noting the tension tightening his posture. iBillion has really done a number on him, but the fact he's at least feeling some pressure, experiencing some guilt, is encouraging.

"Ethan," Mai says, taking his hand, "why can't we go to

Singapore? I'd love to meet your grandmother. Mother will never know, and we can find friends to cover our classes."

Good, common sense. Mai has a head on her shoulders.

"What you mean, Mother never know?" Mai's father says. "She be happy you go to Singapore, you should visit family Thailand too." He turns to Mai's mother, "Right?" She nods.

"Sorry, Dad," Mai says, "*Mother* is what we call our leader."

Then Lynette sees Mai squeeze Ethan's hand and senses the tension drain from his body. "Okay," he says. "We'll do recruiting tomorrow, and Saturday morning we'll go back with you."

Lynette is relieved and thrilled, but she keeps her expression neutral. "That's great," she says, and gives Mai's wrist a reassuring rub. "Grandma's gonna love you. I can tell."

———

One month earlier

"The reason I asked to meet," Sergei says, "is I've come up with something called Protiv-1, a potential solution to counteract the influence of AI fact checking."

This is his first time meeting with the full 1Billion leadership team. He looks over at Mother, who nods approvingly. Magnus, he knows from their dinner a year ago. Miriam, he met when he joined, and has been in touch with recently to obtain recruiting data. The other two gentlemen, sitting on either side of Mother, whose names he's already forgotten, he met for the first time a few minutes ago when he walked into the room.

They asked him to be brief, and he can see why. It's nine p.m. and he's the first of fifteen items on the agenda. When he requested the meeting yesterday he certainly didn't expect or need it to happen this quickly, but it's nice that they're taking him seriously. At Xyloom it can take a good month or two to get on the calendar of a single senior person, and longer to get on the agenda for a standing meeting.

"As you can see," Sergei says, pointing to the recruiting data supplied by Miriam, "BORO algorithms nudge potential members away from 1Billion by influencing the information they receive. My approach should give a gentle nudge in the other direction. We can't change what information people receive, but we can tweak how they feel about it."

He explains that by leveraging a low-level interface to a primitive part of the brain, he'll make consuming negative information about 1Billion induce the tiniest bit of queasiness, and positive information invoke very slight euphoria, so subtle that people will never consciously be aware of the effect. "It won't matter if people feel strongly one way or the other, but on the margins, it should counteract AI fact checking."

He's keeping the explanation simple. But getting to this point has involved a year of dedication, creativity, and luck. He worked harder, and had more fun in the process, than anything he's ever done. He had to solve three problems, all of which seemed impossible when he set out. First was invoking the queasiness and euphoria. Second was injecting his code into implants. Third was making the first two invisible.

"Is this a theoretical idea or something you can actually do?" Magnus asks him. "I thought this type of thing was impossible."

"It's not theoretical, but I'm not sure it will work either. That's why I need to test and calibrate. And that's what I want to discuss with you."

He explains that he needs to conduct a randomized, double-blind, placebo-controlled trial with potential recruits. And, due to how Protiv-1 is transmitted, he needs to have physical contact with them. "My suggestion is we set up a recruiting station in a high traffic location so we can efficiently enroll many people. It's logistically simple and we can do it with a small team."

"Do you have an idea for where? Seoul maybe?" asks Miriam.

"Moscow."

———

One of the few useful skills Sunny learned from Appa is letting a room come to the decision you want without ever saying a thing. After Sergei leaves, she glances at Fernando.

"What do you think?" Fernando asks the group.

Sang-chul speaks up. "He's either bullshitting us or he's delusional."

"If it's too good to be true it usually is," Fernando agrees.

"I'm not so sure," says Magnus. "I'm the one who said it was impossible to hack implants—"

Miriam interrupts. "Who said anything about hacking implants?"

"He didn't say it, and maybe he's not even thinking it, but there's no way what he described isn't hacking, which should be impossible. The thing is, Sergei is exceptional. He's one of the few people in the world who understands the math behind BQCI, and he works at Xyloom. If he wasn't onto something, why take us through all that?"

Sunny agrees. Sergei seems naive about how the world works, but not about technology.

Sang-chul straightens up. "Implant hacking is a class-one crime."

"You didn't seem that concerned four years ago," Miriam says. "If I remember, you even accused Magnus of being a quivering bird. And if it's such a big deal, why didn't Sergei mention that?"

Magnus scratches the top of his head. "I've seen this before. Sergei's an engineer enthralled with a technical solution. More than that, his success would be the first hack ever of implants, a technology whose entire right to exist is predicated on being provably unhackable. He's so focused on the technical accomplishment he's forgotten about the ethical and legal considerations. Or maybe he views the BORO algorithms' inhibition of free choice as a fundamental wrong that he needs to correct. And who knows? Despite his outward humility, maybe he wants to play god."

Nobody responds.

"Let's say you're right and he's not bullshitting us," Sang-chul says, breaking into the sudden silence. "This is where keeping our implants off and privacy shielding this cabin comes in handy. There's no record of our conversation with Sergei and there won't be a record of whatever we decide to do. I personally don't believe that Sergei's solution will work. But, just in case, what we need is plausible deniability. One of us, Miriam as head of recruiting, should tell Sergei we don't believe him, but we also won't stop him from forming a team and running a test on his own."

Sunny looks Miriam in the eye, and Miriam nods.

"Next agenda item," says Fernando.

38

April 7, 2119
376 days before 4-17
Moscow, Russia

Late Friday afternoon. Sergei and his 1Billion recruiting crew are at the Yugo-Zapadnaya metro station for the third day in a row. They started the morning having shared information links with 1,314 commuters and now they're up to 2,088, just ninety-two shy of their goal of 2,180. The goal is dictated by the design of his research study, but as far as Nadya and everyone else is concerned, it's just an arbitrary goal set by the recruiting department.

There's something he's wanted to do with Nadya ever since they arrived in Moscow. If he waits until they find the next ninety commuters there won't be time before their team outing tonight.

"Do you mind taking over approaching commuters?" he asks Isabella. She speaks Russian and her lips are probably fatigued from three days of blowing the trombone. "Contact me right away if you need help or anything weird happens."

He asks Nadya if she'll indulge him by doing something he's always wanted to do but never got around to.

"Of course, Seryozha, as long as it doesn't involve standing outside a metro station."

"Well, it does. Do you know the Koltsevaya line?"

He explains that the line, which opened one hundred seventy years ago, forms a ring around the center of Moscow. Every station is a work of art. "We'll take the metro from here to Park Kultury and proceed clockwise." What he wants them to do is get off at each stop, take in the architecture, then continue to the next station. "When we complete the circle we'll be back at Park Kultury, and if a certain kiosk is still there, I'm getting you a special treat."

Sergei takes Nadya's hand in his and they ride the escalator down to the Yugo-Zapadnaya platform. Kiyevskaya, Krasnopresnenskaya, Belorusskaya . . . at each station he buys Nadya a flower. Yes, this is unnecessary, sappy even, but being back in Moscow and being with Nadya, his wife, has stirred something; and, if they didn't have ballet tickets, he would gladly spend all night sitting next to her riding the metro in circles.

And then, *Dear passengers, when leaving the train do not forget your belongings.* Ring completed. They emerge from underground at the Park Kultury station, Nadya admiring her bouquet of twelve flowers as they ride up the escalator. He looks around.

"Yes, great, it's still here! It's been twenty-five years."

"What?"

"My favorite khachapuri kiosk." He orders two. He's tried the khachapuri at many different places in Israel. It's always good, but never like what he remembers.

"This is delicious," Nadya says.

The cheese and egg filling is the right sour and the right

salty, and the crust is exactly as he remembers it. All the more remarkable because when he was a kid there was still a person here making them by hand, and now they're printed.

Khachapuri in hand, he and Nadya walk down to the Moscow River and stroll along its western bank.

"Would you ever want to move back here, Seryozha?"

"Are you testing—?"

He stops midsentence because he receives a connection from Isabella.

"Something strange happened. We were passing an information link to a boy and he collapsed. When he got up he said his vision was out of focus."

"Where is he now?" Sergei asks.

"He left."

"Why were you passing an information link to a boy? We only recruit adults. How old was he?"

"I'm not sure, perhaps twelve or thirteen. I didn't target him. He approached me and asked about 1Billion. Was I not supposed to share information with him?"

"Did you confirm he opened the link?"

"Yes."

"Did you touch the boy's arm?"

"Yes."

"Did he collapse after or before that?"

"After."

"How long after?"

"I'm not sure. Let me check the timing on my recording . . . after, about five seconds."

"What exactly did he say about his vision?" Sergei asks.

"Not much. Here's the recording."

Isabella: "Are you okay? Let me help you up."

Boy: "I'm okay. I think it was a mini seizure. It happened once to my brother and then they did something to his health system to make sure it would never happen again. Oh. This is weird, everything is blurry and it's like I'm looking through a kaleidoscope."

Isabella: "Can you ask your parents to come and get you?"

Boy: "I live right over there. I can walk home."

Isabella: "Do you want me to walk with you?"

Boy: "No, I'm fine."

"Why are you so concerned?" Isabella asks Sergei.

He ignores her question. "What number is he?"

"2192."

"So you already passed our 2180 target?"

"Yes."

"Why didn't you stop?"

"We were on a roll. I figured the more the better."

"Okay. You can stop now. Tell Mai, Ethan and the others. Let's meet back at the hotel. I have tickets for all of us to see *Artificial Intelligence* at the Bolshoi tonight."

39

April 14, 2119
369 days before 4-17
Outskirts of Pyongyang, Korea

Friday night. Sergei strides across campus to cabin 128054. It's been six days since he returned from Moscow. On Tuesday, he broke the blind, revealing which commuters were randomized into which groups. An instant later he had the results of his experiment. Now he's on his way to present those results to the leadership team.

He steps into the cabin. Mother, seated at the picnic table with everyone else, looks over, smiles, and welcomes him. She gestures at two bowls on the table. Crispy salted roasted seaweed, which he loves, in one, and dried shredded smoked squid, which he does not, in the other. He passes. Snacking is the last thing on his mind.

Stand or sit? There's a place for him at the table, but when he rehearsed, he imagined himself standing, lecturing. He walks to the front of the room.

"Let me begin—"

Fernando interrupts him. "Sergei, one thing first. I want to get your view. I heard that Ethan Tan and Mai Chairat went to Singapore. Are they planning to defect?"

"No, they're just visiting family."

In truth, he's not so sure. He was taken aback when they told him. Nothing wrong with going on vacation. But why the abrupt change in plans? Why not fly back with the group, apply for vacation, and then go to Singapore in a few weeks? And, regardless of Ethan's intentions when he and Mai departed Moscow, Sergei knows Lynette. She's strong-willed and Ethan isn't. She'll use Ethan's time in Singapore to sway him to her fish-rotting-from-the-head view of 1Billion. Anyway, they won't care about Ethan and Mai once they see the results from Moscow.

"Was Ethan acting—" Fernando begins to ask something, but Mother cuts him off.

"Sergei, please tell us about Moscow."

He has four things to cover. First, explain Protiv-1. Second, walk through the study design. Third—the thing he's most excited about—share results. Four, next steps.

Protiv-1. That's what he named it, from the Russian prefix "counter," as in counteract anti-1Billion bias. There's the transmission mechanism and the influence mechanism, both novel.

"Here's how we bootstrap Protiv-1," he says, and holds up a thin, clear, almost invisible two-by-five–millimeter strip. "This releases odorants that carry Protiv-1 code into the implant via olfactory receptors."

He gives it to Miriam who takes a cursory glance and passes it around the table. Magnus is the only one who looks carefully. "How do you control it?"

"Through your implant," Sergei says. He and Magnus connect and look:

Activation Date: [Immediate]
Max Generations: [1]
Placebo?: [Per blind randomization]
Potency: [.001]
[Emit]

"What's *activation date*?" Magnus asks.

Sergei explains that Protiv-1 is autonomous. "The activation date gets encoded into Protiv-1 at time of emission. It tells it when to change from *spread* mode to *influence* mode."

Magnus gives him a puzzled look. Sergei has been working on this for so long, he forgets that no one else knows what those two modes are.

"Before the activation date," he explains, "Protiv-1 spreads by transmitting itself from person to person. It stimulates the body's sweat glands to emit Protiv-1 odorants, which then enter the implants of others via their olfactory receptors."

"After activation," Sergei continues, "Protiv-1 stops spreading and switches to *influence* mode. This is what we talked about a month ago. Episodes of microqueasiness and euphoria are induced as needed to counteract anti-1Billion bias."

"Why is it set to *immediate*?" Magnus asks.

"Immediate activation was used for the Moscow study, so that Protiv-1 was delivered to a single subject and stopped there, with *max generations* set to one as an extra precaution."

"Does *potency* control the strength of the queasiness and euphoria?"

"Yes," Sergei says, "and the current setting is what was studied in the Moscow trial."

Magnus seems to get it.

Sergei shifts his attention away from the Protiv-1 controls and back toward the full group at the picnic table. "Let me go over the study design," he says in his public-speaking voice. "We ran a recruiting station at a metro stop in Moscow. Over the course of three days, we enrolled two thousand one hundred ninety-two subjects. A subject was considered enrolled after two things happened. First, they accepted an information link from one of our recruiters. Second, they came into physical contact with the recruiter, guaranteeing that odorants would travel from one of these strips to the subject's nose. Subjects were...."

This is weird. They're munching on seaweed and squid, looking bored. Are they even absorbing what he's saying? He should tone down the lecturing, draw them into a conversation, but he can't help himself.

"Subjects were randomized one to one into either a control group or a treatment group. For the control group, the strip released neutral odorants. For the treatment group, the strip released the Protiv-1 odorants. In both cases the information shared with the subject was identical, a brief overview of 1Billion containing a 'get in touch' path. Our primary endpoint was the subject going down the 'get in touch' path within seventy-two hours of randomization. And—"

Miriam interrupts him. "What do you mean endpoint?"

Good. At least someone is paying attention.

"The thing we're counting, whatever outcome we're measuring. I know what you're thinking, and you're right, expressing interest in 1Billion isn't the same thing as becoming a member. This is just a preliminary study. Eventually we'll need a much bigger and longer study to assess what we really care about—people joining."

Are they actually thinking that? He can't tell. They

should be. It's not some minor detail. No matter how confident he's feeling, he won't be fully convinced that Protiv-1 is effective until they measure all the way to successful recruitment. He's heard too many horror stories at Xyloom of things that looked promising with proxy endpoints, but later fell apart under larger studies that measured the true outcome of interest.

"On Tuesday, seventy-two hours after the last subject was randomized, I broke the blind. I was floored when I saw the results."

Just as he rehearsed, he raises his closed left fist to shoulder level. "One thousand ninety-six subjects were randomized into the control group, and," he lifts his right fist, "the same number were randomized into the treatment group. In the control group," he shakes his left fist, "fifty-five, or 5.02 percent, went down the 'get in touch' path, while in the treatment group," he shakes his right fist, "seventy-six, or 6.93 percent did."

He puts his arms down. "We can therefore say with confidence that Protiv-1 is effective, at least for increasing interest in learning more about iBillion."

No reaction. Don't they get how huge this is? He developed something considered impossible and has experimental evidence it works. And the six of them in this room are the only people in the world who know about it. Maybe Magnus gets it. But Mother is sitting there waiting for him to continue as if the punch line hasn't come yet.

If any of his fellow Loomies knew about Protiv-1 they would be amazed, shocked, would look at him in a whole new light. He buries that thought. His colleagues would be horrified. And actually, even with this group, maybe it's better to downplay how unusual Protiv-1 is. All they really need to know is it worked, better to be vague about the mechanism.

"I don't understand what the big deal is," says Fernando. "All that scientific mumbo jumbo was leading up to six percent of people did something instead of five percent. That doesn't sound like anything. I could make that happen just by being more persuasive."

Not surprising. He could tell Fernando wasn't following. Recruiting isn't his department and he probably hasn't dealt with this type of thing. But why isn't Miriam saying anything? She knows enough to recognize the significance.

Sergei looks at Fernando. "It *is* a big deal." He opens his palm and bends in his pinkie. "Number one, most things don't work the first time."

He bends in his ring finger. "Number two, 5.02 percent to 6.93 percent isn't a small change, it's an increase of thirty-eight percent."

His middle finger joins the other two fingers pressed into his palm. "And number three, the purpose of the study was to see if Protiv-1 worked. Sure, you could take other actions to increase interest in joining 1Billion. But the thing here, the whole point, is that the subjects in the two groups were treated identically, the only difference being that the treatment group received Protiv-1."

Fernando still looks skeptical.

How else can Sergei explain? He's thinking about that when Mother, who has been quiet until now, speaks up.

"I understand, Sergei. Good job."

Ah, so Mother gets it.

"Let's use it," she says. "How do we do this?"

He's already figured out the next steps. "We need to run a series of small-scale studies to get the potency right. Then we conduct a megastudy that randomizes hundreds of thousands of people and follows them for half a year each to see if they become members. We also need to investigate the long term effects of Protiv-1." He decides not to mention the research they'll need to do into the boy who developed the vision problem.

"How long is all that going to take?" asks Fernando.

Sang-chul looks up. "And how much will it cost?"

"Let's see. Between small studies and then the big one, figure three years. Then once we release Protiv-1, it will take a year to spread organically person to person, so if all goes well we can activate four years from now. If the big study fails to meet its endpoint then we're looking at considerably longer. And, keep in mind, this is research. It could turn out Protiv-1 doesn't work, in which case we'll need to start on Protiv-2."

"The cost?" Sang-chul brings up again.

"Hard to say. Maybe we can work together on a budget, that's not my area. A guideline we use at Xyloom for this type of study is a thousand uni per subject. Our costs, though, should be much lower, maybe a tenth, and we're looking at a quarter million subjects, so rough estimate, twenty to thirty."

Sang-chul jumps up. "Twenty to thirty million uni! Are you batshit crazy? You think we have that kind of money?"

Sergei takes a step back, stunned by Sang-chul's harsh language. He looks over at Mother, expecting her to say something, but she doesn't react or even look surprised. And how is that a lot of money for 1Billion? They don't get it.

"I thought we *did* have that kind of money. Ethan Tan's sister estimated we brought in over a billion and a half uni last year. The funds for the research I'm proposing aren't even a drop in the bucket."

Maybe it wasn't so smart to mention Lynette.

He looks at Mother. She stands.

"Enough," she says calmly. "Sergei, I asked you for your advice on our BORO problem. That was over a year ago. In that whole time all you've accomplished is getting a few extra people to express interest in us, and you're not even completely sure about that. Now you're proposing endless research studies that will take years and cost tens of millions, and you can't even guarantee your thing will work."

He wants to explain that if the outcome was guaranteed, they wouldn't need to run the study; but before he gets a chance, Mother points her finger at him and starts shouting. "You are so timid! So fucking indecisive! Did you run a research study to figure out what to have for breakfast this morning?"

He freezes. Everything turns dark. He takes another step back and supports himself against the wall. He glances at Magnus and Miriam, but they don't make eye contact and nothing on their faces indicates that anything out of the ordinary is happening.

Mother gets closer and now he's sandwiched between her image on the wall behind him and her physical body centimeters in front of him. She screams in his face. He smells the dried squid on her breath.

"Let me teach you a life lesson, Sergei. There is no certainty. And yet you must have conviction, otherwise you get nowhere. You are weak. Have you ever taken a risk? You think you have all the time in the world to get to the perfect answer, but you don't, because we all die."

He shuffles sideways. Why is she doing this? What did he do wrong? It's true, he is indecisive. Is he being overly cautious proposing all these studies?

No. This *isn't* his fault, and proposing studies can't

explain her anger. Maybe this is really about Ethan and Mai. Or bringing up money? Or him mentioning Lynette?

Shit. He hasn't seen this side of Mother before. Could there be some truth to what Lynette was telling him?

Mother steps sideways, getting even closer, making thinking impossible. She cups his face with her hands and starts speaking in a sweet voice. "Let me tell you what I would do Sergei. I'd stop overthinking. Have some confidence. If you believe in what you created, release it into the world."

"B-but," he stammers, "it wouldn't be responsible until we do more studies."

Mother is still cupping his face but she stops talking. He uses the few seconds of silence to collect his thoughts, and then makes up his mind. This is the moment to be strong. To be decisive. He reaches up and removes Mother's hands from his face.

"I'm resigning my membership. My wife and I will leave campus tonight. You don't need to worry about me. I'll keep everything about the study and this conversation secret. You can forget about me and I'll forget about 1Billion."

He starts shaking. He'll need money to travel. He needs to be forceful. He turns to Miriam. "Direct my Xyloom salary back to me. Make it effective now."

"How do you know Nadezhda will leave with you?" Mother asks.

How does Mother have Nadya's name on the tip of her tongue? Panic. Was he too rash? He can't think. He's going to be sick.

Mother takes his arm and walks him the few steps back to the table. He reaches out and steadies himself and then sits on the bench. Mother sits next to him and combs his hair with her fingers, moving it off his sticky forehead. He's nauseous. And the noxious squid.

Somewhere in the back of his brain, the thought—Mother intentionally deactivated her oral hygiene enzymes.

"You don't understand," Mother says to him in a calming, caring tone. "It's not you who needs to keep this conversation secret. It's us. We didn't tell you to try to hack into implants and we had nothing to do with you testing your hack on thousands of people in Moscow. That was your decision."

Hearing it out loud, strange . . . this whole time he's never thought of Protiv-1 as an implant hack. But of course it is. And Mother knows it.

"We're not waiting around for more studies," Mother says. "The way I see it you have two choices. You can release your thing now. It's unlikely to do much, but maybe it'll help our cause, and then you can go back to living your charmed life with Nadezhda. Or you're welcome to leave 1Billion, but we'll report you to the authorities."

Mother grasps his right hand in her two hands. It's oddly comforting. He closes his eyes.

He was so manic, so driven, so caught up in the creation of something technically beautiful that he lost sight of the ethical picture. He crossed a flaming red line the moment Protiv-1 went into the first commuter in Moscow last week. He didn't pause before crossing it, or even notice it. Now it's hitting him. Mother may not understand how big a threat she's making. Implant hacking carries the maximum penalty under international law—forced disconnection and lifetime solitary confinement.

What was he thinking? He should have paused after he figured out how to exploit the olfactory interface algorithm. He could have quietly let Karima know that the flaw in her proof was not just a theoretical problem. Or he could have published his findings and received worldwide recognition; been offered the academic appointment of his choice. Instead he's being threatened by Mother and her leadership team, who still don't seem to get the enormity, significance, and sheer difficulty of what he accomplished. He rests his head on the table.

Mother strokes the back of his head. "Sergei, show Magnus how to release Protiv-1."

Sergei picks his head up. Magnus doesn't need his help. He watches Magnus lift the odorant generation strip to his nose. "You said a year to spread organically to the whole world, right?" Magnus asks.

Magnus seems to take his lack of response as a yes, and he hears Magnus mutter something about a nice birthday present for Mother.

Sergei looks at the Protiv-1 controls. He sees that Magnus switched *max generations* to ten, set *activation date* to a year and three days from now, and is about to emit.

Shaking, nervous, moving as fast as he can, Sergei adds an extra zero to *potency,* changing the value from 0.001 to 0.0001. Magnus doesn't notice. He's activating emit over and over and taking deep breaths through his nose. Magnus must get that each emit has a fifty percent chance of being placebo, and he wants to make sure he gets Protiv-1.

"Is that it?" Mother asks Magnus.

"Yes, if Sergei's thing actually works."

"See," Mother says to him, "that wasn't so bad. In ten minutes we did something that was going to take you four years." She pecks him on the cheek. "Now go back to your cabin, have sex with your pretty wife, and get some sleep before morning dance. And, by the way, Sergei, don't even think about ever leaving 1Billion."

40

July 3, 2119
289 days before 4-17
Haifa, Israel

Fucking conservative GHO. It's such bullshit. One boy goes blind in Moscow and they put a hold on promotion, with no evidence that there is any connection to his algorithm. "Out of an abundance of caution." Six words that won't get you far in life.

Daniel is in his Technion office, alone, fuming. He just disconnected from a meeting with the multinational that has spent the last twelve years commercializing the olfactory interface algorithm. This morning, the company received a notification from GHO. Due to the ongoing investigation of the sudden onset of blindness in a pediatric patient, the root cause of which has eluded GHO scientists, all promotions of algorithms from sandbox to privileged have been placed on indefinite hold. The blanket hold will be lifted once a root cause is established. Or the hold can be lifted on an algorithm-by-algorithm basis with submission of proof of no causality.

After all the work he did behind the scenes to achieve fast-track designation, an effort they never thanked him for, now the company is asking him to prove the algorithm can't cause blindness. Of course they're asking, because positive proof of no causality is an impossible standard, and their scientists aren't up to it.

What choice does he have? Let things run their normal course and wait for GHO scientists to find the root cause? That could delay promotion by years. Or he can drop everything and throw himself into proving no causality. Of course that's what he'll do, and he'll need Karima's help.

There *is* a silver lining. It's always rankled him that he and Karima did all the heavy lifting but will end up with such a small cut of the royalties. He told the multinational that if he and Karima prove things to the satisfaction of GHO, he wants their royalties doubled. They agreed. Almost too easily, he should have asked for triple.

He walks down a flight to Karima's lab, enters her office, and closes the door.

"This is fucking insane," he tells her. "Over a decade of testing. Simulated testing. Animal testing. Flawless sandbox deployment. And all that gets thrown out the window because, first, doctors in Russia can't diagnose why some boy goes blind, and then the idiots over at GHO can't figure it out either."

"Honey, relax. It's not the end of the world."

"Don't fucking tell me to relax. You and I have both worked way too hard for this."

He sees the fear in her eyes. "Sorry," he says.

She remains silent for half a minute, bouncing her leg. "What if there *is* a connection?"

"By what mechanism? Our thing is in the sandbox. And the limbic system has nothing to do with vision."

Their olfactory interface algorithm was deployed world-wide in sandbox mode a year ago, a major milestone, but not the trigger for royalties. The algorithm was originally slated to be promoted from the sandbox in mid-2121, another two years from now. But, thanks to flawless performance, and lobbying, they were on the verge of securing an accelerated promotion date of March 5, 2120. Now, to get even remotely back on that schedule, he needs Karima to work a miracle.

"We start work on this now," he tells her. "Get someone to cover your teaching. Forget about your grad students. Skip committee meetings. We work day and night."

41

September 6, 2119
224 days before 4-17
Outskirts of Pyongyang, Korea

Late at night, lying in bed, on his back, Nadya asleep beside him, Sergei is thinking. It's been five months since he presented the results of the Protiv-1 trial. He hasn't had contact with Mother or anyone else on the leadership team since. There's an ulcer in the pit of his stomach that will never go away. But time has numbed its severity, and there are days that go by, especially when he's consumed with Xyloom work, where things seem almost back to normal.

But tonight is not that. His mind loops endlessly through all the things he could have done differently. How could he have been so stupid? So naive? Standing in front of that table, proud, looking for Mother's approval. So many bad moves. And now there's no way out, at least not that he's thought of yet. He's about to connect his implant and force sleep when he hears Nadya stir.

He feels her rotate onto her side, snuggle close, put her

head on his pillow. Then she's kissing his temple. Her left hand runs over his bare chest, unties the drawstring of his sleeping scrubs, and, with a few tugs, she slides them down below his knees. She climbs on top, slips him inside, and starts nibbling and kissing his right ear. He moans. He hears her whispering, so softly he can barely make anything out.

"Keep making sounds, and don't react to anything I say." And then even softer, "Bring me with you to Tel Aviv next week. Find a reason that can't be shot down. Don't do anything out of the ordinary or say anything about this until I tell you, even once we're in Israel."

He absorbs, and as instructed, does not react. So she suspects, as does he, that everything they do and say in their cabin is monitored. Why does she want to come to Tel Aviv? He'll need to make a compelling case. He's sure Fernando's culture team has been watching him for signs of defection intent. If he and Nadya make plans to be off campus at the same time it could raise alarms. But if regulatory approval happens on his Xyloom project that could be a good excuse. And then the train of thinking crumbles, replaced by the sensation of Nadya's tongue exploring his ear and her pelvis grinding deliciously into his.

———

Two days later, Sergei is in his virtual office when the expected good news comes. The dense logging system he's been working on for a decade has been approved by regulators. This is a major, major accomplishment. His boss schedules a celebration for the following week, to coincide with Sergei's regular bimonthly trip to Tel Aviv. "Could you extend a formal invite to partners too?" he asks her.

He meets with the culture team to request permission

for Nadya to travel with him to Tel Aviv. They reject his request. A runnel of sweat trickles down his neck despite the cool fall weather. He explains that his boss told him she would schedule the party to accommodate his and Nadya's schedule, and will be offended if Nadya isn't there. "My promotion to level five is at risk," he tells them, and only then do they agree.

———

Sergei and Nadya board a supersonic from Pyongyang to Tel Aviv. They're joined by Lara Vega, a 1Billion member neither of them knows and who apparently needs to inspect a dance venue in Israel for an upcoming exhibition. Frustrating, because she's going to be staying with them in the 1Billion Tel Aviv apartment, formerly his apartment. At least she offers to take the couch, leaving him and Nadya the bed.

He and Nadya wake up early to exercise. It's been three years since they've run together in Tel Aviv, but they go right back to their old route, heading south along the beach and turning around when they reach the port in Old Jaffa. On the way back, Nadya diverts off the running path and turns into the city, and he follows. They come to a stop in front of Dizengoff Fountain.

What are they doing here? He looks at Nadya, but still following her whispered instructions, doesn't ask. She takes his hand and leads him into a hotel. This is the hotel where he met Karima. Was that only three years ago? A different life. If only he hadn't bumped into Daniel and Karima, or agreed to meet with her, or had told Nadya the truth, or. . . .

"Turn off recording," Nadya says once they're seated in a corner of the lobby. She seems nervous.

"Why are we here?"

"I remembered that this hotel has a privacy shield from your liaison with Karima. I wanted a place we could speak privately."

So she thinks we're being observed even in Israel? How?

"Remember when we were walking along the Moscow River I asked you if you ever thought about moving back to Russia?"

Yes, he remembers. But why is she bringing it up? Members are encouraged to test each other's loyalty, but Nadya wouldn't do that to him. Would she? If he can't trust her, who can he trust?

"Is this a trick?"

"Seryozha, no, I swear to you."

Of course, he wants to leave, but he can't tell her that, can't even have her think he would entertain the idea.

"Well, sure, I've thought about leaving once or twice, though not for Moscow. I think we would prefer life here. But those are just fleeting thoughts. I like it at 1Billion and have no desire to live anywhere else."

Nadya wraps her slim hands around his. "My soul, I want to tell you something that will change your mind. Promise, no matter how angry you get, to hear me through and not get up and walk away. After you process what I tell you, I believe we're going to decide to stay here and never go back to Korea. But if somehow we do go back, it's critical that nobody ever learns of this conversation. Even if Lara isn't with us in the apartment, never speak of it there because it's under surveillance, just like the entire 1Billion campus, and just like my implant."

What? Her implant?

"Your implant is under surveillance? That's not possible without your consent."

She gives him a guilty look. "I did consent, four years ago, as part of taking on a mission for 1Billion."

"What? What mission?"

"To recruit you."

He stares at her. When he speaks, he barely recognizes his own voice.

"What do you mean?"

"In 2115, five months after I joined, Mother and Miriam Meyer approached me. Mother explained that sometimes 1Billion needs individuals with specialized skills. They identified you as an expert on implant technology and asked me if I would be willing to try recruiting you. I agreed."

No. No. No. He found her, not the other way around. But all those times she kept bringing up moving to Korea. He pulls his hand away. Is she serious?

"Why you?"

"Psychographics. They figured out I was the 1Billion member you would be most attracted to. Miriam said their models showed training me in seduction had a higher chance of success than using an experienced recruiter."

Seduction? What is she talking about? He's never seen her do anything seductive. Could this all be her quirky sense of humor?

No, this rings too true.

"I was trained by Lara. She's part of Miriam's recruiting team. She drilled one mantra into my head: make the prey come to you. She taught me how to fake affection and dangle hints." Her hand twitches toward his, pauses, returns to clasp her other hand. Her eyes glisten with tears as they seek his. "But, Seryozha, none of the training was necessary because I liked you the moment we started speaking at the hackathon."

Everything is a lie.

"Why are you telling me?"

"I need you to understand that ɪBillion is not what it seems. You've been brainwashed, I was brainwashed, and I need to shock you out of it with the truth. I know you, Seryozha. As painful as this is to hear, when confronted with reality you are clear-sighted."

"It doesn't make sense. I made a last-minute spontaneous decision to join your hackathon team. How could you have planned that?"

"We didn't plan that. . . ."

We?

"That was luck, or fate. Our original plan was for me to catch your eye and approach you at the closing reception. I was to build just enough of a connection to exchange contact permission."

This is real. Anger flares hot, and his hands ball into fists, wanting to hurt something. Himself. Her. She screwed up his whole life.

He fights to keep his voice level and not shout. "So getting married was no big deal to you? Just part of the plan? Another little thing you could do to serve ɪBillion? Do our vows even mean anything? Or while I'm in my virtual office doing Xyloom work, you're off sleeping with your dance partners?" He shakes his head slowly, his vision irising down on her face. "Fuck you."

He stands up. He's never used language like that before, even in his head. His heart sledgehammers. She starts crying.

Was that part of her training too? Screw her. He wants to run away, forget about Nadya, forget about ɪBillion, forget about Xyloom even. Go back to Moscow, hide under the covers of his childhood bed.

He can't. If he runs away from ɪBillion they'll report him,

and the penalty for what he did is . . . he can't think about it. But would they actually report him? He can't risk it. At least he can take control of the situation with Nadya. Divorce her. End the lie.

He paces the lobby and rational thought starts to take over. Divorce her. That means he'll need to move in with seven other people. Life at 1Billion with Nadya, no matter how fake this all is, is more bearable than life without her. Is that why she's telling him? She wants *him* to initiate separation? So she can be with someone else? No, she wouldn't need to reveal her secret for that. So why *is* she telling him? He calms by degrees and then sits back down.

"No, Seryozha, please, please, listen to me. Even sex wasn't part of the plan, and if it were, I never would have agreed. The original strategy was for us to get to know each other in virtual space. Then, as ostensibly platonic friends, I would have invited you to Korea. You would have received the usual warm, royal treatment on campus, and I would have hinted that if you joined we could get involved romantically. Miriam's model predicted that after three visits as a guest you would have become a member."

She wipes her eyes on her scrub top. "But instead, something magical happened between us. I'm telling you the truth. Whatever you felt, I felt the same but stronger. I begged Miriam to let me come visit you in Tel Aviv. Miriam was nervous that I would never bring you back to 1Billion, but she also saw it was a good tactic, and she had my implant under surveillance.

"Seryozha, as soon as we embraced at Ben-Gurion, I knew we would spend the rest of our lives together. During the hackathon I fell in love with the precision of your brain, how you sounded, how you looked. And my conviction became total the instant we met in person, when you hugged me, and I ran my fingers through your hair."

He's played the recording of that moment over and over. But he doesn't need his implant to remember it, the electricity of her touch, over in seconds, sealed in his mind. He knew too, then.

She looks him straight in the eye. "When you asked me to marry you, how do I explain? Of course I wanted to. But I also knew that Miriam was watching, or would watch later, and in that moment I decided to leave 1Billion and stay with you in Israel or wherever you wanted to live. I withdrew consent for implant surveillance right then and there."

She's telling the truth. He remembers the moment of fear when he asked her—not a fear of him, a fear of something else.

"You don't know how many times I wish I had stuck to my convictions. Within minutes of withdrawing consent, while I was washing my hair, I was barraged with messages and connection attempts from 1Billion. As soon as we got back to Tel Aviv, Miriam came to see me. I met her at the Sheraton. Later even Mother came in person. All of my friends were telling me, 'Don't defect, we miss you, we love you.' And the other composers kept bombarding me with notes saying how much they needed my artistic contributions."

Mother came to Israel? To make sure Nadya recruited him?

Nadya looks down. "Mother asked me if 1Billion was important to me, which at the time it was. Then she told me you were essential. If I failed to recruit you, it would jeopardize the entire future of the organization. They also cut off my funding. When I asked for my music royalty streams to be restored they dragged their feet, and I didn't want to ask you for money. If I had only told you all of this back then.

"I gave in. I agreed to restore consent for surveillance and I told Mother I would keep working to recruit you. Even so, I found one excuse after another to delay bringing you to Korea."

This too rings true. His anger has long since dissipated. "Nadya, I'm sorry for what I said." He holds her, her face pressed against his shoulder, tears streaming. "Why did you run away after my meeting with Karima?"

The tears come faster. "I'm so sorry. There isn't a day that goes by when I don't think about that. I was under constant pressure from Miriam. 'Find an excuse, any excuse to get angry and come back to Korea. He'll follow you like a lost puppy.' That's the expression they kept using, 'lost puppy.' 'Trust us, Nadezhda, Sergei will follow you like a lost puppy.' And of course it wasn't just me looking for an excuse, they had access to full surveillance so they were constantly giving me ideas: 'he came home late,' 'he gets so absorbed in his work that he doesn't pay attention to you,' 'he never asks you what you want in life.'

"Then the thing with Karima happened. While you were meeting with her in this hotel, they showed me the recording from the fountain out there of Karima whispering in your ear and then the two of you walking into this lobby. Miriam convinced me that you and Karima were rekindling an old relationship, and I believed it. She was your old grad school friend and intellectual equal. And she's beyond beautiful. Miriam told me to confront you, walk out, break contact for a few days and travel back to Korea. She guaranteed you would follow, and you did.

"I still don't know what happened between you and Karima here. But even if you cheated on me, I forgive you a hundred times over, and I want us to stay here in Israel and never go back to 1Billion."

The puzzle pieces fall into place. Mother is evil. And Mother plans long term. And Mother is a chameleon. And Mother is smart.

He can't think of a way out. If only it was as simple as Nadya is saying and they could just stay in Israel. He wants so badly to open up to her about Protiv-1, but other than relieving his burden, that's not going to change anything. It would put her at risk, and by law she would be obligated to report him. No, he needs to keep it to himself. He thinks slowly and carefully.

"Nadya," he says, "I see the full picture now. Nothing you've said changes how I feel about you. I loved you before I knew, I love you now, and I will continue to love you for the rest of my life. And nothing happened with Karima, other than we sat in this lobby and talked about a math problem."

He sees relief flood her eyes. He holds her hands and stares at her beautiful face, the person he expected to spend the rest of his life with, and realizes this might be goodbye.

"I wish we could do as you say and leave 1Billion. But I can't. I'll understand if you want to defect without me."

And then horror.

"Why not? Don't you believe me?"

"I do believe you, but—"

"Then how can you still believe in the righteousness of the group? What justifies such manipulation? Can't you see that even if member intentions are good, the organization is rotten at its core? I used to think mistakes were made by overzealous members misinterpreting Mother, but the more I've thought about it, the more I'm convinced Mother herself is toxic."

"Nadya," he says, wiping her tears away with his thumb,

"I can't say more without putting both of us in danger. You have to trust me. Our choices are these. We both go back to Korea after this trip, hide the fact that we had this conversation, resume our normal life, and see if we can find a way out in the future. Or, you defect and stay here, and I'll go back by myself."

42

April 17, 2120
Thirteen hours before 4-17
Outskirts of Pyongyang, Korea

Sergei wakes up a few minutes before five in the morning, just enough time to make it to the central green for morning dance. Before getting out of bed, he reaches over, takes Nadya's hand, and pumps it twice: a signal they worked out before they left the hotel in Tel Aviv half a year ago. Its meaning is simple, a way to reassure each other of their inner thoughts—I still want out of here. She squeezes back.

At one in the afternoon, having, per his usual routine, attended early morning dance and morning meal and then come back to the cabin and slept for a few hours, Sergei connects his implant and enters his virtual Xyloom office. He's the first one in and catches up on everything that happened since he disconnected yesterday.

8:19 a.m. Israel time. He's on his daily nature walk with Zev. They've debugged many technical problems over the years on these walks. Their trail today is modeled on the coastal forests of the American Northeast, and at the moment he and Zev are paused on a boulder overlooking a waterfall.

"Did you notice how real the woods smell?" Zev asks him.

He breathes in. Evergreen trees, fresh air, pine needles on the path. They do smell exceptionally bright and realistic. "Yeah, this trail is good."

"It's not the trail. Last night the olfactory interface algorithm got promoted out of the sandbox. Over a year early, but the regs accelerated it, deemed it ready. I'm surprised you didn't know."

No. The news, delivered so casually, hits Sergei like a stack overflow. He turns to Zev, seeing his own movement as though in freeze-frame.

"Zev, sorry, I need to take the rest of the day off. Let's figure out this primate thing tomorrow."

Sergei drops out of virtual space. Shit. All of his assumptions and testing of Protiv-1 were based on it activating while the olfactory algorithm was in the sandbox. In privileged mode the algorithm is ten thousand times more powerful. The first thing Protiv-1 does on activation is calibrate, and in theory it should be fine, but he can't be sure.

Why would the regulatory authorities accelerate promotion? They're normally so conservative. Releases get pushed back, never forward.

It's 2:21 p.m. local time. He looks up. Nadya notices his eyes are focused.

"You're back early!"

"I need to meet with Mother."

He's not sure how to find her. They use older style technology for communication and Mother isn't in the directory. He has no idea where her cabin is. In fact, the campus is now so large, with several nearby satellite locations, that she might not live on campus at all and nobody would notice. He stares at the looped recording of a smiling Mother dancing on the back wall of their cabin. Mother is inaccessible. She meets with you, you don't meet with her.

He checks. None of the other members of the leadership team are in the directory either.

He knows he could get Fernando's attention by saying any number of trigger phrases aloud. However, he wants to hide his awareness of the surveillance, otherwise he and Nadya will be inviting even closer monitoring in the future.

"Sang-chul Lee is in my 2:30 dance class," Nadya tells him.

He follows Nadya to her class. He walks over to Sang-chul, who is stretching, and asks if they can step outside the studio cabin and chat for a few minutes.

"Class is about to start, let's talk after."

After is in an hour. There isn't time. He needs to be pushy. "Sang-chul, it's important."

Sang-chul gives him a look, but follows him outside. "What?"

"Please contact Mother. I need to meet with her right away."

"About what?"

"Protiv-1."

"That thing?" Sang-chul rolls his eyes. "What a waste of money. Nothing ever happened."

"What do you mean? It's been slowly spreading."

"Maybe. Or you're delusional. I'm more inclined to believe the latter. I still don't see why you need to meet with Mother, especially on her birthday."

"Something unexpected happened. It's essential I discuss it with her. I'm sure she'll want to meet with me."

He's not at all sure, but he needs to try.

Sang-chul turns back toward the cabin. "Okay, I'll contact her after class if I can. I doubt she'll want to meet with you, but I'll try."

Sergei grabs Sang-chul's arm. "Contact her now please. This can't wait."

Sang-chul shakes off Sergei's grip. "Fine . . . please remind me what your name is."

"It's Sergei Kraev. Our meetings, Protiv-1, Moscow. How could you forget?"

"How long has it been? Two years? You know how many different people and projects I've been involved with since then? It all blends together. Also, I was your age when 1Billion went offline. I was too used to relying on my implant. I never got good at memorizing names, especially foreign ones."

———

Sergei receives a message from Mother instructing him to board a car outside the main gate at three. That's twenty minutes from now. He wants to message back and request to meet earlier, but the message has no return address.

3:13 p.m. The car drops him in the courtyard of a sprawling three-story building. What is this place? The structure is modern and traditional at the same time. The sweeping lines of the roof remind him of the imperial halls of ancient China, the ones you see in period dramas. Decks, cantilevered out from the second and third stories, wrap all three sides of the courtyard.

The garden seems familiar. Then he realizes the entire courtyard is landscaped in a reverse virtual style. Someone has painstakingly taken plants, shapes, colors, and motifs from virtual nature and coaxed them into organic existence. He's been to the reverse virtual gardens in Tel Aviv, but that looks like the work of amateurs in comparison. The cost. . . .

He spots Mother doing pushups near one corner of the courtyard. He walks over and hears her counting in Korean. He's been exposed to enough of the language through dance class that even without his implant translating he knows she's up to ninety-two.

He tries to get her attention but she ignores him. ". . . ninety-seven, ninety-eight, ninety-nine, one hundred." Finally, she stands up, sweating, and acknowledges him.

"Hello Sergei. How is your beautiful wife?"

He ignores the question. "Happy birthday, Mother. What is this place?"

"This, Sergei, is one of my residences. Since you didn't grow up in Korea you may not recognize this part of Pyongyang. It's Ryongsong, where the old presidential palace used to be. I bought the whole complex, demolished the original structures, and built this home. The palace was too ostentatious for my blood."

So his guess was right, she doesn't live on campus.

"Do you know why I invited you here?" she asks.

"Because I asked to meet."

"Yes, but why here? You're the first member ever to visit. I can't have members over because it would be uncomfortable for them. They would wonder why they're in shitty little cabins, eight to a room, and I'm living here. The cognitive dissonance would be too great, even for our leadership team, and it could lead to defections. But you're special, Sergei. You can't leave iBillion." The corners of her mouth twitch upwards. "Come, I want to show you something."

"I have something urgent—" he begins to say, but stops when Mother places her toned, sweaty arm around his shoulders. She leads him toward the residence. There are no doors, but when they are half a meter from the transparent wall separating the courtyard from the interior, a three-meter span swooshes into the ground, like an old-fashioned car window rolling down at high speed, and swooshes right back up after they enter.

He bends to take off his shoes. As he's straightening up, three smiling white-furred puppies come bounding down the hallway. Mother gets down on her knees and the puppies cover her in kisses. He watches, dumbstruck, taken aback by this side of Mother he's never seen, and it makes him hopeful that she'll be receptive to his request.

Then he and the puppies follow Mother into an airy dance studio. One wall looks into the courtyard. The wall opposite that is mirrored, with a barre extending its full length. The two side walls are white and bare, save that each holds a large well-lit painting. Mother stops in front of one of the paintings.

"Do you like it?"

"Mother, I have something urgent—"

"Answer my question first."

He looks at the painting. It has a dark blue background with five red human figures dancing in a circle. It's famous. He knows it, but can't quite remember. He looks it up. Of course, Matisse's *Dance.*

"Yes," he tells Mother, "I do like it. I even saw the original while I was in secondary school. On a field trip to Saint Petersburg."

"This *is* the original, Sergei. I thought you might know it. I didn't. I gave a lot of money to the Korean Endowment for the Arts. Four hundred million uni—their biggest donation ever. They wanted to make a grand gesture. They pulled in favors with the Hermitage in Russia and MOMA in the DU.

They got this painting and the one on the opposite wall on
loan to me for a year. Both arrived yesterday, just in time for
my thirty-sixth birthday party."

Four hundred million. Sergei stares at the canvas, trans-
fixed. Even as some part of him screams, *there isn't time for
this*, another part is mesmerized, in awe of the masterpiece.
The very brushstrokes Matisse applied over two centuries
ago are a meter from Sergei's eyes. He wants to touch them,
and he could; nothing would stop him.

"You have to admit," Mother goes on, "they nailed the
present—what better than naked figures dancing in a circle
to represent 1Billion? Did you know the painting was
commissioned by a Russian art collector, also named Sergei,
and hung in his mansion in Moscow? I was thinking about
you when I learned that this morning. And now you're here.
Funny."

Helpless, he follows Mother to the opposite wall. "This
painting is a study Matisse made for the other one a year
earlier. Today is the first time in history that both paintings
have hung in the same place. Which do you like more? I feel
like when people first become members of 1Billion they
think of our organization like this, with the light-colored
joyful figures, and over time they think of it more like the
other painting with the red, menacing dancers."

Shaking off the spell with an effort, he says, "Mother,
there's something I urgently need to discuss with you."

"We'll talk in the sauna."

Before he can say anything, he's following her back out
of the studio and through several hallways. It's 3:32. Three
hours left.

They arrive at an indoor facility with a gym and natural
wood sauna. He watches Mother grab a towel, and when he
realizes she's about to take off her exercise scrubs, he looks

down. By the time he raises his head, the sauna door is closing. He peers through the steamy window and sees her
obscured figure pouring water onto the coals. Then she lifts
herself onto the upper wooden bench and sit down on her
towel.

He needs to speak with her. He opens the door and
walks in, keeping his eyes down.

"Who wears clothes in the sauna? If you want to talk, go
back out, take your scrubs off, grab a towel, and then come
sit." She pats a spot on the bench next to her.

He walks back out, takes his top off, wraps a towel
around his waist, and slides out of his scrub bottoms. He
opens the sauna door again.

She looks directly at him, apparently completely
unbothered by her own nakedness. She speaks in a scalding
tone. "Be a man and drop the towel. And if you don't have
the balls you can leave now."

Sergei swallows, removes his towel, places it on the
bench next to Mother, and sits. He takes a deep breath,
inhales the cedar steam, and forces his eyes to meet hers.

"Mother, over the past year Protiv-1 has slowly crept
from implant to implant."

"How do you know?"

He labors to keep his head up and look only at her face,
while she does the opposite, making a show of inspecting
his body with her eyes.

"I don't know for sure," he says, conscious of her gaze
lingering on his lap. "But that's what it was designed to do,
and there's a good chance it worked."

"Maybe it worked, maybe it didn't. I guess we'll see if
recruiting goes up over the next few weeks. What's the
problem?"

"The problem is Protiv-1 exploits the new olfactory interface algorithm, and the algorithm was promoted from sandbox to privileged early this morning. I didn't expect that for another year or two at the earliest."

"What the hell is an olfactory interface algorithm? You think English or geek is my native language? You know, you should change your grooming settings to hairless. You could look nice if you made an effort."

He ignores the comment about his grooming. "It's a new way that implants connect with the brain to transmit smells. My design assumed the algorithm would be in the sandbox. I never tested, had no way to test, with the algorithm running in privileged mode."

He sees that Mother isn't following. He needs to forget about the fact that she's naked, that he's naked, and focus on giving a clear explanation. He closes his eyes.

"When new brain interface algorithms are introduced to implants, they're first run in a sandbox for many years, where the full power of the algorithm is dulled in order to protect the host and monitor problems. But, as of early this morning, the olfactory interface algorithm was promoted out of the sandbox."

"And . . . so what?"

"The moment Protiv-1 activates it does a systems check and calibrates itself. I designed the systems check to work with the olfactory algorithm running in the sandbox. In privileged mode the olfactory algorithm has direct access to the brain and is ten thousand times more powerful. I never tested the systems check or calibration in that environment. In theory it should be fine, but what if it isn't? Mother, it could have unknown, possibly devastating consequences."

"Didn't it already activate? Today is my birthday."

"No, not yet, it's set for 6:34 and 18 seconds this evening."

"Why then? You know I was born in the morning."

"I don't know, that's how Magnus set it, probably inadvertently."

"If you're so concerned, why don't you check now?"

He'd been asking himself the same question for the past hour. The only way he can think to check would put a life in danger.

"I can't. Certainly not safely. It will take weeks of careful work to test, and meanwhile Protiv-1 will activate in less than three hours."

She frowns. "Well, what do you want me to do?"

The words rush out of him in an urgent flood. "Use your clout. Get governments to tell their citizens to disconnect their implants for one month. Tell the global community what we've done and give experts a chance to clean up my mess. I'm prepared to face the consequences. Mother, the danger of doing nothing . . . we would never forgive ourselves."

Even as he says these words, which sounded convincing when he rehearsed them in the car ride over, he realizes Mother will never agree.

She leans back, propped on her hands. "Sergei, you've gone crazy. Listen to yourself. You believe your thing spread. And you're saying there's some tiny chance it will cause trouble when it activates. So based on that, you want me to throw away my life and everything we've built at 1Billion? And you want to throw your miserable life away too? Have you lost your mind?"

"No, I haven't—" he starts to say, but she talks over him.

"And even if I did what you asked, do you think world leaders would listen to me? Do you seriously think people would be willing to disconnect for even one minute? Disconnect for a month?" She laughs. The action carries no trace of humor. "That will be the end of the economy, the end of government as we know it. People will starve. War will break out.

"Even if your fears are justified and a few people get queasy, the cure you're proposing is worse than the disease. Sergei, you may be educated, but you have a lot to learn about common sense."

He tries to argue, but Mother shakes her head, a final rebuttal. She pats him on the cheek. "Put your clothes on, go back to campus, and enjoy the special evening meal tonight for Mother's Day."

———

G, B-flat. . . . Nadya sits at a keyboard in a music studio cabin, alone. She's writing a melody for morning dance routine. Her progress is slow. She's distracted, wondering why Sergei needed to meet with Mother. It must have to do with whatever he couldn't tell her in Israel.

She's heard the stories about Mother and doesn't like the idea of Sergei being alone with her. And it's odd that Mother sent a car for him. Where did that car take him?

She thinks back to her early days at 1Billion when she took her turn serving dinner to Mother and the leadership team. Baijiu and beer on a dry campus, Sang-chul staring at her chest, Mother screaming about dinner. Those were all big fat clues that 1Billion was not what it seemed, but somehow, in her enthusiasm, they didn't register. Now Sergei is with Mother, and for all she knows, Mother is plying him with alcohol, forcing him to disrobe, and telling him to relieve her stress. She hopes he has the confidence to resist.

When they took off for Tel Aviv, she was sure they would never set foot in Korea again. But they came back, and it's been seven months, and Sergei still hasn't come up with a plan, at least not one he's shared. She needs to get him to open up about whatever it is he won't tell her so she can help. He's a genius, but not a risk taker. And neither is she, except in comparison.

She fingers a minor arpeggio with her left hand and revises the melody line, humming aloud. She hears a sound behind her and turns around to Sergei entering the cabin. She's relieved until she sees the tension in his body. He walks over, sits next to her at the keyboard, and grabs her hand. She feels him squeeze four times. Code for emergency.

"Did you see Mother?" she asks, struggling to maintain a casual tone.

"Yes. She persuaded me my concern was overblown. What are you writing?"

"A downtempo thing for morning dance cooldown."

Sergei gets up from beside her, grabs the acoustic guitar, sits back down, and tunes it. He strums a few chords and together they start singing, *"Ty u menya odna,"*—"You are the only one." After the first verse Sergei continues singing solo, and after a few more verses, she joins in again with *"Ty u menya odna"* as if they were cycling back to the chorus.

This is a code she and Sergei came up with in Tel Aviv. The people and algorithms surveilling them are not Russian speakers, which means they rely on automated translation and should ignore singing. It's a risky trick and leaves a solid trace. She's nervous, not just because they're using the code, but because whatever's going on, Sergei feels the risk justifies its use. A part of her, though, is also excited—maybe he's found a way out and is sharing his plan.

That hope is quickly dashed. Through Sergei's horribly rhymed verse, she learns about Protiv-1, the accelerated promotion of the olfactory interface algorithm, the activation scheduled for 6:34 today, and even the connection to Karima.

She knows enough about implants and brain interfaces from her many discussions with Sergei that she follows everything he's singing. With a shock she tries to keep from showing on her face, she now realizes what Mother has on him and why he can't leave 1Billion. She needs time to process, but it will have to be later. There's a reason her husband is risking this conversation, and she needs to pay attention.

There is only one way to check
And that is on myself
If I die or am incapacitated
You need to tell Lynette
And Karima and Daniel
Send a burst transmission
And then disconnect yourself
And never reconnect

Be sure to use my name
And mention olfactory interface
The critical thing to do
Before 6:34 tonight
The world must disconnect
My hack is undetectable
So they won't take it on faith
Send a recording of me

If I do collapse
Don't waste time helping me
Inform the world of my hack
And save the human race

You are the only one
Like the moon in the night
Like the pine in the steppe
Like the spring in the year

She sings the last few lines with him on autopilot while her mind races. She needs to think carefully. She'll need to connect her implant to record. These are not her authorized connection hours and her implant is under surveillance. If she's unlucky, she'll only have a few minutes once she plugs in before someone comes to ask what she's up to. If Sergei activates Protiv-1 and nothing happens, then no big deal. She'll say she wanted to record a song and connected by force of habit. But if, god forbid, something happens to him, she'll need to use those few minutes to compose a message and burst it to Lynette, Karima, and Daniel.

Lynette is Lynette Tan. She'll take the message seriously and won't be thrown off just because she can't communicate back—she knows how 1Billion operates.

But Nadya hasn't had any contact with Daniel or Karima since their one interaction at that conference, and as far as she knows, neither has Sergei. They'll be surprised to hear from her, but if she understood Sergei right, Karima is in fact aware of the potential for a security hole and she's sure to act immediately on Nadya's message.

Sergei starts strumming the guitar again. *"Milaya Moya."* This isn't part of their code, but it communicates volumes. If he's taking the time to sing *"Milaya Moya"* with her, he must be more concerned than she understood. Could he be saying goodbye?

She fights back tears, knowing they would look suspicious. She struggles to keep two possibilities in mind at the same time. One is that life will continue as is, and she needs to make sure neither she nor Sergei does anything that gives away their true feelings about 1Billion, making it even harder to escape later. The other is that Sergei is about to take an action that will forever alter him—will it damage his brain, will his personality change, could he lose his interest in her, could he die? A cold terror steals over her. She wishes she better understood what Protiv-1 does.

She thinks back to when she first heard him sing, at the hackathon, a phrase, *"Zdravstvuy, zdravstvuy."* Everything was different. 1Billion was pure, a place for artistic expression, an outlet for her music so much more rewarding than licensing compositions to games. Her team won the hackathon, something she didn't even realize was a big deal at the time. And Sergei, they worked so well together that weekend, each creative in their own way. Then she heard him sing those few notes, the same bard music she grew up with, in his unadorned baritone voice.

And then at Ben-Gurion he was waiting for her at the terminal with a single pink rose. They embraced, and she combed her fingers through his hair, and inhaled his clean, birch smell, and they started chatting in their native language. Their first walk along the beach in Tel Aviv, their first kiss, their first night together.

And now here they are, trapped, everything diminished and minor chords, even the cabin surrounding them transformed from a simple, pure wooden structure to prison barracks. The tears threaten again, and she squeezes her eyes against their sting.

"Where, and in which lands, will we meet me again?" She listens to Sergei sing the final repetition of the chorus. Then he puts down the guitar.

He takes her hand and they walk back to their cabin. People keep passing them, walking in the opposite direction to evening meal. One friend stops them, asking why they're walking the wrong way, reminding them that evening meal is early today, and not to be late, because there will be a special treat for Mother's Day. How are they all so blind?

Back in their cabin. Sergei embraces her, strokes her head, tucks her hair behind her ears, kisses her eyelids.

"Why do you smell like cedar?"

"Later."

She watches him reach into the back of his drawer and pull out a tiny, almost invisible strip. He walks over to the bed, sits on the edge, and looks directly at her. "Stand as far away as you can."

She backs up.

"Are you ready?" he asks.

No, she's not ready. Her husband. Her beautiful husband. He doesn't need to do this. Can't he send out an anonymous warning about Protiv-1? Why does he need to use himself to test? They can leave campus right now. Who would stop them? She starts walking toward him.

"Don't get close. Are you ready?"

He's thought this through and he's determined. She backs up again, connects her implant, and nods.

———

Sergei sets *activation date* to immediate, *max generations* to one, *placebo* to false, and leaves *potency* at 0.0001.

He lifts the strip to his nose.

One second. Two seconds. Nothing. Massive relief. He still needs to test if he feels queasy when consuming anti-1Billion information. But his big concern, that something catastrophic would happen during the calibration phase, washes away.

His thoughts become clear. Maybe it was watching Mother playing with her puppies, or their conversation in the sauna. She's not going to report him. Her bark is worse than her bite. He's sure. He and Nadya are going to leave 1Billion today. They'll walk out the gate and contact Lynette. She'll loan them funds to book travel out of Korea and she'll help them get their income and—

Nausea. Comes a tickle in his mind. Deep in his skull, something sparking. He imagines he smells insulation burning.

An avalanche of scents, smells, odors crashes over him, obliterating everything. The salt smell of the Mediterranean in an onshore wind; the pungent, sewage-like odor of durian at a hawker center in Singapore; the woody, vanilla scent of white birch trees in the Russian forest; the black tea Mama sipped with lemon in their Moscow apartment; the cumin-laced falafel at Wadi Nisnas; Karima's smell of citrus and za'atar; the soft, sensual pear aroma of Nadya's skin and her black sea scent after bathing; Mother's stomach-turning squid breath when....

Something is very wrong. His finger muscles contract, making his hands into claws. He looks down. From some-where worlds away, Nadya cries, "Seryozha? Seryozha!"

He tries to stand, even as he's dissociating, mind exploding from olfactory impressions so overwhelming he could be breathing a toxic, otherworldly soup instead of air. His thrashing legs give under him, arms herky-jerky corkscrewing him helpless on the floor. Ejected from his body, he floats weightless, the metronome in his brain slowing to a crawl. A strange calm comes on him as he sees himself now curled tight in fetal position, spittle on his lips, as Nadya, kneeling, holds him. And then he's pulled like a kite on a string and goes telescoping away into the shuttering dark.

———

Nadya rushes over, holding him as he's thrashing, then stills. Some sort of seizure. "Seryozha!" she screams.

No. No! Health status reports brain death. No. She cradles his head in her arms. Her Seryozha. No, oh dear god *no!* This is her fault! If she hadn't . . . how could she ever have agreed to recruit him? Why did she go through with it?

She closes her eyes and presses her lips against his forehead. Through the cataract of pain, she remembers his words, her mission. She composes a message and attaches the recording and telemetry. She bursts it to Lynette, Karima and Daniel. Seconds later Fernando rushes into the cabin. It's 5:14 p.m.

43

April 17, 2120
Singapore and Haifa, Israel

4:12 p.m. Singapore Time (82 minutes to 4-17)

Lynette looks Emma in the eye. "I know you love music. Who's your favorite group?"

"Daze of Cyan." Emma can't hold the eye contact, but she does answer, so she's not completely incapable of interacting with people in the physical world.

Lynette looks around the apartment. This is her first appointment with Emma and her first time here. Emma's parents aren't home, so it's just the two of them. Typical compact, cookie-cutter condo. She looks past Emma out the window. Nice view. They're on the fifty-second floor, high enough to see Sentosa. She watches a transparent cable car crawl through the sky, shuttling tourists to the island.

She has a good feeling about Emma, who doesn't seem nearly as far gone as her parents explained when they booked the session.

"Okay, here's what we're gonna do. Set your implant to do not disturb. For the next ten minutes you're gonna tell me all about Daze of Cyan. Verbally. Don't use your implant. Keep your attention on me and our conversation. Look me in the eyes. Let's make it to 4:23. I know you can do this."

"You mean just like talk? Like don't share?"

"Yup, you got it."

Emma bites her lip. "Like, let me think, the lead singer, she's, I don't know, like, she shows people she's, like, real. And she writes all the lyrics herself. And, uh. . . ."

"What's your favorite song?"

"Let me look at my playlist—"

"No, use your native memory."

"Uhh . . . like, Shadow of Gany—"

Urgent message. Taking her attention off Emma for a fraction of a second, Lynette reads the summary, sure it will be something she can deal with after this session.

No, she can't, this demands attention now. She's going to have to set a bad example. She places her hand on Emma's leg. "I'm sorry. There's something I need to deal with. Let's pause."

The message is from Nadezhda Maksimova, Sergei's wife. Lynette listens to the full thing and watches the enclosed recording. My god. No. She's never seen anything like it, other than in training simulations back in med school. Telemetry shows brain death. Sergei. It's not possible. She checks the timestamp. The telemetry was recorded moments ago. He needs medical assistance. She tries to reach Nadezhda, but Nadezhda is unplugged. Who can she contact? Her heart begins to pound. Then she listens to the message again and absorbs its broader implications. A trickle of sweat runs down her spine.

The idea that a global implant hack is going to activate

in an hour is absurd. If the message had come from any of her friends she would assume it was a weird practical joke, and if from a patient she would suspect it was another attempt by 1Billion to discredit her. Wait . . . is that what this is? Is 1Billion exploiting her connection with Sergei in some twisted strategy to get her to do something extreme and lose her license again? Retribution for helping Ethan and Mai escape?

No. She trusts Sergei. She examines the message: no question, it's verified. She can't imagine that Sergei, no matter how great his allegiance to 1Billion, would do anything to harm her. Also, even if she allows for that, she can't rule out the possibility that the risk is real, and causing herself professional harm is nothing in comparison. No matter how she looks at it, she needs to warn the world.

Emma clears her throat; Lynette holds up her palm.

But how? How to get people to heed her warning? If she mentions 1Billion people won't take her seriously. Better idea: mention Sergei's connection to Xyloom, a credible and relevant organization. She begins to compose. No time to perfect the wording.

Emergency! Disconnect your implant before 5:34 p.m. An implant hack could cause death. This information comes from an engineer at Xyloom who sacrificed himself by activating the hack early in his own implant. Watch this recording.

She posts the message everywhere, then switches her attention back to physical reality. Emma is still sitting across from her, now staring blankly at the wall.

"Emma," Lynette says, getting her attention. "Listen to me. What I'm about to tell you is serious, it's not an exercise. It's not part of your treatment. I have a friend who's an engineer at Xyloom, the implant company. He sent me a message that something very bad will happen at 5:34. Your implant could damage your brain. You must hard disconnect before then. Tell your parents and everyone you know."

Emma stares, a confused expression at first, quickly hardening to a look of disgust. "That's sick, Doctor. Testing if I can disconnect if I thought my life depended on it?"

"Emma, I'm serious, and I don't have time to explain."

Lynette turns away, connects with Mum and Dad, and tells them to disconnect before 5:30. "Make sure you tell Ethan."

"Lynette, honey, is this some craziness connected to 1Billion?"

"I don't have time to explain. Please just do what I say. Promise."

"Lynette, you sound paranoid."

"Mum, I don't have time to discuss!" she snaps. "Just listen to me, okay? Do you promise?"

A pause, then, "Yes, we promise."

"Dad?"

"Yes, promise."

She allows herself a breath. "Good. And make sure you tell Ethan."

Lynette ends the connection. She should tell Ethan directly. But it could backfire. He's been so angry with her. At first his return to life in Singapore was going okay, but he had a hard time adjusting, wasted his days playing games, and then Mai left him. No time to overthink. She DMs him. No reply.

It's been two minutes since she broadcast her message. There should be a tsunami of activity, her warning echoing around the world. She checks. Nothing. Shit. AI fact checkers must have deemed it conspiracy twaddle. Need to find a different way to get the message out.

———

11:14 a.m. Israel Time (80 minutes to 4-17)

Daniel, wearing only his sleeping scrub bottoms, places his hand against the living room wall and leans his upper body out the sliding door that leads to their deck. "What time's Grandpa coming?"

"Around noon," says Karima, who's wiping the surface of their outdoor dining table.

"Should I figure out food?" he asks.

"I already did. Something special. Grandpa's favorite restaurant growing up was this Mexican place in his town. I searched and found that someone reverse-engineered their whole menu. I'm going to print a caldo. It's like a beef and potato soup. I tried a sample—it's tasty, and no bread."

He streams a yummy emoji, then: "I'll head over and walk back with him."

"I'm sure he would appreciate it, but you don't need to. He's planning to take a car."

"A car? That doesn't sound like Grandpa."

"He's not exactly a spring chicken anymore."

"It's a nice day. I'll walk over, and maybe we'll walk back together, or if he's not up for it, I'll come back with him in a car."

She doesn't reply. "Sound good?" he asks.

"Danny! Look at this message from Nadezhda Maksimova."

"Who the fuck is Nadezhda Maksimova?"

"Sergei's wife."

"Oh yeah, Nadya, she's cute. It's been years, we should have them over."

"Look at the message, Daniel."

He hears the urgency in her voice. He shifts his attention to the message.

What the fuck. A twisted joke? A weird flex on Sergei's part, showing he can fake telemetry?

"This doesn't make any sense," he hears himself say aloud. Why would Sergei do this?

Karima's attention returns to him, strain visible on her face. "Trying to connect with Sergei . . . no response. Nadezhda . . . no response." He sees the strain in her expression turn to fear, and then panic.

"We need to sound the alarm. We need to get this out there." She's speaking fast, stress evident in every syllable.

He shakes his head. Why is she taking Nadya's message at face value? No way is there a latent hack lying dormant in all implants counting down to activation, and no way are they crying wolf.

Words pour from Karima. "Message our media contacts. No, better to go through the military, get them to use the emergency alert system. Contact your unit commander. And contact your friend on the Prime Minister's staff—what's her name?—Lia. Tell her to alert other countries."

He starts pacing. "Karima, slow down. Let's think this through. Implants aren't hackable. If Sergei knows of a problem, why wouldn't he go through Xyloom? Or why wouldn't he give us more detail . . . why all the mystery? And isn't the timing suspicious? Our algorithm was finally promoted yesterday and now he's implying there's an issue with it? Maybe he's jealous of all the publicity and wants to take us down a notch, get us to do something embarrassing."

Even as he says those words he knows they're wrong: Sergei would not do that. He might be jealous, but he would never act on it.

Karima's eyes open wide. "Daniel! He's not playing games. He's brain dead. Dead, are you even listening? That's verified telemetry!"

Her tone sends a chill through him. Could Sergei actually be dead?

"Are you listening to me?" Karima shouts. "Contact your unit commander."

He stops pacing and whirls to face her. He grips her shoulders. "Karima, don't panic."

What's going on? Why are Sergei and Nadya in Korea? It would help if he knew, but he's good at operating with limited information. He plays out various scenarios and plots a course of action. He just needs Karima to follow his lead.

"Let's say we do raise the alarm," he says in urgent but measured tones. "We won't be taken seriously if we don't give a reason, but what is our reason, a communication from an old friend? And then when nothing happens people will question our judgment and we'll lose credibility. No, we need to investigate first. There's time. I'll start digging, see if I can find anything that will get triggered around 12:34, see if I can find any code that doesn't belong, any evidence of a latent hack. You start running simulations. Figure out if anything unexpected happens when you simulate the clock going past 12:34."

He starts up the steps.

"I'll tell Grandpa not to come," she says.

He turns around. "No, don't do that, he wants to see us, celebrate the promotion. We need to take Nadya's message seriously, but let's investigate before we panic."

He bounds up the rest of the stairs.

"Danny, I. . . ."

He pauses and looks at her. "Yes?"

"Never mind."

He walks into the study.

———

4:19 p.m. Singapore Time (75 minutes to 4-17)

AI fact checkers are not going to classify Lynette's alarm as credible. She barely believes it herself. What she needs to do is get the message out over official government channels.

Who does she know? She's been in touch with a midlevel functionary at the Inland Revenue Authority about investigating tax deductible donations to 1Billion. He won't take her seriously, and even if he does, he'll need to run it up his chain of command. There's no time for that. No, she needs someone with juice.

Zelda! Zelda Singh, her old friend from NTU and now Minister of Transport. She hasn't had any contact with Zelda in a decade, other than a brief, unacknowledged congratulatory note when Zelda was appointed by the Prime Minister four years ago. But they were always close, and Zelda will listen to her.

She initiates a connection. Zelda's AI intercepts and responds noncommittally, indicating that Minister Singh will get back to Lynette later. She initiates a high urgency connection. The AI intercepts again. Lynette explains that she needs to speak with Zelda immediately regarding a matter of life and death. The AI asks for details and Lynette begins to explain, but the AI refuses to make the connection or even deliver an urgent message. She clenches her fists and counts to ten.

Does she still have permission to track Zelda? No. No surprise. But that gives her an idea. The Ministry of Transport is close, a few minutes by car. She can physically go there and talk to a human and either get in to see Zelda, or if Zelda's not there, find someone who can bypass her AI.

———

11:19 p.m. Israel Time (75 minutes to 4-17)

Daniel steps into the study, and by the time he sits down, his focus has already shifted to his coding environment. Adrenaline pumping, his thoughts are clear. He forms a plan of attack and moves efficiently and with attention to detail. His military training always kicks in during high-pressure situations.

Within a minute he has access to everything he needs. He starts searching the production implant code for anything out of place, anything that could possibly be triggered at 9:34 UTC, anything that could cause the brain damage Sergei appears to have incurred.

———

4:23 p.m. Singapore Time (71 minutes to 4-17)

"Make sure everyone you know hard disconnects before 5:34," Lynette tells Emma, rushing out of the apartment. She steps into the waiting elevator, rides it to ground level, and gets in a car.

In the moving car, she looks up at the clear sky over the strait, and the glistening sunlight flickering through the canopies of the palm trees lining the road. It's hard to believe catastrophe could be around the corner. And if she's having a hard time believing it, how will she persuade Zelda?

Three minutes later she walks into the Ministry of Transport. No, she doesn't have an appointment, she tells the attendant system. It takes an infuriating twenty-five minutes of refusing to leave to be connected to a human, and then to another human, and then for that person to interrupt Zelda and get confirmation she is in fact willing to meet.

Lynette steps off the elevator onto the top floor. She spots Zelda right away, through the transparent wall of a sizable conference room. Zelda is chairing a meeting with dozens of people. No wonder her AI maintained such a high interruption threshold.

Lynette receives a DM. *Good to see you friend, meeting will wrap up in an hour.*

This is critical, need to talk now.

Zelda says something to the man standing next to her and then walks out of the conference room. "This can't wait?"

"No, it can't."

"Okay, let's step into my office."

She follows Zelda down the hall. They enter a bright room illuminated by sunlight streaming in through a glass curtain wall. Zelda sits down on the couch and motions for Lynette to sit next to her.

"What's going on?"

"Do you remember Sergei?"

"Your Sergei? Of course."

She shows Zelda the message from Nadezhda and the recording of Sergei, and explains that she needs Zelda to broadcast an emergency alert.

"You know this sounds mad, right? And why wouldn't Sergei go through Xyloom?"

"Yes, and I don't know."

"So you want me to broadcast an alert to all Singaporeans telling them they could die if they don't disconnect their implants? And also inform other governments and ask them to do the same?"

"Yes."

"Lynette, I . . . this is so far-fetched. It would be career suicide for me, even more so if I don't get approval from the PM's PR people. I need a covert way to check this out."

Damn. Did she expect Zelda to take action without proof? Zelda's a member of the cabinet. No doubt there are politics, and even asking questions that make her sound gullible or alarmist could be ammunition for her rivals. She needs Zelda to do the same calculation she did.

"Zelda," she says, forcing herself to calm though she wants to scream, "you're right, it is far-fetched, but we're talking about brain damage to everyone in the world, even death. My god, Zelda! Isn't even a tiny risk of that more important than your career?"

"Yes, it is. . . ."

Good, still the same Zelda.

". . . but we have over half an hour. I have a close friend who leads R&D at Brain Duck. Let me get his opinion."

————

11:58 p.m. Israel Time (36 minutes to 4-17)

Daniel receives a DM from Karima. *Find anything?*

He DMs back: *No, nothing. What about you?*

Nothing. I ran three simulations. Here's my log.

He skims. She let each simulation run for several days in simulated time, well past 9:34 UTC, and nothing unusual happened. She also did an experiment in mice, forcing their clocks to skip ahead. Again, nothing concerning, just the expected minor bits of odd behavior from having the implant clock out of sync with the mice's physiological systems.

That's consistent with what I'm seeing, he DMs back.

Grandpa will be here soon.

I think we're okay. You take care of Grandpa, and I'll keep looking into this.

You sure that's wise?

Yes, positive. If something was wrong we would have seen it by now in code or simulation.

Okay. I'll run more simulations in the background. Tell me if you need help.

———

5:17 p.m. Singapore Time (17 minutes to 4-17)

Fifteen precious minutes lost speaking with Zelda's Brain Duck contact. He was certain that it was impossible for there to be a latent hack.

"How do you explain the telemetry?" Lynette had asked him.

"I don't know. Your friend faked the telemetry and stole codes from Xyloom so he could sign it as verified. Or, and this is even more out there, he hacked into his own implant using specialized diagnostic tools he might have access to as a Xyloom engineer. But that there is a latent hack in all implants? No way."

Zelda places her hand on Lynette's knee. "I'm sorry. I

can't throw people into a panic and give the PM an excuse to have me step down. Why don't you hang out here, I'll finish my meeting, then we can go get a drink."

Zelda scooches forward and moves to stand up.

"Wait!" Lynette grabs Zelda's wrist. "I know it sounds crazy. But you trust me, and I trust Sergei. He's"—he *was!* her brain screams—"exceptional, you know that. Ranked first in our class of very sharp people. Isn't it at least possible that he knows something that your friend at Brain Duck doesn't? Please, ask your friend what he means by 'no way' there is a latent hack. Does he mean it's a physical impossibility, or extraordinarily unlikely?"

Zelda stares at nothing for a minute and then shares his response: *Not impossible, but inconceivable. Implants are provably unhackable. In the sixty years since they entered the market, no implant has had its security compromised. That all implants worldwide have a latent hack residing in them, and it's gone undetected—no way.*

Déjà vu. This whole exchange feels like getting others to see 1Billion with clear eyes. People are so accustomed to normalcy, to safety, to security, they can't accept anything that runs counter to their mental model of a well-functioning world. But rare things happen rarely, not never. How to get Zelda to understand that?

"Zelda, please, we're running out of time. It's not impossible, so that means it's possible, and action from you now could save the world. That's not hyperbole."

She sees a change in Zelda's expression. Something finally clicked.

A slow nod. "You're right. Inconceivable does not equal impossible. Like during my second month as minister, when we had our first pedestrian fatality, the first accidental death in the country in forty years. And sometimes sticking your neck out is the right thing to do." She gnaws at her lip. "Let's say we do it. I broadcast an alert and tell people to hard disconnect. How long do they need to stay disconnected for? Even a few minutes will throw things into chaos."

Yes! Zelda's going to do the right thing.

"I don't know. It could be indefinite."

"There's no way I can say that. I'll say we expect the disconnection time to be brief and will be broadcasting an all clear through alternative channels. We'll get better compliance."

"Okay."

"Let me compose something. I should run it by the communications department. But they'll shoot it down, so I'll risk it. If this is the end of my government career, which it probably will be, be prepared for a new roommate."

Lynette takes the few seconds to confirm Ethan is disconnected. He's not. No! She DMs him: *Ethan, please, just listen to me, disconnect.* What else can she do? How about—

"Okay, here's what I have," Zelda says, interrupting her thoughts.

It's good, and there's no time to tweak anyway. Zelda needs to send it with emergency status. That way it will break through do-not-disturb, interrupt sleep, and halt other activity until acknowledged.

"No, I'm doing it as urgent. If it turns out to be a false alarm, which it probably will, I could face jail time for inciting panic."

"We're running out of time, send it."

"We've been racing since you walked off the elevator. Let's slow the pace down, breathe slowly for one minute, be sure we want to do this."

"Zelda, c'mon, there's no time for that."

"There is."

60, 59, 58 . . . 3, 2, 1.

"Sending."

———

12:18 p.m. Israel Time (16 minutes to 4-17)

Daniel has been in the zone for over an hour. He hasn't found anything suspicious or out of place. He switches his attention away from code and thinks. That white and gold dress.

Neutralizing Motivated Perception was a required course for officers. The idea that you only see what you want to see seemed absurd. Maybe others had that problem, but not him. Then the instructor, a psychologist, she showed them a flat, grainy image from a century ago. It was of a woman's dress with white and gold horizontal stripes. Except some of his fellow soldiers said the stripes were black and blue. And they were right. But even knowing that, no matter how many times he looked, those stripes were white and gold to him.

The instructor had them do an exercise. Take an assumption, something you know to be true, and trick your brain into believing, with temporary certainty, that it's false. He remembers it because he questioned her, pointing out that thinking that way was dangerous. Soldiers needed conviction to make flash decisions, he told her.

But now he uses the technique on himself. In his heart of hearts, he does not believe there is a hack. He reverses the assumption. He forces himself to believe, with conviction, that someone found a problem with their olfactory interface algorithm. That person then deliberately exploited the problem to transmit a hack to all implants, one designed to activate fifteen minutes from now and cause brain damage.

For the first time since they received Nadya's message, he feels fear. Not for his reputation, but for his safety, for himself and for Leon, Ora, and Karima. Could there be something insecure in his own implant, in his own brain? In their brains?

He suppresses the fear and regains focus. That a hack could be lying dormant in his own implant gives him an idea. All he needs to do is take a snapshot of his own implant from yesterday, before their algorithm was promoted, replay the audit trail, and compare with the current state of his implant. If there's a hack it should show up.

It takes ten minutes. He finds discrepancies, but they all have innocent explanations, and after filtering them out, nothing is left. No hack. It's not conclusive, of course, because he only looked at his own implant. Still, he feels better.

But actually, what if his assumption about the time frame is wrong? What if instead of being deployed centrally sometime in the last twenty-four hours, it was done biological virus style? One implant infecting another, infecting another—slow enough to evade detection, maybe using olfaction as the transmission mechanism. He needs to repeat his search, starting not yesterday, but with a snapshot from years ago, before their algorithm was deployed to the sandbox. Is there time? He starts.

————

5:31 p.m. Singapore Time (3 minutes to 4-17)

To: All Singaporeans
Date: April 17, 2120 5:31 P.M. SST
Subject: URGENT — potential threat, advise immediate hard disconnection of implants

We have received credible information that in three minutes, at 5:34, implants could malfunction, possibly harming their hosts. Out of an abundance of caution we advise all citizens to hard disconnect their implants now. Leave them disconnected until we send an all clear message via alternative channels, which we will aim to do no later than 5:36.

Lynette receives the message. Then she looks at Zelda. "Thank you. Now—"

Zelda raises two fingers and anxiety appears on her face. "The Prime Minister."

"Include me. We need her to alert other countries."

Lynette's attention is yanked into a virtual conference room with Zelda and the Prime Minister.

"Zelda, what the hell, did you authorize sending that message? And who is this?"

"Prime Minister, yes, I sent the message. This is Dr. Lynette Tan. She's my source."

Lynette speaks quickly. "Madame Prime Minister, we only have a few minutes. Rebroadcast the alert with emergency status. And forward it to other countries."

"Dr. Tan, how do you know implants will malfunction?"

"An engineer at Xyloom. Please, there's no time to explain, you could save millions, maybe hundreds of millions of people."

Prime Minister makes the pause gesture, studies something for twenty seconds, and then looks back up.

"So you're an interventionist. You lost your medical license due to malpractice. You lead a group that works to persuade people to leave some dance group in Korea. Your brother was a member of the group and your boyfriend from college, now an engineer at Xyloom, still is. Is he your source?"

Zelda turns to Lynette. "You committed malpractice? You lost your medical license? You didn't tell me that. Prime Minister, I apologize. . . ."

This isn't happening. . . .

"Please, listen to me, yes, my medical license was suspended, and it was retribution for exposing the unethical practices of the group, but that has nothing to do with this. Nadezhda says everyone must hard disconnect before 5:34."

"Who is Nadezhda? And it's already 5:34."

"Nadezhda is Serg—"

Acute nausea. Lynette tries to complete her sentence, but the toxic smell of burning plastic overpowers her brain. She looks for fire. None. And then there is the scent of soap and kefir, mixed with wet leaves and kopi—Sergei, in the rainforest. The sweet, warm smell of his perspiration, cuddling in bed, her lips pressed against his soft hair.

Her muscles spasm, her body writhes. Her hands seize up. She senses Zelda jerking next to her and feels Zelda's nails scratching at her face. All slows, each labored breath fills her lungs with the dense smoke of a thousand burning tires. She feels Great-grandma's hand on hers, and then nothing.

———

A blue sky and a bright office. Two women, limbs inter-twined, lying on the floor, unmoving. Vomit covers the carpeting. Cleaning enzymes go to work and after a few minutes the carpet is spotless again.

———

12:33 p.m. Israel Time (1 minute to 4-17)

One minute to 12:34. Not enough time to complete his search for discrepancies. So far Daniel hasn't found anything.

12:33:58 . . . 12:33:59 . . . 12:34:00 . . . 12:34:01 . . . 12:34:02

He monitors global chatter. No reports of problems. He let himself get paranoid. Sergei and Nadya must have gone off the deep end.

12:34:10 . . . 12:34:11

He'll wait another minute to be sure and then join everyone for lunch. He'll apologize to Grandpa for being late and walk him back home after to make up for it.

12:34:15 . . . 12:34:16

He checks his feeds. Still no relevant chatter, no sudden rise in requests for medical assistance.

12:34:18 . . . 12:34:19

Fuck, he feels queasy. And something in his head, like rusty scissors snipping at his neurons.

Disconnect your implants! he DMs Karima, Leon and Ora.

His message isn't received. They're already disconnected. But he needs to tell them to stay disconnected.

12:34:22

He stands up, rushes out of the study and stumbles down the stairs into the living room. The air is filled with an acrid, chemical smell; he tastes metal, like the fumes of burning plastic, like the explosives they trained with in his unit.

His muscles seize and his legs go numb. He fights to take a few more steps. He supports himself on the wall, turns to Karima on the deck, and whispers, "Don't reconnect."

44

March 10, 2128
Eight years after 4-17
Singapore Island
Leon Levy

I was twenty years old and had been living in Singapore for eight years. My apartment building had a covered outdoor lobby, and I was sitting in a lounge chair, waiting for a woman named Nadezhda Maksimova. She had contacted me that morning, said she had known my parents, and asked to meet.

She was running late. I relaxed for a minute, breathed in the tropical air, and watched the long-tailed macaques playing in the trumpet trees that dotted our grounds. Eight years after 4-17 there were more monkeys in Singapore than people, and they seemed to know it. I would have liked to stare at the macaques all afternoon, but I owed it to my two-year-old daughter to stay focused on my studies.

I looked through my old-fashioned glasses and resumed working on my quantum cryptography problem set. I couldn't concentrate. Nadezhda's mention of my parents had brought my thoughts circling back to 4-17.

If only Mom had listened to Dad's warning, if she had made a different split-second decision, she would have been with us in Singapore. Or if I hadn't made Mom angry, she wouldn't have disconnected me and Ora, and we too would have perished. Wouldn't that have been easier? But I knew I couldn't go there. I had a responsibility to rebuild.

I knew why I was part of the 0.3 percent. Luck, if you could call it that, and Great-grandpa's clear thinking under pressure. He was right. Death was caused by implants. And it lingered—if he had reconnected us, even hours or days later, even then, eight years later, we would have been killed instantly.

There were four substantial clusters of sub-centenarian survivors. In Israel, there was an extremist ultra-Orthodox sect that refused implants. All of its nearly 52,000 members survived. There was an unusual dance group in Korea that required its 40,000 members to live on a compound and lead disconnected lives. They survived. In the Free States of America, where implants were optional, but in practice rare not to have, there were 19,000 survivors scattered throughout rural areas of the country. And in Singapore, an alert telling people to disconnect was heeded by roughly 70,000.

In Haifa, a few months after 4-17, Great-grandpa told Ora and me what we already knew—we needed to move to a community that had other young people. Great-grandpa, with his aversion to fanaticism, did not want us to become part of an ultra-Orthodox religious group in Israel or what he believed to be a cult in Korea. FSA was of course out of the question. Singapore was the only choice.

We left Israel on a packed supersonic chartered by the

Singaporean government, part of a program to attract skilled pre from all over the world. "I'm having déjà vu," Great-grandpa told us.

Singapore had become a symbol of hope to the millions of centenarian survivors scattered across the planet. Although nobody from the senior levels of government had survived, a senior stateswoman, a former prime minister, took charge, and within a week a new democratically elected government was formed.

Singaporeans understood that in the coming decade the planet would be left with its lowest human population in tens of thousands of years. In recognition of the fact that Homo sapiens could become endangered, the government redefined its mission from safeguarding the country to preservation of the species—the only cluster to adopt the survival of humanity, rather than survival of itself, as its purpose.

The country took stock of its resources. One was a global pool of centenarians with diverse, if somewhat outdated, expertise. In their limited remaining years of life, these centenarians could be called on to solve problems and train a new generation of experts.

Another resource was information. Knowledge, in digital form, would be invaluable in rebuilding over the coming centuries. But it was already difficult to access that knowledge without implants, and unless the computing infrastructure was maintained, access could be lost entirely.

That's why, when the government judged how to apply limited human capital, it prioritized computing.

One initiative was fixing implants. A team of centenarian BQCI experts was assembled and charged with finding the root cause of the malfunction. The goal was not only to learn what had happened, but to then repair implants so we could reconnect them, an idea that was, needless to say, controversial and scary. The team had been working for eight years without success.

A related initiative was building a new generation of computer scientists. Ora and I were selected based on aptitude tests, even though I'm certain that, if not for 4-17, I would have ended up in a very different profession.

After seven years of studying math, computing, and neuroscience, Ora and I understood BQCI. In fact, we were almost certainly the only sub-centenarians on the planet who grasped the theoretical underpinnings of implants. It became clear that if the team of centenarian experts was unable to figure things out, the responsibility would fall on us. And fixing existing implants was only the start. We would need to put safeguards in place so catastrophe could never happen again, restart manufacturing of quantum computers, and reestablish the discipline of BQCI.

It was an immense challenge. One that, even then, we knew would occupy us for the rest of our lives. That didn't depress me. It infused me with purpose. In Israel, homework had seemed pointless. As I sat in our lobby struggling with my problem set, I knew I was building brain muscle the world needed.

I was just getting back into one of the problems when someone approached. I looked up and shuddered because the woman standing in front of me looked like Mom, only paler.

"Leon?"

"Yes. Nadezhda?"

She nodded and sat down in the chair next to me. "Your voice—like your father's," she said, "but you look like your mother."

She appeared pregnant, was at least twice my age, and

spoke in oddly accented English. Her eyes darted around as if she needed continual confirmation that we were the only two people present. A member of 1Billion, the survivor cluster in Korea, she had arrived in Singapore a few days earlier as part of a diplomatic mission. During a meeting in government headquarters, Nadezhda walked into the offices of the prime minister and requested asylum. She refused to leave the building until her fellow 1Billion members departed the island. Her eight children, four pairs of twins, were still in Korea.

"But why do you want to meet with me? How did you know my parents?" I asked.

I struggled to absorb what she told me: olfactory algorithm flaw, Protiv-1, my parents, Sergei Kraev, Lynette Tan, Mother.

It couldn't be true. And if it were, how could I have been the first person hearing it? Could it be true?

She seemed distressed and on edge, but not crazy. And the burst transmission she claimed to have sent fit the facts. Was it the reason Dad was tied up in our study? Did Mom disconnect Ora and me, not because of my behavior, but because she had received and believed, or at least put some credence in, Nadezhda's message?

My thoughts cascaded faster and faster. Were Mom and Dad at fault? If Nadezhda was to be believed, it meant that willful negligence by my parents opened the implant security hole exploited by Protiv-1. It also meant that Mom and Dad could have—but unlike Lynette Tan, chose not to—sound the alarm. With their credibility and celebrity my parents could have saved millions, maybe billions of people. A yawning chasm of horror opened before me, and the whispered word "murderers" echoed in its depths.

My god. Could I live with any of this? Even if I could,

would Ora and I, would my wife and daughter, be in danger once others knew?

Nadezhda was talking to me. "Leon. Leon." Her hand shook my shoulder gently, dragging me back to the now. "Leon, I need you to help me. It's taken eight years of pretending to escape. Pretending to be loyal member. Pretending to like Sang-chul Lee, my assigned partner. Pretending to believe in Mother. I finally earned enough trust to be appointed to diplomatic mission. But real source of trust—Sang-chul knew I would never abandon our children. Except I did. I defected. You need to persuade 1Billion to release them."

I was confused. Back then we knew very little about 1Billion, Sunny Kim, and how they operated. And Nadezhda had thrown so much information at me so quickly I couldn't connect the dots.

"Why would they listen to me?" I asked.

"Because they are in desperate need of technical expertise. Leon, will you help 1Billion in return for release of my children?"

EPILOGUE

April 14, 2221
101 years after 4-17
Singapore Island

Children,

This is my ninety-fifth and final annual message. By the time you read these words I will have passed away and some of you, perhaps most of you, will have attended my funeral.

I received hundreds of questions from you following last year's message. The one I was most surprised to receive came from my seven-year-old great-great-great-grand-daughter Rima Levy. Rima, my story was not intended for children your age, but I'm glad you read it. You asked if I wished my mother had married Sergei Kraev. I've been reflecting on your question these past eight months, and I'm still reflecting.

Children, I'm aware that my revelations, and the public outrage that followed, tainted our family, hurt your career prospects, supplied ammunition to your political opponents, damaged your self-confidence.

You asked why I shared my story. It was out of respect for what we—what you—have built. Transparency is one of the values that separate our Democratic Republic of Singapore from the 1Billion Empire. And yet keeping my parents' responsibility for 4-17 secret, that was the opposite of transparent, an original sin I felt compelled to correct.

A noble choice? Not at all. Your criticism of me for sitting on the secret for nine decades, until the end of my life, and leaving you with the burden, is justified. I hope in time you'll understand and forgive.

My great-great-grandson Kejujuran Zhang, you asked me what happened to Nadezhda Maksimova and her children. I'm ashamed to say I don't know. The more conversations I had with Nadezhda, the more I trusted her. I tried trading with 1Billion, offering technical assistance for the release of her children, but they refused. Three months after arriving in Singapore, with terror and resignation in her eyes, she returned to Korea. I've never heard from her or been able to make contact since.

My great-granddaughter Zoma Levy, you asked if the thing for which I am most famous—reactivating implants—should be attributed to my interactions with Nadezhda. Yes. Nadezhda's information about Protiv-1, which I shared only with Ora, set us down the right path. It became straightforward to find and remove the hack. And then Ora did the hard part—she repaired the olfactory interface algorithm.

Our parents never understood that the flaw they covered up was not just an issue with the proof, but in fact stemmed from a subtle and exploitable logic error in their algorithm. Ora figured it out in a matter of months, and clearly Sergei did too. Why our parents failed to is a mystery we will never be able to answer.

Back to your question Rima. I feel like I've spent much

of my life getting to know Sergei. It started when I decompiled the Protiv-1 code and continued with reconstructing his past and striving to live in his head—all to understand why he did what he did. And after all that, I feel he was a decent human being, no more flawed than most people, and perhaps less flawed than my father.

But do I wish my mother had fallen in love with him? I would not exist. Neither would the 3,203 of you. But that's nothing compared to preventing 4-17. The problem is—and perhaps in my old age I resist counterfactuals—I just can't see it. I knew my mother and she would never have fallen for Sergei; and Rima, as you get older, you'll learn that these things are beyond our conscious control.

My children, even a century ago it was rare to be in my present situation. My mind is sharp, and yet I know with certainty that these are my final days. You may be expecting me to conclude my terminal message with words of wisdom, or optimism about the future, or perhaps even a warning about the fallibility of people and systems. Despite living for almost 114 years, I am still uncertain about most things in life. I have no desire to preach to you with words that carry the weight of finality. I instead want my last words to be these: I'm proud of you and I love you.

Love,
Leon Levy

AUTHOR'S NOTE

I read nineteen wonderful fiction and nonfiction books on topics ranging from dance to cults while writing *The Insecure Mind of Sergei Kraev.* If you would like that list of books, or are interested in anything I may write in the future, please visit ericsilberstein.com and join my mailing list.

Thank you to my editor Dario Ciriello for coaching me, for helping solve hundreds of problems, and of course for editing. Thank you to my proofreader Rick Fisher for being opinionated and debating individual word choices through sixteen rounds of revisions.

I am incredibly grateful to my early readers: Abhinav Seth, Adam Gries, Alex Bi, Andrea Wan, Andrew Silberstein, Ashley McDermott, Bryan Gaensler, Christopher Kreis, Cindy Alvarez, Claudio Migliore, Daniel Navisky, David Abrams, David Hyman, Dima Rogozin, Elizabeth Levy, Elizabeth Navisky, Frances Liu, Gary Silverman, Geanna Flavetta, Gillian Isabelle, Hae-Won Min, Hormoz Solomon, Hui Huang, Jeffrey Liss, Jennifer Couzin-Frankel, Jody Perejda, John Nakazawa, Julia LiMarzi, Julie Hayes, Justin Deng, Kevin Lamenzo, Kris Sarajian, Marc

Schwabish, Meredith Silberstein, Natalka Roshak, Olga Rogozin, Philip Kaufman, Rachel Barenbaum, Rashu Seth, Rob Price, Robert Davoli, Roxanna Sue O'Connor, Roy Rodenstein, Samantha Levien, William Hincy, and Zac Bentley.

Some of you read multiple times and sent back extensive notes. Some of you read once and told me you loved it. Some of you read a few chapters, got stuck, and told me why. All of that was helpful and shaped the final text.

ADVANCED PRAISE

I've read thousands of sci-fi stories, and the thing that stands out for me here is the originality—it doesn't quickly fall into some typical genre or pay tribute to some other great novel. This made it especially enjoyable . . . it deserves to be read and enjoyed widely!

Eric Silberstein's debut novel is a highly original and fast-paced imagining of where wiring our brains and senses to the internet might take us. Quantum computing, dance troupes, mathematical proofs and randomized clinical trials all cleverly intersect in a story that you think you can predict, but which will twist in unexpected ways. *The Insecure Mind of Sergei Kraev* is a credible and realistic view of the near future, with a warning that the fallibility of human beings will always trump technological progress. Enjoyable and recommended.

— Bryan Gaensler, PhD

Sci-fi isn't the genre that I usually gravitate towards but I'm honestly glad I stepped a bit out of my comfort zone. It kept me hooked and I gobbled it down. The tension was real and palpable. The characters spoke with honest emotion and I cared about them. Sergei is everyman without society's required hard, masculine shell. I loved him.

— ROXANNA SUE O'CONNOR

Where do we go from the global disinformation and pandemic of 2020? A history told from multiple voices, an evocative projection of the world we may invent to protect us—and the ways in which humans being human can game any system—this is a fantastic read that I couldn't put down.

— CINDY ALVAREZ

In so many ways, the world Eric Silberstein shows in this debut novel is the one we all want—the world we just know is coming. It is a world of nice things, where humans are online from birth, not merely masters of our technology but, finally, universally enhanced and empowered by it. Neural interfaces connect us to each other while protecting our privacy and gently compensating for our deficiencies.

Inside every utopia there's an unwelcome guest: human nature. What happens when a perfect world is inextricably linked to the minds of its imperfect creators? Are we the reason we can't have nice things after all? Has it always been this way? Silberstein's answer is both an incisive critique and jarring for its feeling of inevitability.

I loved and pitied Sergei for his innocence, his brilliance, and his ability to get lost in a crowd of his own thoughts. For all his talents, he suffers for want of what we all need: to love and to be loved, to feel a part of something lasting; to make things better than they are. Who am I to judge his mistakes? Would I have done any better?

Like all great Sci-Fi authors, Silberstein entices us with a good story, but holds up a mirror. In the end, I reached the conclusion I hope many other readers will enjoy reaching: I am Sergei, and I am why humanity can't have nice things.

— JEFFREY LISS

From the first sentence, I was hooked by the premise and immediate action. Set in the not-too-distant future, it was easy to see how our world could have evolved to the imagined geopolitical climate and technology-laden lifestyles underpinning what is, at its core, a relatable story about universal human concerns—work, love, sex, family. I loved how all of the stories were intertwined and connected but how that unfolded over time, revealing well-developed, authentic characters. Silberstein's vivid descriptions of the foods, neighborhoods, architecture and music of various settings took me on a fascinating global tour that somehow felt both exotic and familiar. I hope it gets made into a netflix series!

— SAMANTHA LEVIEN

The Insecure Mind of Sergei Kraev is a gripping read richly informed by state-of-the-art science. Silberstein brings you into the minds of mathematicians and computer scientists in a compelling portrayal of expediency and ambition colliding to produce disaster.

— N. R. M. Roshak

I really enjoyed *The Insecure Mind of Sergei Kraev*. And I'm saying this as someone who generally is not a fan of science fiction.

The first thing that struck me was that even though it's science fiction, I appreciated the fact that it didn't take place in space or on some faraway planet with space creatures. It was set 100 years in the future and although we have neural implants, people are still people. Once that was established, I felt I was able to relate to the characters and the storyline.

I loved the way the characters' stories all seemed separate and unrelated at the start, but then you were gradually able to see the collision course they were on. Also how it picks up on themes that are simmering in the world today (intolerance, overdependence on technology, using VR as an escape, living in an echo chamber) and carrying them to a conclusion that doesn't seem crazy.

Somehow I managed to feel really sad at the end —I think it's because I liked the characters so much.

— Gillian Isabelle, PhD

The story is engaging, the end is climactic, and as I approached it, I had a hard time putting it down. I felt transported back to Israel by the author's vivid descriptions of familiar places, and while I've never been to Singapore or Korea, I felt like I had. I read *The Insecure Mind of Sergei Kraev* months ago and still find myself thinking about this truly creative book.

— HORMOZ SOLOMON, MD

The Insecure Mind of Sergei Kraev starts with the themes of our current day and fast forwards 100 years into a world we may someday know. A worldwide pandemic, hyper-connected kids, AI to combat fake news and answer our questions. All the while nanobots crawl the microscopic crevasses of our bodies as they heal and clean. Among this setting humanity persists. The familiar inner angels and demons drive the characters through a story of love, ambition, moral culpability, and hope. It's a worldwide futuristic ride perfect for anyone interested in a fresh and fun story that can help us begin to understand the time we live in now.

— KEVIN LAMENZO

ABOUT THE AUTHOR

Eric Silberstein lives in Newton, Massachusetts with his wife and two children. He holds a BA in Computer Science from Harvard.

www.EricSilberstein.com